SECOND CHANCES

Blood Brothers #3

MANDA MELLETT

CONTENTS

PROLOGUE

I'm no stranger to fear. *Real* fear.

It's not that delicious fear that comes when watching a horror film, hiding your face in your hands while silently screaming for the heroine *not* to open that door. It's not that vague feeling of unease when you hear an unexplained creak in the house. It's that bone-deep fear when you're anticipating something dreadful to happen, and there's nothing, absolutely-fucking-nothing you can do to stop it, no way to escape the consequences of your actions. Like standing in front of an avalanche rushing down the hill knowing there is no chance of getting out of its path. Inevitable and unavoidable.

Deep-seated fear is my constant companion. No waking breath can be taken without it. No word uttered or action performed without my heart beating too fast, my palms sweating, and involuntary shivers trembling through my limbs in case I say or do the wrong thing. Fear haunts my dreams every night as I lie sleepless beside him. Each day the fear grows worse, knowing the time might be close where he goes too far and kills me. The possibility increases exponentially with the slightest thing I do that he could perceive as wrong. No, I'm no stranger to fear.

It didn't start out that way, of course. The man I met and got involved with was a gentleman in every sense of the word—handsome, kind, caring, and rich. But then he began to change, and slowly, oh so slowly, his true colours began to emerge. It took me a while to notice, and even longer before I admitted the abuse; in the beginning making excuses for his actions and blaming myself. Then, as the situation deteriorated, my sense of self-preservation told me I had to get out. But by the time I'd come to that decision, the noose had already tightened around me, strangling me as it held me captive, caught in his trap; his own personal plaything and punching bag.

Most people would find it difficult to understand the hold this man has over me and just how hard it is for me to break free. Until they hear his name. Then they understand. Ethan St John-Davies. One of the richest, most powerful and influential men in the UK.

CHAPTER 1
Zoe

Having a tyre blowout is frightening enough; the sudden lurching of the car, the loud bang making me jump, then the glance in the review mirror showing me rubber flying out behind. And all the while, I desperately fight the car's natural inclination to pull to the offside, struggling to persuade it onto the safety of the hard shoulder, hopefully without hitting another vehicle or causing a major accident.

But that's not the reason why, only seconds later when the implications of what's happened hit me, I sit with my head resting against the steering wheel, violently shaking. *I'm going to be late!*

I've suffered the repercussions for not being on time before; what he called my 'correction'. Shit! Let's call it what it is: good old-fashioned abuse. Last time I was lucky to escape with a blow to my stomach and right kidney, followed by a brutal kick to my ribs. Lateness, for whatever reason, is a punishable crime in Ethan's world.

Practicing deep breathing, trying to calm my nerves using techniques I'm so well versed in—a daily exercise to suppress my anxiety—I start to wonder whether it would be better just to sit here and let fate fall as it will. A person's life expectancy is apparently only an average of forty minutes if you stay in your vehicle when broken down on a motorway. Will I be crushed by a heavy goods vehicle before he comes for me? He could find out exactly where I am; he has the ability to track my every move if he so wants. Every second of every frigging day.

For just a moment it's tempting to wait in the car and take my chances, but despite the months of living in hell, I've still got higher expectations for my life than ending it splattered over the highway. So, pulling myself together, I grab my phone and step out. Then, multi-tasking while climbing over the safety barrier, I look up the contact for the AA. Changing a wheel is, I have to confess, beyond me, and even if I knew what to do, my hands are nowhere near steady enough to turn a nut. I can only hope the road recovery experts will be quick to help.

I select the right number, and am ready to dial when a truck pulls up behind my car, and a chap gets out. There doesn't seem to be anything wrong with his vehicle, making it obvious he's stopped close by me on purpose. Immediately I feel uneasy—I don't know him from Adam. I'm a woman on my own, easy prey for someone with suspect motives. Then, as I realise no one could do worse to me than Ethan's already done, my fear of the stranger begins to recede.

I stare at him curiously as he walks purposefully towards me. He's not the type of man Ethan would send, definitely not. No, this man is well below his station. He's wearing dirty and well-used navy overalls open to the waist and shrugged down around his hips, and a once-white T-shirt covers his chest. He looks tough and rough, but even so, as he stomps towards me, any worry about the legitimacy of the reason why he's stopped disappears when I catch the concerned expression on his face, and hear his opening words uttered once he's within earshot. His clear worry for my safety dispelling any lingering fears.

When I'm able to hear him over the noise of the traffic racing past, he assures me he means me no harm. "Hey, sweetie, need help? That's your rubber all over the road, isn't it? Want me to change your wheel?"

He might be my knight in shining armour, but things aren't as simple as that. *What is the right course of action?* There would, of course, be consequences to a wrong decision. Or the right one for that matter, depending on Ethan's mood tonight. Glancing suspiciously up at the traffic camera just a hundred metres further up the road, I can't forget it's relaying and recording everything I do. It's all too easy for Ethan to get access to such systems; it's even possible he has someone watching me at this very moment. But whether someone's monitoring it in real time, or will call up the video to examine it later, the end result is the same. Ethan would be able to discover whatever decision I make.

Although it is kind of a stranger to stop and offer assistance, the right action is not to accept, and definitely not to include him in any escape plan. Oh no, I've already learned in the worst possible way how brutal Ethan can be if I involve anyone else.

So, staying dumb of my greater plight, I just wave my phone at him declining his offer of assistance. "Just calling the AA now," I explain, "Thanks for stopping, though."

He looks surprised that I'd refuse his aid, and then, misinterpreting my anxiety, he holds out his hands in a gesture of reassurance open and facing up as if to show he's no threat. "Hey, love. I just stopped because it looked like you were in a spot of bother." He walks over to the car and checks the rim of the now tyre-less wheel, then glances up. "The AA will probably take an hour or more at this time of day," he scoffs, "If it's just the tyre and you've got a spare I can have you on your way again in a few minutes?" His voice rises at the end of the sentence, so I know it's a question.

Staring at him, I'm amazed a complete stranger would bother to fix an unknown person's car; I'd almost forgotten there can be kindness in the world. But then his words sink through the fog in my brain, and I realise he's offering me the chance to get back on the move again. If he can change the tyre quickly, maybe I won't be too late home—and maybe the outcome won't be as bad as I fear. Perhaps Ethan wouldn't bother to check the camera feed if I get home on time? Quickly I make a decision. Nodding at him, I manage to summon up a smile, the expression feeling strange on my face, "Thank you. That would be fantastic."

Taking the keys from my outstretched hand, he locates the spare fast; it's only a space saver which will slow me down, but at least I'll soon be on my way again. As I hover behind him I begin to shiver in the cold winter air, my hands wringing and twisting together. I bite my tongue to curb any words to hurry him along as I can see he's working as fast as he can. He wastes no time swapping the wheels over, rolling the one with the shredded tyre across to show me. "Reckon you hit a nail or tack, love. Just bad luck."

Bad frigging luck. You've got it, mate.

"You alright? You look a bit shaky. It can be a shock." He's staring at me, his face kind, open with concern. "You gonna be okay to drive?"

Yes, I'm in shock. I'm trembling, but can't find the words to explain to this helpful man that the best way to alleviate my fear is to get back on my way as fast as I can. Putting as much confidence in my voice as I summon up, I reassure him I'll be fine. From his expression, he doesn't believe me, but I turn away before he can say anything else, throwing a quick 'thank you' over my shoulder. Digging around in the passenger footwell, I locate my handbag from where it fell on the floor during my mad swerve to get the car off the carriageway. Extracting my purse, I offer to pay him.

He laughs, waving his hands in refusal, pushing away the notes I'm holding. "Just happy to help a beautiful woman." He smirks as he throws the compliment out, but there's no malice or threat in his face. Reaching into the pocket of his overalls he pulls out a card, "Name's Josh, sweetie. Give me a call if you ever get stuck again."

Glancing down, I see he's a mechanic from the local garage. Pocketing the card without thinking, and thanking him profusely once again, I take back my keys and go to my car. A flash from his headlights shows he's waiting until I get moving, and then I see him following at a safe distance as I increase my speed along the hard shoulder until I'm going fast enough to slide out into a welcome gap in the rush hour traffic. A minute later, looking in my rearview mirror, I see he's also successfully navigated the almost constant stream of cars. By this time my saviour's a few vehicles behind.

Flicking my eyes to the dashboard clock, with no further problems I calculate I'll only be a quarter of an hour late; perhaps Ethan will overlook it. It's not like I don't have a good excuse. Allowing myself to relax a little, my eyes dart back to the road as a van speeds past, hoots, and the driver waves. I'm pootling along at fifty on the spare, and he's got his foot down. I even manage a smile as I recognise Josh, and give a quick wave as my Good Samaritan disappears, merging with the vehicles in the fast lane.

But my optimism soon fades. It doesn't take long for me to realise that I'd underestimated how quickly the rush hour traffic would build up. Nor had I made any allowance that the dark clouds, which had been threatening all afternoon, would unleash heavy sleet and hail; apparently providing more than sufficient reason to cause the whole motorway to come almost to a complete standstill.

By the time I pull up outside the large ornate gates and impatiently wait for them to slide open, I'm nearly an hour late. With a sinking feeling of dread, I make my way slowly along the sweeping drive leading to the front of the mansion, taking care not to kick any gravel up onto the manicured grass either side. In the mirror, I see the gates automatically close behind me, locking me inside my prison as securely as any high-security detention centre.

My apparent freedom this afternoon was an illusion, a taste of normality solely to mock me. The GPS tracker in my car, Ethan's illegal, but unlimited access to CCTV footage, together with the not unlikely possibility he could have had someone following me, curtails any thought of escape.

Like it had flashed through my mind briefly when the mechanic, Josh, had come to my aid, I'd also had the fleeting thought of confiding my plight to the dentist I'd been to see today. But I have already learned my lesson of what happens to innocent people if I try to enlist their help. Ethan made sure I only needed one example of that. He allows me a modicum of normality, permitting me occasionally to go off the estate, but it's only one more way to toy with me, allowing me a brief glimpse of the life I'm missing. That I was allowed out at all is a privilege. That I'm home late will be something for which I'll have to pay.

I park, switch off the engine, then remain in the car for a second trying to compose myself, erasing any trace of guilt that could appear on my face. It's not my fault I'm late, but if I look like I need to shoulder any blame, Ethan will jump on that weakness immediately.

Suddenly the driver's door is pulled open. I look up into my tormenter's face.

"You're late." His tone is emotionless.

Eighteen months ago

"Hey, girlfriend!" As I pulled Sophie in for a hug and a kiss, she turned her head and accidentally ended up giving me a smacker on the lips.

"Hi yourself, babes!" The grin almost split her face in two, as I slapped her lightly on the arm.

"Carry on like that they're going to think we're a couple of lessies."

She immediately pulled away, glancing around as if evaluating the quality of the males in the pub. She's like that, always looking for her next conquest. I barked a laugh at her, and together we went to the bar and ordered a round of drinks. While waiting to be served she started regaling me with all she'd been up to, and didn't stop talking, except to nod briefly at the bartender and give her choice of vodka and coke. By the time, we were sitting at a table in the corner where we could gossip to our hearts' delight my mouth had already fallen open.

"Both of them? Together?" As she smirked her confirmation, I found myself wondering exactly what goes where in such a situation. I was far less worldly than my friend, whose primary goal in life seemed to be collecting as many and varied sexual experiences as she was able to. But this particular story had rendered me speechless.

Now it was her turn to give me a slight rap on the hand to get my attention. "So what's up with you, bitch? 'Bout time you got laid, isn't it? How long's it been now?"

Sophie and I had a long friendship going back to our Uni days when we shared a flat together. Living a fair distance apart, our contact nowadays was limited to these Friday girls' nights out which tended to follow the same pattern. Each time we met, she would entertain me with her long list of conquests while I sat back and listened. Not that I didn't enjoy living vicariously through her experiences, it's just that occasionally I'd have liked to have some of my own stories to reciprocate. And she's right; it had been an awfully long time since my last sexual encounter with anything that wasn't battery operated, and even that, like the others before it, hadn't been anything to write home about.

I had nothing to compare with Sophie's adventures. Oh, I'd had a few intimate liaisons sure, but had never seen much point in it myself; a few fumbles, then he, whoever it was, did the deed and left me cleaning myself up, waiting for him to leave so I could have a session with my trusty vibrator. Okay, the first time was understandable, with both of us virgins and neither having a clue what to do; the whole rather unfulfilling and embarrassing, and, in his words, messy event, saw us amicably agreeing to part ways just a short time later. But, as years passed and after several more tries with various partners, which always left me feeling similarly unsatisfied, I was not overly fussed to repeat the experience. Hence my envy of the way Soph appeared to put it all out there, and the enjoyment she got from doing the dirty deed.

But needing to contribute something to the conversation, I took advantage, when she paused for breath, and just dropped it in there, my voice animated, "Guess who I'm working for?" Watching her shrug, as obviously it was impossible for her to answer without me explaining, I continued excitedly, "Ethan bloody St John-Davies!"

"What? He's like one of the richest men in the country, Zoe!" After a quick flash of her eyes letting me see I'd caught her interest, she grabbed her phone out of her bag. "Go on, tell me more." She gazed intently at the screen, fingers of *one hand flying over the keys, but waving her other to show she was still listening.*

"I'm working on a project to renovate a 16th century walled garden on a massive estate; his estate." I gestured towards the picture of the handsome looking man who'd appeared on her phone.

She seemed to be enraptured by the image, "I could so do that! Wow! Just look at him! And look at that house behind him. It's a fucking mansion! Is that where you're working? Do you need an assistant? Have you met him?"

Ignoring her questions and wanting to give the answers in my own way, I continued, "So, there I was, Soph, digging in a trench on the hottest day of the year so far. You can imagine the state of me; sweat pouring off me, my tank top sticking to my boobs. And you know what trouble I have with my fair skin—even Factor 50 hadn't stopped me turning bright red."

A chuckle. "You weren't looking your best then, babe?"

I huffed. "About as far from it as you can frigging get! My hair was plastered to my forehead, and, I'd been digging down into the subsoil, so vile stinking mud covered me from the head to toe!" I wait for her snort. Soph, a fashion buyer for one of the top chain stores, had never understood my love for my profession that had me getting down and dirty, in a quite literal way. There it was! I smiled at her derisive sniff.

"Anyway," I continued, "Suddenly I hear voices, and it's him! And all I can think about is what I look like and how I must smell. I tried to hide, but Rod—he's my boss—decides it's an excellent time to introduce me."

"You actually bloody met him? What's he like?"

"Gorgeous!" I tapped my finger on her phone, "In his case, the camera doesn't lie. And it certainly doesn't show you his rather tight backside. Soph, his gluts are something else!"

Now her mouth hung open, "I'm surprised you noticed, Zoe! Go you!"

"Well, when he asks if I'm a woman labourer, Rod only bloody tells him I'm the landscape architect on the project!"

"I thought you were just an assistant?"

"I did, too. But Rod, bless him, has given me the project to manage, with him just overseeing I'm doing things right. Workwise it's a tremendous opportunity, Soph!"

Her eyes narrowed as I deviated from what interested her most, "Hey, babe! Get back to the good stuff!"

"Okay, so he introduces me…"

"I got that bit, babe. Now get to the fucking part."

My drink almost shot out of my mouth as I spluttered, "What the heck?" I gave her a long stare, and she returned a rueful smile. "So," I ignored her interruption, "He introduces himself in this really upper-class cultured voice, you know, pronouncing his name as Ethan 'sinjun' Davies. I brush as much dirt as I can off my hands, and he holds his out for me to shake. Hah! Then I notice him wipe it off on his trousers. Don't think he's used to mud."

"I doubt he ever gets his hands dirty, babe. According to this website he's a billionaire and that is fucking multi-million-pound estate you're working on. He'll employ minions to do everything for him." She tilted her head to one side, "So what happened next?"

Taking the opportunity to have a sip of my drink, I

thought for a moment. Yes, I'd done internet searches too when I'd arrived home that day, and something inside of me tingled when I saw him described as one of the most eligible bachelors in the UK. I wasn't going to tell Soph just how much he'd fuelled my fantasies over the last few days, and how many times I'd regretted he did not see me looking halfway decent! What girl could truthfully say she's never wanted to be Cinderella?

"Nothing, Soph. He went his way, I went mine," I told her, honestly. "To tell the truth, we've been working on the site for a month now, and that's the first and only time I've seen him. I doubt I'll see him again." I pointed to her empty glass, "Another?"

Present day

"Why are you late, Zo?" His voice is calm, but the vein pulsing on his forehead betrays his false equanimity.

Knowing any embellishment is likely to be greeted with a sneer of disbelief, I offer him the pure and straightforward truth. "I had a tyre blowout, Ethan. On the M25." A tremor comes naturally, "It was scary, but I managed to get onto the hard shoulder..."

Already he's lost interest in my explanation. Instead, he's looking down at the car. When he doesn't immediately see anything amiss, he starts to walk around it. I see the moment he notices the space saver wheel on instead of the proper one as he begins to nod slowly. "Must have been frightening, Zo. Are you're okay?"

Ignoring his faked concern for my wellbeing, it's a game

he likes to play, I answer him nonetheless. "I'm fine. Shaken, but not hurt. It could have been worse."

"Good. That's very good, Zo."

I hate the way he shortens my name, but wouldn't dare pull him up on it. The first time he used it I had butterflies in my stomach, thinking it signified that I was important enough for him to give me a unique nickname, but now I've learned to be wary. Ethan doesn't do nice. Or hasn't done, for a very long time.

"Come, dinner's waiting, but it will probably be ruined by now." He puts his arm around my shoulders in an affectionate gesture.

I make every effort not to flinch, and somehow the words come out of their volition as he mentions the spoiled meal, "I'm sorry…" Shit! Never apologise.

"Well, it can't be helped, can it?" he acknowledges mildly.

Have I got away with it? Surely not! He won't let an opportunity like this pass by.

I scarcely dare to breathe as he leads me into the stately home that has been my home for almost a year and a half now. We enter via the grand front entrance and cross the spacious hallway with its impressive staircase leading to the upper floors. He helps me off with my coat, and hangs it up, a demonstration of his well-bred manners. His hand goes to the small of my back in a gentlemanly fashion as he guides me into the formal dining room. Why he insists on always eating here, I'll never understand. The long antique table, dating from the sixteenth century, could easily seat twenty people, and we look lost sitting opposite, one at either end. Early on I took an instant dislike almost bordering on hatred, to the portraits of his ancestors hanging on the walls which seem to look down on me with censure, their creepy eyes following me wherever I go as if wondering how I, a mere commoner, dare to eat in this room. As usual, I keep my eyes downcast and try to ignore them.

A long sideboard takes up one side of the room, the top of which currently covered by tureens on warmers. Ethan takes me straight over to the food, only letting go of me to lift the lids of the containers. In one, there's Coq Au Vin, usually a favourite of mine, but tonight does nothing to tempt me, I've no appetite. In another, there are roast potatoes, and the last holds mixed vegetables. The latter have suffered from being left too long, runner beans, carrots and peas well past their best, shrivelled and dried. Ethan fills two plates, piling one high with a generous helping of the ruined veg as if to make a point. Then he nods to my usual seat and puts the overfilled plate in front of me. He pours red wine into a glass for himself then, with a sneer, pours a glass of white for me. Red wine gives me a nasty headache, and he only indulges me at home. In public, I have to drink the right wine with the meal.

We eat in silence for a moment, or in my case; I pick at my food.

"Lucky I took out AA membership for you." Again, his voice is reasonable and calm.

I swallow rapidly, almost choking on the piece of chicken I'd been chewing. *Ethan knows!* I look up to see his piercing eyes staring at me as if he can see the thoughts in my head. With a sneer that I don't understand, he turns back to his food, clearing his plate. My own is still almost full.

Suddenly he holds something up and waves it at me. "Explain this!" His shout echoes around the room.

I can see what it is from here; it's the business card my saviour Josh gave me. He must have got it out of my pocket. *Shit!* I look up at him. "He was very helpful to me, Ethan. He's a mechanic. When he saw I'd broken down, he stopped and changed the wheel for me."

Ethan's face darkens, "And you were going to tell me this, when?"

With a feeling of dread, I keep silent knowing I'd already missed my chance to come clean.

His face tightens as he glowers, "What other services did he offer you?"

I shake my head. Remaining calm and keeping my voice even is hard, but I call on the months of practice to help. "None, I had a blowout as I said. He pulled up behind me and offered to sort it out for me. He was very quick. I thought it would be faster than waiting for the AA." My eyes, meeting his at last, silently plead for him to believe me.

"Get me your phone." His voice is cold, icy.

He means immediately. Putting down my cutlery, I go out into the vast hall and collect my bag. Pulling out my iPhone, I hand it to him before retaking my seat at the opposite end of the table, needing to retain the distance between us. He puts in my passcode that he knows by heart.

After a second, he looks up. "You didn't even try to ring the AA. Were you with this man? Did you let him touch what is mine?" His voice has deepened, his face glowing red; the first familiar signs he's starting to lose control.

"No! Of course, not!" I deny it as forcefully as I can, while still trying to keep my voice relaxed. If I show my fear, he'll interpret it as guilt. "It happened just the way I said. He pulled up before I could get a chance to ring anyone, and I wanted to get home to you as quickly as possible. I thought it was the fastest way. I didn't want to be late, Ethan. I know how that disappoints you." My heart's beating so frantically I think it's going to jump out of my chest. I've tried like I always try, but whatever the truth of the matter I know that he'll choose not to believe me. What he thinks could have happened is sufficient for him. I start to feel sick, the small amount of food I've managed to swallow churning inside of me. *How bad will it be?*

"You didn't tell me about him. You left that little tidbit out, didn't you? You tried to keep it from me. Now that makes me very suspicious, Zo. Very." His words come out fast as he stands up and marches to my end of the table, pulling me roughly to my feet. Without giving me time to prepare, his fist goes hard into my face; I hear a crunch, and see stars. *Jesus! Has he broken my nose?*

I reel, but he holds me tight, not letting me go. Hanging onto my arm he drags me towards the door. Once there was a time he was much more careful about leaving marks where people could see them, not wanting others to see the damage he'd caused, but recently his brutality has been growing steadily worse. Now he no longer cares, and right at this moment, I'm about as scared as I've ever been.

I should know better after all this time, should be aware that making any protest or trying to fight the inevitable will only enrage him further, but maybe the blow to my head dazes me. Instead of giving in and letting him take me where he wants to, I yell, "No!" and put my free hand on the door-jamb, holding onto it with all my might as he tries to pull me through,.

I could have so easily missed the glint of glee in his eyes as he lets go of the heavy door, pushing against it to slam it closed. The thick wood smashes against my wrist, and I let out a blood-curdling scream as I'm immersed in pain so bad I pass out for a fleeting moment. When he opens the door, he's laughing as he starts to haul my almost limp body across the floor, out into the hallway. *No, not now, please, I can't take it!* Full senses returning I protest, "Ethan, please, no!" My voice is a wail as I cry out through my tears.

He ignores my pleadings, dragging me with one hand while the other extracts a key from his pocket. In my agony, I've no option but to go with him downstairs to the basement, to that dreaded room he calls his play room, the place I've come to call my torture chamber. Opening the door, he manhandles me inside, throwing me across the spanking bench, but not tying me down. He doesn't have to; I've no fight left in me. All I can do is hope that what he's going to do won't be unbearable.

Reaching round my waist he undoes my button and zip, yanking my trousers down to the floor and ripping off my lacy underwear. Cruelly his hand crushes my naked mound, his fingers invading me, "This is MINE! You let another man touch it." He smacks his hand down hard, once, twice, and then again.

"No, I didn't!" I scream out, "He didn't touch me!" But it wasn't worth my breath to voice the denial. As one firm hand holds me down, I try in vain to struggle knowing he's not going to believe my innocence. It suits him not to credit the truth.

Another harsh spank, his palm hitting with enough force to bruise, "You're MINE! This belongs to ME, no one else. I'm going to remind you of that," he tells me, then adds, as I hear him lowering his zip, "I'm taking what belongs to me."

CHAPTER 2
Kadar

Head bowed, I stand by the unmarked grave almost hidden in the grounds of the great palace in Al Qur'ah, the country's capital. The grave which contains a man who I'd thought too larger than life to die. A man who I expected would be around so much longer than the sixty-three years Allah had allotted him.

Who would have thought a brain aneurysm would have taken Emir Rushdi as fast as a lightning strike? And who'd have thought that I, at just thirty-four years old, would be picking up the reins of the country; becoming Absolute Monarch of Amahad, a small but strategically placed Arab state with a coastline on the Persian Gulf? Stunned at the loss of the man I called father, I'm nowhere near ready to take his place. Despite training me to follow in his footsteps since the day of my birth, he'd died long before I felt sufficiently prepared to take on his role. But now, by chance of birth, I'm the ruler.

Yesterday, alongside my brothers I bathed our father's cold body, washing him three times as is our fashion, feeling no emotion. Even after we wrapped his remains in a shroud and buried him in the earth, my heart remained numb. Then, today, the new deference proffered to me by the senior government officials as well as the household staff brought home my great loss. With it came the realisation that I *am* the emir, and there's no one else to whom I can turn or pass this burden. The resulting tide of grief drove me here to my father's graveside, this pile of earth which will soon become overgrown, any sign that anyone had ever been buried here hard to find. No tomb, no mausoleum, nothing to mark the passing of a monarch. Our way of showing even a ruler is simply a man, destined just like anyone else, to return to dust.

Here I stand, paying my last respects to the man who sired me, and who had left me such a legacy. An inheritance I've never been certain I wanted, and one which, without doubt, I'm not yet ready to collect.

The warm desert air whispers around me, and I strain to hear just one final word from the former ruler. But there's nothing. He left everything unfinished; letters half-written, contracts waiting to be signed. Meetings arranged with foreign dignitaries, negotiations due to be held with the Amahadian tribes. These are just some of the balls I now have to pick up and run with. Me. No one else. The overwhelming responsibility is mine alone.

It's now my duty to keep the desert sheikhs united and supporting the Crown; a formidable task when even at the late emir's funeral there were sideways glances and overheard comments that I was too young to lead. And decision making starts now, today.

Do I rule like my father and continue to put barriers in the way of progress? Or govern as I would want to, exploiting our new found oil wealth to modernise the whole country? An ominous cloud hangs over me, and an air of uncertainty sweeps throughout our lands. Amahad, a country of two halves; the progressive and multicultural north always at odds with the desolate desert of the south, where life is harsh and steeped in traditions of the past. Even if I give my all to succeed, others are just waiting for me to fail. And the result of failure would be the loss of my throne—if I'm lucky I'll be deposed, if I'm not, I could face assassination. It's a dangerous legacy that I've been left.

"Why, father? Why did you leave me now?" The cry escapes me almost as a howl, but I need not suppress my feelings here; for this short space of time I'm left alone and given privacy to grieve. Sinking to the ground, I let handfuls of earth run through my fingers. "I'm not like you; I'm not strong enough." I let my head fall forward, the last gesture of obeisance towards the man who I admired not, perhaps, for the manner in which he did things, but how he managed to keep everything tightly controlled. I have to follow in his footsteps, but I'm not sure the shoes will fit.

****

The palace of Amahad is vast. With so many of the ancient rooms fallen into disuse, some have now been repurposed to serve more modern functions. One such area, located on the lower floor, has been turned into a gymnasium and is reserved for the use of the royal family. As my brothers and sister have made their homes elsewhere, it's not unusual that I have the massive space to myself. Especially since my preference is to get my workout completed in the early hours before most of the palace is awake.

Even as Crown Prince the work demands were substantial and now more so that I'm the emir. While I'd have loved to have had the time to devote to more pleasurable ways of keeping fit— riding, one passion of mine which I never now seem to have occasion to enjoy— I need to maximise the benefits, while minimising the time taken, to maintain my level of fitness. My physical capability to protect myself essential, particularly now I've taken the throne.

This morning, a week to the day after the death of my father starts like any other. Changing into my exercise gear, I first complete my warm up then start the programme of exercises my personal trainer had compiled for me. Sweat starts to build as I perform the series of lunges, squats, and bench presses and the range of other activities in their prescribed order, and then repeat them again. I begin to feel the rush of endorphin release as I push my body to its limits, the exertion helping to focus my mind. As usual, the despondency with which I start my exercise is replaced by a more positive attitude as my brain clears, allowing solutions, not problems to take the fore.

After one final circuit and now decidedly feeling the burn, I finish off and take a much-needed shower. Energised to start my day, I turn my mind to the first item on today's agenda, an important meeting, but this one at least with a man I can call a friend.

An hour later, I'm ready and waiting as Sheikh Rais enters my office. Before seating himself across the desk from me, he performs a deep bow that I return in deference to his status and reputation, earned by his prowess on the battlefield and renowned sharp intelligence. He's one of the most powerful and influential of the desert sheikhs, the leaders of the tribes in the southern desert. Rais is a man just a couple of years older than myself, and, like me, educated for the most part in the west. Unlike me he seems better able to marry his staunch traditional background and upbringing with the values learned during his years in England and more able to stomach the atrocities he sees almost on a daily basis.

If his scarred face wasn't enough to show he's no stranger to the harsher side of life his bearing—shoulders up and back, chin raised in ever ready challenge and piercing eyes— would indicate this is a man to be reckoned with. A good friend to have on your side, but a man no one would relish as an enemy. When Rais speaks, even an emir would do well to listen.

"Thank you for staying on in Al Qur'ah after the funeral." Well aware the desert sheikhs are often a law unto themselves it's wise for me to request their presence, not demand, so I voice my appreciation that he accepted my invitation to this meeting.

"My pleasure, Emir Kadar."

"No formalities between us, Rais. I wanted to talk with you as a friend."

He breathes in deeply, and then sighs, "And you need those, Kadar."

"It's bad then?" I don't need to explain I want to sound him out on how much truth there is in the rumours that have reached the palace. It would be useful to get the gist of how the leaders of the other nine tribes are positioning themselves in relation to my succession to the throne. He'll be well aware why I wanted to see him today.

Creasing his eyes, Rais seems to be pulling his thoughts together, "No one likes change, Kadar. An old shoe might be more comfortable than a new one, at least until it starts to let in the dust. There's always comfort in the devil you know."

I huff a laugh, "Devil's probably the right word."

"You see that. I see that. Doesn't mean others do," he frowns.

Wiping my hand over my face, I park it briefly on my chin. I find it difficult to believe that the previous emir had so much support in his manner of leadership, which to put it simply, was to rule with an iron fist. "My father never gave an inch. His way was always the right one."

"But one which my fellow sheikhs were comfortable with," Rais pauses before adding, "Myself, not so much. But at least we all knew exactly where we were."

"Which was where he told you to be. He'd allow no questioning of his decisions or policies."

Rais laughs, "His advisors had an easy job of it, they just said yes to whatever he proposed or waited until he told them what advice to give."

He's hit the nail on the head. But enough about the old emir and the way things used to be done. Today it's more important to discover what's happening now and the reliability of the gossip that's been reaching the palace, "What's the view of the Haimi?" I ask him about his tribe,

"How are your people on the ground feeling about the change in ruler?"

He shrugs, "Take Muzaffar, for example, his methods would probably not be condoned by any international court of human rights. But they work." Rais says, referring to the man who's responsible for interrogating any jihadists captured while crossing our southern borders. "Your father celebrated his skills in extracting information, and there's no doubt the intelligence he's obtained over the years has saved lives. No one likes using torture, but you try to restrict that…" He breaks off and shrugs.

Leaning back in my chair, I fold my arms and bow my head. I want to improve our international reputation but as my father refused to censure the practices of people like Muzaffar, we've already got committees of the United Nations making noises. Even though there haven't been outright complaints—to be frank, anyone who would have raised such a grievance would no longer be breathing. I receive reports to the palace, of course, but we don't make them public record. Nevertheless, wind of how we operate has reached prying ears. I don't want to get on the wrong side of the UN, but on the other hand, I know where Rais is coming from. The desert's a brutal place, and desperate measures are necessary to protect the tribes and their way of life.

Already I've started to make changes. Only yesterday I signed the dictate outlawing death by public execution when I found out two of our tribes, the Qaiquw and the Khabi, still continue the practice which has received condemnation and has been prohibited throughout the world. I'd been horrified to find it still regularly carried out in some parts of my country. Luckily, as the custom was limited to just the two tribes, it hadn't come to the notice of Amnesty International for which I could only be grateful. But I've yet to face the fallout from my decree against carrying out the death sentence in the presence of spectators, and putting an end to that barbaric tradition might require subtle negotiation. I also reduced the number of crimes punishable by the death penalty, revising the ancient list and removing, amongst others, burglary, blasphemy and theft from the list. Which means we need new prisons built… My work is never ending.

"Anything else?" I ask him.

"I know the men of Ghalib's tribe, the Hagra, are worried about some of your proposed changes to the justice system." Rais continues his precis of the current situation.

Although we'd long since giving up the practice of amputating the hand of a thief, and no one has been stoned in Amahad for decades, lashing is currently still permitted for some crimes. It's well known I'm planning incarceration, imposing fines or, in some cases, community service as the only available punishments for all crimes, except the most severe. So along with the gaols we'll need courts and jury system in place to administer it all. The northern cities already function this way, in the desert, though; the decision of the appropriate sentence is at the discretion of the tribal leader. They've worked that way for centuries.

"And your view, Rais?"

"It's something we need to do."

I'm glad he's on my side; having led his tribe for ten years now he's had the time to demonstrate his strength as leader and garners a lot of respect from the other sheikhs. Something I've yet to do. "What else should I be aware of?"

Now he laughs, "I heard the tribes are terrified of women learning to drive."

I give him a weak smile, it's a trite example, but behind it lies a myriad of issues. In the northern cities, Amahadian women can wear what they like, drive and work. But in the desert, though such matters are not prohibited by custom they're not encouraged either. And it's well known I want to unite the country, so there is consistency across the nation. My father declined to impose equal rights on the desert tribes, turning a blind eye to their refusal to come into the twenty-first century.

"There's concern about how far your reforms are going to go, Kadar, and how fast and how much it will affect them."

"Amahad needs to change if we are to establish our position in the international arena. We must improve our reputation to take our place in the world marketplace. If sanctions are raised against us our country could be ruined financially."

"I can't argue with you about that. But you're treading a thin line, and must proceed carefully to avoid revolt."

I know how everything hangs in the balance. It's all I've been thinking about since my father died. My choices are to continue to ignore the outmoded practices by the desert tribes, or do something about them. Part of the problem is that our largest military base is located in the southern half of the country, with most of the soldiers drawn from the desert people. The possibility of a coup is therefore not an idle threat.

"Are *any* of the sheikhs voicing support for me?" I hardly dare vocalise the question and dislike the hesitation before Rais responds, as it douses any lingering hopes of an easy transition to the throne.

"Sofian, Wahid, and Ghalib are pushing for time to let you prove yourself, and are wary of any attempt to depose you. What viable alternative is there? No one else has been groomed to lead Amahad. And you're best placed in the international arena."

Nodding, I know that's probably as much as I could hope for. But there's something I have to ask, "What about you, Rais? Would you want my position?"

Tilting his head to the side, he looks me in the eye, deep lines appearing on his forehead. He's garnering his words, letting me know I'll hear an honest answer, "There's talk, of course. I've been tentatively approached, but my relative youth," he pauses to point his finger at himself and then towards me, "Is an issue, same as with you."

At thirty-four I don't feel particularly youthful, but it's not my view that counts. Again I dip my head up and down in agreement, then jerk my chin towards him, "Who's the most opposed to me?"

He snorts, "You really need me to tell you that?"

"Abdul-Muhsi," I answer for him, giving an exasperated sigh and letting my head fall into my hands.

"He's the only one who believes himself a contender for the throne." The look of disgust on Rais's face shows exactly what he thinks about that.

"Has he much support?"

Rais narrows his eyes, "Only from his own tribe, as I understand it. Though I don't doubt, he'll be canvassing others."

"I already know I'll need to keep a close eye on him."

"Yes, you will." If I hadn't already been aware of my number one enemy, the sheikh who claims his right to the throne on account of his distant relationship to the royal family, the force in his reply would have convinced me.

There's a moment of silence between us; Rais hasn't told me anything I don't already know. But neither has he brought me much comfort.

Standing, Rais walks over to the window, gazes out into the gardens, and then returns to my desk. I glance up at him, knowing he's not finished with our conversation. I raise my eyebrow.

"The monarchy needs constancy, Kadar. I know your brothers stand next in line should anything happen to you, but if you provide an acceptable heir, then I believe you'd have more backing behind you. Much of our country is very traditional, as you are aware."

Leaning forwards, I steeple my hands and rest my chin on my fingertips. "The proposal was voiced at the funeral, and I have agreed to it." I reply bluntly. To be honest, I'd consent to almost anything that would provide some stability for myself and for Amahad. This particular issue hadn't been a price I'd factored in to have to pay, but in the scheme of things, what's the loss of my personal choice and freedom if it buys peace?

Rais rearranges his fierce features into an approximation of a smile; it does little to gentle his expression, "Following the custom of marrying a woman acceptable to the sheikhs, or at least the majority of them, would cement your allegiance to Amahad in their eyes. The ultimate personal sacrifice, so to speak."

I know. My father had followed the same path, the one I'd always hoped to be able to avoid. While Rushdi and my mother Hafsa seemed happy enough until her death at my sister Aiza's birth, it was still an arranged marriage. It's archaic, in this day and age, to be forced into an intimate relationship for political reasons, but at this point, if it avoids upheaval in Amahad, I'll go along with it.

I know I'm the only person who can lead my country, none of the sheikhs have the experience, knowledge or connections to do so, whatever they might believe. Putting any one of them in my position would return Amahad to the medieval times, and place the development of the oil field—on which our continued financial health depends— in jeopardy. I'm not naïve enough not to acknowledge the sheikhs wish to have some control on their ruler through the wife I take to my bed, but if martyring myself on the matrimonial altar is what is needed to keep Amahad from descending into civil war, that's what I'll do.

In truth, I've no real feeling about it either way. I've never had a woman as a permanent fixture in my life, there's no one I've yet met who'd I've seen myself wanting to spend a lifetime with. I've been too wedded to my country to have time to play the field. Like most men, my cock's not too fussy about which particular hole it sinks into, so I've no real concerns about my ability to impregnate the woman of their choice.

Rais takes his seat again. He himself is a widower with a seventeen year old son so has no personal interest in who might become my wife.

I frown at him as he smirks, "Jibran's eldest daughter is quite attractive. I could do that easily. I'd avoid Tamir's — she's a bit of a shrew. And Nazmi's? I doubt you'd be the first to plough that."

His comments break the tension and make me laugh. "It's been suggested I marry King Asad of Alair's daughter, to unite our countries."

"Fuck!" the expletive is drawn out of him as he splutters, "She's hardly out of nappies."

"She's sixteen," I correct him, a wry grin on my face.

The corners of his mouth turn up as he studies me, as though wondering whether I'd stoop so low. I leave him guessing, but the answer is a definite no. While some women might not see marriage to a wealthy ruling sheikh as a punishment, I'd never put someone so young or presumably innocent in that position. No one will be forced into my bed; the woman I wed will come willingly or not at all. And I don't worry there won't be plenty of eager contenders for the position. I can only hope to find someone to my taste.

I've had enough of this subject, so change it. "You'll keep me informed of anything you hear, Rais? Your counsel is always welcomed."

"Of course I will. I'll keep my ear to the ground. Any rumours of any substance I'll be sure to let you know. You have my support, Kadar, you can bank on that."

I stand and round the desk to take his hand, drawing him to me, slapping him on the shoulder a couple of times. "Rais, I'm always grateful to you and our friendship."

He reciprocates my actions. "Take care, Kadar. And watch your back."

As he takes his leave and exits my office, I feel a shiver running down my spine. While normally just a figure of speech, the possibility that one day soon I might find cold steel stabbing between my vertebrae is a very real possibility and not one I should be dismissing lightly.

CHAPTER 3
Zoe

I come to, finding myself lying on the cold stone floor of the basement playroom realising I must have passed out from the pain, and that Ethan just left me where I'd fallen. Pulling myself up stiffly I wonder how long I've been lying here; the house is dark and quiet, suggesting it might have been hours. Without bothering to rescue my ruined underwear, I pull up my trousers, wincing as the material scrapes my tender skin. And then I freeze as I feel wetness trickling down my legs. *He didn't use a condom.* No! How could he? Did he forget? Or is this just another way to entrap me? Not being able to tolerate the pill I'm completely unprotected. *Shit!*

A violent tremor brings me back to myself, forcing more immediate concerns to the forefront of my mind. Pulling my ruined blouse around me, unable to use the sleeve due to my swollen wrist, shivering with cold and pain wracking my body I shuffle through the eerily still and silent house, making my way through the corridors into the surprisingly modern kitchen at the rear. This part of the property is the domain of Mrs Denton, the cook, who the St John-Davies family have employed for decades. Ethan holds her in high regard due to her long service and how she cared for him when he was a child. Which explains why her realm was completely overhauled and refurbished to restaurant standards just a couple of years ago.

Switching on the harsh overhead light, I approach a corner cupboard, one I've visited far too often. Reaching up with my good hand, I grab the bottle of painkillers, tipping just two into my hand. Ethan will have counted them; I daren't take more. Catching a glimpse of myself in the mirror on the door of the cupboard I falter at the sight; dried blood covers my face, and one of my eyes is already puffed-up and starting to blacken. Gingerly I reach up and touch my swollen nose; if it's not broken, I'll be lucky.

Only once before has he hurt me this badly, and that was the first, last, and only time, I made any real effort to escape. And I was the lucky one; at least I hadn't ended up in a wheelchair like my dear friend Sophie who'd dared to help me. Oh, the police had it down as a hit and run accident happening just a day after Ethan had brought me back. Only I knew it wasn't a coincidence; he might not have been the actual driver, but Ethan had been responsible for setting it up. He'd admitted as much. And there wasn't one darn thing I could do about it. The business he's in, the influential friends he has make him so untouchable it would have been signing my death warrant were I to report him.

And that was when he'd told me the same, or worse, would happen to anyone else who dared help me escape. He'd commit murder to keep me with him. It was an effective threat. How could I put anyone else in danger?

How did I let myself get trapped like this?

Things weren't always this way. For the first few weeks,

even months, there was no sign of the man he really was. And when the monster did emerge, it started so gradually it took time to notice. First, it was verbal—little put-downs and off-the-cuff remarks that left me uncertain and unsure of myself, aimed to eat away slowly at my confidence. Then it was a slap, as though in play, but soon the teasing disappeared. Of course, he was solicitous and apologetic after he hurt me, and like an idiot, I forgave him. Every single time. Until the day he introduced me to his playroom. I can't even remember what I did wrong on that occasion, but in that soundproofed room he'd made certain I'd never do it again.

Now he's playing a game, trying to see how much pain I can take. Each day he becomes crueller, and I've can no longer deny that to stay will be the death of me. And he'll get away with it. He can get away with anything. *I have to escape.*

I nod back at my reflection with renewed determination then, looking down at my wrist, I see it's swollen and worse, out of shape. It looks broken. But I doubt Ethan will let me get treatment for it, leaving it to heal as it is as a permanent reminder of what happens when I defy him.

As always, I need to look after myself, there's no one else to help me. Rummaging around to see what I can find to bind it with, I reach down for a container, the one holding medical aid for the guard dogs that patrol the grounds at night—they're better cared for than me. I find some Vet-wrap. It sticks to itself, so I can wrap it around my injury easily enough with the other hand, making it tight enough to hold it in place, hoping that I'm keeping it in a good enough position to heal, gritting my teeth as I do so. When I've finished, it still throbs, but the bandage is at least stopping that jarring bolt of agony every time I move. *I'm right handed*, I try to think positively, *it could have been worse.*

Finished, I switch off the light and leave the kitchen, making my slow, painful and weary way up the staircase and through the hallways of the vast house until I come to the master bedroom, dreading going inside. The very last place I wish to sleep tonight is in Ethan's bed, but that's where he'll expect to find me in the morning.

Without even the energy to brush my teeth, I remove my clothes awkwardly and struggle out of them using my one good hand. Naked, as he likes me, I ease myself under the covers, swallowing my gasps of pain as the sheets rub on the fresh bruises from my earlier beating, lying on my side to try to find a comfortable position which doesn't hurt too badly. He snorts in his sleep, rolls onto his back and begins to snore loudly. *I hate him.*

Aches course through my body; I don't think there's any part of me that doesn't throb or sting. It's impossible to sleep. So I lie, my eyes open, plotting how I'm going to leave, determined, this time, I'm going to get away, but all the while knowing I'll need all my wits about me. If I escape, he'll come after me. Nothing and no one gets away from Ethan St John-Davies. *But I will.* The pain makes me determined.

To escape, Zoe Baker has to disappear off the face of the earth.

Seventeen months ago

We'd missed a couple of weeks for one reason or another, but when our next girls' night out came around I was so eager to see my best friend I arrived early. Tonight I'd got news of my own, and I was almost bouncing in my seat with excitement, impatient to share. Being terrible at keeping secrets, as soon as Sophie walked into the pub and slid up the bench next to me in our normal booth, she noticed something was different and threw me a sharp look.

"Well! You've either got fucked or fucked up!" she announced, as she took a sip of the vodka and coke I'd already bought for her and grinned widely, "Spill!"

I almost spat out my mouthful of wine, and a short laugh burst out of me at her crudeness. Taking a tissue out of my bag, I blotted it over my lips to dry them.

"Come on! Which is it?" She looked at me carefully, "Or have you just been playing too hard with your BOB."

"Sophie!" Admonishing her, I quickly glanced around to make sure no one heard her reference to my vibrator, then put her out of her misery, "Ethan St John-Davies has asked me out on a date!"

Her gasp is loud, "He fucking what?"

"Shush!" I chided her again, noticing heads turn at her exclamation, "Calm down a bit and I'll tell you what happened."

"Well come fucking on then, don't leave me hanging!" Her eyes were wide open; she was as shocked as I'd expected her to be.

Grinning, happy and pleased with myself, I think back to

that day and explain how it all came about. "It was last weekend." In my head, I'm back there, "It was Sunday" I start," Sundays are the crew's day off. So I decided to take advantage of the peace and quiet, going back to the site alone to see how things were coming along." I had a mental picture of the scene. There I was, sitting on the raised bank, enjoying the warmth of the sun utterly engrossed in the drawings I was holding; glancing up now and then as I compared the diagrams to the restoration already completed. I was smiling to myself, happy that the work all seemed to be moving ahead at a good pace, pleased with the progress. Thinking I was all alone, unexpected footsteps approaching on the gravel path startled me. I jumped, and turned so quickly I dropped my papers, and they went flying everywhere in the slight breeze. Trying to gather them up I tripped over a clump of grass landing on my knees. Frigging hell! I'd literally fallen at Ethan St John-Davies' feet. Could I have looked more of a clot if I tried?

Sophie was laughing her head off. "You fell at his fucking feet? Way to go, Zoe! What happened next?"

"He helped me up." I could see it all again. As a hand reached out to assist me, I looked up to greet my employer, immediately regretting this yet another inauspicious meeting. My rags to riches dream rapidly fading into the distance; I summoned up a polite greeting, "Mr St John-Davies! Good afternoon." Brushing the earth from my legs, I felt blood rushing to my cheeks turning them red with embarrassment. Trying to regain some measure of dignity, I forced myself to meet his eyes, and used my most professional voice, "I'm just taking a look to assess how things are coming along."

He studied me carefully; his head cocked and an appreciative smile on his face, "Excepting the dirty knees, Miss Baker. I prefer today's look."

"Zoe, please," I grinned, taking his words as a compliment, even enjoying his brief allusion to my clumsiness. Apart from the aforementioned knees, I was turned out quite well today, wearing a simple yellow sundress which I knew was flattering, emphasising my narrow waist and adequate breasts and well as the flared skirt serving to hide my overly wide hips. I'd left my blond hair loose, so it hung in a cascade reaching just below my shoulders. And, simply because it was a lovely day, I'd put a flower in my hair. I looked very different from the mud-covered urchin he'd first met.

His steady appraisal, followed by a slow, careful nod of approval suggested he liked what he saw. A fact made apparent when he dropped the formality with his direction, "Call me Ethan." Then he raised a quizzical eyebrow and pointed at the blueprint in my hands. I passed it over to him, and he looked at it, glancing from the paper to the garden in front of us. "Your work?"

"Mainly, yes. But Rod's overseen it all." I gave due credit to my boss while part of my mind was thinking how good my role in this project would look on my CV.

"How much longer until it's complete?"

"Hmm," I considered, mentally calculating the work remaining. The torrential rains recently had set us back a bit, hence all the mud in the trench, "If the weather stays with us, about a week to ten days."

"So, a week to ten days. And then I won't have an excuse

to see you again. Right." He looked closely at me, and then another smile lit his face. "We must do something about that."

Tilting my head, I raised my eyebrows, not quite understanding what he was getting at and not wanting to make a fool of myself by reading in a meaning that wasn't there. But that's when he stunned me. Taking my hand, he brought it to his lips and kissed it then, keeping hold; he stared deep into my eyes, "When I'm no longer your, er, employer, I'd like to take you out for dinner," he paused, "Zoe." In a deep and oh, so sexy voice, he completed his invitation with my name, stretching it out, so it sounded like it has three syllables. My stomach dropped, and I shivered, even though the temperature was in the mid-twenties. The invitation so unexpected, at first I was unable to respond. My eyes were glued to his as I tried to think of a suitable reply.

Well, I was certainly not going to turn him down, this rich handsome man who had occupied my thoughts so much over the last few days, particularly when I'd been having some time out with my battery operated boyfriend. For a fleeting moment, I wondered what he'd be like in bed. Maybe he'd be the one to show me what I had been missing. He already had my lady-parts throbbing.

He was waiting for a reply, his brow furrowed as though he couldn't comprehend why I was taking so long to give him my response, but I was tongue-tied unable to believe one of the richest men in England was asking me out. Fuck! Breaking our locked gaze, I managed to get some sense back. When I was sufficiently pulled together and over my shock, I told him my answer in a breathy voice that sounded nothing like my own. "I'd love to," while mentally I was giving myself a high five. Ethan St John-Davies was asking me on a date? I knew it wasn't a proposal of marriage, but even so. Frigging heck! It was hard to prevent myself thrusting my fist in the air and shouting, Yes!

Sophie's mouth had dropped open. "Fucking hell, Zoe. When you get back on that horse you do it properly, don't you? You've landed yourself a fucking thoroughbred stallion!

Present day

The next morning I feign sleep as the bed dips signalling Ethan is rising, but I sense his malevolent presence standing by my side, and know he's looking down at me. He's not fooled. If he were, he'd move away or wake me, but he waits; I hear him breathing and the scent of his expensive aftershave wafts over me. Knowing it will only make things worse to continue to pretend reluctantly I open my bleary eyes. They feel swollen and sore.

"Why do you try my patience so, Zo? You know I don't want to punish you." He speaks so reasonably, his voice so full of regret it would be easy to believe I bring all my beatings on myself. In the beginning, his censure had worked, and I'd forgive him, accepting that I'd been the one to try him too far, that it was me who'd pushed him over the edge. Lying here now, I scoff at myself. Who would ever have believed that *I'd* become *that* woman? The one who exonerates her man, and takes the culpability for his violence on herself? But it starts oh, so slowly; you don't notice the trap closing until it's snapped tight shut. At first, you think you're must be mistaken, the man you met and put your faith in would never do something like that; that it must be something to do with you. Then, as the abuse gradually escalates you realise there are no longer valid excuses to be made, and find you've sacrificed your very soul into a monster's hands.

Experience tells me the correct response, "I'm sorry, Ethan." My throat is dry, so my voice is hoarse.

I see him staring at me for a long moment, but am no longer fooled he bears any remorse. He's examining my injuries, taking pride in his handiwork and admiring the view.

After a pause, he leans over and kisses me. I make sure to control my instinctive response to pull away. "Rest today. It's Mrs Denton's day off, remember? So you'll have to get your own breakfast."

"That's okay, Ethan. I'm not very hungry," I reply, hiding my pleasure that she'll be gone for hours. The emptier the house is, the easier it will be to put my plan into action. Not that the elderly lady could stop me, of course, but she'd report any unusual activity to her beloved Ethan immediately. She dotes on him so much I doubt she believes him capable of doing any wrong. My constant injuries? Well, I'm clumsy in her view. That's all it is.

As Ethan continues to watch me intently, it would be impossible for him to miss the pain I'm in, that my nose is probably broken, or I need medical help, but I know better than to ask. My nerves on edge, it seems an age before finally, he takes one last glance, then brushes his hand possessively, almost lovingly over my shoulder; the caress making want to cringe. Then, at last, he leaves.

As his footsteps fade, my repulsion and fear gradually recede as cautious anticipation and excitement start fizzing inside. Last night was the final time he got to abuse me.

Sixteen months ago

"How did your date go? I can't fucking believe you went out with the richest man in Britain? Go you, Zoe!" Sophie's face was a picture as she leaned forwards, "Tell me he's got friends, babe. And when I can meet them."

I laughed at her, "It's early days yet, girlfriend. But I'll keep my eye out for you. And he's not the richest man, just one of them."

She waved her hand at me, "He's way up there, babe. But come on, spill the beans. What happened on your date? Did you fuck?"

I sighed, and gave a sad shake of my head; that was probably all she wanted to know. "It was a great evening. He was such a gentleman…"

I proceeded to give her a blow by blow account. Ethan had been so solicitous, full of praise for the work that the team and I had done, starting off our evening by telling me, "The walled garden is magnificent! I very much admire what you've achieved there."

I'd just taken a mouthful of the most delicious salmon pate I'd ever tasted in my life, and answered him once I've swallowed it. "It was a team effort, Ethan. I can't take all the credit." I smiled at him, relishing the sight of the gorgeous man sitting opposite me in the poshest restaurant I'd ever been to. I'd known dining out with one of the wealthiest men in the country would be daunting, I mean, he wasn't exactly going to take me to Prezzo's or Frankie and Benny's and expect me to select the cheapest thing on the menu or to share the bill.

I'd been worried that I'd make a fool of myself. Choosing what to wear had been bad enough, but I also wasn't sure I knew the right etiquette for a highfalutin restaurant. By the time he arrived to pick me up in an expensive sports car, I had worked myself up into a state of panic. But I needn't have got myself into such a tizzy, right from the start of the evening, Ethan put me at my ease as he complimented me on my simple black cocktail dress as if it was a designer label and immediately relaxed me with his charming manner.

He continued to act the perfect gentleman, pulling out my chair and waiting for me to be comfortable before seating himself. But his manners shouldn't have surprised me. His family was listed in Who's Who and could trace their ancestry back to the Norman Conquest; he'd known nothing but high society all his life. Giving an inward smile, as I sat down and let him push in my chair behind me, I recalled how I tried tracing my family tree and had to give up at the beginning of the twentieth century when finding a great-grandmother called Ann Smith had proved nigh on impossible. Idly I wondered how Ethan's blue blood would mix with my very average red. And then gave myself a mental slap. This was just a dinner date, for god's sake.

And Ethan himself? Well, to say he was easy on the eyes would be an understatement. He was just under six feet tall; his short, dirty blond hair groomed to perfection, his blue eyes sparkling and bright. He was certainly fit and had to work out in some way, I could tell by the way he moved, his muscles flexing beneath his clothes. He had a rounded face, a slightly weak chin—the only down point that I noticed— and clean shaven. His grey suit was tailored to fit, nothing off the rack for him; the faint sheen of the material screaming quality and money. He was wearing a white shirt open at the collar, and no tie. Underneath his skin was bronzed, and I could see a light smattering of hair across his chest. This man had everything!

The number of knives, forks, and spoons on the linen table cloth had me flustered until he stated he'd ordered a taster menu, a meal of seven small courses and despite my fears, I found it was pretty easy to select the cutlery following the outside-in method. The set meal allowed us to get to start getting to know each other without being sat behind menus for half the night, and provided a topic of conversation as we discussed the food we were served. Ethan dominated the discussion, but that didn't bother me, I was quite happy hearing about a life so different and alien to my own. And who was I to debate whether the oysters were English or imported? As he spoke his voice washed over me like a silk caress; I could have listened to the cultured accent all night. No, I didn't resent him monopolising our discussion.

Ethan liked his food. A fact explained when I found he was all but brought up by the family's cook, Mrs Denton, spending more time in her kitchen than he did with his mother. I interpreted that to mean he didn't have a particularly happy childhood and was an only child. When I asked whether he had any pets to keep him company he told me animals in his household didn't last long, for some reason and, in the end, his parents stopped letting him have any. Though the comment struck me as strange, I was full sympathy for what sounded like a lonely, albeit privileged, life for a little boy.

He was funny and made me laugh, playing down his role as CEO of a multi-billion pound electronics corporation specialising in communications, supplying the police and military in our country as well as abroad. He preferred to concentrate instead on relating the antics of Deena, his middle-aged secretary, for whom he seemed to have nothing but respect.

After the meal, he drove me home and said 'goodnight' at my front door with no expectation of being invited in. When he did nothing more than shake my hand, I felt a glimmer of disappointment realising that was probably going to be my last chance to see how the other half lived. But with his parting words he invited me to an elite dinner and dance river cruise down the Thames the following Saturday and I jumped at the chance. Who'd have thought such a wealthy, handsome, kind and charming man would want anything further to do with me?

"Fuck me, babe! You're going out with him again? Jeez! Why couldn't I have seen him first?"

I gave Sophie a playful slap on the wrist.

Present day

As I lie and wait, giving Mrs Denton time to leave for the day, I realise it would be all too easy to stay, just like I've stayed all the other times before, telling myself, "just one more day." But today, I know, I've run out of time. Another night like the last and I might not capable of going anywhere.

Finally I think I can take my chance. Carefully I pull myself out of bed, holding onto the bedstead until a wave of dizziness passes. Hugging my hand across my stomach I go to the bathroom and wash, making sure to scrub away all evidence of what at last I admit can only be called last night's rape; I certainly didn't consent to it.

Studying my reflection in the mirror while picking up my make-up case, I start to apply a thick base of foundation, disguising my black eye as best I can, and reducing the redness around my nose. Touching my face is painful, but I make myself do it. Close up I look like a battered woman whose gone a few rounds with Mike Tyson; from a distance, I think I'll pass muster. I've no doubt once Ethan finds that I'm gone I'll be the most wanted woman in England.

Having done as much as I can to hide my beaten features, I gaze at my reflection again, remembering how he warned me, "There's no place you can run to, no place where you would be able to hide. Nowhere that's out of my reach." I shiver even though the room is warm and take a deep breath. *You can do this.* Despite the pain, or perhaps because of it spurring me on, I know I've got no alternative. It's past time to break out of this prison.

Dressed, and prepared as well as I'm able, I lift the edge of the expensive and luxurious bedroom carpet and take up the loose floorboard I'd found by accident soon after moving in. One hundred and ten pounds is a pitiful amount, but it's all I've managed to save from the meagre spending money Ethan gives me. Taking out the banknotes I put them in my purse.

Standing up straight, I briefly close my eyes and breathe in deeply. *This is it!* The next step will commit me to my escape; I have to steal from him. Exhaling the air from my lungs, I start towards the bedroom door without a backward glance, taking nothing with me but my handbag.

Cautiously I step out into the corridor, pause and listen. Hearing no sounds, I continue through the vast house, making my way down the staircase and to his home office. It's not worth looking for the keys to my car; Ethan will have taken them, or he'll have programmed the gates so my remote won't work. It's one of the ways he keeps me, prisoner, here. But the garage is full of his collection of luxury cars, and I've spied on him enough to have seen he holds the keys in his locked desk drawer in his study.

I'm trembling so much it's hard to use the heavy antique letter opener to jemmy the drawer open, particularly being able to use only one hand, but failure isn't an option. I try harder, desperate, and when at last the lock springs open, slivers of wood fall to the floor. No going back now, not with such damage clearly visible. I suppress a shudder as I imagine what the 'correction' for that could conceivably be, but spare no remorse for the damage I've caused to the valuable eighteenth-century desk. Step One —getting a means to escape—is complete, and I allow myself a small smile of victory. Standing back with the keys to the BMW in my hand I take another deep breath to fortify myself.

Taking one last look around his study, I flinch, remembering the punishments that have dolled out here, far too many to mention. Then, my horrified eyes land on a business card on the desktop; it's the one the mechanic gave me yesterday. I can't leave it behind in case Ethan decides to visit him, so I pick it up, hoping he hasn't already memorised the information, remembering anyone who comes to my aid is in danger. Turning the card between my fingers, I recall Josh offering his help should I ever need it, well, perhaps today's the day I'll take him up on that. Along with my nervousness, I feel a glimmer of hope. *Maybe, this time, I can succeed.*

I take nothing else with me except a photo of my mother and myself, together with her husband of the time —I forget which number he was—and it joins Josh's business card in the pocket of my jeans. It's a shame I haven't a clue how to open the safe; Ethan had confiscated all my personal documents from me after my first attempt to escape. But as I'll be assuming a new identity, what does it matter I'm leaving everything that identifies me as Zoe Baker behind; my birth certificate, driving licence and passport? I'm going to become someone new.

After checking the coast is clear I leave the main house and make my way to the garage, entering by the side entrance. Pressing the button on the remote, I jump guiltily as the doors of the smart BMW unlock with an overloud beep but recovering quickly, slide into the driving seat. It's an automatic, part of the reason I choose it, but however easy to drive I won't be using it for long. As soon as he knows I'm missing, Ethan will activate the locator on the tracker or will be tapping into the Automatic Number Plate Recognition system used by the police. Highly illegal, but then Ethan plays by no one else's rules. Adjusting the seat, I feel a wave of dizziness, a combination of fear and pain, and I have to wait for a moment, willing it to pass.

At last, with a small tingling thrill of elation, I drive towards the garage doors, waiting for them to automatically rise at such a painstakingly slow rate they seem to take forever to open. As soon as there's sufficient room I go through and out onto the long driveway. Resisting the urge to put my foot down, not wanting to draw unwanted attention, I drive sedately across the gravel track down towards the massive iron gates protecting the property. As I head for them, I'm holding my breath, but the car's remote works and they start to open when I'm just a few metres away. Step Two—escaping the house—is accomplished.

CHAPTER 4
Kadar

During the weeks following my meeting with Rais, other desert sheikhs had come to the palace, mainly to try and discern how my rule was going to be different to that of my father's. More than one had expressed the view that change was to be avoided. This early on in my reign, however, I wasn't ready to share much more than what was already known but the fact that I'd agreed to marriage for political expediency seemed to be welcomed universally. The meetings were cautious on both sides; the sheikhs and I wanting to find out each other's views, while not giving too much away. I was left with a cautious confidence that they would give me at least some time to prove myself, although no particular period was specified or even hinted at. But of course, not all the sheikhs came to meet me.

I'm surprised and not a little concerned when I receive a request from Abdul-Muhsi for a personal audience with the emir, but I clearly have no option other than to agree to it, while making sure I'll have my most senior guards present. I don't trust the man as far as I could throw him, and given the excess weight he carries, that wouldn't be far at all. I'm suspicious over the reasons for this meeting, but doubt he'll come straight out with a challenge for my throne. *Even he's not so stupid to do that, is he?*

The Kassis royal family have had good reasons not to trust him for years now, but recently his insolent behaviour has been escalating, culminating a few months ago in a confrontation with Nijad. If Abdul-Muhsi had has his way, Cara's head would no longer be on her shoulders. Even my father, a staunch supporter of most of the desert sheikhs and their methods of rule, had been wary of the leader of the Qaiquw tribe and Abdul-Muhsi's opinion that as a second cousin, his right of succession should be given serious consideration. Apparently Emir Rushdi's sons, with their extensive international education in the west, were worse placed to rule than a sheikh who'd never stepped outside the Arab nations.

So expecting this morning's meeting is set to be difficult, I only hope to glean useful information about how Abdul-Muhsi would go about his challenge as, eventually, challenge for my position there will surely be.

When ten o'clock comes around, punctual as always, my personal assistant, Richard, allows the desert sheikh into my office. Abdul-Muhsi enters with his customary arrogant swagger, and I take a second to view him. A scar, from a wound my father gave him, stretches from eye to mouth. Their fencing bout, some thirty years ago, had been billed as a friendly one, but even then the tribal leader wanted his rival out of the way. Rushdi, however, was the better swordsman and hadn't been fooled by Abdul-Muhsi's sudden feint then parry; a thinly veiled attempt to get in a fatal blow. The clash of sabre's forced my father's blade up, slicing across his opponent's face earning another black mark against the Kassis family.

Younger than Emir Rushdi by about ten years, the desert sheikh is a shadow of his former self. His belt, now empty of weapons due to the diligence of my guards, sits high over his fat belly, and I feel a shudder of disgust. Not at his excess weight, but the thought that a man in his position should let himself go to such an extent, a vast contrast to the other tribal leaders who are still able to stand and fight with their men.

He's scowling, but whether to express his feelings or a permanent feature as a result of the scar, it's impossible to tell.

"Kadar," he greets me, dipping his head in an almost imperceptible movement. He might be insulting me, or claiming his relationship with the royal family by addressing me so informally, but I don't deign to sink to his level.

"Sheikh Abdul-Muhsi," I respond, with a more polite bow. "I'm honoured you've come all this way to meet with me. Please be seated." I indicate the chair the opposite side of my desk. When he takes it, I sit down. I don't offer refreshment; not seeing any reason to extend what I'm certain will be an unpleasant meeting.

My open manner at least draws some civility from him.

"I was sorry to hear about your father. It was a shock to us all."

I know he's lying through his teeth. He'd probably dance on Rushdi's grave if he knew where it was, but I incline my head, accepting the platitude.

"What can I do for you, Sheikh?" I want to move this meeting along.

He looks down as if examining his hands, and then raises his narrowed eyes to meet mine. There's a shifty expression in them. "It must be very difficult for you, Kadar, to be thrust so unprepared into this role. I have every sympathy for you. And," he adds, staring at me intently, "I offer you my every support and guidance."

His condescension astounds me. "I expect support from all the sheikhs," I tell him, not wanting him to forget I'm the emir of Amahad, and he answers to me. Unless he wants to lose his status.

There's a flash of anger in his eyes, and his olive-skinned cheeks grow darker, but he attempts to hide his irritation at my reminder, "You misunderstand, I intend to offer you *my* services. I am prepared to relocate here to the palace to help you begin your rule."

Which interpreted means he wants to get in on the seat of government. "I can't ask you to do that," I reply, keeping my expression impassive, successfully shrouding my revulsion at this snake of a man, one of the cruellest and most ruthless of any of the tribal leaders. I'd heard murmurings of attempts to replace him as the head of his tribe, but any contenders seem mysteriously to disappear before they can enact a challenge.

"It would be no problem," he hastily seeks to reassure me, every word coming out of his mouth making me inwardly shudder. "You've spent so much time abroad your knowledge of Amahad—particularly the southern desert is limited… "

"My understanding of my country and of my duties as ruler are not in question." Not for the first time in my life when faced with this bastard, I wish my father's blade had struck a few inches lower and removed him permanently from our lives.

"I only meant to suggest… " he blusters.

"That you know the needs of the desert tribes better than I do myself?" Again I've interrupted him. There may well be some truth in what he's saying, but he's certainly not the person I'd go to for advice.

Once more his eyes narrow. He seems to be considering how to continue this conversation. I just want him gone.

"The desert sheikhs have concerns about your ability to rule them," he continues, not knowing when to give up, "With me by your side you'd offer them the confidence you have their best interests at heart."

Close enough by my side to put a blade through my ribs?

"I was not aware you speak for all the tribes?"

He doesn't. I know that, and he knows that. His eyes narrow, and his brow furrows. His hands clench in his lap. This man wants power and doesn't care how he gets it. Unable to tell me that he's got the backing of even the majority of the tribes, he tries to stare me down, but I don't give an inch, meeting his gaze with a reciprocally arrogant one of my own. In the background, I can hear my usually stoic guards shifting on their feet, as though getting ready for my instruction to throw him out of my office. But however attractive that option might be, it's a route I'll have to avoid the temptation to take. He might not speak for all the tribes, but I have to bear in mind that he might speak for some.

He's the first to look away, breathing heavily, seeming to

force himself to relax. After a brief pause, he starts again, his voice now almost friendly, "I hear you've agreed to take a wife?"

He's surprised me with the abrupt change in topic, and the transformation in his approach. I become wary of his motive. But I play the game.

"I have," I agree, "From a selection prepared for me by my advisors. The daughters of the desert sheikhs, if they wish, will be on the list."

Now Abdul-Muhsi sits forwards, the palms of his hands resting flat on my desk. At his movement towards me, I see my guards stiffen, their hands going to the weapons in their belts showing me I'm not alone in my concerns about this man, though I doubt he'd be so stupid as to attack me in my own office.

"I have no daughter," he states.

Ah, so that's it. I'd forgotten that he has only sons. If I marry into one of the other tribes, he'll have even less power. I suppress my grin.

"You must look outside the country for a wife. Perhaps from Alair," he offers.

This time, I don't point out the daughter of King Asad is young enough for me to have sired her, I just nod diplomatically as though considering the option.

"She's a pretty little thing," he states with a leer on his face, "I've considered her for myself."

By Allah! Completely shocked I take in a sharp breath, "I thought you were already married?" Had his wife died? I hadn't heard of it.

"As a second wife," the repulsive excuse for a man

explains, "But I'll make no move until you decide on your choice."

While Muslims are permitted to take up to four wives, polygamy is not nowadays practised in Amahad or Alair, and his suggestion shows the extent he's wedded to the old ways. Asad, I know, would have an apoplectic fit were Abdul-Muhsi to ask for his teenage daughter's hand, so I have no fears such a mating would go ahead. But the thought he can even think of it gives me further insight as to what kind of man he is.

The bastard's watching me, as though waiting for me to thank him. Having to say something, I say, "I will, of course, consider your suggestion." I don't add that I wouldn't contemplate going down that road for a moment. "Now, you will have to excuse me, I have another meeting."

Making no immediate move to take the hint and go, he sits back again. "My offer to assist you stands, Kadar. I am willing to give up my home and move to the palace to aid you. My knowledge of the ways of the southern desert is unsurpassable."

And it's precisely those ways he's talking about that are the ones I wish most to change.

But I have to be polite, not wanting to give him further excuse to malign me, "Thank you, Sheikh. I will give thought to the matter."

He hasn't finished, "You are threatening our way of life, Kadar. With your changes to the judicial system, you are taking away our ability to govern the southern desert as we need to. You have lived in England too long and do not understand that to tie our hands in how we deal with those who break the law will result in chaos. In the desert, retribution must be swift, and punishment must fit the crime."

I could explain to him that progress and modernisation are essential. I could speak to him of the wealth that will come from the oil field and of the foreign nationals who will be working in the desert, using their expertise to extract the liquid gold that will be for the benefit of us all. I could elucidate the importance of international relations and spell out that seeing a man flogged for eyeing up his neighbour's wife in the wrong way or having a hand chopped off for stealing a goat would gain us a poor reputation, and threaten the exploitation of our new found riches. But it's not worth the breath I'd use in doing so.

He can't read the look of derision on my face, or doesn't interpret it correctly as he continues, "Your father understood us. Emir Rushdi assured us shortly before his death he abhorred the heathen ways of Al Qur'ah and the northern cities, and that he was going to ensure a return to the Muslim religion being the only one tolerated in Amahad. You need to make sure to see his visions come to fruition, Kadar. We must rid this country of the infidels."

Sadly, I shake my head, knowing my father lived for peace between the cities and the desert, but would never have threatened the freedoms of the north in such a way. We've been multi-cultural and religion tolerant for centuries. I grow tense and am hard put to keep a tight rein on my temper, knowing Abdul-Muhsi is lying, but not wanting to call him out on it and show my hand. Not just yet.

It annoys me that this one man seems to believe he speaks for all the desert sheikhs as though he's above them all; as if he's already emir. And that will never happen. Unless it's over my dead body.

To my relief, his time's up. A buzz from my intercom and Richard informs me the participants for my next meeting have arrived.

As he realises I'm not going to respond, he stiffens and then pulls himself to his feet. Again he leans over my desk, his face taut, his eyes narrowed, his mouth sneering, "Take care, Kadar, there are those who think you not suitable to be their ruler, and who might rise up against you. You should consider your position. A young man such as yourself, educated as you are could go anywhere in the world and make something of yourself—just like your brother, Jasim. If you stay here as emir, your future, and your life, might be shorter than you would wish."

My guards were not employed for their inattention, and both take a step forward at the same time, a low growl audible from their direction.

I stand, forcing my body to relax, not letting my fury show, "You'd do well not to threaten me, Sheikh."

His hands come up in supplication, and he casts a quick glance over his shoulder, seeming to realise the position he's put himself in. I see his Adam's apple bob as he swallows rapidly, and seeks to reassure me, "No, Emir Kadar," using my title must stick in his throat as he continues, "Obviously I'm not talking about myself. We're family, after all. I just wanted to make sure you realised the risks of treading the path you have chosen. I hear others speak and so I'm only passing on what has come to my ears. I only wish to help and support you, as family should do." And with that passing shot, he finally turns and leaves the room.

Definitely a snake. And I'd best remember a very poisonous and slippery one. Even the air seems cleaner once he's gone.

He's right on one point; I can't afford to alienate the desert sheikhs. But what he doesn't know is that I've already got ideas how to go about that. A proposal to keep the tribal leaders on my side, while ensuring the needs of the desert are balanced with those of the cosmopolitan cities. A plan that Abdul-Muhsi would hate.

How far would Abdul-Muhsi go to depose me? That's the unanswerable question. And what support does he have? The hairs on the back of my neck stand up as his threat echoes in my head. If he had his way my reign would be a short one, as would my life.

CHAPTER 5
Zoe

I daren't drive far. As soon as Ethan realises I've left the house, he'll get a trace put on both me and the car. And I'm not so naïve as to think after last time's attempt he'll have hidden GPS trackers in everything I own. So I only travel a couple of miles from his estate into the nearest town, Guildford. Parking in the city centre's multi-storey, I leave the keys inside as it's served its purpose. If it's stolen, it will help spread a false trail.

Quickly I enter the already busy shopping mall and take out as much cash as I can from the first ATM I see. I can only get out a measly six hundred pounds, the total of the maximum three hundred pounds I'm allowed from each of my debit and credit cards. Then, entering the first clothes shop I find, I take next to no time purchasing an entirely new set of clothing, right down to underwear and shoes. I put it all on in the changing room, exiting the shop carrying a bag full of anything and everything that could have been tagged by Ethan. Finding the nearest bin, I dump everything I'd left the house with, including, reluctantly, my iPhone, old bag, and purse.

A stall selling wigs is my next target. I buy a couple and walk away, my head now a mass of auburn curls. The final stop I make is Boots, where I purchase the morning-after pill after being subjected to a rather intense, but sympathetic scrutiny by the pharmacist. I know he's seen my black eye when he doesn't question my purchase, limiting his conversation to just giving me clear instructions as to its use. With relief I put the little box in the handbag I'd bought along with my new clothes. I want no lasting reminder of Ethan St John-Davies. Lastly, before leaving the shop, I buy painkillers and bandages.

So far I've paid for everything by credit card, Ethan's of course, he cut up my own long ago, telling me he would support me which in reality, was just one other way to control me. I drop the cards in another handy litter bin, removing any temptation to use them again. I'd rather starve than have him find me. Pausing only a second as I say goodbye to my past, I take the first step towards my future. Hiking my bag up over my shoulder, I exit the shopping mall by dipping out through the back entrance of a shop and start walking.

As I'd discovered from his business card, Josh, the mechanic who'd so kindly helped me the day before, doesn't work too far away, and his garage can easily be reached on foot from the town centre. At least I don't need to take a taxi where the cabbie might remember me, nor use a bus that will have CCTV. Marching on, I ignore the throbbing in my wrist, ruefully thinking, at least the past year has taught me how to cope with pain and how to ignore it. And that makes me sad; I'm now so far removed from the girl who used to scream blue murder at the slightest little scratch. No one should have to put up with abuse or be proud it's raised their tolerance for being hurt.

I know this detour might be futile, Josh might not even be working there today, but in that case, I'll have to summon up a Plan B quickly. I don't know this man at all, I had only met him for a few minutes, yet something about the vibe coming off of him yesterday tells me he'll help me if he's able to. And he gave me his business card for a reason, even if the assistance I'm going to ask for today might not quite be what he intended. But the other reason for going to see him is to warn him. If Ethan remembered the details on the business card I'd been so stupid to keep, he'll need to be prepared for a visit.

In the end, the garage is easy enough to find, a sign swinging and squeaking in the chilly winter breeze shows I've arrived at the right place. Out front, there's a man bent over, looking under the bonnet of a car, and even from the rear, it's easy to recognise the man who I'd met the day before. Going over I stand close to him, waiting for him to extract his head from looking at the engine. Whether he sees my legs or just senses my presence, I'm not sure, but it's no time at all before he straightens up. The fact he doesn't recognise the woman he helped yesterday pleases me, suggesting my disguise is working. I'm a different person today, with the wig, the bruises I'm sporting and the way pain makes me hunch over and move like I've aged twenty years overnight.

I give him a little help. "You changed my tyre yesterday?"

He stares at me, looking very closely at my face. His eyes widen, and I see the exact moment it all drops into place. He puts down the wrench he was holding and takes a step towards me, growling out. "Shit, girl! What the fuck happened to you?"

As he straightens, I give him the short answer, "I was late home."

It takes him a few seconds, then his mouth drops open in shock as the implication of my words sinks in, and I see his whole body tense with rage, his reaction showing me I was right, he *is* one of the good guys. Clearly fighting to keep his anger under control, his hand touches my chin, and I try not to pull away. With an unexpected gentleness belying his large frame, he moves my face so he can see me more clearly, his scrutiny full of compassion. His eyes drop down to my left arm, and he sees the bandage not completely hidden by the sleeve, "Your hand?"

I shrug. "It's my wrist."

"Have you seen a doctor? Do you want me to take you?" I try to ignore the concern in his eyes. Sympathy won't get me anywhere.

"No, and I won't, can't go." Surprised, he's looking for more of an explanation, so I give it to him. "He'll trace me."

When he understands my fear of being found, he starts to tell me, "There's a woman's refuge…"

Shaking my head violently, I reject his suggestion, but give him my reason, "No, he's too powerful. He'll get me back, and I'll put other people in danger." I swallow a couple of times and put my good hand on him arm. "Josh, I'm sorry, but he saw your business card. I've taken it now, but he might have noted your details. You need to take care. That's one reason I came here, to warn you."

"You've left him." It's a statement, not a question, but I still nod my confirmation. "Thank fuck for that. And there's no need to worry about me. I can look after myself."

Like yesterday, I notice his build. He's a big, powerful man, but then he doesn't know what he's up against. Again I shake my head, "He's dangerous, Josh." I need to explain just how much. I swallow my mouth suddenly dry. I tell him exactly who he's dealing with, spelling it out by giving him Ethan's full name, and then try to make clear the risk he could be in. "I tried to run before, a friend of mine, Sophie, helped me. She…" I break off as tears come into my eyes then continue with new determination. "She's in a wheelchair now. I haven't dared contact her since the accident, in case he hurts her again."

"What the fuck?" He sounds so angry I take a step back.

While he's still processing that information, I prepare him for the favour I'm going to ask him. "Josh, I had to run. I couldn't stay." I wave my good hand at my face; there's enough evidence there. "I'm worried Sophie, could be in danger. I haven't been able to ring her as he might trace I made the call." I swallow a couple of times, "Josh, you offered me help if I needed it…"

"I did. Just tell me what I can do?"

"It's Sophie, Josh. Could you possibly speak to her to warn her? Tell her to take extra care?"

"Fuck! Of course, I can! But why would he go after her? Are you going to ask her to help you again?"

"No, I'm not going near her. But Ethan might use her to try to get at me. Threaten her, hurt her. To persuade me to come back. He could even kill her. You don't know what he's capable of." My hand comes over my mouth to stifle a sob, and I feel sick. It's all down to me, if I hadn't got mixed up with Ethan in the first place, Sophie would still be walking.

"The fucker would really do that?"

I draw in a deep breath, but despite the additional air in my lungs, my admission comes out as a whisper. "Ethan St John-Davies would do anything." Now the sob escapes me. The mechanic's eyes narrow as he watches me, frowning. After studying me for a moment, he suddenly yells out,

"Horse, get out front!"

The biggest man I've ever seen in my life somehow squeezes through the door at the side of the garage and comes across to us, his gait rolling like a cowboy's. Josh takes him to one side and mutters to him for a moment, filling him in on what I've told him. 'Horse' well over six feet tall, and build like a brick shit house. I've never seen such large muscles. He's wearing a cutaway T-shirt that reveals full sleeve tattoos down each arm. My gaze moves up his large frame and settles on a face that is certainly easy on the eyes. He has a gold earring and dark hair just long enough to flop over his forehead. As he listens to Josh I watch his face muscles clench, and his eyes darken. He's nodding in agreement. At one point in their discussion, I hear Horse ask incredibly, "*The* St John-Davies?" As Josh confirms it, Horse just replies, "Fuck!"

After a couple of minutes, Josh comes over, "Come with me."

I follow him into an untidy but surprisingly clean office and watch as he spins around, rummaging in a cluttered desk to find what he wants, before turning back. "Write your friend's name, address and telephone number on here, love." He hands me paper and pen. "Horse will check it out and make sure she's not bothered."

"He's got people working for him, Josh."

"So have we."

I realise I don't know quite who these people are, but his confidence is probably misplaced, and I'm impelled to utter another warning. "You can't underestimate him."

The enormous man with the strange name clears his throat. "I'll make sure he doesn't come near your friend."

Casting a grateful glance towards Horse, it occurs to me although I don't know these people at all; there's something in the giant's voice and the way they are both looking at me that gives me confidence that if anyone can keep my friend safe, they will. I quickly jot down Sophie's details, while offering up a silent prayer that I haven't brought trouble to anyone else's door. Horse takes the piece of paper, stares at it for a second, then nods at Josh. He disappears out the back of the garage, and shortly after I hear the throaty sound of a powerful motorbike starting, and a few seconds later the loud roar as it takes off down the road.

Turning his full attention back on me, Josh asks, "How the fuck did you get mixed up with a man like that?"

Fifteen months ago

This time it was my fault I'd missed the last few of our get-togethers—Ethan kept me busy— so I was eager to see

Sophie again tonight. Tonight she beat me to the pub and was already waiting when I arrived and thankfully had already lined us up with a couple of shots. As soon as I was within hearing distance, she yelled out, "How's it going with lover boy?"

Laughing at her eagerness to know all the details, remembering how she'd been on at me for ages about finding a man, even going so far as to set me up with a couple of disastrous blind dates, I quickly put her out of her misery. "Oh, Sophie, he's gorgeous. He's so gentle and kind! I've moved in with him. I live in a fucking mansion now. Servants, the lot! I don't have to clean, cook or even do my own laundry!"

It wasn't often I was able to shock her, but I saw that's what I'd done when her mouth fell open. "Blimey, that was quick! So, what's the fucking catch?"

"No catch!" I giggled at her, "He's amazing. So generous. So attentive and caring. He can't do enough to keep me happy."

"What?" Her face creased, and she looked incredulous. There was no jealousy there; she was genuinely pleased for me. "Shit! You've hit the bloody jackpot babes." Then her face tightened, and her eyes narrowed with suspicion, "It's moving a bit fast, isn't it? You're actually living with him? Have you given up your place?"

I shook my head and grinned at her. "Yes, I've terminated the lease. Let's face it, it was a crap place in anyone's eyes, and Ethan persuaded me to let it go. It feels right, Sophie girl. He spoils me something rotten, and I want for nothing."

She went silent for a moment, as if considering what even I had to admit was an impulsive action, jumping straight in with both feet. I kept my face impassive, making sure none of my lingering doubts about giving up any refuge showed. Then she asked, in her unique way. "So what's he like to fuck? Must be good if you moved straight in. Tell me you did the deed before you committed? You can't live with someone without putting him through his paces first. What's his dick like? Large, medium? Does he know what to do with it? Ah, waiting a fucking minute! Don't tell me it's tiny? You're living the life of Riley, but there has to be a snag somewhere. Still, I suppose if he's got the money, the size of his prick probably isn't so important as long as he can use his hands and mouth. Does his tongue compensate?"

"Sophie!" I covered my mouth to stop my shocked giggles escaping, partly wondering how she could ask so many questions without stopping to draw breath. "Why is it all you can think about is sex?"

"Hey, Zoe, bless you, you're beautiful, but sex is what makes the world go round. But if you're telling me he's got a big dick, then go you! You've won the fucking lottery!"

"I am not discussing the size of his appendage with you," I told her, primly. In all honesty, I wanted to change the direction of this discussion and fast.

She gestured with a hurry up movement. "Come on, spill the fucking beans!"

As I raised a querying eyebrow, she clarified in her unique blunt manner, leaning forwards and smirking. "Is he a good ride?"

"I, er…" I thought back over the past couple of months and wondered what I could tell her. After our dinner date, Ethan wasted no time or money courting me, continuing to be the perfect gentleman, but never taking things further than a goodnight kiss or holding my hand. Against my protests, he insisted on giving me expensive gifts of perfume and jewellery and totally spoiling me. I'd never had a man treat me so well before. It wasn't until our third weekend when we'd taken that all-important next step. He'd booked a lovely five-star hotel in Brighton where we shared a room and slept together for the first time. To be honest, no bells pealed in heaven, but we just needed time to get used to each other, didn't we? Ethan enjoyed it, although, if I'm honest the repeat performance the next morning left me equally unsatisfied while he roared out his climax. And the sex hadn't improved much since then, but I was probably expecting too much. My expectations of the earth moving came from the romance novels I'd read, and not from real life. Except for someone like Sophie perhaps, she was unique, not every woman was could come from penetrative sex, though perhaps a little foreplay would have been nice. Ethan seemed happy enough with our sex life, and I enjoyed everything else about living with him, so where was the bother? So, a little reluctantly, I confessed, "Not great. But that's me, not him."

She slammed her empty glass down on the table. "For goodness sake, babes. What do you mean it's not him?" Her eyes widened.

"Well, I, er, never… Not with anyone else either."

"You've never come before? Christ, Zoe, your first

experience was losing your virginity in a drunken fumble on the back seat of a car. And the men you hitched up with after that were selfish pricks. I'm not surprised you didn't get much out of them. But you must have come sometime, what about with your BOB?"

Sometimes I regretted how much I confided in my friend. My face went red, and I quickly glanced around to make sure no one was within earshot. "Well, of course," I hissed. I didn't add my BOB was now out on the rubbish tip after Ethan happened to find it one day.

I saw her face tighten, "You can't live with a man who's too selfish to get you off. Doesn't he know the woman always comes first?" She waggled her eyebrows. "If he's really a gentleman he knows that."

"Sophie, you might think sex is important, but I don't know what all the fuss is about." I started to get annoyed. "I've never come with a man; I doubt I ever will. In every other way, he's perfect for me. There's more to life than sex!"

Eyes open wide she stared as though she couldn't believe I'd said that, and subjected me to an intense scrutiny. To get a moment's peace, I collected the dead glasses and took them up to the bar; splashing out on another round even though it was really her turn. As I waited for the drinks order to be filled, I risked a glance back at her. She was still watching me intently, her gaze moving from my head to my toe.

When I returned to my seat, she put her head on one side. "You look different, babe. Hey, I'm not saying it's a bad fucking thing. But your clothes, hun, they're not you."

I heaved a sigh. Instead of an old pair of jeans and a comfy jumper, I was wearing smart black slacks and a pale pink pure silk blouse. "I told you he's generous, Sophie. And he likes me to wear what he's bought for me." I waved a hand down at myself. "I could never afford to buy stuff like this before, but now I can I love it. This is me!" As I added the last bit, I wondered who I was trying to persuade, her or me? Whichever, I'd not done a good job of convincing her if her expression was any indication. I decided to move this on, "Now, Soph, can we please change the bloody subject? I'm happy—happier than I've ever been! Can't you just be pleased that I've found someone?"

Another critical look. I started to think this evening was a complete fuck up, and perhaps I should just summon the car to take me home. Ethan's chauffeur was on standby to collect me as I was drinking tonight; I held my tongue on that bit of information, expecting my friend would find something to criticise about that too. I looked up at her from underneath my eyelashes, hoping she'd leave the subject alone. But she had one more thing to say.

"Do you love him?"

Did I? Now that was the question. I was 'in love' with him; I loved the life, the money. But as a partner for life? The jury was still out on that. As an answer, I gave her a dismissive shrug and then turned the conversation back to her. "What about you, Soph? Anyone sweep you off your feet yet?"

She glared, knowing exactly what I was trying to do, but my expression must have shown her she'd got as much out of me as she was going to. She mumbled something under her breath that I didn't catch, and probably wouldn't want to have heard in any event.

With a shake of her head, she reached out and touched my hand. "I love you babes, and I'm always here for you. Remember that!" Then, after downing another good part of her vodka she started telling me about the latest fiasco at her work. Soon she had me in stitches as she described a workmate who'd embarrassingly left his fly undone revealing his Flintstone boxers. Telling me, to his chargrin, they've since nicknamed him Fred, the matter of my new boyfriend was thankfully dropped.

CHAPTER 6
Kadar

ave we any other business to discuss?" I address
Sadiq, our newly appointed Minister of Finance. In
English, his name translates as sincere or truthful, and I
only hope he lives up to it. The previous occupant of his
post had proved to be anything but. It was Cara, my sister-
in-law and the other participant at this meeting, who had
exposed his predecessor's treachery.

"Nothing from me, Your Excellency," Sadiq politely
dips his head.

I wipe my hand over my brow. It's been a hectic month
since Emir Rushdi died, and one in which I've had to
become immersed in state business with no time for
anything else. What with trying to get an oil field
constructed in the Southern Desert while maintaining
peace with the desert tribes—following the warnings from
Rais and Abdul-Muhsi, rumours have increased that some
of the other leaders are now vociferously voicing doubts
about my ability to rule the country—my days are fraught
with problems.

But now another meeting is over, and I can cross it off
my very long list. Every minute of every day I have to
concentrate on projecting an image of a confident man to
the world, while underneath I'm struggling, trying to come

to terms with the role life's unexpectedly thrust upon me. Trying to second guess the outcomes of each of the decisions I have to make. Trying to do my best for Amahad.

"Kadar, can I speak to you for a moment?"

Cara interrupts my thoughts. I sigh, narrowing my eyes, unable to spare the time but equally incapable of resisting the woman who's over half way through her pregnancy now, absolutely glowing, her ballooning tummy clearly visible. And despite my impatience at yet another delay before I start on the myriad of other tasks waiting for my attention, I would be a fool to dismiss her or what she might want to say. My sister-in-law has a well-earned reputation for uncovering trouble and while the last thing I want is another problem on my plate, if she's got anything I need to know about, it would be stupid to delay hearing it. I throw her a quick nod of agreement then watch as, with a deep reverential bow, Sadiq leaves us.

"What is it, Cara?" Switching to English, the language I used throughout my youth while being educated at Eton and Oxford and that I'm as comfortable speaking as my native Arabic, I raise my eyebrows and stroke my hand across my chin as I wait to hear what my brother's wife has to say. Taking a moment to admire her I realise how she's grown into her role. In the last few months, she's picked up enough of our language to be able to hold her own even during complicated financial discussions, sometimes to our detriment. We can't hide anything from her now, and occasionally I forget her fluency to my cost.

She shakes her head, in answer to my question. "No

glitches or anything Kadar, don't worry. The country's money is safe. There are only the usual problems, as you know. I'd rather be with Nijad."

The 'usual' refers to the fact that the current unsettled situation following my accession to the throne has forced her to relocate to the main palace in Al Qar'ah as a precautionary measure, rather than staying in the desert city, ▯alm▯▯, with her husband. Although the challenges since my father's death have so far only been verbal, both my youngest brother and I have fears that insurgents may be plotting to actively contest my supremacy. In the event of acts of violence or, Allah forbid, an outright civil war, Cara is better protected here in this cosmopolitan city, rather than among the more primitive and often volatile tribes in the desert.

"So what can I do for you?" I know I sound haughty, but I have a massive pile of paperwork to address. Glancing across at the myriad of contracts and other legal documents I need to wade through, I heave a deep sigh then wave my hand to encourage her and let her know I'll hear her out.

"The harem," she starts.

It was the last thing I expected her to say! Even though I'm in the middle of sorting out at least a dozen problems, the mention of the ancient building makes me guffaw, "Missing the Desert Palace?"

Now it's her turn to narrow her eyes, and she's unable to hide the blush that comes to her cheeks. While not in a strict twenty-four-seven Dominant/submissive relationship, both she and Nijad like to play so part of the harem in their home, the Desert Palace, has been transformed into a Dom's Dungeon. *She's not going to suggest something similar for the palace here in Al-Qar'ah, is she?* My eyebrows rise, as I consider it. I've played such games myself—out of the country, of course. An emir, or even just an heir to the throne, has to preserve their integrity on home ground. I am a Dominant, but I'm not sure I need an actual dungeon to amuse myself. And not being married, I have no one in Amahad I can play with, or not without becoming the source of unwanted gossip.

"Kadar, get your mind out of the gutter." Cara rebukes me with an easy smile.

Again I sigh, now thinking back fondly to the time when I used to intimidate her. It seems I can do that no longer. Perhaps I'm losing my touch. "Spit it out then, Sheikha."

"It's a beautiful place, Kadar, or it was once. It's just decaying now."

I know the harem has a special place in Cara's heart, and it's one part of the palace she grew to know extremely well when she was incarcerated there during the weeks when we thought her to be a thief. It was also the place where her child was conceived, where Nijad proposed to her, and where they spent their wedding night. It doesn't take a genius to guess what she might be thinking. "You want to renovate it?"

She nods slowly and blushes again, making me intrigued. She gets out of her chair, walks across my office to the windows and an open door leading into the gardens, and gazes out while she starts to speak. "Even the word 'harem' brings forth evocative images." She swings round to face me with a twinkle in her eye, and throws out a challenge, "You aren't planning on using it for its original purpose, are you, Kadar?"

I snort. One of the so-called benefits of occupying the Amahadian throne is that ancient laws dictate I have sole access to the harem. I can't deny the idea of a bevy of concubines awaiting my pleasure does hold some attraction, especially as I've not been able to spread the royal seed except via the efforts of my hand for longer than I care to remember. But that really would be a step back into the dark ages. "No, my dear, I am not."

"Well," her eyes shine with excitement, "Why not renovate the harem so that we can offer it as elitist accommodation for people wanting to act out their fantasies? Perhaps a honeymoon couple or someone who wants to propose?" She pauses, and as a flush crosses her face, I suspect she's recollecting Nijad's marriage offer. Not that either of them has ever admitted the details of that event, but from her behaviour and my brother's enormously satisfied grin on his face immediately afterwards, I always understood the occasion to have been somewhat special.

But I can't quite grasp the idea. "Not sure if you'll be able to find people to volunteer for the role of a eunuch. Considering the er, physical adaptations required."

She laughs, a lovely tinkling sound, making me realise yet again why my brother fell in love with her. She came here a shy woman, completely lacking in self-esteem and has grown into an entirely different person, blossoming in her relationship despite the original auspices. An arranged marriage of two such different types shouldn't have resulted in wedded bliss. *But who can predict anything?* As I watch her returning across the room, my mind flits to my own forthcoming nuptials; a second marriage of convenience in the Kassis family, wondering briefly whether there's any chance that I could be as lucky. Then, as she takes her seat at the conference table once again, with a surprising grace for a heavily pregnant woman, I realise my own chance of being so happily wed is probably next to nothing.

Cara throws a glance my way and takes a moment to consider her thoughts then, as she continues to try to persuade me, I pull back my attention to what she's saying. "The harem's got its own entrance that can be isolated quite easily from the rest of the palace, so no security issues there. And maybe even the foreign dignitaries who visit might like to experience a bit of the exotic?"

I can't stop a smile spreading across my face as I find some light relief in trying to picture the president or king of one of our allies lying back on luscious cushions, experiencing his bit of the exotic by being catered to by semi-nude belly dancers and concubines waiting to service him. But perhaps they'd appreciate that, and it could help improve our international relations. I end up grinning and chuckle, "So what do you suggest?"

"I'd like to take it on as a project; employ someone who can design both the alterations required to the building and restore the gardens to their former glory. Someone who can be both sympathetic to the history and provide twenty-first-century comfort to the accommodation." She's taking this seriously.

I groan, "Cara, renovating the harem is right off the bottom of the list of things that I need to address at the moment. We've got a potential revolt happening in the Southern Desert, and I'm attracting international attention as to how I'll deal with that, as well as an oilfield to get off the ground and developed. I can't get involved with something like this. I simply haven't got the time."

Sitting back in her chair the smirk on her face lets me know I've played straight into her lap. "I have. I've got the time. I'll take on the project. It will give me something to do now I've here in the main palace, and not in Amahal."

Personally, I think she's got more than enough to do incubating my soon-to-be niece or nephew inside her, but then what the fuck do I know? I'm not a woman. I think about it for a moment. There's no point in having a harem any longer, and if left to itself it will just disintegrate into dust without renovation. It can't hurt to let her take such a project on, although I'm still to be convinced of the benefits. Still, there's part of me that would be loathe to see any aspect of the fabric of our rich history neglected and left to crumble away. Putting my head on one side, I consider her. Is a restoration proposal something to satisfy her nesting instincts, perhaps?

I come to a decision. "If," I hold up my hand to emphasise the point, "If Nijad agrees to you taking on the extra work, I will give my agreement. But only on the condition that you assume responsibility for the whole of the project—and that means every single detail! I have no time or inclination to be involved in any way at all. Any issues you deal with yourself."

She jumps up, runs around the table and hugs me. "Kadar, thank you!"

I can do nothing but hug her back; she's so demonstrative since she's come out of her shell. "Nijad hasn't said yes, yet." I remind her.

"He will," she assures me with a grin.

As she leaves my office, I shake my head. She's probably right; she's got her husband twisted around her little finger. *No woman*, I think emphatically, *is ever going to have that sort of power over me.* I lean my head back and then move it from side to side trying to get the kinks out of my neck. Cara's presence has provided a welcome interlude in my day, albeit probably putting me behind. Damn this role, damn my destiny. *For fuck's sake, why did my father die?* I don't need these millstones hanging around me. I close my eyes. It's bad enough that Cara's had to relocate, and Nijad's exposing himself to danger again. The tribes don't trust me without trying my authority, testing my strength. And the jihadists are just waiting for a chance for us to show weakness so they can cross over our borders. The burden to prevent radicalisation affecting Amahad such as has spread to other Arab countries lies with me. Everything rests on my shoulders.

CHAPTER 7
Zoe

I realise Josh had asked me a question, and it's a good one, *how the fuck did I get involved with Ethan in the first place?* His raised eyebrows show he's still waiting for an answer, so I go for the simple version, "I got involved with him because I was stupid, alright? And now I'm getting away." I don't want to say anymore.

He knows there has more to it than that but doesn't press me, changing tack to ask, "Have you got somewhere to go?"

Shaking my head, I admit, "Ethan's got every resource he could want behind him, Josh. All I know is I've got to get as far away as possible; somewhere he won't bother looking. I can't leave any trail."

Leaning back against a workbench, he folds his arms across his chest. "Tell me how I can help? Do you want to stay at my place for a while? At least until your injuries have healed?"

The offer stuns me. How can this man, this stranger who met me for the first time yesterday, and then for only a few minutes, be so kind; so willing to assist me? All I'd thought he'd agree to do was get a simple but urgent message to Sophie, but now he's offering me a place to stay? But it would be too easy an answer.

"Josh, I can't thank you enough for the offer, but it's too close to home. And I don't want to involve you any further," I pause. There is a way he could help me. "You could give me a lift to the station if you wouldn't mind."

"If you're sure that's what you want to do." He looks at me steadily for a moment and sees the answer in the set of my features. Then he throws a glance over at his van emblazoned with the name of his business and gives a small shake of his head. Rummaging in his pocket, he comes out with a set of keys dangling in hand and tells me we'll 'borrow' one of the cars he's got in to fix. I hastily agree, knowing if Ethan had remembered his details he'd probably leave no stone unturned and check out routes taken by all vehicles registered to the mechanic who'd helped me.

Josh picks up his coat, not seeming to care he's going to have to close up his business for a while. "Let's get you going then; I suspect you don't want to dally." He leans over and grabs a beanie and scarf from behind the counter. "Put these on, pull the hat right down. That's good. Not the height of fashion but they'll do the job." He nods encouragingly as I do as he suggests. "If you keep your head down no one will recognise you. And, look, love, if you need anything, anytime, call me." Again he stares at me intently, until I agree.

Then I remember. I smile weakly, "I haven't got a phone."

He wipes his hand over his face, thinking. "Easiest thing to trace, I suppose. Hang on." He goes over to the desk again and tips out the contents of a drawer, coming back to me with an ancient looking Nokia. "I bought this as a spare, never used it. It's not registered to me. All you need to do is to buy a sim."

Words are inadequate to convey the depth of my gratitude. Thank heavens I met this man yesterday. Someone must be watching over me. Before we leave, I ask for a cup of water, and under Josh's angry gaze down a couple of the painkillers I'd bought, delaying taking the morning after pill due to the possible side effects the pharmacist had explained. I can't afford to get sick until I reach a place of safety and I've got a couple of day's leeway before it would cease to be effective. He shakes his head when I wrap my good hand around my left wrist and quietly swears when I grimace in pain. But he doesn't say anything; there's nothing he can say.

I follow him through the garage and out the back where a white Audi is parked, and get in the passenger seat. After thinking for a moment, he suggests, "Going back into Guildford would be a giveaway, it's the first place he'd look. It's only an extra half-an-hour's drive to Morden; I'll take you there, and you can disappear into the tube network." I don't have to think twice about it; it's a better plan, the train service in town has limited options. *Adapt and improvise, isn't that a motto I read somewhere?*

Luckily the traffic's not too bad this time of day, so we make a good time, getting to the underground station just before midday. Now I'm strangely reluctant to leave my new friend, but making myself bite the bullet I get out of the car, putting my head back inside for just second to say an insufficient 'thank you'. He reaches over, and we shake hands a little awkwardly, I smile weakly, thinking to myself, *when I'm safe, I'll contact him,* but then I remember, if Ethan recorded the details on the card, he'll track incoming calls to Josh and the garage. Best I don't get in touch. I can't afford to be anything but paranoid. So, turning my back on the mechanic who's still waiting in the car, I go into the station. Approaching the ticket counter I purchase an all zone travel card with cash. Step Three of my plan—get as far away as possible.

I've played this out in my head so often. Josh was right; escaping onto the tube network is the place to start. Although it's riddled with CCTV, I've changed my appearance, and the mechanic's scarf and the beanie cover most of my face and head. It's winter and the weather's turned cold, so I'll look no different from everyone else who's dressed appropriately for the season.

Morden Underground Station is on the Northern Line, but instead of taking a through train, which would take me directly to the mainline station, I take the first tube that arrives at the platform, making a change onto the Victoria Line at Stockwell. This takes me to Euston Square, and then a quick walk will take me to Euston station from where I could catch a number of trains heading all points north. To avoid detection I use the knowledge I'd picked up when living as a student in the area, and don't take the direct path, instead doubling back on my tracks and taking a convoluted route around the side streets to get there.

I know Ethan and the lengths he can, and will go to, to find me—I can't afford to take any chances. He'll be using any dirty trick he can. So as per my plan I do whatever I can to evade detection. At Euston, I buy a ticket for cash to Birmingham, and another for Watford Junction. Feeling like I'm in a spy movie I change to the second, dark brown wig in the Ladies, then hover between the platforms checking no one is paying me any particular attention and leave it until the last minute before I decide which service to get on. It looks clear, so when the Birmingham train is just about to leave, I jump on.

My nerves are shot, I'm running purely on adrenaline as I sit shaking on the train, hugging my aching wrist to me, waiting to be exposed, keeping my head down to avoid the surveillance cameras in the carriage. When the guard comes to check my ticket, I give a guilty start. Then I have to fight down panic when anybody walks past me, which they do with frightening regularity, my seat, unfortunately, being situated halfway between the buffet car and the toilets. Every moment I think I'm going to be discovered, but eventually, the train pulls into the station, and I reach my first destination safely.

I find an information desk with a helpful local map on the wall and discover there's a shop well-known for low-priced clothing not too far away. Ethan's dressed me in designer clothes for the past sixteen months, but that life's lost to me. Now I have to replace my wardrobe at rock bottom prices, buying cheaply and ignoring any ethical arguments about how the store sources its wares. Quickly, I grab enough clothes and underwear for a week as well as a cheap rucksack to put everything in. In the shop entrance, I put on a new waterproof over my jacket and swop the beanie for a fedora I've just purchased. My appearance again hopefully sufficiently changed, I return to the station where I use more of my precious cash to buy a ticket for Glasgow, almost baulking at the price which seems exorbitant, but telling myself it's worth it to leave another false lead.

Time's getting on now; it's nearly five o'clock. Even if he hadn't discovered it earlier, by now, Ethan is certain to know I've absconded. I've no doubt he'll be using every means at his disposal to try and locate me. It's a race against time to find a safe haven. He'll be getting all the CCTV footage analysed, probably using facial recognition software, as well as calling in favours from the many people he's got under his thumb. He could even set loose his private army. There's nothing I'd put past him. He'll report me to the police for some reason, and get me listed as a missing person, or perhaps even a criminal or lunatic. I lived with him long enough to know the way he operates; little does he know all his boasting and threats serve to help protect me from him now. *Can I do enough?* Whether I can or not, I'd rather die on the run than like a mouse in a trap.

As jumpy and cautious as prey being chased by a hunter, I find the right platform and get on the next train I've chosen, making my way to a vacant seat. My wrist throbs, my back aches, I want to sleep, but daren't close my eyes. As the train starts to move and is soon thundering over the tracks, I sink back into my seat, as much on edge as I was on the last journey, finding this no less tedious than the first. Finally, after watching station after station fly past, I leave the train at Crewe, and then board a local service for a place called Ludlow, a town I've plucked out of the air. I've never been before, and I don't know anyone who lives there. But as far as I am aware, neither does Ethan.

I arrive at the quaint medieval market town in the late evening, not quite knowing what to do. Walking into the main street I'm unable to shake the feeling that everyone is looking at me, or that someone is following me, but after ducking into doorways and waiting for someone to appear at last I accept it's just my nerves making me so jumpy. Just up the road I find a friendly enough looking pub and go inside. I don't buy a drink, not wanting to linger in any place for long. The landlord doesn't seem to mind that I'm not there to buy anything, but only to ask if there is a cheap bed and breakfast nearby while trying as best I can to hide my face from curious customers. The cheerful chap behind the bar directs me to a slightly run down but clean B&B on a side street, which, on entering, I find has an available vacancy.

Giving my name as Claire Ranger, using my middle name and a surname picked at random, I'm shown to a room with a freshly made, but obviously well used double bed. Finally alone, I sink onto it, uncaring that the mattress is lumpy and has seen better days. I rub my hand over the tired, faded but clean duvet cover, I realise I'll be that tonight I'll be sleeping alone. It's a comforting thought.

A few moments later I visit the tiny en-suite bathroom where I splash cold water on my face, gazing into eyes reflected by the mirror, hating the haunted look that stares back at me. But slowly, as I watch the corners of my mouth turn up in the beginnings of a smile and it's at that point jubilation starts to bubble up inside me. *I've escaped! I'm out of his clutches.* Unlike last time when he found me and dragged me back within hours, this time I've had freedom for a whole day.

My smile turns into a grin as I realise Ethan can't hurt me anymore. He'll never think of looking for me here in this out of way town in the West Midlands. He's no connection to the area, and neither do I. Pulling my shoulders back I stand up straight. Step Four complete. I start to laugh. For all his assets and money, little old me has beaten him. I imagine him ranting and raving as he initiates the hunt for me and I giggle. *I got away!* I've no frigging idea what to do next, but I've escaped him. Tomorrow's another issue, but for tonight, I've won. I allow myself a moment to revel in my success.

Returning to lie on the bed, I switch on the tiny TV hanging on the opposite wall. The last occupant of the room must have left it on Sky News, so it comes to life just as the newscaster is going through the main stories again. When I see the picture and hear the headlines, vomit rises to my throat and I only just manage to make it to the en-suite and puke into the porcelain rather than my hands. They'd had a recent photo of me on the screen—without bruises of course—and I can hear the newscaster's words coming through from the bedroom.

"Billionaire's girlfriend, Zoe Baker, who is suffering from severe depression, has disappeared from their multi-million pound home in Surrey today. It's unclear at this moment whether she left voluntarily or whether she has been abducted. Mr St John-Davies is appealing to anyone who might have seen her to come forward and is offering a reward of a quarter of a million pounds for information that will help locate her. So far no ransom note has been delivered, and Mr St John-Davies has told Sky News that he is extremely concerned about her safety. The number to ring if you have any information is…"

I switch off the TV with trembling hands. Of course, Ethan's concerned about my safety. He's setting it up so I won't be found alive.

Oh shit! Is my disguise good enough? I knew he'd use everything he had at his disposal to try to find me, but didn't consider he'd get almost everyone in the UK on his side by using such a plausible appeal and offering that incredible reward. *Oh God! The man at the pub, the customers, the B&B owners and God knows how many others may have seen me. Could they have recognised me?* Could they even now be thinking of lining their bank accounts?

Frantic thoughts race one after the other through my mind until I try to think rationally and calm myself. They described me on the news as blond, but I arrived here with mousy brown hair. Surely no one would link me with the missing woman, even if they'd seen the story? And they wouldn't have paid me that much attention, would they? My hosts hadn't given me a second glance. To them I'm just another anonymous guest; one among the many they must have staying here.

Running through my decidedly limited options I know I've got no choice but to sit tight for tonight and just hope that no one is already coming for me. It's below freezing outside; I'd die of hypothermia if I tried to rough it. I'll just have to pray that I'm safe.

But every footstep outside my door makes my heart beat faster, and even when all the guesthouse lights go off for the night, I can neither close my eyes nor relax despite my lack of sleep over the past thirty-six hours. If these are my last moments of freedom, I don't want to waste any of them. So I lie awake all night, and worry.

Fourteen months ago

Another month had passed before I met Sophie again. She greeted me with her easy smile, motioning to my wine she'd bought already. She barely let me sit down before she started. "How the fuck are you? Wouldn't have minded a phone call, babes, or an invite to that fancy mansion you live in!"

I sat down opposite her, trying not to grimace. Ethan had been particularly rough the previous night, taking me well before I was ready for him, pounding into me for what seemed like hours before getting his relief. I'd known something had upset him at work, and he needed to relieve his tension, so I tried to respond as he wanted me too, giving him the release he desired. I really can't understand how other women apparently enjoy this sex thing, but it was a subject I didn't want to get into knowing my friend's view of it is at the opposite end of the spectrum to mine.

"Sorry, Soph. I've been so busy. What with work and starting a new life with Ethan. We have so many functions

to attend, so when we get to stay in it's a luxury, and I'm just dead to the world. How's you?" I'd lied to my friend. Something I never thought I'd do. I might not tell her everything, but an out and out untruth? The fact of the matter was Ethan had become extremely possessive. Jealous of any time I spent away from him. In truth, the parties and evenings out we used to enjoy had trickled down to almost nothing as he wanted me all to himself. Our evenings consisted of me reading or watching TV with my headphones on while he sat and worked. He liked me in his line of vision at all times. I didn't make phone calls as it was too awkward in his presence.

"Same old fucking same old." Sophie grinned, "Hey, you ought to have seen the fella I met last week. He was an electrician doing some wiring at work. Well, we got chatting, and one thing led to another. Let's just say I'll never look at the broom cupboard in the same way again."

"Soph, you didn't! Not even you would do that!" I covered my mouth but was unable to suppress my snort of laughter.

"I fucking did! I couldn't walk straight the rest of the day." Her grin widens. "Another thing crossed off my bucket list. Now, what's going on with you and Ethan? I'm not joking about that visit; I'd love to see how the other half live."

I tried not to squirm; there was no way I could invite anyone back to Ethan's mansion. I lived there, but I wasn't comfortable enough to treat it as though it was my home. I attempted to distract her. "Didn't anyone see you?"

"No. And don't change the subject. How's that man of yours treating my bestie?"

I'd always enjoyed the evenings spent with Sophie, but tonight seemed to drag. When she questioned me about Ethan, there wasn't much I found I wanted to share with her. Sure, I was living what appeared to be the perfect life, but it wasn't quite everything I thought it would be. Eventually, my friend took over the conversation, telling me after the electrician she'd hooked up with a guy from the solicitors she'd met when dropping some documents off. She'd packed more fun into one day than I've had in four months! Certainly, she'd had more orgasms—and she'd described every single one! Surreptitiously I kept glancing at the clock, and when 'last orders' was called, I couldn't help but be relieved. As we made arrangements to meet again, I resolved that I had to do something to change my relationship with Ethan in the meantime.

I enjoyed his company, but, while I'd never admit it to anyone else, I'd come to accept he was a selfish lover, uncaring about my satisfaction as long as he got off. Such a contrast to the caring person he was proving to be in other parts of my life. Perhaps he didn't realise? I mean, I'd never come out and admitted it before.

I decided I had to man up and talk to him about my needs, however difficult a conversation that was going to be. But I neither had the experience or the audacity to find it easy to ask for what I wanted in the bedroom. Sophie wouldn't have had any such problem! It's not even as though I was going to ask for much, all I wanted was a little more warming up, and him to touch me where I needed him to.

Hearing about Soph's experiences made me determined

to address the subject for both my sanity and comfort. So, knowing delaying the conversation wouldn't make it easier, the very next evening, while he was removing his clothes getting ready for bed and I was already naked and waiting under the sheet, I took a deep breath and started telling him my problem as tactfully as possible.

"You fucking what?" I didn't know what reaction I'd expected, but it certainly wasn't for him to get angry. "You're complaining? You want me to touch you like a slut?" I shrank back against the pillows as he approached me, his face is red. Belatedly I realised, to him I was criticising his technique, his manhood. As he stared down at me, I'd never seen him so enraged. "It's that fucking whore Sophie, isn't it? You're not going to see her again. She's a bad fucking influence on you. You really want to copy her whorish ways?"

Wiping his hand over his forehead, he looked exasperated, "If you don't like it, Zoe, you know where the door is."

I didn't know what to say, anything that came out of my mouth at the moment would probably be the wrong thing. I was aghast Ethan thought he could prevent me seeing my friend, but now wasn't the right time to protest.

He continued to stare down at me; his features were tight, and then he dropped his bombshell. "And you know that cow was fucking with your ex behind your back, don't you?"

I gazed at him in horror. "Sophie wouldn't…"

"She's been bragging about it, you stupid bitch! Laughing at you behind your back. And she's probably like a bit of my action if she could get it. But I'm faithful to you,

though fuck knows why. You don't fucking appreciate it, do you? Make your choice; it's her or me."

With a cold feeling inside and remembering how Sophie loved to talk about her conquests, I started to believe him. Although the relationship I'd with my ex was both short and unremarkable, and we'd only had sex the once, it still hurt me to think she might have got there first. Had he been comparing me to her? He certainly hadn't wanted a repeat performance with me. And if she had, I could so imagine her gossiping to all and sundry about it. What he's telling me all at once seemed credible, I could even picture her laughing at me behind my back.

"Well? Make your choice!"

I swallowed a couple of times; I didn't want to lose him. "You, Ethan. I choose you." What choice had I got now he'd told me my best friend was a cheating liar?

He grabbed my shoulders with both hands and shook me violently, then pulled me off the bed, pushing me down to my knees. "Now you better give me a fucking blowjob like the slut you are. And I better fucking enjoy it!"

Anything to appease him. Feeling about as turned on as a turkey being made ready for Christmas I put out my hands and ran them up and down his shaft, then I slid them down to his balls, rolling his heavy sacs around and squeezing them gently.

"Oh for fuck's sake woman! You can't even do that right!" Ethan took hold of my hair and fisted it tight in his hand. Roughly he pushed my head to the tip of his cock, forcing the drop of pre-cum around my lips. I opened my mouth, and he pushed inside with no finesse. Luckily he wasn't a

big man, and though he thrust to the back of my throat, it wasn't too uncomfortable. He controlled me, fucking my mouth. I felt like he was treating me like the whore he'd called me; I was just a vessel to be used. It wasn't long before I felt the swelling in his prick and his warm semen gushing into my mouth. He held me in place, forcing me to drink every drop.

Then he straightened, his limp cock falling out of my mouth. I glanced up and didn't like the expression on his face, a trickle of fear ran down my spine. He'd still got hold of my hair, and for the moment, he wasn't letting me go. "Your mine, slut and don't you forget it. You're fucking lucky to be here. I should just throw you out. You're as common as muck; I should never have bothered with you in the first fucking place, just left you in the gutter where you belong." Before I realised what he was doing, he backhanded me across the face. Shock flooded through me; No one had ever hit me before. I was stunned.

"Now, perhaps, you'll remember. I don't want to see that sluttish side of you ever again." He released me and stormed off to the bathroom.

The next morning he brought me flowers and chocolates and apologised profusely, I'd caught him on a bad day, he told me; he'd never wanted to inform me about my best friend's betrayal in that way. I never mentioned his bedroom technique again.

Neither did I see Sophie again.

Then I lost my job. It was winter, after all, and contracts had tailed off, but I hadn't expected that it would be me that the team would choose to let go, Rob had seemed to see such promise in me. But whatever the reason, the result was the same. I was unemployed. Ethan graciously offered to support me, telling me to use my talents around the estate if I wanted to do anything. I soon stopped mentioning finding new employment; he got so disappointed at even the idea of me working away from home. He was giving me the life of luxury, and I was made to feel guilty I wasn't more grateful to him.

Two weeks before Easter I asked him if my mother could come to visit for the holiday, and his virulent response was unexpected, spitting out he didn't want a whore like her in the house, forbidding me from ever contacting her again. I didn't understand; her only crime was deciding that being a single mother wasn't for her, and taking to married life with a vengeance. By that time she was on husband number six and living with him in the South of France. She'd never had much of a real maternal instinct, but she was my only close relative. Of course, I had to make the mistake of telling Ethan he was wrong to think so little of her.

I shouldn't have stood up to him. That time, he blackened my eye and followed that with a vicious punch to the stomach. I'd been uneasy about our relationship for a while by that point. Sure, I enjoyed not having to lift a finger or worry about anything, but I could no longer be blind to the wrongness of some of his actions. That was the final straw; I had to leave him. If my mother couldn't come to me, I'd go to her. She'd give me house-room while I was getting myself sorted with a new job, I knew she would.

The very next morning I packed my bags and told Ethan I was leaving and wouldn't be coming back. He was all apologies, of course, all hearts, flowers and incredibly loving. Oh yes, he could turn on the charm when he wanted to, and I even thought I saw tears in his eyes. So I agreed to stay until he got home from work to give us a chance to talk things through.

Of course, that was my next mistake. I'd seen Hargreaves around the place before but had never taken much notice of him. He acted as Ethan's chauffeur, butler, and bodyguard, and was the only live-in servant, the rest all departed at six o'clock each night unless there was going to be a function held in the house. Before that day, I'd not really had much contact with him nor understood the extent of his duties. Having stayed to have what I'd expected would be a cosy makeup chat with Ethan, instead, I was subjected to a night of cruelty when Ethan took me to his play room for the first time, with Hargreaves, a willing participant.

At least he didn't let Hargreaves rape me; Ethan was far too possessive for that. But he let him wield the whip. My correction for wanting to leave him.

As he examined the cruel marks left on my back the following morning, even Ethan knew a simple apology wasn't going to suffice. This time, he booked flights for a break away to the Seychelles, leaving that evening. There he spoilt me, he cried and vowed he'd never hurt me again. Taking advantage of his remorse and feeling brave, I explained things have to change if he wanted me to stay. He must never hurt me again, and he would have to support me in finding a new job. We had a wonderful holiday, and I started to think I must have imagined and exaggerated how bad it had been. But then we returned home.

It wasn't long before the gloves came off, and the violence escalated, as did Ethan's dire threats if I ever even suggested leaving him again. As time went on, Ethan gave up making any attempt to justify his actions, and I came to realise I was seeing the real man, he was a monster in well-cut clothing. I had to escape, but now I knew there was no chance of me simply walking away.

So I waited until he was away overnight on a business trip. Taking only an overnight bag, I got in my car and drove out of the grounds. I had no job, no money to my name and Ethan had successfully isolated me from everyone I could have depended on. But now I knew he was a liar, warping the truth as it suited him. And I'd come to realise Sophie would never have cheated on me; she'd got more than enough men dangling without having to take a rather unexceptional one of mine. She'd always been there for me, my best friend, and despite that I'd not seen her in ages, she'd help me, I knew she would.

I turned up at her front door and knocked. It opened, there was a moment's pause, and then I was being hugged so tightly it I knew how right to I'd been to dismiss Ethan's accusations. And when she saw the bruising on my face she put together the story without me having to say the words. With no hesitation, Sophie gave me sufficient money to make the trip to the South of France, plus a little extra on top to tide me over. I couldn't have wished for a better friend.

I was so, so bloody stupid, not realising then just how much Ethan would want his possession back. I didn't get far; I was stopped by the police on a trumped up charge while driving down the M20 towards Ashford. It was only later I realised he must have used the number plate recognition system to find me.

Hargreaves came with him to get me. I had ribs broken that night, but the physical pain that I went through was nothing compared to that of my friend. Ethan's retribution was swift; Sophie would never have the use of her legs again. As a persuasive tool to make sure I didn't try to escape again it was very effective. I knew then, if I wanted to get away I'd have to do it all on my own.

He wasn't just a monster; I was living with a madman.

CHAPTER 8
Kadar

As I wash my hands, my attention is caught by a glimpse of my reflection in the gilded mirror above the sink. Leaning closer, lines which I've only recently noticed are clearly apparent, an indication I've aged rapidly in the three months since my father's death. It's hardly surprising given the number of challenges I'm dealing with; it's impossible ever to relax and switch off entirely. *Will the stress end up putting me into an early grave like it probably did the last emir? All work and no play won't just make me a dull boy; I suspect it might make me a dead one.* Looking down, I see my hands have started trembling and have to make a conscious effort to still them. My heavy workload is taking its toll on me, but I can't afford to show weakness, and I can never let anyone know I feel like an elastic band stretched taut, ready to snap.

I'd made the excuse of a bathroom break to adjourn the meeting for a short time, needing space to control my temper. But it didn't help. I'm still fucking angry. Can't they see I've got enough to deal with? With everything else I've got on my plate, Cara's bringing this request to me now? Why hasn't Nijad told her I simply couldn't take on anything else, especially something this trivial? Sometimes

I wish he could control his wife, but he only seems to want to do that in the bedroom.

Closing my eyes briefly, I inhale deeply and try to damp down my temper then, walking with my back straight and with new resolve, re-enter my office where my brother Nijad and his wife, Cara, are waiting for me, ready to resume the meeting. Taking my place, I'm unable to miss the curious looks thrown towards me. I pretend I haven't noticed.

"So, will you do it?" Cara asks enthusiastically, seemingly unaware she's putting yet another demand on my time. She leans forwards as she speaks, well, as far as she can with a seven-month baby bump in front of her. Honestly, at the size she's grown, she looks like she's having twins. Her face is flushed and excited. Animated, happy. All the things I'm not and I can't help but resent her for that.

Glancing at my brother, I don't miss that while I seem to have grown older over the past few months, Nijad's looking younger than ever. Since his marriage, he has reverted to his playful and relaxed self. His wife seems to have steadied him, their union giving him a maturity that enables him to make rational decisions, unlike the previous knee-jerk and often violent reactions he'd earned a reputation for. I envy him. He doesn't have to carry the burden that our father's death placed on me. Deep down inside, I know he's doing everything he can to support me, but it can never be enough. Sometimes my envy of what I see as him living the ideal life while I'm slowly killing myself for my country makes that elastic band inside me snap. Like right now.

My eyes zoom in on my target, my lungs fill with breath, and then I direct the full force of my anger on my brother's wife, "For fuck's sake, Cara. Don't you think I've got enough problems to deal with? I can hardly afford the time to go to England as it is." I remain standing, my fists clenched by my sides.

Nijad jumps to his feet, moving, so he's between his wife and me. "Brother!" he growls in warning. "Cara, leave us," he continues, glancing behind him quickly as he throws the command over his shoulder. The tone of his voice lets me know this time I've pushed him too far.

His wife doesn't obey him. That doesn't surprise me. But I ignore her; this is between my brother and me now. "You think you can take me on?"

Nijad dismisses my challenge with a snort. "Oh, I could beat you, brother, there's no doubt about that." He shakes his head, his expression showing his disdain, as his eyes find the ever present bodyguards standing stoically against the wall, "But you've got the upper hand, haven't you? I can't lay a bloody finger on my Ruler! Don't think I'll fall into that trap!" With an abrupt change of emotion, he turns his back on me and exchanges looks with his wife. When he touches Cara so gently on her arm, the light contact such a loving gesture, I feel envy at the depth of their affection, knowing the relationship I've agreed to is likely to be cordial at best. The hardness directed at me disappears in a second; his voice softening as he addresses his wife. "Please, go, Cara. I need to talk to Kadar alone."

It's clear she doesn't want to leave, and the way her eyes flick between us, I know she's concerned our discussion is about to get physical. She all but threatens me with just one look, the narrowing of her eyes promising retribution should I hurt her husband. Her intimidating stare makes me want to laugh; she's like a gazelle threatening an angry tiger. Admiring her bravery, I let the anger disappear from my face, holding out my hands in supplication. With a sharp nod and with palpable reluctance, tossing a last glare at me and a fleeting supporting smile to Nijad, she vacates her seat. "There's too much testosterone in here, anyway," she retorts, having to have the last word before leaving me alone with my brother.

This altercation between us has been brewing for a while; it's not just about what I think is Cara's unreasonable request.

"Leave!" I wave my hand imperiously towards the ever present guards that attend me then turn back to Nijad, snarling once the men have left us, "There, we're alone now if you want to take a swing at me, brother."

Nijad's interaction with his wife appears to have to have calmed him down. Taking off his headdress and throwing it onto a vacant chair, he goes to another and seats himself again. After giving me a long, careful look, he tells me, "You're turning into our father."

His words make me pause, giving me food for thought. Shuddering, I quickly recognise the truth in his succinct response. My need for violence slowly seeps away, and I let out a sigh. Emir Rushdi's approach to everything had been to show his strength, never weakness. To fight, not talk. To never doubt himself for one moment. Removing my own headdress, I take a seat beside him, realising I'm going to have to choose another way. Rushdi would never have bared his soul. To anyone. But perhaps Nijad is the one person who would understand.

"He trained me, Ni. All my life, everything's been to prepare me for this role, to follow in his footsteps, to rule as he did. But I'm not him." Placing my hands palms down on my table, I stare at him. "I can't see another way of doing things but carrying on the way he did, but it's not working. I can't be that man; I haven't got it in me. And it shows. He kept control of the country; control that I'm fast losing. We all know he was a bastard with almost no humanity in him, and now I understand why. To be emir, to be the absolute ruler, you can leave no room for error."

"You don't want to end up like him," Nijad tells me, sympathetically.

Sighing I turn, glad I've dismissed the guards, needing the privacy to be frank with my brother. "I'm afraid if I don't emulate his rule, continue at least some of his policies, everything will fall apart." Pushing away from the table I put my elbows on my knees and rest my head on my cupped palms. "But it's hard, Nijad. All his life he was trying to mould me into his likeness, but he died long before he'd completed the job."

"Thank fuck he did, Kadar. Your path must be a different one." Nijad's concerned for me, "You are not him, and never will be."

To be honest, becoming a replica of Emir Rushdi is a horrifying thought. "I accept that, Ni, and that times have changed. Have been changing for a while, but our father thought he could resist the advance. We've got oil deposits to exploit, and, although he refused to admit it, international relationships to nurture and maintain. Heaven help us if we lose the trust of the USA and Europe. If we can't control our country, then I can foresee foreign troops being deployed here. The oil discovery changes our position as a world player."

"Don't forget the Russians," my brother drops in. He goes to help himself to a cup of coffee. Holding the pot in one hand he waves it at me, and I shake my head, I've had enough caffeine this morning.

When he sits down opposite me, I nod slowly. "It's too much for one man, being an absolute ruler, there's too much power, too much responsibility. What if they manage to depose me? Is there anyone stronger who could rule in my stead?"

"Certain people might think they could, but no. You've been trained since birth for this role, brother. No one could do a better job, definitely not Jasim or me. I agree, you've been dealt an impossible hand. You never had the opportunity to prove yourself as a leader while our father was alive. He expected, as we all did that he'd remain healthy for many years yet and then, when he eventually started failing, you'd gradually take over his role. Instead…" His voice trails off; there's no need to state the obvious. Rushdi had died before he'd completed his reign.

I decide to let him in on my plans that I've been thinking about for quite a while now, and over the couple of months, putting time and energy into researching how it could work. "I'm going to put a government in place." I'd had the idea long before my father died. Of course, he'd never have considered it. But in the twenty-first century, it seems archaic that a wealthy and powerful if small state is governed by the will of one man.

Nijad takes in a breath and raises his eyebrows. My statement has surprised him, and he immediately seems taken with the idea. "That's a huge leap forward for Amahad. But the right one, brother. This government would be elected, I presume?"

I shrug. "Yes, but the how needs to be determined. In the cities that's the only way, but for the tribes?"

"The sheikhs will assume they'll represent their people," Nijad speaks the truth.

"Exactly. Can we have two forms of representation?" It's something I've been pondering. On my forthcoming trip to England, I'll be meeting with their representatives from the Electoral Commission to get some advice. The UK is one country that has democracy down pat.

"What about the Mullahs?"

"I'd prefer the people to elect who they want speaking for them. I don't want the religious leaders to have too much power."

Nijad looks deep in thought. "It's complicated, isn't it? And if you automatically include the sheikhs you'd potentially give power to someone like Abdul-Muhsi." He grits his teeth on the name and frowns.

"Surely he'd find little support?" I sound more optimistic than I feel. I recall Rais couldn't confirm whether or not he had the others behind him.

"I think we ought to take him out of the equation altogether. He's a dangerous man."

In all honesty, I can't deny it's a suggestion that I've not thought of too, but ordering the killing of a man, however much he might appear to be my enemy, is not the way I want to start my rule. "A last resort, I think."

Nijad looks at me sharply. "You think he'd hesitate if he had you in his sights?"

Again, I heave a heavy sigh, as I remember the thinly veiled threat he'd made in my office. Nijad's right. Sheikh Abdul-Muhsi thinks I'm too weak and disagrees with my policies. But for now, I find it hard to believe he's got the support to take me down, either in numbers of followers or the financial backing to attempt a coup. Taking him out would be one solution, but I'm not naïve enough to think others wouldn't emerge to fill the void. "I'll bear it in mind, Ni. *Tamm 'iinsha' husud lmjrd 'ann 'aghdab.* The envious were created just to be infuriated." I quote an old Arabic saying. So long as Abdul-Muhsi covets my position, it's not going to be easy to appease him. As my brother nods, I realise the friction between us has diminished, and I know what I have to do. Changing the subject, I even summon up a smile, "I'll go and see Cara, and apologise."

"She'll understand. You've got a heavy load on your shoulders, brother. Does this mean you'll agree to her request?"

I give a chuckle, which releases some of the tension inside of me. "Can anyone refuse her?"

My brother gives a hearty laugh, and we exchange grins. I know *he's* certainly never been able to.

After Nijad exits the room I wait a few minutes, getting my thoughts in order. Trying to dismiss this feeling of hopelessness that's come over me, I make myself put all the negatives to the back of my mind, focusing on the positive steps I am taking instead. Amahad had been my legacy since birth; I just have to man up and deal with it. At least I can rely on the support of my brothers.

Once I think I've got my head on straight, I go to Cara's office and prepare to eat humble pie.

Cara is one of the loveliest people I know, both in looks and in personality, quick to forgive and forget. When I explain I've come to hear her out, she says nothing about the rudeness with which I dismissed her earlier, but gets straight down to explaining her request with a welcoming smile that no one would be able to resist.

So I give her time. But soon I realise I'm listening to her words, but am unable to grasp her reasoning. "Wouldn't it be easier to bring the woman here?"

"You're going to England, Kadar. It would only take a few moments of your time, and save her a long, possibly wasted trip to Amahad." She pouts, and I realise any attempt to dissuade her would be futile. Her heart seems to be set on it.

"She's your only candidate?" I sit back and listen while my sister-in-law explains that there were very few applicants wanting to help her with her pet project of renovating the ancient harem. Easy to explain why; Amahad is rapidly gaining an unfortunate reputation for political unrest—another reason for my forthcoming trip to England to meet with the government there. I won't be asking for military support, but to ensure we're on the same wavelength with our strategic response.

But now Cara is aiming to hijack part of my limited time in London to interview her candidate in person. On paper, I have to agree she looks ideal, but anyone who's ever been in the position of taking on a new employee knows the person in the flesh might be very different. I steeple my fingers as I think about the practicalities. If she came to the embassy, it really wouldn't take up much of my day. But I'm still annoyed I'm being pulled into this project against my express wishes. I thought I'd made my position clear that I wanted no hand in it.

"Please, Kadar. I have a gut feeling about this woman." She's looking at me with doe eyes, her hands rubbing her stomach in an unconscious movement, drawing my attention to her unborn child, the first baby to be born into the royal family since the birth of my young sister, Aiza, twenty years ago. The first of a new generation. Returning my gaze to her face I know, much like her husband, I'm unable to deny her anything. Cara's done so much for her adopted country, and her gut feelings are not to be ignored; indeed, Amahad owes its current financial stability to her intuition. With a deep sigh, I respond. "Alright, set the interview up. I'll meet with this woman and let you know what I think of her qualifications and suitability."

The way her face lights up is sufficient thanks and reward for me. It will only, hopefully, be half an hour out of my life, but my agreement has given her so much pleasure. She's almost too delighted, and I have to wonder why this is so important to her. She could easily have arranged the private jet to fly her candidate here.

Something is up, but I can't put my finger on it. And when Nijad walks in, the need to get to the bottom of Cara's reasons for her request flies out of my head altogether.

"We have that meeting, Kadar," he reminds me as he enters, his robes billowing out behind him.

I notice he doesn't say which meeting, but the scowl on Cara's face makes it clear that she knows and doesn't approve. She meets my eye. "Go, Kadar," she waves her hand in dismissal. "I've said all I have to say on that subject already." Yes, we've had many discussions about my proposed marriage.

It's something else I admire about Cara; she doesn't keep flogging a dead horse. And this is definitely a lost cause. I will do my duty, however unpleasant, just another obligation on the emir, though this particular one comes attached with manacles and chains. A life-long commitment.

Having followed Nijad through the palace, we reach the more modern government wing. Entering my office, he holds the door open for me, and I precede him, pausing just a second to mention to my assistant, Richard, that he's to come in once the event organiser arrives. Shutting the door behind me, I wave Nijad towards the table then move towards it myself, leaning over to take the fresh pot of coffee that's just been delivered and pouring two cups. I offer him a pastry, but he declines. I sit, and I lean back in my chair. "You're a lucky man, Nijad."

He nods slowly realising I'm referring to his wife, "I know." He's quiet for a moment, and I suspect he's reflecting how it could have turned out so differently. "Are you still going ahead with the marriage arrangements, Kadar? Wouldn't your plans for an elected government make the need for it redundant?"

I shake my head, "That's not going to be achieved in a day, it will take time. Since I've given my agreement, the sheikhs at least have something else to focus on other than my shortcomings."

"So this is still your plan?"

It's my turn to nod, but I can't hide my grimace. 'This' is a farce of a ball where prospective brides will parade before me. "It seems I need a wife."

"Arranged marriages aren't that bad." He grins at me to give me encouragement, but he was lucky, he got Cara. It's why I wanted him here today, to provide both moral support and proof positive that the course of action I'm taking need not necessarily turn out to be as bad as I fear.

Too keyed up to sit for long, I stand and walk over to the window, but right now can't appreciate the sights of the beautiful garden outside. Instead, I think of my duty as monarch to marry and produce an heir. The bride will be carefully chosen, and to that end, my advisors are already working on a possible selection for me. Plans are underway to hold a ball in just three months' time so I can meet suitable women and thus have some semblance of choice, but as my coupling is expected to form a beneficial political alliance for the country, my options will be limited. But, enough, I'll do my duty when the time comes. I have to; a marriage of state, another expectation on the emir. My advisors tell me the right match will help stabilise the country, and that's all that matters.

Turning back to my brother, I change the subject to keep my mind off my life sentence with an arranged bride. "How do you read the situation in the southern desert, Ni?"

"As we were discussing earlier, it's all comes back to Abdul-Muhsi. He worries me."

"How are you dealing with that?" Nijad is Sheikh of the Southern Desert, his role to guard the borders and keep Amahad secure. But nowadays his job is extends beyond that, preventing dissidents among our populace.

"Sheikh Rais is acting as a liaison, but the time for talking might be done. We're increasing the garrison in [illegible]alm[illegible]."

My brow furrows as he mentions the military base in the desert city, and I remember his suggestion to dispose of Abdul-Muhsi. But do his people share his views? I don't want to set tribe against tribe, use our soldiers to fight our own citizens. "We must completely exhaust the negotiation route before taking up arms, Nijad. Amahadian against Amahadian is more than I can stomach."

I don't wait for his answer before I turn back to the view outside again. It's only during the last few decades that all the desert tribes were united to come under the one umbrella of the state. Amahad is a progressive country, but some of the smaller tribes such as the Qaiquw and Khabi are still strict Muslim, still veil their women and see any modernisation as an act of the devil. Easy pickings, for the jihadists trying to start a religious war. Do I fight to keep us all united? Or let the rebellious tribes combine with our neighbouring country, Ezirad? And what would be the implications for either, bearing in mind the recent discovery of a new oil field running beneath both our countries? It's a fucking minefield and one that I must carefully weave my way across. Our very last option is to declare war. I'll do anything to prevent that, even bind my life to the desert sheikhs' choice of the woman they wish me to marry.

CHAPTER 9
Zoe

My initial joy at having escaped evaporated fast after I'd seen that news report. I'd hardly slept a wink, so woke lookine worse than ever with bloodshot and bleary eyes. *But I can't give up now.* Understanding that lying on this shabby bed in the B&B, afraid to show my face in case I'm recognised, worrying even at this point the police or Ethan's men might be coming for me will get me nowhere. I'm better off to keep moving.

As I count my remaining funds, I realise what a fix I'm in with just over four hundred pounds to my name. *That isn't going to last me long.* Part of me resents how much I'd spent on tickets I didn't use the day before, but if it has Ethan running around in circles it has to be worth it. But that leaves me the question of how I'm going to be able to support myself and there's only one answer, I have to find work. But who would want to employ a woman with no history, a broken wrist, and a bruised and battered face? A woman on the run?

For a moment all I want to do is curl up and cry when it hits me how much I've lost. I was a graduate with a promising career, now I'm without friends, all alone in an unfamiliar place. But just when it seems like my melancholy is going to pull me under, the saner part of my brain reminds me no matter how bad my prospects seem right now; they look one hell of a lot brighter than if I'd stayed with my abuser.

The thought gives me the impetus and courage to leave my room, I check out of the B&B, relieved when the receptionist doesn't give me a second look. My hat once again pulled well down over my face, I start walking, using my feet to save money, with no particular destination in mind. Each car that passes, each person that I see causes shivers of fear to run down my spine. With every step I take, I'm scared that someone will recognise me, and decide the chance to become two hundred and fifty grand richer is too good to miss. Hurting and tired I plod on, convincing myself even if I end up penniless, dying of exposure and hunger, it would be on my terms, not his.

I barely have to walk a mile out of town when my guardian angel gives me a prod with her guiding hand, and I came across a plant nursery with a small shop out front and a vacancy sign for an assistant in the window.

I stand, looking at that sign for a very long time. If I'd been seeking work in any other circumstances, it would have been a heaven-sent opportunity. With my qualifications, I could do the job standing on my head, or could have if I didn't have one hand in a sling. But even injured I could give it my best shot. I need money, and walking on further provides no guarantee I would find a better option.

Another minute passes while I wait undecided. What if the person inside recognises me? What if walking in and asking about the vacancy means the end of my liberty?

Then, knowing I don't have little choice; I decide to take the gamble.

Slipping my hand out of the sling and taking it off, I shove my ruined wrist into my pocket for support and so my injury isn't immediately visible. Taking a deep, shaky breath, I enter the shop and instantly came face to face with a woman who has to be close to seventy. But it's her kindly countenance I notice first, a vibrant, welcoming smile that spreads from her mouth to her eyes and which, after only a few seconds, turns into an expression of concern as she takes in my battered appearance which I apparently hadn't done enough to disguise. It was to be my first lesson that it isn't possible to hide anything from the sharp-eyed Ida.

I'd already made sure the shop was otherwise empty, but I keep casting furtive glances towards the door on the lookout for customers as I introduce myself, "My name's Claire Ranger, and I'm enquiring about the job you're advertising out front..."

Her intense stare makes me falter; then I feel defeat flood through me as she takes my arm and with an unexpected strength for her advanced years, pulls me into a small office behind the shop. All at once certain she's seen me on the news and is about to make the dreaded call, tears fill my eyes, and I debate running, but truthfully I'm on the verge of giving up. *If the first person I meet sees right through me, I'm never going to be safe.*

But the older woman surprises me. Keeping her hand on my arm, but relaxing it into a gesture of comfort and support, she starts to speak, her words crisp and clear in a tone of voice that suggests she would take no nonsense, "I'm Ida. I don't get many customers this early in the day, but someone might have walked in. It's best you don't work in the shop, deary, but in the greenhouse out back, you'll be well out of sight."

I stare at her, my mind unable to fully comprehend her words.

Then her smile returns, the expression totally transforming her face, and holding out her hand out to me she repeats her introduction, "I'm Ida. Ida Wilkinson. I'm offering you a job, love. One where you can keep out of sight, and out of the way. No one will find you here."

****

"Shit!" *Stupid fucking wrist!* I stare at the mess on the ground from yet another dropped plant pot, still having no strength in my left hand. At least, after two months it no longer hurts, except for a slight ache when I overuse it. It's just weak and looks horrible. Usually, I try to avoid looking at the ugly twisted mess that used to be a delicate set of bones and tendons joining my hand to my arm; you don't need to be a doctor to see it hasn't healed right. But having evaded Ethan for sixty days now my wrist is a permanently reminder, a warning to always to be on my guard.

Bending down, I sigh, then start sweeping up the peat and putting it back in the pot. Luckily the plant wasn't damaged. My task completed, I get back to my feet, glancing around the nursery, letting the tranquillity of the greenery and flowers surround me, continually thanking whichever deity was looking out for me the day I met Ida. It's still hard to believe how lucky I was.

For two months now, she's kept me safe and out of sight, here, just outside of Ludlow, in a small garden nursery where I've found my personal sanctuary. A place to mend, heal and regroup, beginning that first day when she nursed me as I suffered the nausea and weakness brought on by the morning after pill I'd eventually taken.

Ida has put up with my clumsiness while I learn to cope with having just one good hand, and gradually, as I've healed, I've been able to contribute fully in my role as her assistant. Sometimes, to my chagrin, my physical weakness reappears and this is not, unfortunately, the first pot I've dropped. Oh well, another one bites the dust, as Ida would say, nothing to do but pick myself up and carry on. I'm alive, and free. What else matters?

Today continues along the same lines much as any other as Ida and I follow the routine we've settled into. When the shop closes I help her prepare dinner. We eat then sit down in front of the telly for the evening. Tonight, as usual, we get into a debate about the flimsy plots and whether the villain will eventually get his just desserts in the soap we're watching and that I've become addicted to since I've been here. I'm not sure the program is entertainment as much as giving us an opportunity to shout advice at the TV. But a change comes this evening as Ida switches our entertainment off when EastEnders ends. I cast a surprised glance across to her, knowing one of her favourite dramas is coming up next, and it's odd she doesn't want to watch it.

I'm used to Ida's probing looks, but tonight she seems to have something particular on her mind, and I shift uncomfortably under her assessing gaze. She doesn't leave me in suspense for long. "I worry about you, Claire." Poking at the dying embers of the fire she tries to get it to burst into life again; shovelling in some coal, but she's left too late. It was only when the small, but cosy sitting room in Ida's cottage had started to grow cold that it occurred to either of us to do something about it. "Damn, not sure it's going to catch now!"

"I'm going up soon, anyway. Don't worry about it on my account." Not feeling in the mood for an in-depth discussion tonight, her opening words make me suspect if I don't make the escape to my bedroom I'll be in for some of Ida's home truths.

With regards to the fire, the old woman is on a mission. Grabbing a sheet of newspaper, Ida holds it over the fireplace, gripping it tightly on each side to prevent it being sucked in as air is quickly drawn under the grate. In only a few seconds, the time honoured method has the desired effect as a flame appears with a roar behind the paper. Expertly, Ida whips the paper away with a triumphant exclamation, and I grin behind my hand. This old lady refuses to be beaten by anything. I have to admire her. I've seen that trick before, but wouldn't have the confidence to do it myself; I'd probably end up burning the house down. "That should do it! Now where were we?" She sits back on her heels, thinking for a moment, "Oh yes, this just won't do, Claire. You can't keep on like this."

I sigh, hoping she'd forgotten the topic of conversation

she'd just started. Having been engrossed in watching her get the coal blazing I'd missed my chance of evading it. "But I'm safe here, Ida. I've been here two months without any problem, so surely we can assume Ethan has no idea where I am."

She gives me her sharp look, the one that shows her natural intelligence honed by extensive life experiences she's so far only hinted at. "Physically you're safe, yes. Hopefully. But it's your mental state I'm worried about." Holding her hands out to take in some of the warmth of the now rejuvenated fire, she continues, "You're just a young woman. Now you're healed you shouldn't be hiding out here; you should be out living life, seeing friends your age. Not stuck working and living with an old biddy like me."

Letting out another sigh, I explain it to her again. "Ida, even if I wanted to I couldn't. You know that. I'm at risk the minute I step out of this place. I can't even take a chance of going into Ludlow." We watch the news avidly each evening, and though admittedly, my disappearance is no longer headlines, every now and again, reference will be made that Zoe Baker remains a missing person, and of course, there's always mention of the extravagant reward offered for information as to my whereabouts.

But worse, I'd found my story splashed all over social media too; I'd used Ida's account rather than my own to keep an eye on it, I'm not stupid after all. But I did grow cold when I found trying to trace me had become almost a craze amongst Facebookers and Tweeters, with madcap theories circulating of where I'd gone. Search parties had been organised to follow up the many reported sightings. The only comfort I took was that Ethan had to be wasting his time rushing up and down the country following up on the rumours; even over the world if the gossip there had been a sighting of me in Reykjavik, the capital of Iceland, had been taken as at all credible.

Am I imposing on Ida by staying here so long? I start wondering whether I may have outstayed my welcome. She's been wonderful, giving me a home and a job that at least makes me feel useful when I'm not dropping and breaking pots, and her wonderful upbeat company. But I know she's used to living on her own. A shiver runs through me at the thought of having to find somewhere else to go. I haven't got the guts to come straight out and ask her. I don't know what I'd do if she turns me out. Not wanting to prolong the discussion, I give an exaggerated sigh, and say 'goodnight' going to bed with a heavy heart, worrying I might shortly be on the lookout for a new sanctuary.

****

"Hey, Claire!" Glancing up, I see Ida's back from doing her shopping in town. She goes and does her weekly shop at Tesco once a week on Tuesdays.

"Ida!" I greet her, "Did you get everything you wanted?" I wait for it, trying to hide my grin, knowing how this is going to play out. She always forgets something and spends the rest of the day moaning about it. She blames it on her age, but I know she's as sharp as a tack and her memory's probably better than mine.

"Everything except for the one bloody thing I went there for. Tea bags! Would you believe I forgot to get the goddamn tea?"

She walks towards me and though her response is as expected, her customary smile is missing, making me wonder what's wrong. Her hand, usually as steady as a rock, is shaking as she holds out a sheet of paper, and I watch her approach in consternation, something warning me I don't want to reach out and take it. When she's close enough, she passes it to me without speaking. Glancing at her face, I see her lips are pursed, her brow pulled down in a frown. Dreading what it could be, but unable to put it off any longer, I look down at the freshly printed flyer she's given me. It's got my face on it, and the wording asks if anyone's seen this person, and, in big letters, a sum doubling the last reward for information. I'm now worth five hundred thousand pounds. Half a million frigging pounds!

An incredulous laugh bursts out of me, but any amusement quickly flees as I realise Ethan's nowhere close to giving up. "Where…?"

"Post office in Ludlow," she tells me, answering before I finish my question.

Shit! That's far too close for comfort. Does that mean his net's closing in? *How the hell did he trace me here?*

Ida's face is full of sympathy; she knows my fears without me having to express them, "He could just be widening his search; it could be a coincidence."

"But it might not." I feel tears pricking behind my eyes. My haven doesn't feel safe anymore. Cursing under my breath, I start to think. We haven't advertised the fact I'm here, and I'd put good money on Ida keeping it close to her chest. I don't work in the shop, but it is possible someone's seen me working out back. It is a glasshouse after all.

"Come." She puts her arm around my shoulders and leads me into the house adjoining the nursery, "I've got enough tea bags left to make you a cuppa, and you look like you could do with one."

I could do with something stronger, but it's not even lunchtime yet so I can't make that suggestion. Instead, I go with her and sit at her small kitchen table as she fiddles about putting the kettle on and rinsing out then warming the old fashioned teapot. No just dipping bags in a mug for Ida, she has to go through the whole darn ritual. But watching her going about her task is settling, and allows me to start thinking about things rationally instead of in blind panic.

"There's that job in Amahad," Ida states knowing my objections to it as she carefully pours boiling water into the pot. A couple of weeks ago she'd found a position advertised online. It was right up my street; a job that combined both parts of my landscaping and architecture degree. A fantastic opportunity to renovate an exotic sounding building and gardens. And the best part of it? It was more than three thousand miles away in an entirely different part of the world. Ignoring my concerns about the practicalities, Ida had gone ahead and had applied on my behalf. When she'd told me what she'd done I hadn't been worried; I knew there wasn't a chance in hell I'd land it, there'd probably be hundreds of more experienced people applying.

But to my astonishment, last week there had been a phone call to the shop's landline. Ida had summoned me in, and before I could protest I'd found myself speaking to a woman named Cara Kassis who was responding to my application. With a sigh I started to tell her I had to withdraw as it would be impossible for me to take the position, but she was speaking over me with such enthusiasm about the project I was soon hooked.

As Cara continued to describe my ideal job, I quickly found myself drawn in and responding in kind. After half an hour we were getting on like a house on fire, my suggestions on the approach to the works tallying exactly with what she had in mind, and we were soon both discussing something close to our hearts. I got carried away, believing it was something within my reach, until at last she remembered herself with a laugh and said she better get down to the formalities. It was then I had to let her down, admitting I had no passport, and would be unable to get one. However well matched, I wouldn't be able to take the job in any event. She asked, of course, but I didn't tell her why I couldn't get documentation. I couldn't trust anyone with the truth, however friendly they might seem. It was an awkward end to the call, and I never expected to hear from her again.

As my heart speeds up, I realise things have changed now and are forcing my hand, whether I want to or not, it seems I need to get on the move. I can't take the chance that leaflet in the post office window wasn't just coincidence. What if Ethan has he traced me to the area where I'm hiding? Or worse, knows exactly where I am? I shudder as I look at the steaming cup that Ida's placed in front of me, perched on the saucer she insists on using, not sure if I can drink it, my stomach in knots.

Ida waits patiently for my response. It would be the obvious answer, yes, but it's impossible. "I can't go to Amahad. You know why."

"That email last night didn't suggest it would be a problem." She raises her eyebrows.

The email she's talking about came out of the blue. It was from Cara Kassis and asked me to attend an interview with Kadar Kassis at the Amahadian Embassy in London on Thursday, two days from now. It had a strange message at the bottom.

Don't worry about the passport; there are ways around it. Be certain to tell Kadar 'Cara said so'"

I didn't understand the footnote. I may not be well travelled, but even I know that you need to show your identity papers before leaving any airport in the UK, and before entering any foreign country. So I'd dismissed it out of hand. It wasn't worth the danger of the risk of exposure travelling down to the capital, just to be told what I already knew. But were things different now? Should I give it more consideration? Could this Kadar person possibly do anything for me? Would it be legal? *But what the hell do I care if it isn't?* If the threat of staying here has increased significantly, perhaps I should take the chance?

What if even now Ethan has plans in motion to take me back? Just the very thought makes me shudder and glance nervously at the door, half expecting to see his car pull up outside.

As if she knows what I'm thinking, Ida touches my arm then taps the paper I'd forgotten was still in my hand. "Half a million pounds for information on where you are, Claire. I wish I could, but I can't promise you're safe here any longer. That's one heck of a lot of money." Leaning forwards, she places a gentle, motherly kiss on my forehead, "I'll miss you, but I think it's time for you to move on. I don't know if anyone has noticed you're here, we've tried to keep you well hidden. But, well, people who work in glass houses shouldn't assume they're invisible."

"You think someone's seen me?" I appreciate Ida's take on the proverb.

"I don't think we can take the chance that they haven't," she insists, concerned.

With a sinking feeling, I know she's right. But I still have doubts.

"It's an interview, Ida. I can't even prove who I am. You're supposed to take proof of qualifications as well as identity, and I've got nothing! I can't even use my real name! I can't prove my relevant experience, and I've got no references." I grow angry, realising once again how much Ethan has ruined everything for me. I have the opportunity not only to escape but a chance at the job of a lifetime; one I would have jumped at even if I didn't have other reasons to flee the country.

"I don't know why, but I've got a good feeling about it. I think you clicked with this Cara person, Claire. I believe the interview will simply be a formality." She pauses for a moment, "It's time to take hold of your life again, and if that has to be thousands of miles away then so be it. I will miss you, though. I've enjoyed having you here." The kindly old woman puts her arms around me, and I lean into her embrace, thanking her without using words. Perhaps she's right.

So despite my apprehension of the risk, I'll be taking, my mind starts working out practicalities of traveling down to London. I made it up here without being detected; I'll simply have to be just as careful and reverse the process on the way back down. More cautious, even, as almost the whole country is on the look-out for me. *Half a million pounds! Shit!*

Just the thought of being so far away and out of his clutches sounds so attractive, I owe it to myself to try. As I am, hiding out here with Ida, I'm only existing, not living. I can't let Ethan steal the rest of my life as well as the time he already has. The knowledge that his search might be homing in on my whereabouts is the push I need to pull me out of the stupor I'd descended into. It's clear I can't wait here and stagnate any longer. Ida is right; I can't let Ethan continue to dictate my life. Pulling away from her arms, I let a smile come to my face. "I think I've got call to make."

A knowing grin slowly spreads over Ida's face as she pats me on the back in approval.

Standing, I turn and start walking away but then pause as the perennial woman's problem suddenly hits me. "Ida, I've got nothing to wear! I can't turn up to an embassy in a cheap pair of jeans!" I swing back around to face her.

She just laughs. "Isn't that what next day delivery's for?"

I gape at her, then chuckle. *Of course, it is.* Feeling more positive for the first time in months I take a step towards Ida's office and also towards my future. A future, hopefully, not overshadowed by the threat of Ethan. Taking out the untraceable phone Josh gave me all those weeks ago I ring the embassy and leave a message saying I'll attend the interview. Next I have fashion websites to browse through.

I've gone from rock bottom when I saw the leaflet Ida brought with her back from town to feeling a light-heartedness I haven't felt for a very long time. It might come to nothing, but for the first time in almost two years, I feel I'm taking charge of my destiny.

CHAPTER 10
Kadar

Sitting at my office in the Amahadian Embassy in London I glance out of the window. It's early spring in England, when snowdrops are just past their best and daffodils and crocuses begin taking over from their little white friends. I have to admire the lushness of this country, coming as I do from the land of sand, where gardens are few and far between; the cost of keeping plants and flowers alive—sacrificing our most precious resource to keep them irrigated and watered—often too high to pay. Even the rain that's slanting down from the murky grey London skies doesn't bother me; the sight now such a rarity that I relish it.

In many ways, England is my second home, but it's my brother Jasim, the middle child of the three Kassis brothers, who has made it his first, hardly returning to Amahad at all now. The strictness of my father, both in his parental duties and his rule, drove him away. He now works on our behalf as an unofficial ambassador, and plays an important role, being in charge of exploiting our newly found extensive oil reserves. I can't resent him for emigrating, given the significant and valuable burden Jasim shoulders for us. Having a close member of the family in such an important position means I have someone I can trust at my back.

And now I watch as he comes forward to greet me, dressed in his stereotypical tailored suit, probably coming from Saville Row; costing more than an average person's monthly salary. His hair has grown, I notice, just touching his shoulders, but perfectly coiffured, of course. Even in the breeze, it falls back to its styled position with just a flick of his hand over his forelock. He moves with the grace and stealth of a panther, and I can see from rippling of his muscles under his jacket that, like me, he's kept up his fitness regime. I hold back my sigh of envy. Jasim is the only one of us who has any choice as to how he lives his life, and who he spends it with—something currently very close to my heart as I'm about to be shackled to a wife for nothing other than political reasons. But despite my jealousy of his freedoms, he has so far remained a bachelor.

"Kadar! It's good to see you!" He holds out his hand, takes mine then hugs me towards him with his other arm. We've not always got on, in fact, we very nearly fell out completely when I involved him in our plans to bring Cara to Amahad and force her to marry Nijad, but we've settled into an easy enough relationship again since. Now, releasing me he pulls back, his eyes narrowing, "You look like shit, brother."

Trust Jasim to give it to me straight. "Nice to see you too," I reply dryly, but I'm unable to deny the stresses I've inherited are visibly wearing me down.

His dark eyes examine me carefully. "You need to release some of that tension." As I cock my eyebrow at him, his face splits into a wide grin, and I'm not surprised when he continues, "I know the best way to do that. Come to the club tonight."

I laugh in response; it was a predictable offer for my brother to make. Jasim is part-owner of an exclusive BDSM club in London; the cost of membership so astronomically high as to make it extremely elite, and safe enough for people such as myself to be assured of anonymity when playing. I've been there many times before, usually managing a visit whenever I've been able to come to the UK, and admire the excellent setup. I hadn't considered a visit this trip with everything else I've got to do, but all at once it occurs to me Jasim just might be on to something. An opportunity to relax and unwind sounds very attractive; I haven't allowed myself any release except for one that's been self-administered for a very long time. The chance to wipe my mind free of all problems Amahadian, even for just a short while, is extremely tempting. It doesn't take me more than a couple of seconds to mentally run through the meetings I'll have to shift before deciding to take him up on it.

So, that's how I find myself, after a good catch-up dinner with my sibling, entering Club Tiacapan, located in a mansion on the outskirts of a park to the south-west of London. As always, I'm impressed by the décor and facilities as well as the size of the place, which, while already large, Jasim's told me, is still insufficient. Preparations for an extension are underway as there are always more applications for membership than space to accommodate the number of people who want to join. Even the sky-high fees don't negate the desire for a safe, clean, and well-managed place to play.

As ruler I'm tied to Amahad, so nowadays it's rare I can afford the luxury of coming here, but I still retain a locker where my clothing and well-stocked toy bag is kept for those odd occasions when I can. Feeling much like I'm coming home, I go into the changing room, emerging after a few minutes dressed in tight leather trousers and a leather vest. I feel I've shrugged off my persona along with my outer clothes; I'm no longer emir, but a Dom.

Proceeding through the impressive atrium and out into the main room, my tension drifts away as I begin exchanging nods with people I recognise as I make my way to the bar, briefly greeting a member of the British parliament and then a well-renowned judge, calling them by their assumed names. Here, I have no fear of exposure, any one of us would risk too much by revealing the proclivities of the other. Then, when I see another familiar face mixing drinks, a grin spreads across my face at the welcome sight.

"Master Ralph! You still here?"

"Where else would I be?" The man in his forties who seems to be a permanent fixture behind the gleaming mahogany bar answers in his deep voice, his barked laugh immediately making me feel back among friends. "Getting a bit hot in your part of the world, isn't it, Master K?"

Knowing how he keeps up with current affairs, I realise he's not referring to the weather. "We're trying to lower the temperature." I respond, obliquely. He doesn't press me further; Club Tiacapan is a place to forget the outside world.

Without asking he passes me a whisky; a top shelf single

malt, straight up without ice as nature intended, knowing full well how I like to indulge when outside of my home territory. There's no question or censure; here it doesn't matter who I am or what I do as long as I obey the club rules which are simple enough. No exchange of bodily fluids in the main room—private rooms are available for that—and strict adherence to the principles of safe, sane, and consensual, or in some circumstances where all parties are aware and agree on Risk Aware Consensual Kink. The use of the traffic light system for safewords is obligatory.

Taking a sip of the excellent whisky I let the atmosphere of the room flow over me, the heavy rock music playing at a volume that allows Doms and subs still to communicate, but loud enough for the beat to provide a useful accompanying rhythm for those using canes and floggers.

I hear a whip whistle through the air, and as I cock my head to one side, Master Ralph answers my unspoken query, "Master Jonathan is playing tonight."

I turn to see. A large area has been cleared to allow room for the eight-foot single tail to be used safely without endangering the onlookers. Jon's skill and expertise are widely admired, so it doesn't surprise me a small crowd has gathered to watch. Another crack, and from my viewpoint I can see the tip kiss across his sub and wife, Mia's back. What I can't see, but would expect, is the slightest red mark which will feel like a small sting despite the loud sound which I know increases the anticipation of the strike and expectation of pain. I wouldn't be a good Dom had I not been at some time on the receiving end of the experiences I put my subs through. Picking up on the way

Mia relaxes into the St. Andrews Cross I hope that she will be able to let her emotions go tonight.

Master Jonathan, co-owner of both Grade A Security and Club Tiacapan is a close friend of the Kassis family. Therefore, I am only too well aware his wife recently suffered an early miscarriage which her doctors have sadly put down to damage left over from the abuse she suffered when only a teenager. The fact Mia became pregnant at all is a medical miracle, and to lose the baby was devastating for the couple and particularly hard on Mia. But she's a strong woman, brave enough to rise above the horrors of her past and Master Jonathan is an exceptional Dom. And, if I'm any judge of the matter, he's already got Mia close to subspace where she'll be able to let go of her pent up emotions, if only for tonight.

The depth of their relationship makes me examine my predicament. Even if I wasn't about to enter into a political arrangement tied up with a marital bow, would it have ever been possible for me to love a woman as much as Jon loves Mia? The depth of affection I can see clearly demonstrated by the light touch, though heavy mind fuck, of the man whipping his wife across the room? Have I even got that much emotion in me, or has the ability to feel anything been killed off by my single-focused upbringing? I've never cared for anyone in my life, except so far as it was obligatory. Raised separately, and differently from my brothers, it's only in adult life that we've developed any closeness, but even now I would be hard pressed to say I regarded them in any other way except as the best of friends. Am I capable of feeling that elusive emotion, love?

Shaking my head, I try to rid myself of self-analytical thoughts. I'm here to have fun, and forget everything else. Turning back to the bar, I watch Master Ralph pour drinks in his role as the bartender for the night and let my mind drift as the screams and sighs of submissives and the clear odours of sex and arousal waft across the room. I was right to come here tonight; I needed this.

"Master K?"

A soft voice at my elbow brings me out of my thoughts, and the sight causes a smile to come to my face. The girl, now kneeling in a perfect submissive pose at my feet is someone I know well, a regular in the club, and I've played with her on a number of occasions in the past. She's my kind of sub, able to cope with and enjoy some of my more extreme tendencies. "Diamond. It's lovely to see you. Stand, let me look at you!"

Diamond, an experienced submissive, gracefully unfolds herself and rises to her feet, her head still bowed. She's wearing one of her favoured baby doll costumes. I had been in two minds whether I was going to play tonight or simply enjoy the atmosphere and imbibe my senses, feeding on others' pleasure, but suddenly I realise I can't turn down the blatant offer in front of me. Placing my finger under her chin, I tilt her head towards mine, turning it this way and that, soaking up and enjoying the beauty in front of me. I know what I want to do. "Would you enjoy being bound tonight?"

Her breathy voice and the dilation of her pupils would give me the answer even if she didn't give voice to the words. "If it pleases you, Master K."

I find it pleases me very much. "Your limits the same as they were?"

"Yes, Master K." Her face is already growing flushed with excitement, and I suspect she's already aroused.

I regard her for a moment. "Are you comfortable with Shibari? With RACK?" From previous experience, I know that she is, but still have to check that she understands the concept of risk–aware consensual kink, and will place her total trust in me.

She nods, then immediately corrects herself, knowing I need a verbal answer. "Yes, Master K. Thank you." Now her cheeks take an even pinker tinge and I hear the slight breathlessness in her voice; her growing anticipation is impossible to miss. I have a well-earned reputation as a proficient rigger, having taken years to study and perfect the art, a sideline followed during my diplomatic trips abroad and knots being something I can practice in privacy, even in the palace. Her glazed eyes show me she is eagerly looking forward to giving me her complete submission tonight.

With a nod and quick grin at Ralph—Diamond's not the only one looking forward to this—I pick up my bag in one hand, take hers in the other, and lead her to an empty stage that I can see is already equipped with what I need.

The babydoll costume looks good on her, but it has to go. My voice lowers to a dominant tone, "Strip!"

I don't wait to see her obey me. I know that she will, and from previous play, I've seen she's an exhibitionist and not worried about showing her skin in public. Leaving her to undress, I open my bag and take out a coiled length of rope. Glancing behind and eying her, I realise the eight metres of red silk is going to enhance her flawless pale skin perfectly. I'm going to thoroughly enjoy myself tonight.

She stands, naked, feet apart, hands grasped behind her in the small of her back, her eyes lowered to the floor, breathing deeply in and out as she gets herself into the correct mindset for our activity. I take a moment to enjoy the view, my eyes feasting on her generous curves; not a model-thin body, but one I know will become even more beautiful with the careful placement of my ropes. I drink in her the splendour of the exquisiteness nature gave her, considering how best to enhance it. As I take my time deciding the effect I'll be aiming for; I sense people gathering around us, taking the opportunity to see a skilled rigger at work. I don't object to an audience, they know as well as I do that it's not just the end product which will be a thing of beauty, but the steps I'll take to get there, and I've no objection to others sharing the experience with me. I may not have played here for a while, but my reputation hasn't faded.

Taking myself to a place generally kept hidden deep inside of me, I mimic her deep breathing for a short while, clearing my mind of everything else and ignoring the appreciative mutterings around us, focusing solely on her, my subject, my blank canvas. Moving slightly back from her, examining her from head to toe, I begin to see in my mind not only where I want to get to, but how I'm going to arrive there.

At no point does Diamond raise her eyes or show impatience at my delay, which only heightens her level of expectation. If the red flush now spreading all over her body is anything to go by, she's already enjoying the undivided attention of her Dom, even though, as yet, I haven't laid a finger on her. My one word of command has readied her and excited her.

The music changes, a rock ballad starts, its melodic beat with gentle rhythm increasing the air of entrancement surrounding us. It is time to begin. I inhale deeply once more then, taking a firm hold of the rope, I close the gap between us and start wrapping the red length around her wrists, fastening them in position, slipping my fingers between the silk and her skin to ensure the knot is firm, but not too tight. Her posture shows she trusts me implicitly, but her breathing has speeded up. She's beginning to succumb to my control. Giving oneself totally over to a Dom, however experienced the sub, is a step full of anxiety, much like climbing over a barrier and launching into space for a bungee jump. Deep down she knows it's safe, but the subconscious desire for survival makes her question the decision to take that leap, or, in this case, to give over her power. I smile to myself, knowing as she's bound more tightly and I take more and more control, such fears will disappear, and there will be no room for nervous thoughts in her head, no room for thoughts at all. And on her journey to subspace, I'll be rewarded by sinking into Dom space, a place where I'll no longer be contemplating the burdens that otherwise plague me.

Breathing in and out, letting all tensions fade away, I bring the rope around her body, binding it above and below her breasts, and tie a knot in the middle. I step away for a moment, taking a second to examine my handiwork. Diamond is tall for a woman, and her shapely curves cry out for the caress of my rope. Already her breasts protrude nicely, her nipples even now erect and just right for clamps. But refusing to be distracted from my primary task I make myself wait before adding such adornments. Moving back to her luscious form, mindful of the advanced state of relaxation I'll be putting her in, I adjust the suspension hook above her and, utilising the loop I created while binding her chest, attach her, so the hook is taking her weight. Using the pulley at the side of the stage, I hoist her up until her feet are just above the ground.

Next, I draw the rope around her slender neck, taking care to tie it off so that the knot cannot slip and tighten, leaving it lying around her throat like a necklace. The rope lies loose, but the veiled threat of strangulation causes her breath to quicken. After ensuring there can be no pressure on her tender throat I lose no time as I move on, taking the red silk around her back and looping it tightly around her waist, and then around her ample hips.

With a grin, I hold the rope against her measuring it and then place a knot in its length. Passing it under her crotch I know the place where I've tied it will rest against her clit when it's secured it to the binding around her waist. At the moment, it's only touching it gently, but any movement will cause stimulation. As my hand brushes against her, I check how wet she is, then give another satisfied smile. There's no doubt she's enjoying this.

As I start to bind her left leg creating red diamond

patterns, a beautiful contrast against her creamy white skin, I feel the transfer of power between us as though it is a physical thing. With my rope I'm embracing her, gradually taking away any opportunity for her to move, but we both know she retains all control. A mere uttering of her safeword would have her free in an instant, but she won't need to use it, and neither will I have to use the sharp knife I've got ready, close at hand should I need it. Diamond is no stranger to suspension play or the feeling of giving her total trust to someone else. As I truss her tighter, she'll lose any ability to move, and will achieve an endorphin high that, at this precise moment, is only in my hands to gift.

So far I have avoided binding her knee, so when I reach her ankle, I'm able to bend it up. Sliding the silk up and through the pattern I've made I tie it off, her leg bent, and positioned slightly to the side. I then give the other leg the same treatment. It's not only her getting high; I'm also achieving that incredible state as I feed off the total submission she's offering to me so beautifully.

Finally, I tie off the rope, tucking the end neatly against her body, and step back to better admire my handiwork, appreciating the red diamond patterns covering her skin, marking her as mine if only for tonight. I don't hurry but take my time. A small step to my right which me to my toy bag, now unable to resist decorating her. I have a new pair of nipple clamps with red beads on the chains that will provide the finishing touch on my completed canvas. Her erect nipples don't need much attention before I clamp them, they are already begging for my touch, her body tenses, and a small gasp escapes her lips as I pull and tweak them, and then at the sharp bite, she briefly tenses then relaxes again with a sigh. I grin, seeing her rush of arousal, my nostrils inhaling her personal scent; it's heady stuff.

Now she's properly adorned I hoist her up higher into the air, and the action causes her to spin slightly. She's an incredible sight; her legs are stretched wide, allowing me a full view of the moisture dripping from her pussy snaking like a snail trail down her thighs, glistening in the lighting as she rotates. I can't suppress a smirk, knowing that the knot I placed above her clit will be rubbing against her gently as she swings, not enough to cause her to orgasm, but keeping her level of arousal high. The dazed expression and beatific smile on her face show me I've achieved my objective. She's now deep in rope space.

A gasp of approval from behind reminds me I have an audience, in all honesty, I'd forgotten they were there, and that they're enjoying the same sight as me. As I'm viewing my subject and handiwork with pride, a voice sounds at my elbow.

"Another faultless display, Master K. It's inspiring to watch a master rigger at work."

"Thank you." I turn and acknowledge Ralph, noting that he's left his bartending role and is now wearing a red dungeon monitor's vest. I can't leave Diamond tied up for too long, and if I did, Ralph would soon be on my back reminding me to cut her down as the woman herself is in no state to be able to safeword out. The close attention paid to all subs is one of the reasons Club Tiacapan is such a safe and popular place to play.

I almost wish I had a camera with me to record my work for prosperity, the artwork I've created tonight is one of my masterpieces, though it owes much to the curvaceous beauty who's allowed me to shape her. But cameras and phones are strictly forbidden in the club for a very good reason. Not everyone appreciates the kink we engage in.

After one last lingering look on my beautiful sub for the night, I bring her down, taking her off the suspension hook and gently lowering her to the floor. Using the knife, I quickly cut her out of her bindings, rubbing her legs and arms gently to get the blood flowing again. As she comes back to herself, she has tears coming from her eyes—clearly experiencing the highly emotional feeling reported by subs as the ropes are removed—protesting the sudden lack of restraint, so I replace the sense of the bindings by holding her tightly in my arms. Master Ralph appears with a bottle of water in hand, and I encourage her to take a good, long drink. I hold her for a long time until she's moving, trying to straighten of her own volition.

"Master K!" She turns her dazzling blue eyes onto mine, "That was, that…"

I laugh softly, knowing she's unable to describe the experience and sensations she's just been through. For myself, the intense concentration the task involved and the feeling of inebriation as though I was drunk on her submission had certainly lessened the degree of tension that had its hold on me when I entered the club tonight. She doesn't have to thank me; I should be the one thanking her.

CHAPTER 11
Zoe

Although a million miles away from the expensive designer clothing I used to wear, I'm dressed smartly enough in a black trouser suit with a white blouse underneath and turned out better than I have been for months. I'm also wearing my dark-haired curly wig, thick dark foundation that hopefully hides the natural fairness of my skin tone, bright red lipstick and heavy eye makeup that unfortunately makes me look only just the right side of a whore. But I've achieved an image unlikely to be associated with that the old photograph of me displayed on the numerous posters I've spotted plastered all over the place. Some faded and weathered tattered and torn bearing witness to Ethan's long search for me. But many are fresh, showing he's still looking, and warning me—I can't afford to relax.

My journey to London, though stressful, is without incident, and I arrive safely at the Amahadian embassy without hassle at eleven forty-five for my twelve o'clock interview with Mr Kassis. Reporting to the reception desk, I can't interpret the rather odd look I get from the receptionist when I identify myself, ask for the man in question and say why I'm there. But when he looks it up on the screen in front of him, he finds my name easily enough and confirms my appointment. Still throwing a strange glance at me, he nevertheless points the way I need to take. That necessitates, apparently, a rather thorough security check, requiring me to remove my jacket and shoes, and having to submit to being patted down, luckily by a female guard. But of course, I've never been to an embassy before, so assume they take security very seriously in this type of place.

While they subject me to the measures designed to give them a feeling of safety, it has the opposite effect on me, and I start thinking about the lies I've told about my identity and the fact I've nothing with me to prove who I am. Would it be viewed as a crime that I'm asking for a job under false pretences?

As I'm escorted up in a lift to the second floor, I worry I might fold and admit my deception if I'm questioned too hard, or will inadvertently give something away. On the other hand, if by some miracle I *can* pull this off and land the job I may have no need ever to worry about Ethan again. This contract is only for six months, but who knows? I might be able to get further work out there, or, with the money I could save from the generous salary, go somewhere different in the world. With those more positive thoughts in my head, I pull my shoulders back and do my best to look the confident professional I used to be. There's too much riding on this for me to fail.

The lift stops with an abrupt jolt, and after the seemingly necessary brief pause the doors slide open, and I step out into a waiting area where I'm politely invited to take a seat; presumably the downstairs reception has reported my arrival. At twelve noon precisely, the person with the plaque on the front of his desk announcing his name as Richard, and showing his job title as 'Personal Assistant,' gets to his feet and tells me, "His Excellency will see you now."

Excellency? What's going on? Hang on; there's been a mistake. I get to my feet but make no immediate a move to follow the man. Realising I'm not following, he turns back to gesture me forwards.

"Er, sorry, I think there might be a mistake," I start, rummaging in my bag as I scramble to get the copy of the email out, "I'm here to meet a Mr Kadar Kassis."

The look of disbelief he throws me is comical, and as I'm expecting him to apologise and take me to a different office, his next words floor me when he replies in a rather bored voice, "Yes, His Excellency, Sheikh Kadar Rushdi Sadiq al Kassis, Emir of Amahad is the man you're meeting with today, madam." He shakes his head as if I'm stupid.

A sheikh? A real life *fucking sheikh*? And the title emir? Isn't that like the king or something? What the freaking heck is going on? *Is this a trap?* I freeze, unable to move while mentally running through my options at the speed of light, rapidly recalling the research I'd done on Amahad. It's an absolute monarchy; the emir has total power over everyone in his country. That includes everyone in his employ. *The man at the top of the food chain is just the type of person Ethan would consort with.* Have I been conned? And if so, what the bloody hell do I do now?

I've been tricked! I came here expecting to meet with a

lowly frigging envoy. I must have been set up! While realising, I can't have been as careful as I'd hoped, all the blood drains out of my face. The confidence I'd regained under Ida's care seeps away as I rapidly try to think how to escape.

As I'm standing there, mouth hanging open, looking like an idiot, I notice the door to the main office is open, and I see a man standing there, a man, tall and intimidating, wearing an aura of command around him like a cloak. *I can't do this! Is Ethan in that room behind him even now?*

"I thought you said my twelve o'clock was here, Richard?" The voice is deep, authoritative, with only a touch of an accent. He also sounds slightly bored. As he looks around the anteroom, his eyes meet mine, and I see something flare in them for a second. But then just as quickly it's gone as if it was never there as he stands back and gestures for me to precede him into the room.

I've no alternative but to do as he directs. I'm not stupid; there are embassy officials and guards enough that I wouldn't be able to run even if I tried. They wouldn't believe any excuse I could offer. If indeed I'm delivering myself into Ethan's clutches, he'll have already convinced them to believe a story that suits his purposes. Taking a deep breath, I smooth down my suit jacket to give my trembling hands something to do, and enter the powerful man's office, hesitating just a second to scan the large space, feeling some relief when, apart from the emir, the room is otherwise empty. *Perhaps Ethan's running late?*

"Please, take a seat." The door closes behind us, and the Monarch of Amahad indicates where I should sit. Like a victim waiting for the executioner's axe to fall I do as instructed, and take a moment to survey the man who's moved behind the desk and seated himself in the chair opposite. His height and build remind me of Horse, who'd promised to protect Sophie, but he's even more intimidating; a strong, virile man with confidence and power oozing from him. His smart business suit is definitely not something bought off the peg or via next day delivery. A handkerchief, perfectly matching his tie, peeps out of his top pocket and as he sits he undoes his jacket button revealing a tailored waistcoat underneath. Were it not for his assistant's introduction and his olive skin, his smart mode of dress, his dark hair cut short around his head and a short beard on his chin he would look like any typical businessman.

His generous lips are pressed together giving him a stern appearance as he, in turn, examines me with dark, brooding eyes, making me lower my gaze, feeling overawed and afraid as if I've just stepped foot into the lion's den. Like Ethan, he's wealthy, dominant, and probably uncaring as to whom he steps on to get his way. *Not every man's like Ethan,* the common sense part of my brain tries to calm me. I lick my dry lips and swallow hard, not wanting to be the first to speak, but feeling increasingly unsettled as the silence stretches on and his scrutiny continues. Just as I feel I need to blurt out something, anything, he clears his throat.

"Thank you for coming here today, Miss Ranger. My sister-in-law, Sheikha Cara has asked me to meet with you on her behalf."

I raise my eyes in astonishment. *He's talking about the interview!* Could my fears be for nothing? Could this be exactly what it's supposed to be? Then I shake my head in confusion. The woman I spoke to, Cara, Cara's a Sheikha? But she sounded so normal, so down to earth? So, well... English! I swallow rapidly, feeling even more out of my depth.

I try to speak, but nothing comes out but a squeak. Everything about this meeting unnerves me. Even if this isn't a way to hold me until Ethan arrives—and part of me still believes that's an entirely possible outcome—there's no way on earth I'm going to be taking a job as a humble employee of people of this calibre. No, this job is not for me. I've been around people with such prestige and power for long enough to know I'd be too far out of my depth. Memories of the strained dinner parties I'd attended with Ethan, where those present only tolerated me because of my relationship with him, come to mind. These are the kind of people who chew someone like me up and have no remorse spitting out what's left. And right now, there's not much remaining of me, to begin with. Their conversations would revolve around money, making more of it, and expressing outright disdain for those who didn't haven't enough; laughing with cruel amusement at the struggles of the have-nots in their vain attempts to better themselves, and throwing condescending looks at me. I can't work for these types of people; I'd never survive it again.

I realise I've been I've been preoccupied with my thoughts when a cough brings me back to the present. I blush in embarrassment.

"We're to conduct an interview here today, Miss Ranger. I suggest you give it your full attention." The emir sounds like I'm wasting his time, which I am, having decided there's no way I'll be accepting a job offer from a person like him. In any event, I've blown my chances by sitting here, made up like a clown, and struck dumb.

I struggle to find my voice when I do it comes out as a gasp. "I'm sorry, this is a mistake." I'll make my escape now, get back to Ida's, and hopefully, in time, come up with some other plan.

I've surprised him. He leans forwards, elbows on the desk, his chin coming to rest on the back of his hands which he holds clasped in front of him. His pose seems almost threatening, his gaze direct and focused. Something has caught his attention; there's hunger in his eyes, he looks like an owl hovering over a petrified field mouse that waits frozen, anticipating sharp talons to descend. I'm right; I couldn't possibly work for a family such as this. Sheikha Cara is his sister-in-law, not just a humble palace employee. And in my experience, wealthy women can be just as, if not more, spiteful than men. Puzzled, though, I recall she hadn't seemed like that during our telephone conversation, which had flowed so naturally as if we were already friends. Had it just been an act? People from a powerful family like this would only see pound signs and have the innate need to dominate, to control and abuse little people such as myself. My suspicions rise again. What would people of this ilk want with someone like me? *He must be acting for Ethan.*

I decide not to wait to find out, and stand up, my body

visibly shaking. "No, I have to go. I'm sorry." I make an about turn to face the door.

"Stay." The gentleness of the deep velvety voice almost belies it is a command. Almost. My body obeys and I still.

"I'd prefer to speak to your face." A suggestion, but it has me rotating. He nods in approval, and with an officious wave of his hand indicates the seat again. I'm not sure why I'm following his instructions, almost against my will I do as he's ordered. He's still leaning forwards, but the fierce expression has smoothed out into one of curiosity, and he no longer appears quite so threatening. I try to control my breathing, but my hands continue to shake as I clasp them in my lap, my right hand gently massaging my crooked wrist hidden under my jacket sleeve. I know my nerves are shot to pieces, and make an effort to pull myself together, starting to reconsider whether it's unreasonable to accuse this man even mentally as being from the same mould as Ethan, who abused more than my body, who destroyed my confidence and my ability to trust.

The emir gives me a brief moment, and then, with another nod, starts to speak again, "I know you have spoken to my sister-in-law, Miss Ranger, though possibly it was not a long conversation and you perhaps did not pick up on the force of her personality. You see, she is someone I would hate to disappoint," he laughs, disparagingly. "Even I, as emir, would be concerned if I had to return to my country without completing the task she allotted me. I need, therefore, to beg you to stay and for us at least to conduct this interview in a civilised manner."

My eyes widen, Cara, a woman, has such power over

this incredibly self-assured man sitting in front of me? I see by the twinkle that comes into his eye that to some extent he's joking. His assessment of his sister-in-law's character has caused his face to soften; the predator momentarily suppressed. But I doubt it will be satisfied for long. That's how men like this work, they pull you into until they have you tight in their clutches, and then the mask is removed, and their true face is revealed. The face of a monster.

"You could tell her the interview took place, and I wasn't suitable?" I offer the lame excuse, hoping he will accept it.

"Ah, but that would not be truthful, would it? And I always tell the truth." He doesn't sound like he's teasing now.

I stare at him, trying to read from his face if it is true he never lies. Don't powerful men get where they are by at least bending the facts to suit their purpose even if they don't come straight out with downright falsehoods? In my experience they do. So I don't believe him. I can't lower my guard. I've learned that lesson at least.

He leans back in his chair, picks up a pen and taps it against his teeth. "So, Miss Ranger. Shall we proceed?" He pulls some paper towards him, "Tell me about yourself, and why you wish to work in Amahad?"

Is he actually going to go ahead and conduct an interview? For a moment, I have a mental block. Sure, I've come to this meeting expecting I'm going to asked questions, but at this point, my thoughts are all over the place. An interview for a dream job is a faraway location? Now I truly feel like a fraud I am. It was one thing talking to another woman on the phone, a woman who at the time I'd thought was another employee like myself, but quite another to speak to a real life influential sheikh. Particularly since I'm here under false pretences, and as soon as he knows I can't prove a thing he'll see right through me.

He stares at me, waiting. Realising I look like the village idiot, the business-like manner he's adopting helps summons up my professional pride. Suddenly I find myself clearing my throat and starting, "I've got a joint first class honours degree in landscape gardening and architecture. When I saw the job advertised, I knew I had the right skills necessary for the role, and when I discussed my background and experience with, er, Sheikha Cara, she indicated that I sounded just the person she was looking for to renovate the harem." I break off, unsure what to say next and uncertain what I'm trying to do. *Do I want this job or not?* My wrist throbs, reminding me that if real, this chance of employment in Amahad is my escape out of Ethan's clutches. *But what would I be escaping into?* Frying pan, fat and fire come to mind.

He steeples his hands, his strong chin resting on his fingertips, "*My* harem, Miss Ranger."

It's his tone of voice, a mesmerising drawl as he stakes his claim, making clear his ownership of the evocative sounding place, that draw my eyes sharply to his face like metal filings to a magnet, and there's an unsettling churning in my stomach which has nothing at all to do with nerves. Unbidden, the vision of a bevvy of women waiting for his attention comes into my mind, and out of nowhere, the sudden thought of what it might be like to be one of those women makes my stomach muscles clench. A woman with nothing to do but to wait for the summons to go to the bed of this powerful, commanding man. I look at him as if seeing him for the first time. Now I'm able to see that his tailored suit is giving him a false air of civilisation and that underneath lies a desert warrior, a proud, untamed man. A man who could use his strength to harm a woman, or to protect her with his last breath. And there's an aura surrounding him, a sense of pride suggesting he's someone who wouldn't just use a woman for his satisfaction, but would see to her needs first. *Careful, Zoe, you're projecting just what you want to see. Ethan fooled you, remember?* My brain might be giving me sound advice, but my body betrays me as unwanted fantasies rip through me, causing my nipples to harden.

Tugging my jacket tighter around me, I force myself to remember the man across the desk from me is exactly the type I should stay away from. He's a man who exudes dominance through every pore, everything I should avoid. How did just four words resonate within me, and trigger such a physical reaction? It must surely be nerves that cause me to blush as I dare to glance up at him.

He hasn't missed my reaction to his words in the slightest. One side of his mouth is turning up in a small, crooked smile, and his eyebrow has lifted as though in question.

As I'm beginning to dread the direction the conversation might take next, an interruption comes by way of a knock sounding on the door. I start, blood draining from my face as I *know* it signifies Ethan's entrance, or perhaps he'd send Hargreaves to collect me. I knew I'd been tricked. I've no fight or protest left as I sit, twisting my hands in my lap ready to accept my fate. I don't even look up as the door opens, but see through my periphery vision that the emir's assistant is entering alone, carrying a tray.

I'm hardly able to comprehend the normality of the situation as Kadar gestures for Richard to place the tray on a side table, and then he rises. "Can I offer you refreshment, Miss Ranger? Coffee?"

A violent shiver runs through me. I might have a reprieve from being delivered into the hands of my nemesis, but there's something about Kadar that suddenly seems equally dangerous. His voice arouses feelings that should stay forever dead, and I shrink back into my chair, scared and overwhelmed.

If this interview is real, what exactly is the position I'm being interviewed for?

CHAPTER 12
Kadar

I must still be running on the after effects from last night's intense experience; I don't think I've come down from a Dom's headspace yet. *My harem?* What the fuck made me lay claim to that part of the palace which has lain in disuse since my great-grandfather's time? As Richard causes us to break off this particular discussion, I cringe inwardly, particularly when I can't fail to notice the reaction of my visitor. Her nervousness is palpable, the blush that's risen to her cheeks so obvious. Does she think I'm interviewing her for a role as a concubine? And for fuck's sake, why is that thought making blood rush south, my cock coming alive like that of a teenager who's not yet learned to control himself? As I feel myself hardening, I turn my body away from her, embarrassed by my unexpected reaction.

She's nothing particularly special or out of the ordinary, pretty enough I suppose, her dark hair seeming at odds with her pale complexion as if the colour isn't natural. It looks like there's a nice enough figure under those dreary looking clothes, though currently, she's holding tight to her jacket as though it's armour to protect her, and I can't tell much about the body underneath. Her eyes are large, but her nose is slightly crooked, I suspect it might have been broken at some point, but that just serves now to give her character. Her makeup is overdone; bright red lipstick demands me to focus on her mouth, forcing inappropriate thoughts of those lips into my brain. *What would they feel like around my cock? What the fuck is making me think about that?* And what is this sudden and intense desire to see her naked of both her clothes and the heavy cosmetics that seem to spoil her face? It has to be the lingering effects of last night; this is no way to conduct an interview. I tell my unruly cock to stand down. It's reluctant to obey.

Pushing irreverent thoughts aside I wait for her nod in answer to my question, and then prepare her coffee, offering her cream and sugar before passing it to her; the simple tasks giving me the much needed time to bring myself under control. A suit was a mistake today; my traditional robes would have better hidden my reaction. Once I'm sure I'm adequately concealing my body's betrayal, I move back and sit down again. I sip my drink, and retake the reins of the interview, resolving to keep it on track this time. Her nervousness is not lost on me, and I know I have to try to put her at her ease, embarrassed I seem to have scared her. But in some ways, that helps. I need her relaxed and off guard for the next part of the conversation.

"I'm well aware of your discussions with the Sheikha, and she has told me how happy she is with your approach to the project. You should know that the harem has been in disuse for over half a century. And you should also know that I have no plans whatsoever for that part of the palace ever to be used for its original purpose again." Perhaps I put unnecessary stress on the last sentence, as well as pause, to let that sink in. I want no misunderstandings between us. I'm only too well aware of the fascination that just the word Sheikh can conjure, let alone when it's linked to a harem, and the last thing I want her to think that anything other than a landscaping job is on offer. "Our meeting today is to verify your experience and qualifications for this venture." So far, Miss Ranger and the interest Cara has in her remain a mystery to me. Why had my sister-in-law become so enamoured with her in such a short time? Was it simply a lack of other candidates and an overwhelming desire to see the restoration work started? Or was it something about this woman herself?

Miss Ranger hadn't been aware I'd witnessed her interaction with Richard when she'd arrived for her appointment. I'd been standing at my already open door, taking my first impression of the candidate. She looked like any other applicant until my assistant had divulged my title. Another woman might have been impressed she was to be interviewed at the highest level, but she'd seemed terrified by the idea. I immediately grasped she'd been expecting a palace lackey, someone who'd be easier to fool. Oh yes, I'm already aware that Miss Ranger has secrets. I just didn't expect to be so intrigued to find out what they are.

She'd stood, looking so frightened, for a moment there I thought she was going to about heel and run. In my head, I'd already decided I'd chase after her if she did. *What was that all about?* Of course, I would hate to disappoint Cara, but in reality, my sister-in-law holds no sway over me. Why should I care if her candidate turned tail and fled? I could have used the time to catch up on work from some of my other meetings. Fuck, I've got enough to do going through my notes from the Electoral Commission and catching up on the rest of the work I neglected last night.

But something about this scared woman calls to me. It's obvious there's a mystery here; I knew that before she arrived. But what is it about my position that frightens her so much? What is she hiding? And, lurking at the back of it in my mind is the question why would a young woman like her want to come halfway across the world to the volatile country of Amahad? These are questions I need answers to, more relevant, to some extent than whether or not she can do the job.

She's looking down into her coffee cup as if trying to find her answers buried at the bottom. Watching, I can almost see wheels turning in her head, different thoughts manifesting themselves as they flit across her expressive face. Then her shoulders slump as if she has given up. A reciprocal drop in my composure mimics hers, and I'm at a loss as to why I don't like to see this woman so defeated.

It's at this point in an interview when I would expect an applicant to start getting out their documentation and appropriate certificates to back up the spoken words. But I'm not surprised when she doesn't. Richard is diligent with his research. It's time to show my cards.

"Miss Ranger, I have to ask, who are you? Any applicant for work in the Palace of Amahad has to be subjected to vigorous background checks; you must have realised that. And I regret the searches we have done don't reveal anyone of the name you're using with the qualifications you claim, nor who attended the university you state you did. Either you are lying about your experience, or you are not who you say you are."

She seems to shrink into the chair as if I've dealt her a physical blow, but it's the look of complete desolation on her face that undoes me. If she were any other prospective employee, I'd be showing the door by now, but she's very different to anyone I've interviewed before. Telling myself it's not because she caused such a blatant reaction from my cock which is still half hard, I wait to see what she's going to do and am not surprised when once again she gets to her feet.

"I'm sorry I've wasted your time," she mumbles, turning to leave.

"Wait." My firm instruction has her pausing. "Sit down. Answer my question." Warriors have flinched at the tone I'm using so I've no doubt she'll obey.

She complies, and when seated, places her head in her hands. As moments tick by in silence, I start to think she's not going to speak at all. Her fingers rub her forehead as if to ease an ache there, and for the first time I see she has a disability, she moves her left wrist awkwardly. As if it's a familiar gesture as she moves her hands back down to her lap and unconsciously rubs it as she raises her eyes to meet mine.

Then, she says, quietly, "I'm sorry, you're right. I'm using a false name. But I'll be in danger if I give you my real one. Look, I'll just go now, and we can forget all about the job. You won't employ me, so there's no point continuing this."

I regard her carefully, she's wearing no mask; I can read people well enough to know that her lack of protest at my accusation of falseness shows her inherent honesty. But the question remains, why did she use a name without building a background behind it? She's no con-woman; Richard could find no history, constructed or otherwise. She's a mystery I want to solve. Even though, of course, I can no longer consider offering her a job.

"You've entered the Amahadian Embassy under a fake identity." I point out to her, my voice letting her know this was no innocuous crime. That in itself is a serious offence. Then I soften my tone, "Why, Miss Ranger, or whoever you are? I'd like you to tell me why. Your honest answer, please. You must understand that in today's world I cannot let such a transgression pass. You must either tell me, or I will summon my guards, and you can explain to them. The UK police will also need to be informed."

Her eyes widen, her mouth drops open, and an expression of almost sheer terror comes over her face. "No!" she shrinks back into her seat, "Please no! Not the police!"

She's guilty of something; I just don't know what. If she's committed a crime, the correct authorities will need to be involved. But just at this moment, I don't intend to do that. There's a story here, and I'm intrigued to learn what it is. I encourage her to confide in me, "Talk to me, tell me why you are here. Then I'll decide whether or not this needs to go any further, or whether I will let you leave. But you need to give me something. And I want to hear the truth."

Her head drops lower then she lifts it again, now staring straight into my eyes, making it impossible for me to doubt her when she says, "Because my life's in danger." She drops her attention to her twisting hands once more.

Sitting back sharply, my forehead furrows as my eyebrows rise. The words seem incredible, but there's so much sincerity in her voice I have no doubt she believes them. Who the fuck would want to hurt someone like her? "Miss, er…" I skip the introduction as I have no idea what to call her. "I am Sheikh Kadar, Emir of Amahad. You are at the Amahadian Embassy, and thus on Amahadian soil, and hence, if there's a valid reason for it, under my protection. I would like to know your real name, and why you believe you're under such a threat."

In response, she shakes her head, so when I continue, my tone is cold and formal, "You have come to my embassy using a fake identity. You must understand that in the current circumstances of political unrest, I need to ensure you are not a terrorist trying to gain illicit entry to Amahad, to the very Palace of Amahad in fact, our seat of government. Perhaps for some nefarious purpose which could cause my country harm. To gain information maybe, or to plant a bomb?" Inwardly I believe the chances that this innocent and ill-prepared woman is a suicide bomber to be less than none, but I use the extreme example in the hope she'll confide in me.

I see the moment the implications hit her. Again her eyes come up to meet my unyielding stare, and this time, she's shocked. Her voice is just a whisper as she rejects the accusation, "I'm not a threat to you. I'm not a terrorist."

I'm sure she isn't, but I lean forwards quickly, making her flinch back, "Tell me who you are, and give me a reason for not turning you over to security."

Another silence. Her head turns away as if looking anywhere but at me. I'm just about to prompt her for an answer when I hear her say, so softly that I almost miss the point when she decides to trust me, "Zoe Baker," she sounds defeated as she repeats, "My real name's Zoe Baker. But I can't prove it. I have no documents to show you."

Though I don't believe she's on some reprehensible mission, I don't want to give asylum to a criminal. I probe further, "So we would be able to find Zoe Baker graduated with a first class honours degree if we looked?" Has she even got the qualifications she says she has?

Although she's looking down at her feet, there's positivity in her voice that assures me she's speaking the truth. "Yes."

"What about your birth certificate? Driving licence? Passport? Can you produce at least produce them?"

Now her head shake shows she's going to answer in the negative. "I'm unable to get hold of them."

The question is, of course, why not? "If you've lost them you should be able to get copies." I provide the obvious answer.

Again that shake of her head, this time, more violently, and she raises her eyes to mine momentarily. "No, that's not possible." She sounds utterly crushed.

Tilting my head to the side, I try to understand. Why can't she get copies? It raises one obvious problem that she must already be aware of. Shrugging I point it out to her, "Without a passport, Miss Baker; it's hard to see how you could come to Amahad at all. Even if you hadn't lied about who you are."

This time when she meets my gaze the look in her eyes is almost challenging, "I know, I've explained that to Sheikha Cara, but she said it's been done before. She said if you told me that would be a problem I was to remind you of her."

Despite the seriousness of our conversation a laugh barks from me. *Oh, Cara, you can make me smile from three and a half thousand miles away.* Yes, indeed there's been a precedent set when my brother Jasim and I kidnapped Cara and brought her to Amahad to force her into an arranged marriage with our younger brother Nijad. But it was a gamble misusing my diplomatic immunity in that way. I'd done it once and had thought never to do it again. Is it a risk worth taking for this unknown woman? I can't understand why the thought even crosses my mind.

"Apply for new documents. Have you looked into it properly?" I suggest again. It's the most straightforward route. Maybe Richard could help her if she doesn't have the nounce to do it herself? With a passport, she could travel to Amahad without a problem. *Fuck! Why am I even thinking about that?* I can't risk letting a woman we know nothing about, and who's already lied to me have the run of the palace. What am I doing even contemplating it?

While I've been lost in my thoughts I realise she's said something I don't catch, her face is turned back down facing the floor, her voice muffled. One hand seems to be gripping her other wrist, rubbing it as if relieving pain.

"Pardon?" I ask her to repeat her comment.

Again her face lifts, and now I can't miss the sight of tears glimmering in her eyes, making me believe there's a background to her story that I cannot begin to guess.

"I can't," she whispers. And then she anticipates my next question, answering before I ask it, "I can't let him find me." Now she shows some animation, "I'm sorry. Please, this has all been a terrible mistake. Please let me just go."

"Sit!" I wait to make sure she's not going anywhere. "Define 'he,'" I instruct sharply, using my most dominant voice.

Her eyes close as though in pain, a tear escapes and she brushes it impatiently away, she sighs loudly and seems to come to a decision. "My ex-boyfriend. If he finds me, he'll kill me. He abused me. Mentally and physically." As if to offer proof she raises her left hand and gingerly pulls back the sleeve. I recognise the twisted and gnarled healing of an untreated injury; a simmering rage begins inside me as I suspect there are other less visible wounds she carries. As she covers her wrist again, she continues, "I escaped from him, but I had to leave everything behind. All the documents proving who I am. He'll never stop trying to find me, and he'll succeed if I come out of hiding and apply for replacements. That's why I wanted this job. It would take me far out of his reach."

The damage to her wrist suggests she isn't exaggerating that he'd hurt her, but would he actually kill her? Who could this man be if she believes he'd know if she applies for replacement documentation? Is there any real basis for her concern? Perhaps if I weren't the emir of a country where part of the population seeks to depose me, if I weren't daily aware of threats against my person I would dismiss her fears. But the expression in her eyes mirrors that which I see so often reflected in mine; and that tortured, but silent appeal for asylum makes me realise that, at least to her, her fears are real. I wonder just who is threatening her, and what is his power that he could have so much assumed reach? As I find myself accepting what she believes is the truth I feel a chill running down my spine; the same feeling that has kept me alive in battle before, the sixth sense of something very wrong. With an audible indrawn breath, I ask the obvious question. "Just who is this man?"

She squeezes her eyes shut even tighter as though the very words cause her pain, "Ethan St John-Davies."

Cupping my hand around my chin, I wonder; I've heard the name before, my brother Nijad had a run in with him, oh, it must be four years ago now? I don't know much about him, just that he on that occasion he proved himself to be violent. A rather nasty man, if I recall correctly. And that's enough to convince me to press the button on the intercom, summoning Richard. He enters immediately.

"Miss Ranger, I'm sorry, Miss Baker I suppose I should call you now. Will you please go and wait outside with Richard for a few moments? I need to make a phone call." I expect her to comply immediately, but she hesitates, and I'm shocked by the desolate expression on her face as if all hope has gone.

"You're ringing Ethan?" Her eyes grow wide in shock and horror, "Please…"

My hand slashes through the air. "Do you think I'm a man who'd send someone back to their abuser? I'm trying to help you, woman!" I get to my feet, and she takes a step back, apparently frightened by my outburst. Immediately I feel remorse, realising she's wary of any man exuding this type of anger, whatever the provocation. I make an effort to calm myself, holding my hands out, palms facing her, trying to convey my rage is not directed at her, "Please. Just give me a few moments and we'll talk again. Trust me."

She stares at me as if trying to read my thoughts, and it hits me how hard it will be for her to trust anyone if she's on the run. I put everything I can into my expression to appear honourable and watch her give a defeated shrug as it slowly dawns on her that I hold all the power here, and whatever my plan is, she has no choice in the matter. Accepting she's leaving her fate in my hands she walks out of my office, shoulders down, her spirit crushed. Her defeated posture makes me angry; no woman should ever be made to feel like that.

I stare at the closed door for longer than I should. No longer having to control myself, I to give rein to my rage, my hands clenching into fists. What kind of a man is violent to a woman? The sight of her wrist! What other scars does she carry? My nails dig into my flesh, stopping only just short of drawing blood as the thought of what she must have been through making me want to murder this bastard with my bare hands. How could anyone mistreat *her*? How long was she with him? Her words suggest he held her captive. I'd thought her timid, unsure, but now I realise she's broken, damaged. Who is the real Zoe Baker? Surely not this beaten and crushed woman I've seen today? The woman who unwittingly calls to the Dom inside me, exciting me to rise to the challenge of putting her back together? It hits me that I can't let her walk away without taking care of her problem. I vow to do whatever is necessary to keep her out of his reach. And if that means taking her to Amahad, that's what I will do. Damaged goods, no, damaged is too mild a word for it; the woman I see today is shattered into pieces.

Once the decision is made, I hesitate no longer before taking action, reaching for the phone and dialling a pre-set number.

I'm lucky; Ben's available and answers immediately. "Carter."

"Kadar." My introduction is equally short.

"Sheikh? Or should that be emir now?" It's not particularly new; I'd been the ruler for more than three months now. I hear the grin in Ben's voice, though; our friendship is too old to be tied up in formality. He'd come to my rescue when I foolishly ditched my bodyguard one day, many years ago, when I'd been following my cock rather than my head. An ex-SAS man in the process of setting up his own security company, Ben had foiled a kidnap attempt and managed to keep the incident out of the ears of the palace saving me a whole heap of embarrassment. I owed him for that and had given him a hand starting his business, Grade A Security, in return.

"It's good to hear from you. I heard you gave quite a

demonstration in the club last night. Impressed a few people. Are you coming for another visit? Always an experience to see a good rigger in action."

"Flying visit, Ben, so not this time, unfortunately. Just here for a few meetings then I'm going back. Last night was my one break away from work."

"Not a social call, then?"

"No, I'm after some intel." I consult the pad where I'd written down the name. "I want to know all you can find out about a man called Ethan St John-Davies."

I can hear his sucked in breath whistling through his teeth. "Sinjun. Ethan *Sinjun* Davies" He corrects my pronunciation. "Nasty piece of work. What do you want to know? Do you need an in-depth report or just the headlines?"

"You know of him? Give me what you can, now."

"Okay," there's a pause, I presume Ben's pulling his thoughts together. When he starts speaking again, it's interesting how much he knows of the man straight away. "Right, he's landed gentry, parents are dead, so he inherited the lot. Even after death duties, he's one of the richest men in the UK. He's also the CEO of ElecComs; it's a huge company specialising in electronics and communications, including military and surveillance equipment. You can't go far in this country without coming across his software. Or, for that matter, him knowing about it. Nearly all the CCTV and such like in Britain, and some countries abroad, use his systems. There's a lot of suspicions he abuses his power, and rumours he has certain influential individuals under his thumb."

"Such as?"

"He works very closely, too closely some say, with the police. And some politicians, and has some senior government officials in his pocket. Word is he's got info on them that he uses to keep them in line. As I said, through his company there's not much he can't find out if he wants to. And his hackers would probably give Cara a run for her money." My sister-in-law's hacking ability has put her in deep water before, but I know she's quite exceptional, and if he's got better…

"Shit." No wonder Zoe was so paranoid, he'd be able to find her.

"He's not a man you want to cross. Too fucking powerful; too many friends in very high places. Chatter says he has his own army of mercenaries and people who antagonise him do so at their risk. Are you going up against him, Kadar? Because I'd think twice about it if I were you."

I'm thinking hard. "Ok, Ben, here's the story. I've got his ex-girlfriend in my office, well, she's with Richard outside at the moment. He was abusive, she left him, and now she's so terrified for her life that she wants to take a job in Amahad."

"Fuck, Kadar! You've got *Zoe Baker* there? Jesus fucking H Christ!"

"You know of her?"

"Everyone does! Well, just about everyone does who's not deaf and blind, and even they probably do as well by now. Everyone's on the lookout for her; there's an enormous fucking reward for information on finding her. How the fuck she's kept under the radar for this long is unbelievable. She must be one very smart cookie."

"She's terrified, Ben." I have my answer; she wasn't exaggerating.

"And she's right to be. If he finds her, I have little doubt he'll kill her. He'll get away with it too." Ben's voice goes hard, "Insider info says he's done it before."

"Shit and bugger it." I'm repeating myself, my expensive Eton and Oxford education flying out of the window as I find myself lost for more adequate words. Zoe Baker is in real danger. "She doesn't seem to have involved the police? Is it worth her reporting him?"

"Not sure who'd be brave or stupid enough to take him on. He'd wriggle out of anything, and she'd just be putting herself at risk if she came out into the open."

If I had any doubt before it's gone now; she's coming back to Amahad.

"He came to Club Tiacapan once, Kadar. You should ask your brother about that. Ignored safewords and Nijad had to pull him off a woman before the Dungeon Monitors could get there. He was barred after." I don't bother telling him I remembered the incident that had got both Nijad and St John-Davies banned. Nijad's had been lifted, though. Ben continues, "Understand he made a bit of trouble for Jasim afterwards, but with the kind of clientele the club attracts he didn't get far."

I'm not surprised, the carefully preserved privacy of the club meant that Jasim's contacts are probably as widespread and of the same calibre as St John-Davies'. I think quickly. "Have you got anyone available to put on Zoe until I leave on Saturday? I need to get a passport sorted for her. She left his house leaving all her papers behind."

"You want help with the passport?"

"I'll get an Amahadian one for her."

"Okay. Well, Sean Cooper's available? You know him from the club I think, and he's one of my best. I know you'd probably prefer Jon, but he's not doing close protection work anymore. I'll make sure he takes the lead from the office side, though."

"Sean would be great." Jon Tharpe used to be Nijad's CPO until *the incident*, and after that would often provide his bodyguarding duties for myself or Jasim. Until he met Mia, of course. Ben's right, I would have liked to have Jon working with me again, but someone else would do. To be honest, all of the Grade A close protection officers are well trained and efficient.

We conclude the conversation with Ben sending best wishes to Cara and Nijad, hoping the birth of their baby goes well.

Putting down the phone, I'm relieved Ben's got someone available. I know Sean, he's a good guy, albeit with a rather unique deviant sexual slant, even in the world of kink. I've met him at Club Tiacapan and seen him in action. It's as if the guy can't make up his mind what he wants to be. He's a switch, can top or bottom, and is bisexual to boot. Even I, as a man, can admit he's extremely good looking with charisma which makes him attractive to either sex, he can dominate the ladies, or be submit to the men. Or vice versa. He's also a skilled fighter, excelling in hand-to-hand combat using his martial arts. A sharpshooter and sniper.

Yes, Sean's a good guy to provide protection to Zoe. Except… I feel a strange burning sensation inside me as the thought slams into me like a twenty-ton truck; I'd rather he didn't come within a hundred miles of Zoe. A blind man would be able to see she's submissive. Shame Ben didn't suggest Harry; he's happily married and in his forties. Perhaps I should ring him back and insist he assigns someone else.

I just about manage to pull myself together before I reach to pick up the phone to request a replacement officer to provide close protection. Last night's Dom space must still be affecting me, otherwise how on earth could I be feeling possessive of a woman I don't even know?

CHAPTER 13
Zoe

Who is this man? I know he's Kadar Kassis, the Emir of Amahad, but who is he underneath all those trappings of state? And why am I so confused about him?

As I sit in the outer office, worried who he could be calling, my fears that he's in league with Ethan may have dissipated, but I'm still scared that even an innocent enquiry about my name could trigger alarm bells and somehow lead to giving away my whereabouts. That huge reward—*half a million fucking pounds!*—for information would be tempting to many people. And I know nothing about Kadar, only what he's shared with me.

As I wait and wonder, my mind goes back to that day when I first met Ethan, and how he took me in so completely. A shiver runs down my spine. Is history repeating itself? There's a magnetism about the emir which lures me in. And when he mentioned the harem… heaven forgive me, but I felt such a sudden strong desire. And when he offered me his protection I could have melted into a puddle at his feet. *Shit! Am I forever doomed to find wealth and power a turn on? Is that all it takes to ensnare me?*

Sitting, hunched up in the comfortable visitor's seat, my arms around my knees I wonder why on earth I'm worrying about my reaction to Kadar. He's hardly likely to have even noticed me, except as a problem he'd like to solve. He's an emir, for goodness sake, so far out of my reach, it's laughable. It's not going to be a repeat of Ethan; I'm not that naïve to believe I've so much appeal that I could catch the attention of any wealthy, powerful man. I've got real problems to deal with rather than worrying about something that will never happen. No, what I should be more concerned about is now he knows my secret, what's he going to do with the information?

Once again seated behind his assistant's plaque, Richard looks at me curiously as the tension and worry clearly show on my face. I can't seem to stop wringing my hands together in my lap; I only just managing to hold in my scream of frustration. And now there's him to worry about, too, Richard, another one who knows my real name as Kadar had let it drop. Is he trustworthy? Is his loyalty to the emir worth more than the reward for revealing where I am?

My eyes keep flicking to that closed office door, concerned I haven't a clue what's going on behind it. Is Kadar contacting the authorities? If he calls the police I'm done for, they won't believe my word over Ethan's. They might not give me straight back to him, but he'll find out where I am, and somehow I'd soon find myself in his clutches again. I'll never be safe in this country, not with such a large bounty on my head. But I'm stuck here; without a passport, there's no way I can leave. Putting my head in my hands, I feel like a mouse in a humane trap. I'm not dead yet, but I'm at the mercy of others to set me free.

It seems like I've been waiting forever, but the clock tells me it's only twenty minutes when Richard leaves the reception area, quickly returning with a selection of sandwiches and places them in front of me. I don't think I'm hungry, but my stomach growls at the sight of food and without giving it too much thought I start to eat.

I'm halfway through the plateful when the outer door opens once more and in walks one of the most good-looking men I've ever seen in my life. He's tall, not broad or muscular, but his face has an elegant and symmetrical bone structure with high cheekbones, drawn in cheeks and an angular jaw covered with designer stubble. I can see his long dark eyelashes from where I'm sitting; they're the type any woman would die for. His blue eyes twinkle as he crosses the room, and his blond hair, a shade darker than my own natural colour, reaches to his collar in a shaggy but expensively styled fashion. His face could easily grace the cover of a woman's magazine, and I'm curious why he's here. He's not dressed for a meeting with a monarch; he's wearing tight dark blue jeans, a light blue shirt and a casual blazer left unbuttoned. I have to acknowledge he's utterly gorgeous as he gives me a wink and a friendly smile, and as I nod back at him, I find I'm comparing him to the ruggedly handsome sheikh. My assessment awards preference to the other man. I give myself a mental slap.

Richard uses the intercom to alert the sheikh of the newcomer's arrival, and to my surprise, he then ushers both the stranger and me into the inner sanctum. The emir gets to his feet and shakes the stranger's hand warmly, clasping it as though greeting an old friend.

"Sean Cooper. Thank you for coming over so quickly. Please, take a seat. And you, too, Miss Baker." His manner seems to have changed. Now there is no doubting he is a ruler, in charge of a whole country, his tone is commanding. He waits until we've complied with his instruction. "Sean, you've been briefed?"

Not wasting time, Sean answers with just a quick nod. The emir turns to me, his dark eyes piercing, "Miss Baker, I've been putting some plans in place, and I hope you will approve. You will be coming to Amahad with me when I return on Saturday, and you will take up employment, as previously discussed with my sister-in-law, managing the project to renovate the harem. We'll be flying by private jet, and you'll be will travelling on Amahadian papers. I trust that is acceptable?" He asks the question, but it comes out as more of a statement.

I close my eyes briefly, trying to assimilate he's just told me. In just two sentences, Kadar has thrown me a lifetime. I take a moment, allowing myself to enjoy the immense relief that I'll be out of the country in just a couple days. After the stress and strain of the last few months, it seems unbelievable that I'll be away from Ethan's clutches *and* doing a dream job I've been trained for. When I open them again, I can see he's still waiting for me to speak. "Thank you, Your Excellency. You don't know how much this means to me," my voice is breathy; I can feel tears pricking in my eyes. Happy tears this time. Maybe there is an escape for me.

"You have made a bad enemy," the emir tells me. All at once his face grows fierce. "I have no time for men who hurt women, Miss Baker. Unfortunately, this is not my country, and I can make no retribution for you. But rest assured you will be safe in Amahad. I give you my word."

The ferocity of his statement and tone in which it's delivered surprises, but also comforts me, and makes me reconsider my belief that all men who wield power are the same. Something in his voice, the way he holds himself as he gives me his promise, makes me believe it's not an empty one and that his word is something I can rely on. I meet his eyes, and nod my thanks, hoping I'm conveying my gratefulness sufficiently without words which, for the moment, seem to escape me.

The emir is now all business. He accepts my thanks with a sharp nod, but no particular warmth in his eyes. With relief, I acknowledge if there's any attraction it's all on my side, and I need to bury it now. He's saving my life, and I couldn't ask more of him that that. Quickly I pull my attention back when I realise he's still speaking.

"This is Sean Cooper, he's a Close Protection Officer, and he will be providing protection for you until you are safely on the private jet."

That makes me look up. *He's a bodyguard? Never!* "You're arranging protection for me? But Ethan…" I was going to explain Ethan was more than a match for one man, particularly this one sitting next to me who seemed more suited to use his assets to sell aftershave.

The man in question smiles and leans towards me as he sees my confusion, "You'll be safe with me, Zoe. I'll make sure you arrive at the airport without any problems." He oozes confidence, and when I open my mouth to try and get him to understand who he's dealing with, he pre-empts me, holding up his palm to face me. "I'm well aware of St John-Davies," he tells me, "And I know what he's capable off. Don't worry; I'll keep you out of harm's way. That bastard won't get near you." He even reaches over and pats my hand in reassurance.

For some reason the Sheikh frowns at the gesture, his eyes alighting on the back of my hand before his gaze moves up again, "I'll make sure you have all the flight details, Sean."

I look from the incredibly beautiful apparent bodyguard who evokes no reaction from me to the stern-faced Sheikh, and the thought of going with him to his homeland gives me butterflies in my stomach, and once again my nipples harden, betraying my attraction. *What the hell is wrong with my libido today?*

The emir is looking at me strangely, and I feel my cheeks reddening as I hope to God he can't read the thoughts going through my head. After a moment's steady appraisal, he turns back to Sean. "I have another meeting; I'll leave you and Miss Baker to acquaint yourselves." He stares at him for a moment, his face becoming fierce, almost threatening, "I'm leaving her in your capable hands, Sean. I trust you will treat her appropriately." *Was it my imagination there was an emphasis on the last word?*

And with that, we appear to be dismissed. I leave the room with my new bodyguard, the person who tells me he'll be my shadow until I reach the safety of Amahad, reassuring me yet again of my safety under his protection. In the reception area, he pauses to scrutinise me, examining me so intently that I shuffle my feet and look down.

"That's a wig." It's a statement, not a question, but I confirm it anyway.

"I know he can access the CCTV, he'll be using the software that analyses faces too," I tell him, my fears suddenly taking over from my more jaded thoughts. "I have a hat and pull it down. It's worked so far."

Sean nods, "We'll take a cab back to my office, and then I'll take you to a safe house for a couple of days. I'll be staying there with you."

I hadn't got as far as thinking what I'd do in the unlikely event I was offered the job. Now I realise I can't just disappear without seeing the person who, for the last two months, had become so vitally important to me, like a second mother. I can't leave Ida without saying goodbye. And I also belatedly realise I've nothing with me for an extended trip. So I say, a little desperately, "I've got to go back to Ludlow, I need to pack my things and see my friend who's been keeping me safe."

With his head on one side, he considers my request, "I can't promise that, pet. Let me think on it for a while and see if it's possible to sort that out." Asking Richard to organise a cab to come directly to the embassy, he makes a couple of calls while we're waiting. I try to eavesdrop, but can't hear everything, though it sounds like he's arranging for somewhere we can stay. When the taxi arrives he gently rests his arm on my lower back to guide me, and I jump, my heart beating furiously. And when we sit side by side in the cab I move as far away as possible, unconsciously rubbing my wrist.

My bodyguard throws me a look of sympathy, "He really worked you over, didn't he?" He stares for a moment, concern in his eyes, "You've nothing to fear from me; my job is to keep you safe. And I'm excellent at my job."

"I'm sorry, Mr Cooper."

"Don't apologise, pet, and for God's sake call me Sean." His twinkling eyes are still on me; I look away and out of the window as if interested in the cars, lorries, and buses surrounding us. "I've sorted things out. We're going up north and can stop off at Ludlow. We're not staying there, but as long as we can do so without risking your safety, you'll be able to see your friend for half an hour or so."

It's more than I'd been hoping for, so I throw him a grateful smile. He refrains from touching me again during the short journey, pointedly keeping his distance as we collect his car—a nondescript SUV belonging to his company apparently—and begin the drive out of town. I breathe a sigh of relief once the metropolis is left far behind and we're driving along the M40 heading north. There are roadworks, and delays which seem to have no reason, as we swap onto the M42 and then take the M5. Sean doesn't talk much. He drives competently and takes the holdups in his stride. He's always alert, and I can see he's constantly checking to make sure no one's following us. At one point he turns off the motorway into a service station and then straight out the other side, remaining vigilant the whole time. When he does speak his voice is firm and confident, and I begin to relax, recognising his proficiency in his assigned role, and starting to believe he'll be able to keep me out of Ethan's clutches.

It's nearly six o'clock before we pull into onto the driveway in front of Ida's house. Getting out of the car I stretch, all my muscles feeling knotted from the long drive as well as the tension of the day. I glance around; the closed sign is on the shop door as it should be—the nursery closes at five. The greenhouses behind are quiet with only the soft sounds of the automatic irrigation system murmuring through the air. I beckon Sean to follow me as I walk around the side of the house which has been my home over the past couple of months.

Approaching the front door, I get my key out ready and open my mouth to call out a greeting to Ida, but Sean reaches around and takes the key from my hand, and indicates I should remain quiet. Entering the house first, he signals that I should stay outside. But I'm not used to this cloak and dagger stuff, and eager to tell Ida my good news. I'm only a step behind him as he softly walks across the hallway and into the small sitting room.

"Who the fuck are you?" a male growls from the inside.

I immediately realise that I've made a mistake as I move into the room alongside Sean, but curiosity overruled me. My bodyguard throws out his arm and tries to push me behind him, but it's too late, I've already seen Ida sitting frozen, her face white as chalk and the man standing over her with a gun in his hand.

The gunman's seen me too; I can't get out of sight now. A slow grin spreads across his face, "Zoe Baker. The ticket to my fucking fortune." He waves me in with his gun. Sean holds me back, but the unknown man menacingly points the barrel at the head of my friend, his threat palpable.

Sean releases his hold on me, and I step forwards. "Fucking bitch!" He slashes the gun across Ida's face, "I knew you were lying when you said she'd gone."

My hand goes to my mouth in horror, and I move to go to the old woman who's rubbing her sore face, her hand coming away red with blood. But the gun now pointing straight at me brings me to a halt.

The gunman turns his attention to the person behind me. "I believe I asked you a fucking question. Who the fuck are you?"

The voice I hear surprises me. Gone is the confident man I travelled up with. Instead, Sean stammers out in an effeminate squeak, "Boyfriend." He sounds terrified. Some bodyguard he is. So close and yet so bloody far. Another two days and I'd have been far away from here. *Why, oh why was I so stupid to think coming back was a good idea?*

"Well, I'm taking your girlfriend with me. You gonna try to be a hero?"

"You're the one with the gun." There's a quiver in Sean's voice. Jesus! Could the person employed to protect me sound any more ineffective? I'm desperately hoping my bodyguard is putting on an act, and he's going to pull something out of the hat to save me, but at the moment he seems so weak and useless my shoulders slump in defeat.

"However much he's paying you, I'll double it." Though she's hurt, Ida's voice is clear and vigorous, such a contrast to Sean's.

Targeting his weapon around each of us, in turn, the gunman answers her. "Have you got a spare million lying around then?" He gives her a disdainful look. When she gives a sad little shake of her head, he trains the weapon back on me, "Didn't think so." He takes a step towards me. "Come bitch, time to go."

As he goes to takes another pace, Sean moves to my side as if giving us room to get out of the door. Just as I'm thinking how despicable he is not to make any effort to save me he moves in a blur of action, his body twisting and his leg coming up seemingly unnaturally high as his foot swings out kicking the gun from the man's hand. I've seen on TV where a karate expert can smash planks of wood with their feet, and the way the gunman is holding his wrist it appears to have shattered the same way. I don't feel any sympathy. Sean follows up his move by linking his hands together and bringing them down on the back of his head. The gunman crumples to the floor unconscious. Without pause, Sean reaches into his back pocket, extracts a pair of handcuffs and secures the man.

Seeing my look of surprise Sean chuckles and winks, "You never know when they'll come in handy, pet." His voice has changed completely and is deep, dark and authoritative now.

"You're a useful man to have around. Must admit you had me fooled for a moment there." Ida's contemplating Sean thoughtfully and getting to her feet, her hand still resting against her cheek. I run to her and hug her, and then stand back to see the damage. Gently Sean moves me out of the way and raises his hand to her chin.

"You're going to have a bruise there." Another voice change, this one soft and full of compassion, "He broke the skin, but it's only superficial. You won't need stitches."

"I'm alright," Ida moves his hand away and gives a little shake. I knew she was a tough old bird, but she's excelling herself today, "It's Claire, *Zoe*, I'm worried about."

They seem to have some silent communication over my head. Sean's nodding at Ida as he speaks to me, "Pack your stuff, little one. We're leaving as soon as you are ready."

"But Ida? Him?" I wave to Ida, and then down at the unconscious body on the floor.

"I'll take care of him," Sean gives me a gentle push in the direction of the stairs. Reluctantly I start to move. As I leave the room, I catch sight of him pulling out his phone and being inquisitive I pause with my foot on the first step, listening to his side of the phone call.

"I've got a package needing collection. It needs to go into cold storage for a couple of days."

That's it. Apart from giving the address, Sean says no more, apparently expecting the person on the other end to understand what he means. I run up the rest of the stairs and go into my room. I gasp when I see the mess, the man had obviously already been up here, I assume looking for clues as to where I'd gone. But there had been nothing to find, my communications with Amahad had thankfully been by email on Ida's work computer. Quickly stuffing my cheap clothing into the rucksack I'd arrived with, I collect my toiletries from the small bathroom. With one last backwards glance at the room that had felt such so safe before Ida returned from the post office with that flyer. I hurry back downstairs.

I find the bastard now conscious but trussed up with his ankles tied and gaffer tape across his mouth. His eyes flick to and fro furiously, hatred zooming out like laser beams. He doesn't look so threatening now. He looks more like a slug as he rolls around frantically trying to find some way to get free. But he's not going anywhere. Sean reaches into his pocket and pulls out a pair of surgical gloves; my eyes widen, and I wonder what else he keeps on him. He looks at me as my eyebrows rise.

"I was a boy scout—always prepared." As he speaks, he picks up the gun and checks the bullets in it. "Know how to use this, Ida?"

My mouth drops open as my friend confirms she does with just three words. "Ex-Army Officer."

"Takes one to know one," Sean smirks knowingly. "Here, take these. We only want his fingerprints on the weapon."

A look that frightens me transforms the face of the woman I thought I knew well, and her words send a chill down my spine. "Haven't used one of these in years. Might get in some target practice. Wonder if I'll still be able to hit his kneecap?"

The gunman stills, his eyes now full of fear.

"Get her out of here." Ida's eyes don't move from the man on the floor.

"We can't leave you with him," I say, horrified at the thought.

"Yes, you can," her voice is firm, "You don't know who else has found out you've been staying here."

Sean pats her on the back, "My colleagues aren't far away, Ida won't be on her own for long."

"I'll be okay. Just go." She allows herself a quick glance

at me and gives me a reassuring smile, "I'll be all right, Zoe. Just get yourself somewhere safe."

I realise she doesn't know. "I'm going to—"

"Stop!" She spits out the words, "I don't want to know."

Sean walks over to the prostrate man. "You hear that? Zoe's disappearing again and this woman has no idea where she's going. Prick." He punctuates his words with a sharp kick to the ribs. Having witnessed the strength of his legs that had to have hurt. But as I recall how the gunman had pistol whipped Ida I find myself wishing he'd do it again.

Without getting in her line of fire, I go to the woman who sheltered me and give her a fierce hug, her free arm comes around me, squeezing me to her. "Thank you… for everything." The words are inadequate; Ida had saved my life. She's done so much for me, "I can't…"

She stops me from saying anything more. "Just keep safe, and keep that fire burning inside you. Promise me."

"I'll try." I hug her, holding her tightly to me, this kind friendly woman who had taken me in when she didn't know me from Adam and who had ended up getting herself hurt as a result. It's hard to pull myself away, but she shoos me towards the door, with her action, telling me to get going.

Outside Sean sees the worry on my face, and takes a moment to reassure me she'll be okay and won't have to wait long alone with my would-be kidnapper. As we get to the car, he even makes me giggle when he says, "Hey, you know I think they'll have to prise that gun out of the old girl's hand. She seems rather taken with it and is having far too much fun!" I agree, it's a side of Ida I hadn't seen before.

But as we begin to drive off, my amusement fades as the events of the day catch up with me, and I start to shiver. I turn up the heating on my side of the car but it doesn't help all that much, I can't seem to stop feeling cold. *I'm not cut out for all this stress. I had a normal life until I met him. Now I've been face to face with a loaded weapon and another friend got hurt because of me.* Tears start to fall, and there's nothing I can do to stop them.

Sean speaks only to let me know there are tissues in the glove box and lets me cry out the amalgamated tensions of the last few hours without offering false comfort or minimising the seriousness of the situation. When he gets a brief call, he tells me the package was successfully collected, and Ida is safe. The relief makes me a little calmer. It also helps when he tells me his firm, Grade A, will be keeping an eye on the elderly lady in case Ethan has any thoughts of retribution as she'd taken me in. At least that's one thing off my mind.

I'd expected a long drive back to London and, lost in my thoughts, I hadn't taken much notice of my surroundings or the direction we were travelling in, so when we arrive at a house on a residential street after just a couple of hours of driving, I have to ask where we are. Apparently, this is the outskirts of Manchester; we weren't making the longer journey back to the capital after all. He pulls the car into the garage and takes me inside the house, putting in a complicated code on a state of the art looking gadget to open the door. It's late, and I'm tired, completely done in for the day. I watch as he carries in our two bags, even forgetting to offer to help. He must keep a go-bag packed ready in his car. *Definitely a boy scout.* When he drops my rucksack in a small upstairs room, I decide to go straight to bed, noticing nothing other than the bed looks clean and there's a comfortable duvet I can snuggle beneath. Despite all the thoughts churning around my head, including the fact I've had a man hold a gun on me today, everything seems too much for my tired brain to cope with and I fall, almost immediately, into an exhausted sleep.

CHAPTER 14
Zoe

Waking early the next morning feeling more refreshed, and still unbelieving I've been offered the chance of a dream job as well as the opportunity to get my life back on track, I go downstairs to find Sean already up and making tea and breakfast in the small neat kitchen, somewhat dressed. Somewhat. He's only wearing a pair of jeans, and even they aren't properly done up. Succumbing to the fact I'm only human, I don't fail to clock he's got a body to die for, tanned and hairless without an inch of fat on him. His six pack is clearly defined as is, rather unfortunately, the V of his lower abdominal muscles angling down towards the open zip. A slight glimpse of curly hair tells me unless he's wearing tiny bikini briefs, which don't seem his style, he's gone commando. It's all a bit too much for me this time of the morning.

My eyes shoot up then look away in embarrassment, and I feel blood rushing to my cheeks. His smirk tells me he knows I've been checking him out. As he turns and bends to take milk out of the fridge, I glance back to see the denim of his jeans stretching over his tight backside. I can't help but lick my lips; I can appreciate a fine specimen of manhood as well as the next woman.

"Can't you put some clothes on?" my voice comes out as a squeak.

"Thought you were enjoying the view," he teases holding up the milk bottle and at my nod pours some into each cup. He pushes a mug over to me, and waves at the sugar bowl.

I shake my head at the sweetener. "What's not to like?" I answer his question. "Just a bit early for me." I think of Sophie as I return his banter; she'd probably already have got his jeans off or at least round his ankles by now. I feel a bit lightheaded; I've not been in this sort of situation before. Ethan would never appear so underdressed—the only time he was naked was in bed, and he always disrobed in a business-like manner. Mind you; he didn't have Sean's body which seems made for flaunting. I don't know this man, yet his attitude beams a ray of sunshine into my life. I manage a small smile while asking a silent question. *Is he flirting with me?*

He grins, crossing to his bag that he's left at the foot of the stairs and taking out a T-shirt pulls it on. It's black, sporting a Lynyrd Skynyrd logo with a skull, crossbones and wings suggesting he's a rock fan. It looks a size too small for him and if anything, enhances his well-defined muscles. With another smirk he lowers his hand to his crotch and slowly and deliberately takes hold of the zipper, making a real show of it as he pulls it the rest of the way to the top. Then he fastens the button. "Better?" he winks, knowing my eyes are transfixed to his actions. He comes and stands in front of me.

My reaction to him is just an appreciation for a perfect

masculine form. His blatant sexual attraction is surprisingly non-threatening.

Putting his hand under my chin, he tips my face up, "You can admire, but not touch. I'm your bodyguard, and I'm off limits to you."

I almost spit my tea over the counter, "You…"

Laughing, he backs away. It's funny, but I feel I can trust him.

To get us back on track, I ask him, "Have you heard any more about Ida?"

"Yup, the package was collected shortly after we left." He reconfirms what I already knew, then adds, "Our first-aider checked her out, she didn't need medical attention. She's a tough old girl, isn't she? We're giving her protection, but I don't think they'll go looking for you there again."

"I didn't know she was ex-army, but it figures now. Makes sense." I watch him as he returns to the stove placing bacon under a now heated grill, "You're a chameleon." I take a sip of my drink as I move to a different subject.

"What do you mean?" He breaks eggs over a bowl and whisks them.

I gesture towards him, "I can't work out who you are. You keep changing."

He glances over and grins, "Not surprised, pet. I haven't discovered who I am myself either. If you figure it out, please let me know." After throwing me another cheeky wink he goes back to his task gathering plates and cutlery and then dishing up omelettes and bacon. He puts toast in a rack with butter in the tub beside them. I take a bite; he's a surprisingly good cook. Not having eaten much the day before my plate's soon clean.

I help him wash up. We're just going to be hanging out here today, he tells me, and then leaving early tomorrow to catch the flight. I don't mind, after yesterday's excitement I could do with a day to relax. But soon after breakfast, he gets a text. Reading it his mouth tightens.

I'm immediately on alert, "Problems?"

He shakes his head, "No, but you're going to have to put up with me a bit longer. Apparently, I'm coming with you to Amahad. Kadar seems to think you warrant a CPO out there too, or at least until you get settled. Looks like he's starting to realise the reach this St John-Davies chap has."

Unable to suppress the shudder as he speaks that name, I idly flex my wrist as two of the things he says stand out. One that he's familiar enough with the emir to call him by his first name, and secondly that it appears I'll still be at risk three thousand miles away. "Has something happened?" There goes my relaxed feeling for the day. I'm not going to be free of this tension which holds me in its grip. His next words don't help either.

"Not really, but the reward for information about you has just gone up to a million pounds."

"Christ!" I stand up so quickly the chair I'm sitting on falls over. "What is it about me? Why does Ethan think I'm worth so frigging much and want me back so badly?"

Sean shakes his head, looking at me carefully. I've not put my wig on today, so my natural blond hair flows down over my shoulders. He's quiet for a while, and just when I think he's not going to say anything he begins to speak, "You're quite beautiful pet. Not classically, but you have a natural beauty, a typical English rose. That's one reason." As I shake my head in denial and disbelief, he runs his fingers through his hair, "But mainly he considers you his possession, and you got away from him. He's a man who enjoys the chase. You're proving more of a challenge than he thought, and he's not the kind of person who'll just give up. By evading him, you're defying him. The trouble is, the longer you stay out of his reach, the greater the consequences will be."

I know that, and give a small shudder, "He'll kill me."

Now he's nodding, "Yes, I think that would be his end game." His confirmation isn't encouraging; it would have been nice for him to have contradicted me even if it would only have been a blatant lie. I'd like some reassurance, however unrealistic it might be.

"He's insane." He has to be totally mad. What kind of man would go to the lengths he has to get his ex-girlfriend back? I mean, a bloody million pounds? I know he's got money to throw around, but surely I'm not worth that!

"He's not mad for wanting you; any man would. You are attractive, as I said, and you've got a spirit a man like him would like to break."

I run my fingers over my nose, slightly crooked now with a small scar at the top. "Not any longer. He's already broken me. He's broken my nose, wrist, ribs… And he's broken me mentally too. I can't even remember the woman I was before I met him."

Sean comes over and stands close; he's so tall I have to

look up to see his expression. His hand hovers in the air for a second as though waiting for my permission then, gently, he touches my face, "I didn't know you before, but you have an asymmetry which gives your face character and doesn't detract from your attractiveness in any way. No need to worry about that, pet." He pulls his hand away, and I feel strangely bereft. He takes a step back. "And you're not broken. Fuck, woman, the way you've evaded him for so long, that would be challenging even for a trained expert. And you didn't even fucking panic when a gun was pointed at you yesterday. I'm bloody amazed at the way you held it together."

Briefly, I feel a sense of pride at his praise, but then throwing him a quick grin I can't resist it. "Well, I was *fucking* working out what to do when my brave bodyguard wimped out on me."

"Good ploy that works every time." His cockiness makes me laugh. I can't deny it had proved successful.

Wanting to get off the depressing topic of Ethan, I ask him a question I've been curious about, "How do you know the emir?"

"Kadar? I know his brother, Jasim, better. He co-owns a club with one of my bosses." If he's surprised at the complete change in direction, he doesn't show it.

"Oh?" He's intrigued me, "What kind of club?"

He tilts his head to one side for a moment as if considering whether or not to answer. When he makes up his mind he approaches me with a broad cheeky smile, his finger coming up to tap me on the nose, "A very exclusive private members club. A BDSM club."

I gasp, "BDSM?" I'm pretty sure what he means, but I'm hoping I've got it wrong.

At my quizzical look, he steps in with a clarification, "Bondage, Dominance or Discipline, depends on how you want to interpret it. Submission, Sadism, Masochism. Basically, whatever your kink."

Oh! Shit! And Kadar's brother's into this? Does this mean Kadar is too? And Sean? Feeling a wave of dizziness, I back away from him only stopping when the kitchen counter gets in the way of my retreat. The amusement fades from his face.

"What's the matter, pet?"

Swallowing rapidly, I open my mouth a couple of times, before letting him into one of my darkest secrets, "Ethan," my voice is almost non-existent, I cough to clear my throat and try again, "Ethan had a playroom. He had every kind of whip, flogger or cane that you could imagine. He had handcuffs and equipment he would fasten me too. For the past year, I've been tied up and beaten. Sean. I couldn't escape him; he would torture me for hours. There was nothing remotely enjoyable about it. So you can see why I wouldn't trust a man who'd go to a club like that. Or how I could understand why any woman would want to go. If you go to a club like that, it makes you no better than him!" I start to tremble, tears in my eyes. My saviours are no better than the enemy I'm running from.

He moves close, invading my personal space, I press myself into the counter as far as I can. "You can't compare what that fucking bastard of a man did to you with what goes on in the club. Listen," as I try to turn my head away, his hand comes up to hold it in place, "Listen to me." His voice lowers and becomes commanding. Almost against my will I look up into his eyes. "Safe, Sane, and Consensual. That's the overriding principle we practice. What Ethan did to you was not consensual. You had no choice in the matter, and it obviously was not safe or sane. Yes, he might have had the equipment, but he obviously hadn't a clue what to do with it. He was a sadist, pure and simple, and someone who wouldn't be tolerated in a halfway decent club." He gently tugs on my chin, moving my face upwards so he can look into my eyes. "Club Tiacapan, Jasim's club, banned him a few years ago."

I straighten in surprise; I hadn't known that.

"Presumably, that's why he 'played' at home. No club would tolerate his kind of 'play'. Do you understand me? The club's full of consenting adults, nothing happens that anyone doesn't want to happen, there's no corollary with what happened to you. Do you know what a safeword is, darling?"

I give a quick shake of my head. I'm still shivering, trying to understand what he's saying, desperate to give him the benefit of the doubt and to process what he's telling me.

"A safeword stops all play," his free hand strokes my hair. Although I feel suffocated by his closeness, the caress calms me. "You would say your safeword to stop anything happening. Of course, your Dominant wouldn't want to take things that far; he'd be a piss poor Dom if he didn't already know where your limits were."

"Was Ethan a Dom?"

"Fuck no, Ethan's a bloody cretin. He's barely got his man card."

I draw back my shoulders, "Well this BDSM stuff might be all well and good for someone else, but I'm certainly never going to submit willingly to any man."

His grin is almost a leer, "You just keep telling yourself that, darling. You," he taps me on the forehead, "You, are submissive to the core."

"Don't be fucking stupid! I didn't ask Ethan to hurt me. I didn't give Ethan control he took it! He stole it from me!" My anger comes blazing to the fore.

"Listen to what I'm saying! Ethan is a fucking prat, an arsehole. He robbed you. You didn't give your control over to him; he took it! That's not what Dominance and submission are about. In a proper relationship, a submissive has all the control—they can stop the scene at any time they like. The Dom only has the power that his sub lets him have."

I push him away with my hands, and he immediately frees me. Despite the direction the conversation has gone in, for some strange reason, I don't feel threatened by him. I turn round more concerned at the word he used. *Submissive? Fuck no.* Let a man hurt or control me again? *Never.* I shudder at just the thought of a man even touching me sexually again. My thoughts return to the handsome sheikh. Is he really a Dom and into the kind of things Sean's spoken about? The emir's authoritative way of speaking, his imposing voice, the way he issues commands, do they add up to something that would terrify me? Or are they just because of his position?

"Sean," I begin, hesitantly. "Is Sheikh Kadar a Dom? Does he play at that club?"

His face is impassive, giving nothing away, "That, pet, is something I cannot tell you."

I'm not going to get any more out of him; I can see that by his serious expression. But is it because he doesn't know, or is he just not going to say?

CHAPTER 15
Kadar

Rubbing my hands across my face as I unsuccessfully try to focus my attention on the paperwork in front of me, I realise sorting out my country's problems isn't consuming my interest at this moment in time. Sitting in the Kassis private jet, I've got other things on my mind, such as waiting for my special guest. No, not a guest, my new employee, I'd do well to remember that distinction. Inwardly I curse at the distraction just the thought of her is causing, and that I'm allowing my concern for her safety to override my ability to work.

For the tenth time in probably as many minutes, I glance out of the window. Although I have Richard waiting for Sean and Zoe with diplomatic papers as well as the woman's new Amahadian passport, getting through security at the airport still carries a risk of exposure. In the intervening days since that rather bizarre meeting with Zoe at the embassy, I've found out more than I wanted to know about St John-Davies. It's true he's a force to be reckoned with, and seaports and airports are bound to be littered with extra surveillance to help him find her.

So now, as I watch a white saloon drawing up, I inhale sharply as I wait to see who steps out and then let the air out in a rush. *She's here!* A wave of relief floods through me, inexplicable in its intensity, and I lean back in my seat for a second, at last able to breathe normally again. *Thank Allah, I got protection on her.* If she hadn't had Sean with her when she went back to that house in Ludlow on Thursday, she wouldn't be here today, might not even be breathing any longer. The thought that I'd have lost her before having a chance to properly get to know her makes me go cold. But she's here, and she's safe. Just a few more minutes and we'll be in the air and out of that fucking monster's reach. Once on the royal family's jet, she'll be under the protection of the Emir of Amahad.

Rising to my feet, I go to greet her at the door, noticing she's climbing the steps to the plane as though in a trance and hasn't seen me yet. At the top, she steps inside, acknowledges the polite greeting from the flight attendant; then her eyes widen as she notices the luxury of the interior. I hadn't factored in that the pretentiousness of the Kassis jet, kitted out in my father's time would have been such a surprise to her being so accustomed to such ostentation myself. She takes it all in, and it's then she spots me and her cheeks blush bright pink, making her look a typical English rose, her otherwise pale skin an attractive contrast. I hold out my hand and when she reaches me, clasp hers.

"Welcome, Miss Baker." I hold her hand a little too long before I remember myself and let it go.

"Zoe, please Your Excellency. And thank you." She seems shocked to see me, and her voice falters on her greeting. Instead of coming closer to me she steps back as though seeking the protection of her bodyguard, Sean, who's ascended the stairs behind her, and he puts his hands on her arms to steady her. Taken aback by this demonstration of familiarity I throw him a sharp look and see him shake his head and throw me a quick grin in response. But still the question comes to my mind, *has he claimed her*? Or is she just taken aback to find me wearing the traditional robes of my country and the golden agal of my office securing my headdress?

Putting thoughts of their possible relationship aside, I stand back allowing her to precede me into the plane and, with just a light touch on her shoulder, direct her to the seat opposite mine. As I sit down, I study her briefly. She's wearing that godawful trouser suit again—the one she wore to the embassy—but today her shirt is pink, almost reflecting the colour of her cheeks. Hands twisting in her lap, teeth nibbling at her bottom lip she looks incredibly nervous.

"You're safe now, Miss Baker, Zoe. No one's going to hurt you." All that I am makes me want to reassure her.

Her eyes flit quickly to mine. "I can't tell you how grateful I am, Emir Kadar. I can't quite believe I'm leaving it all behind," a pause, then she adds, "That I'm leaving *him* behind." The words are the right ones, but there's hesitancy in her voice that suggests I've still some way to go to get her to relax.

"We'll be taking off in a couple of minutes. And call me Kadar, please, I'm sorry but using my title still makes me look around for my father."

Either what I've said or my tone of voice seems to break the tension between us. Her eyes soften with compassion,

"Did you lose him recently?"

I nod. "Just over three months ago."

"I'm sorry." Her brow furrows, as the thought occurs to her, "So you've only recently become the emir?"

I nod to confirm that indeed I have, and accept her sympathy graciously. "Fasten your seat belt. We're taxiing to the runway."

"Oh!" I see she hadn't noticed the plane moving as she glances out of the window with a start.

In no time at all it's our turn for take-off. As we leave the ground and the runway disappears beneath us, she seems absorbed in watching England fade into the distance behind, oblivious to my presence. I can't begin to guess how she's feeling leaving her old life behind, heading towards a new one that currently, she knows nothing about at all. Cognisant she's much to think about and to come to terms with, I leave her to muse and pick up my paperwork once more.

It's an unfortunate irony that the first matter vying for my attention concerns arrangements for the darn ball I agreed to. My advisors have compiled a list of likely women acceptable to the country and are asking for my approval. *Fuck it!* I put the document at the bottom of the pile, unwilling to give it a minute's consideration given the presence of my companion.

Soon we're airborne and shortly after, reach cruising altitude. The seat belt lights go off, and the flight attendant comes down and offers us a meal. I frown, remembering how on the way out she'd blatantly offered me more services than are written in her job description, but I had turned her down, unsure whether she viewed the opportunity as a perk of her job or a duty. Whatever, I'm pleased to see she's all politeness when she notices I have a female companion with me for the return trip. I also observe she's also done up all the buttons on her tunic today.

We order food from the vast range of delicacies offered, and a short while later eat our meal exchanging small talk. Zoe indulges in a couple of glasses of wine with her food and gradually starts to look more relaxed in my company. At first, I have to coax her out of her shell, but soon she responds, looking me straight in the face and asking questions. I find it's surprisingly easy to chat with her, and use the time to satisfy some of her curiosity about the country that will soon be her new home. I avoid touching on the reason for her being here today, not wanting to add a sombre note to our conversation.

As she finishes her food, I have a desire to see to her comfort. "There's a bedroom at the rear of the plane. And some new clothing laid out for you." I indicate her current clothing, "Your suit will be far too warm for Amahad."

I can't fail to see that as soon as I mention the word bedroom, she stiffens, and I feel a burst of anger. Does she think I'll take advantage of her? "I'll get Lisa to take you down." I gesture to the flight attendant. "And there's a lock on the door," I add the last through gritted teeth.

She flushes red again, this time with embarrassment as she realises she's given herself away. "I'm sorry, I didn't mean…" She's flustered, waving her hand in apology and dismissal of the unspoken accusation.

I sigh deeply and shake my head, "You've been through a lot, Zoe. Go, have a rest, a shower, change. You'll feel better prepared to face your new life after freshening up."

She bows her head, "Thank you, your…Kadar. I'll take advantage of your offer." She gets up so fast I suspect she's grateful of the opportunity to escape from my presence. But my name on her lips makes me smile.

As she follows the flight attendant down to the rear of the plane, I motion Sean to join me. "She's like a cat on a hot tin roof!" I exclaim as he sits down.

He's obviously as angry about it as I am. "She's been used and abused. She was conned into what she thought was the perfect relationship and then it all went sour. That bastard isolated from her friends and family, and now she's frightened to contact them in case she puts them at risk. She doesn't trust anyone, Kadar. You, me or any member of our sex."

I feel my gut clench in anger. Someone as lovely as Zoe should be treated with hearts and flowers, not violence. I realise what Sean's telling me and know what I have to do, "I'll contact Cara before we land and make sure she's waiting to greet her. I suspect she'll feel more comfortable in female company for now."

"I think you're right. Bastard did a fucking number on her."

"She's safe now. She's under my protection."

Sean narrows his eyes, "Make sure she knows there are no strings attached." At my sharp look, he adds, "She's a beautiful woman, Kadar, and I've seen the way you look at her."

"I thought you were interested yourself," I retort.

He laughs, but there's no mirth there, "I've nothing I can offer her, I don't do relationships, and my kind of play wouldn't be hers."

Frowning, I tell him, "That goes for me, too. So we'll both be leaving her alone."

There's nothing more to say on the subject. I bury myself in my work again; Sean seems to get lost in a best seller. Shortly before we land, I send Lisa back to wake and prepare Zoe for our arrival. Despite my assurances to the bodyguard, my gut clenches when I get my first glimpse of Zoe in the traditional clothing of my native land. In a soft peach, long sleeve silk tunic and matching trousers, she seems to move more gracefully than I've observed before. When I see Sean close his book and rapidly blink as he brings his eyes into focus, I realise it's not just me she's affecting. But what makes me take a good long look is her hair. She's no longer wearing a wig, and now she looks more like the photographs my investigators had managed to dig up. Her natural hair is a light blond colour, straight and fine, and falling just past her shoulders, complimenting her pale skin and rosy cheeks. It's shine matching the shimmer in her steel blue eyes. With her face washed clean of the heavy makeup, she looks almost beautiful, only the slight crookedness of her nose marring her complexion. I'm glad I'm wearing a robe and she can't see the effect she has on me. In a western style suit, Sean's not so lucky; I can see him adjusting himself, hiding his reaction under the table. I throw him a warning look and then turn to greet her with a smile.

"Thank you," she indicates the clothing. "You'll have to let me know how much I owe you for it."

"No need. Consider it an advance in your wages." Forcing my voice to sound unaffected I explain, "You can wear western clothes if you prefer." I don't want her to feel pressurised, or that she has to dress to please me.

She smiles shyly, "I know—I saw the selection in the bedroom. I chose this; it's…" She waves her hand down, unwittingly drawing the attention to both of us to the way the tunic hides, but somehow clings to and emphasises her feminine body underneath. "It's lovely, I've never worn anything like this before, and I can feel how cool and comfortable it will be."

"Lisa should be packing the rest of the clothing for you."

She starts at that, and I realise she thought she was just to select one thing from the variety I'd had provided for her. For some reason, she's not pleased. "No, I don't want you to do that. The clothes; they're far too expensive for me to accept."

Her rebuttal reminds me she must be well used to designer labels from the wardrobe Ethan would have provided knows quality when she sees it. Sean's looking at me with interest, wondering how I'm going to handle this. I could play the card as absolute monarch; she's technically one of my subjects now as she's travelling on an Amahadian passport, as well as my employee. But insisting she takes them that would make me an absolute prick. I lean back in my chair, watching the emotions flit across her face.

"If you don't like them…"

She grimaces, "I do like them, but…"

Realisation dawns, "He dressed you, didn't he?"

I can see a tear come to her eye as she remembers. "Yes," her voice is soft, low. "I never had a choice. I had to wear exactly what he told me too."

"Not the same thing here at all." I sit forwards, "Zoe, you left Ethan with nothing more than the clothes on your back, presumably anything you've bought since was for the English winter. The clothes you've brought with you, well, they're not going to be suitable for the climate. You didn't have time for a shopping trip to prepare for Amahad, so I asked for clothes to be provided that will be comfortable in my country. If you don't like them, choose a couple of things to tide you over then I'm sure Cara will be happy to take you shopping, or you can replace them online. If you do like them, keep them. As I said, consider them an advance on your wages." I've caught her attention.

But the brief shudder that runs through shows how much she's struggling to accept my gift. *Fuck, this is difficult.* I'm starting to realise just how fragile she is and knowing what to do for the best is like walking on egg shells. I try to make it clear to her, "Zoe, what you do is your choice!" I throw a glance at Sean; he gives me a look of approval. Just at that moment, the pilot informs us that we should prepare for landing.

As she sits and searches for the seat belt, she remembers her manners. "Thank you, Kadar. That sounds sensible. I'll accept the clothes as an advance. But I *will* be paying you back. And I won't wear anything I don't feel comfortable in." She holds my gaze for a second, as if to impress on me this is her decision, and then her attention is taken up with the sights out of the window, now eager to get the first view of her new home.

As the plane flies lower and my country comes into sight below us, my heart begins to swell with pride. We circle round the moderate sized city of Al Qar'ah, the capital of Amahad snuggled against the coastline, and then move a little further inland towards the airport where the runway looks like it leads off into the hot desert. The sands shimmer beneath us as we descend. It's early afternoon, and will be hot when we land. The wheels engage with an audible clunk, then, as we touch down in my native land, I feel as though I can breathe properly for the first time since I left. Despite all the problems, this is my home.

As warrants the return of the ruler, soldiers of the Royal Guard gather in formation as the steps are brought to the plane, and diplomatically I don't rush to disembark, allowing the delay while they get themselves sorted on the ground. A limousine flying the national flag is waiting to take us away from the main terminal, and outriders on motorcycles have assembled to escort the royal car through the city to the palace. Two black SUVs wait on the sidelines, trying to appear inconspicuous but in reality containing the elite of our security forces. It's a stark reminder of my sometimes fragile grasp on Amahad that I need to take such precautions, even on my home territory.

When I receive the signal all's ready, we descend the stairs. I hear a small gulp beside me, and looking down into her pretty face I see Zoe's eyes are wide. She hesitates, pausing to let me go in front to be first out of the door with the words, "You really are the monarch, aren't you?"

I smile at her and take her hand, so she's forced to walk beside me. "Welcome to my country, Zoe. I hope you'll be able to make a new start here. A new life."

And I do; I sincerely hope that she will be happy here, and maybe on occasion, our paths might cross. But I won't be seeking her out deliberately. This ends for me, now, or will the minute I hand her over to Cara. Much as I know I'll regret saying goodbye to my broken flower; it will be a final parting. It was part of my reasoning why I decided that Sean could accompany her to my country; he can help her get settled as well as provide her with protection. And if forcing them together means anything starts between them, well, I'll have to bury that jealousy deep inside me.

I am the emir. I have to do my duty. And my obligations to my country mean I'll soon be marrying a woman selected from those with the right pedigree. I cannot, and must not, explore this strange attraction to Zoe Baker any further.

CHAPTER 16
Zoe

A new life? That's what I wanted. So why do I feel so out of depth and lost? I should be over the moon excited. When we'd left the plane the air was so hot and dry it brought home I'm on another continent, and now, sitting in the air-conditioned comfort of the royal car as we drive through the streets of Amahad's capital city, taking in the scenery as we skirt round an intriguing looking souk and head up a main highway towards the palace, I can't help but wonder whether I'm doing the right thing. I'm over three thousand miles away from Ethan; he doesn't know where I am, so I should be feeling safe here.

But for some reason, sitting between the model-gorgeous bodyguard on one side and the stern, but handsome Sheikh on the other, I feel small and overawed, and I have to remind myself to take air into my lungs. Both men have pledged my safety, but am I safe from them? And why do I feel my stomach rolling when I'm near to Kadar? Is it just that the power he has that overwhelms me? The reception at the airport, the outriders now surrounding the car; demonstrating that with all his wealth, even Ethan could never compete with him. Ethan's status was bought with money. Kadar had been born to it.

I'm still mulling things over when we enter the gates of the palace compound and drive along the long, perfectly straight driveway towards the palace itself. I notice houses dotted around the walls, all with views out into the impeccably maintained gardens but I don't have long to take in all my surroundings as, only minutes later, we pull up to the main entrance.

Even before I'm out of the car, I see a perfectly poised and unquestionably pregnant woman coming towards us and have no doubt this is Sheikha Cara, the woman who I clicked with so quickly during that long phone call, the person who is responsible for bringing me here today. She comes forward quickly as though impatient to greet me, her hand outstretched in welcome, a beaming smile on her face. The sun reflects off a gorgeous choker she's wearing round her neck; it's made of white and yellow gold and dotted with diamonds which sparkle in the light.

"Zoe, I'm so glad you're here at last! I can't wait to get to show you the harem and start discussing your plans for it!" She immediately puts me on the right footing; I'm here to work. For some reason, that grounds me.

"Thank you, Your Excellency. I'm ready to see it as soon as you want to take me."

"Oh, for goodness sake call me Cara! We weren't formal on the phone, were we?" I notice she throws a look at Kadar, nodding to him in greeting, but asking a silent question with her eyes.

"I think Zoe needs to get settled before you put her to work, Cara."

Turning back to me the Sheikha smiles, the expression

allowing her natural beauty to shine through, "I decided to put you in one of the houses in the compound rather than a suite in the main palace as I thought you'd like your own place. Sean can stay there with you while he's here."

I glance at my bodyguard, who tells the both of us, "That will suit me fine. I'll be here until you've settled in, Zoe, and we've monitored what St John-Davies is up to. I'll check out the security and make sure you'll be safe."

Kadar gives a short laugh, "The system better be to your approval, Sean. Grade A installed it!" He grows serious as he turns to me, "I hope you will be very happy here, Miss Baker. Now my sister-in-law will make sure you have everything you need. You'll be working directly with her, and anything you want or need she'll be able to get for you. Goodbye, Miss Baker."

I don't miss that he's swopped to the formal use of my title and last name as I take the hand he holds out, our fingers touching briefly before he quickly pulls away. With a quick bow of his head, directed at both myself and his brother's wife, he strides towards the palace entrance, his robes billowing out behind him in the hot air. Immediately he is surrounded by a dozen or so men, questions being thrown at him from all directions. I hear his rapid-fire answers, seeming to address diverse topics all at once, some queries he answers in English, some in Arabic, some with German, and then with what I believe might be Japanese. Realising I'm seeing the emir in action, I watch until he disappears from sight.

His goodbye sounded final.

And so it has to be. In this land where he is the ruler and where everyone seems to want to have a piece of him; there's no place for even a friendship with a lowly employee. Part of me feels almost liberated at the loss of his dominant presence, but that relief is admittedly tinged with regret. I hardly know the man, but I'm going to miss him.

Cara must have been watching me. When I turn back, slightly embarrassed I'd spent so long watching her brother-in-law, she quickly hides her grin, transforming it into an easy smile. Gently she touches my arm, "Come, Zoe. I'll show you where you're staying."

I follow as she leads me away and around the side of the palace, Sean behind us carrying the luggage. He has his bag slung over his shoulder, and wheeling along the designer pull-along suitcase containing the additional clothes I seem to have ended up with. A palace guard has appeared and I'm embarrassed to see he's carrying the cheap and out of place looking rucksack I'd bought a lifetime ago from Primark. I'm still not comfortable about the outfits Kadar provided for me, his actions a little too close to what Ethan would have done. But I park those thoughts, for now, too interested in seeing my new home.

The palace is so huge it's a good ten minutes' walk through the extensive grounds before we come to a functional structure of a house backing onto the outer wall, one of a number of identical abodes I'd noticed on the way in. It's a basic square box, but as Cara opens the door, I can see comfortable looking rooms furnished in a western style and stairs leading up to the upper floor. It's cosy and surprisingly homely, with a range of authentic pots and ornaments dotted around taking away what could otherwise be a cold, empty feel. Examining what will be my new home, I agree it's far less daunting than having to stay in the grand palace. Throwing a glance over my shoulder I see Sean checking out the alarm system, and the quick nod and look of satisfaction appearing on his face presumably means he thinks it's adequate.

"There's a fully stocked fridge and larder here." I follow Cara into the kitchen that, while not large, seems complete with all the necessary equipment, "You can either cook for yourselves, go into the city where there are some great restaurants or, of course, you're welcome to come eat in the palace if you want."

"This is fantastic!" I tell her with a grin; already starting to feel at home.

"Oh, and a car will be delivered for your use."

I grasp her hand, "I can't thank you enough for the opportunity, and everything you've provided for me. It's brilliant, far more than I expected."

"It's going to be lovely to have another English woman around the palace." She holds my hand a little longer than necessary, "I hope we can become friends. I'm sorry I can't stay and help you settle in, but there's a state dinner tonight which I've got to attend." When her face screws up, I take it it's not particularly one she's looking forward to.

During our encounter Sean has stayed in the background, taking everything in, but not contributing to the conversation. Now he steps up, "That's alright, Cara. We've got this covered from here."

Cara nods but throws him a strange look that I can't decipher before going out of the door.

As soon as she's gone, I feel his presence behind me, Sean's hands gently stroking my arms. I pull away, still uncomfortable with a man's touch, however innocent. I turn to face him, wanting to get things on a practical basis, "Hungry?" His intense eyes drink me in for a moment, and then he steps away, nodding in agreement.

The kitchen has been stocked with familiar items, probably shipped in from England. I'm glad as I'm able to pull together a quick meal. Eventually I'd like to find out more about the indigenous food of Amahad but for now, the recognisable packages and English instructions are comforting. One unexpected find is wine and beer in the fridge, I thought these items wouldn't be available in a predominantly Muslim country, but am grateful as we're able to enjoy the alcohol with our dinner. Night falls quickly in the desert, and it's not long before my mouth opens in a wide yawn after the eventful day. I'm not surprised I'm tired as I'd had a drink with the meal on the plane and now I've indulged in yet another couple of glasses of wine.

Upstairs there are two bedrooms, and I've already claimed the one with an en-suite, leaving Sean the smaller room and the separate bathroom. I put my new and old clothes away, slip into my nightie I brought from home, and slide under the sheets. As I lie awake, strange sounds from outside reach me; voices and the occasional shout in the exotic language foreign to me, but native to Amahad, and the calling of night birds I can't identify. The wine, the journey, and the excitement of the day have my eyes quickly closing, and soon I fall asleep.

Twelve months ago

Lost in my book, absorbed in the plot, I was rapt with the sexual tension between hero and heroine who reach levels of arousal and fulfilment that I couldn't believe to be true, and surely could only have come from the author's vivid imagination. If only that sort of pleasure existed in real life.

Reading was my only recreation, my one escape from the reality of my lonely existence. I had no friends, or none I could contact; I wasn't allowed to go out to see them, or even to call them on the phone. I lived solely to serve this man who held me captive.

Caught up in the plot, I forgot the time, becoming engrossed as the characters reached the scene's, as well as their own, climax. Then I glanced up at the clock. Shit! Ethan would be home in ten minutes. I had to get a move on!

He liked me dressed for dinner, full makeup—the works. I threw down my book and raced to my wardrobe, selecting one of his favorite dresses. Stepping quickly out of my jeans and tearing off my top, I slipped the dress over my head. Next, I grabbed a pair of stockings out of the drawer and pulled them on, ripping my fingernail through one, causing a long and very visible ladder. Damn! I get out another pair, this time taking more care attaching them to the suspender belt he preferred me to wear. Dressed, I rushed to the bathroom and tried to put on my makeup as best I could with a shaking hand, ending up stabbing myself in the eye with the mascara wand. My eye watering, I rubbed it, my whole eye became blackened. With shaking hands, I cleaned it off and applied it again. Foundation, face powder and lipstick. Done. Putting a brush through my hair, I realised I'd no time to put it up, so I pushed it behind my ears. With a last quick glance in the mirror, I raced downstairs.

To find Ethan standing in the hall, waiting for me, tapping his watch.

"I'm sorry," I gasped out my apology, "I didn't notice the time."

"You have a clock in your room?"

I could only nod, my whole body trembling with fear.

"Can you tell the time?" Ethan asked with a sneer.

Again I nodded, frozen to the spot as he stepped closer.

"So why are you late? Why do you come down to dinner looking like a slut? Look at you! A child playing with makeup for the first time could do a better job than you!"

There's nothing I could say, no excuse I could offer that would have been accepted, so I stayed dumb. His hand came up, and I tensed. As I looked into his cold eyes, I saw a flash of anger. He formed a fist, and I knew what was coming, but there was no way of evading it. I couldn't run; that would only have made it worse, enraging him further if he had to catch me. I waited, he did nothing. Tears pricked at the corners of my eyes. Why didn't he just get it over with?

When his fist made contact with my stomach, I doubled over in pain. He hit me again, this time, taking advantage of my bent position and finding a kidney. I fell to the floor, and he kicked my ribs.

At last, he stepped back, "Stupid bitch! Now get to the dining room or dinner will be cold."

I knew I had to pull myself up and move to the table as quickly as I could. If his dinner was ruined, he'd start on me all over again. Gingerly I got to my feet; my whole body feeling like it was on fire. Tears of pain ran down my cheeks, but I made no sound, no protest. I stumbled into the dining room and took my seat. On the sideboard were bowls of vegetables and a plate of roast meat.

He sat at the other end of the table and bellowed out, "Now serve me, bitch."

Closing my eyes briefly I took a breath, not too deeply as it would hurt my bruised, or quite possibly broken, ribs. Again I pulled myself up, the exertion causing pain to course through me. I filled his plate, asking his vegetable choice politely, and then delivered his meal to him.

"Now your own."

I'd lost any appetite I might have had, but if I didn't make the attempt to eat I'd anger him further and prompt a lecture about wasting food cooked so lovingly by Mrs Benton, probably accompanied by more pain. So I put some items on my plate, feeling his eyes on me, knowing my painful exertions were bringing him pleasure. Tentatively I put my loaded fork to my mouth and tried to chew, but the ache in my stomach made me retch. With an effort I swallowed it down, and took another mouthful of meat, all the time aware his gaze was burning into me.

He nodded in satisfaction. "Good girl!" he said condescendingly, as I forced another piece of meat down.

Present day

The next thing I know is someone waking me, saying my name loudly right by my ear. I scream and move to the far side of the bed, my heart beating fast in terror; *how could he have found me? And where am I?* I flail my hand, but I don't locate the light that's usually by the side of my bed. Luckily before I can get into a full blown panic a lamp is switched on—it was the other side of the bed—and I see it's Sean standing beside me, not Ethan. My hand on my chest, I try to slow my rapidly beating heart.

"Shush, Zoe, you were having a nightmare," his voice is soft and calming. I'm grateful he keeps his distance and makes no move to offer physical comfort.

I close my eyes, hoping to prevent the tears of shame falling down my cheeks, embarrassed I'd disturbed him. I have nightmares all too often. Ida used to wake me, calm me, and make me hot chocolate to help me sleep again.

"Is there anything I can do? Do you want me to stay with you?"

Shaking my head, I decline his offer, too embarrassed by the night terrors which make me feel so weak, wondering whether I'll ever be free of them. After all these months Ethan still has power over me. He comes to me in my sleep, and I can even feel the pain he inflicts. It's as if my memory insists on replaying everything back to me. "No, thank you," I tell him, wiping the tears from my eyes, "I'll be alright now; I'd rather be alone. I'm sorry I disturbed you."

He perches on the side of the bed, careful not to touch

me, but makes no attempt to leave. Instead, after a moment, he starts to speak. "I served a couple of tours in Afghanistan." His voice is quiet, "Well, let's just say I saw things I wouldn't wish anyone to see and did things I would never have believed myself capable off. The worst mission was a bodged extraction. We were supposed to bring out ten young girls taken from a village. We got there too late and couldn't save them. We only found their tortured bodies. Even after I returned to England and was discharged, those girls' faces would visit me, night after night after night. Teenagers and even younger who'd never have a chance at life." He pauses for a moment, leans forward, his elbows on his knees, one hand cradling the other. "I know what it's like to have nightmares."

I'm stunned he's revealing so much of himself and am saddened by his story. "It wasn't your fault, was it? That the girls died?"

"No, we couldn't have done anything more. The intelligence we were given was naff, and we'd searched in the wrong place first, causing the delay. But something like that always haunts you and doesn't stop you thinking whether there was anything that you could have done differently. But we weren't in control, the terrorists were. The girls never had a chance."

"Do you still have nightmares?"

He shakes his head, "Not so often, now. I left the service four years ago, couldn't cope with more—that wasn't the only incident but by far the most horrific. I got therapy, which helped me see that I'd been helpless in the situation. That there was nothing more I could have done." In the dim light from the lamp, I see his eyes turn to me. "Just like you. You were a victim, but I bet you're blaming yourself, wondering why you let him fool you in the first place? Wondering why you let yourself fall for him? And why you didn't leave when it first got bad. I know you are, Zoe. That's to be expected." He pulls himself up straighter, laser eyes almost burning me, "It's not your fault; nothing was your fault."

Deep down I understand what he's saying, but I can't help thinking that a different person wouldn't have been taken in by Ethan. *How could I have been so stupid?*

"Not every man is like him," Sean tells me what I already know, even if it's hard to accept.

"How can I tell, Sean? Perhaps other people have an abuser detection meter, but mine's faulty. I don't feel I can trust anyone to be what they appear on the surface."

Reaching out his hand he slowly strokes my face, and calmer now, I don't flinch away. "You'll get there. It just takes time. Are you feeling better now? Ready to go back to sleep now? I'll stay if you want me to."

I give him the appropriate positive and negative responses and he leaves me alone. I don't turn off the light, keeping it on in the hope it will help keep my virtual monsters at bay, if not the real ones. My talk with Sean seems to have settled me, and thankfully the rest of the night passes without another appearance from Ethan.

The next morning I wake surprisingly refreshed and excited. I'm in Amahad; I'm going to do the job I was trained to do. And there's no one here who's going to tell me scrubbing around in the dirt is unladylike!

While we're eating breakfast, a package is delivered with ID cards for both Sean and me, together with a map of the palace and an invitation to meet Cara in her suite at ten o'clock. Suspecting it will be more comfortable in the heat, I select Capri pants and a long-sleeved T-shirt from the selection Kadar had provided, hoping it's demure enough not to give offence. I'm still not certain what the dress code is in the palace, but know this practical clothing will suffice when I'm crawling around checking foundations. *I can't wait to get to work!*

With plenty of time to spare, Sean and I leave the small house and go over to the Palace, crossing through the public areas. Then our passes are checked as we enter the entrance to the private quarters. When we arrive at Cara's suite of rooms, Sean goes off to do whatever bodyguards do when they're not on duty. Apparently, the palace guards will take over my protection from here.

Cara greets me warmly, but I notice getting out of her seat is a bit of a struggle. I indicate her stomach, "When are you due?"

"Still two months to go," she answers, an easy grin coming to her face, "And I can't wait. I already feel like an elephant!"

We discuss the baby for a few minutes and then I ask her whether what I'm wearing is suitable. It's the opening for a discussion and first lesson on my new home. "You can wear what you like here. You wouldn't be popular if you went topless bathing, but otherwise Amahadians are reasonably permissive. The citizens wear western or Arab dress in the capital. Amahad is multicultural and any religion can be practiced here. Of course, out in the southern desert, the nomadic tribes are a bit more traditional, but Kadar is trying to bring them into the twenty-first century." Her face drops slightly, and her natural smile disappears, "It's not easy protecting our ways; fanatics are continually trying to cross over our borders to fuel a religious war. That's why Nijad, my husband, isn't here, and why I am. Matters are escalating, and while he needs to be in the desert city to direct operations there, he prefers me to stay and have our baby in the safety of the capital."

I feel sorry for her, "How often do you see him? Can he come to you?"

"Oh yes, he's never away much longer than a night or so. And he'll be here for the birth—it's only a two-hour helicopter ride away. But, come, it's time you saw the harem and the work you've got in store for you."

I love her positivity and friendliness. Even now I know she's akin to a princess, I can see no airs and graces, and I quickly forget her status as she opens the door to the suite and ushers me out. As I take in the almost intimidating opulence of the hallways of the palace, my companion looks so comfortable you would think she had been born here, but to my surprise, she explains she's only lived here a few months. Her friendly chatting helps me relax as we make our way through long corridors with alcoves outlined in gold paint off to the left and right, and past gleaming white marble pillars.

Glancing at the walls decorated with beautiful tapestries and paintings which can only be originals, I feel I'm in a museum, and again I'm amazed how Cara, of equally common birth as me, seems to be taking it all in her stride. Emphasising her status, but almost ignored by Cara, are the guards and servants bowing in obeisance as we pass. She greets them simply with a nod or a smile. *Perhaps one day I'll get used to it too!* But for now, I'll just appreciate the unique experience of working in a royal palace.

We descend from the living quarters and enter the state rooms of the palace. As she points out the ballroom, dining room and library, large and small sitting rooms I start to move closer, thinking if I lose sight of her I'd be lost forever, wandering round in circles trying to find my way out. At last leaving the magnificence of the main palace behind, we come to corridors with plain stone walls and instead of marble underfoot are uneven flagstone floors. We're alone here, except for the discreet guards following behind, and our footsteps echoing on the ground becomes the only sound we can hear. Eventually, we come to a set of massive ornate golden doors which have clearly seen better days. My companion and guide pauses, as if for dramatic effect, giving me time to see the tarnish and dirt, allowing me time to start a mental list of what needs to be addressed in the renovations.

With a flourish, she pulls the doors open. "The Harem!" she announces, unnecessarily. With a feeling of awe, I step inside. The guards take up their post outside the great doors and stare resolutely straight ahead, not even taking a peek into the forbidden area. A sense of reverence comes over me. Until the emir makes the decree to lift the restrictions, this is a women only domain.

Touching Cara's arm and indicating the guards, I whisper softly, "What would happen if they came in?"

"Beheading, castration…something like that," she replies, laughing. "I need to speak to Kadar about rescinding that ancient law."

It's is not difficult for me to fall immediately in love with my new project. The harem is gorgeous and beautiful, and there's such an aura of mystery the very air seems to pulse as if the building has a life of its own. Strangely I don't associate it with kidnapping or keeping women against their will, but of sensuality and love.

"Hey, let me show you round. I know every inch of this place." Cara has a glint in her eye as she speaks and I expect there's a story there, but it seems that it will be one for another day as she moves on, offering no explanation. "There are cubicles or bedrooms if you like, around this central pool. The water must have drained away long ago because of the crack in the base."

I walk over and look down mentally jotting notes of what kind of expertise I'd need to bring in to complete the restoration. I notice a beautiful mosaic on the bottom of the pool, broken because of the crack, and I wonder whether there might be a local artisan with the skills to return it to its former glory. As I nod to confirm I've seen all I need for now in the central area, Cara leads me through to the bathrooms, all but one in a state of disrepair. I love the old Victorian plumbing, but the pipe work needs replacing, and much the ancient porcelain appears to be damaged beyond repair.

Once I've had my first glimpse of the inside of the

harem, she takes me outside. What once used to be a beautiful garden with paths, raised flower beds and palm trees all surrounded by a high wall now seems a desolate area. Paths and walls are crumbling, the raised beds spilling over onto the paving. The ancient irrigation system has rusted away. There's a tremendous amount of work to be done here, and I'm excited to start, feeling a longing to get my hands dirty. My primary role will be planning and designing, then employing and directing the craftspeople to complete most of the physical work, but here, outside in the garden; I won't be able to resist joining in.

The sun's blazing down, and I find it a little too much not yet being acclimatised to the heat. Seeing me wilting, Cara walks me back into the harem and shows me a secret door. I tilt my head, curious, as she seems to stand in a trance in front of it. After a moment, realising what she's doing, she turns with a quick laugh, "Memories," she explains, looking a little embarrassed. But she doesn't elaborate further.

I notice she looks tired, but then again, she is carrying a baby inside her. "If you've got things to do, Cara, just leave me here, and I'll start getting a better feel for the place and what needs doing."

I'd apparently read her correctly, as she quickly agrees with the idea and we spend just a little longer discussing the practicalities of how she wanted to be kept up to date. She introduces me to Asif, one of the men still waiting outside. He's a fierce looking man armed to the teeth who's apparently been assigned as my personal guard, and who, thankfully, speaks quite good English. We swap telephone numbers and agree that he'll be my escort to and from the harem, allaying my fears I'll get lost in the maze of palace corridors. Asif nods at Cara's suggestion that he'll act as interpreter when I need to go out into the city or meet with local craftsmen. We seem to have all the important details sewn up, so Cara takes her leave, and I'm, at last, left alone in my new workplace.

For a moment I'm satisfied to sit on the crumbling surround of what was once the central pool, soaking up the atmosphere. Cara's asked me to come up with some designs and suggestions for making the place work as a sensual retreat. Getting myself into work mode and opening my bag, I take out my laptop and sketch pad and begin, in my usual way, by staring at a blank sheet of paper. Gradually different notions and ideas start to come to me, and soon the ground around is covered with half started drawings and scribbled out diagrams on the discarded sheets of paper.

By the end of the first day, I'm toying with an idea that excites me. The more I look around and develop concepts in my head the more animated I get. Could it be I'm on the right track? Is this something that might interest Cara? Unable to wait any longer I use the phone I've been given to ring the Sheikha and make an appointment to see her the following morning.

The next day Asif takes me, not to the Sheikha's suite, but to the newer part of the palace housing the government offices. He leads me through the busy area where people are working hard behind computer screens, just like any workplace in every other part of the world, and then through to where the senior government staff work. An assistant announces my arrival, and then opens the door to a large private office. Sitting behind the desk, evidently hard at work, is Cara. My face shows my surprise, and she grins, quickly filling me that she assists the Finance Minister, and that she occupied the role until she'd helped Kadar find a replacement. She goes up in my estimation. I mean, it was already obvious she is a very intelligent woman, but I didn't expect to be seeing her in such an important position in what I had foolishly assumed to be a very male-dominated world.

After a couple of clicks of the keys, she closes a program on her screen and then gestures me to a small conference table located by an open window. Soft perfume wafts in from the scented garden outside, and the view over the palace grounds gives me some ideas for the exterior of the harem. I must have been gazing out lost in my mind as a polite cough brings me back to the present.

"Sorry. Right," I open my laptop, and pull up my design programme, but slightly close the lid as if Cara doesn't agree with the basic premise then there's no point going further. I take a breath, "The harem has an atmosphere — and I'm planning the decoration to keep it that way." At Cara's nod, I think she understands exactly what I mean. "It's romantic, sexy." Another nod. "Soooo," I string out the word, hesitant to suggest my idea, "What about making it a destination for hen parties?"

Cara stares at me for a moment, her lips part, and then she claps in delight as her face breaks into a brilliant smile. It's at that instant I know how she's bagged herself a sheikh;

she is a gorgeous woman, animation lighting her face showing off her loveliness. I pull myself back to the business in hand. "We can employ," I hold up my hands to demonstrate I'm putting the next words in quotes, "'Eunuchs' to serve them. And I haven't been yet myself, but I understand there are a night club and a casino in the city, and of course, they can have an arranged visit to the souk."

"Camel rides at sunset into the desert!" Cara's eyes glaze as she catches on with the idea, "Zoe, that's a brilliant proposal!"

Now it's time to open my laptop to show her the quick design that I've come up with. It will need more work, but my initial idea is to keep the cubicles as they are, and I've come up with some designs for decorating the walls with murals of concubines relaxing semi-naked awaiting their sultan. Apart from restoration, I don't plan to do much other than enhance and repair what's already there. The place is designed for a bevy of women, so why not maximise on that idea?

We spend time throwing around ideas of what kind of packages they could offer but are brought back to earth by the thought that Kadar needs to be on board. Though Cara doesn't think there'll be any problem; one of his main aims apparently is to put Amahad on the map as an international tourist destination.

A buzz from her intercom interrupts us and alerts her to another meeting, so we part. I'm surprised that she hugs me before I leave, holding me close and then keeping her hands on me as she steps arms-length away. Her eyes examine me carefully. "You're looking more relaxed already, Zoe. I must admit, when I was talking to you that day on the phone, I knew you needed this job, as much as we needed you to do it. Now I'm so glad we're going to be able to help each other."

She's given away that Kadar has probably shared at least some of my story, so I tell her the truth, "I do feel safe here. And I know I'm going to love my work."

She nods slowly, a sad look crossing her face. But as I shake my head she realises I don't want her sympathy. The moment breaks, and I leave her to her to get on with whatever she has to do.

* * * *

A couple of days later I lose my personal bodyguard when Sean returns to England. Intelligence has confirmed Ethan is still chasing his tail in England and appears to have no knowledge I've left the country. Grade A Security have been keeping note of his whereabouts, and has confirmed he's still tracking down rumoured sightings of me; though, unfortunately, he hasn't yet gone as far as Iceland. It's considered safe for me to rely on the palace guards now. While I miss Sean's cheery presence, I quickly find I prefer living on my own, and not having a constant bodyguard around means that I can start to live a normal life without worrying that Kadar is laying out considerable expense employing people to keep me protected. Or worry myself wondering why such an important man is so bothered with my protection in the first place.

It's been a very long time since I could feel like an ordinary girl, but gradually as time goes on, I stop looking over my shoulder. Day by day the harem draws me, its atmosphere exotic and enticing. Even if it weren't my job, I'd feel the compulsion to spend time there. The environment seems to soothe me; perhaps it has something to do with it being a place forbidden to men. Whatever the reason, it enables me to produce some of the best work I have ever done as I draw up plan after plan reflecting the designs I have in mind.

But it's not all toil and slog; I have all the time to myself that I need. In the evenings, I enjoy reading extensively, learning as much as I can about the harem's history and past occupants to help me reproduce the authentic atmosphere. In its heyday, I glean, it would have housed women and children, the wives and concubines of the Sultan, who were kept sequestered away from the world. Some were there by choice; others undoubtedly kidnapped for the ruler's pleasure. My romantic leanings lead me to wonder what it would be like to be abducted by a handsome sheikh, and in my mind, such a kidnapper always bears an uncanny resemblance to Kadar.

My imagination runs away with me to such an extent that one evening, when Asif comes to take me to the small house which has fast become home, I send him away, deciding instead to spend the night in the harem, excited to have a real chance to soak up the ambience and try to get some more ideas on how to replicate the atmosphere of bygone years in the restoration. Spending the dark hours alone here seems an exotic adventure. And it's perfectly safe. No males would enter under the threat of death. Or castration. *Nope, I can't think there are many men who would risk that particular punishment!*

One cubicle remains furnished, and I know the reason has something to do with Cara, but she still hasn't explained fully why. She's told me it was the place where she and Sheikh Nijad spent their wedding night, but there seems to be more of a story to it than just that. But in any event, it's in this fabulous bed, surrounded by ornate hangings, where I am going to lay my head tonight. It does feel a bit awkward bedding down where a marriage was consummated, but I dismiss those thoughts quickly as there's no other option, and it can't be unlike staying in any hotel room where goodness knows what might have gone on.

As the skies darken and night falls I use the facilities in the one working bathroom, strip off to just my underwear, and lie on the bed. Although there are covers I deign not to use them, the night is warm, and I have no desire to snuggle under a sheet for the sake of it. Closing my eyes, I breathe in the tropical smelling air, soaking up the romance and imagining how I could enhance the sensuality for the future guests by the use of evocative scents I could bring out with the right planting arrangements in the garden. Roses and lavender would have to be thought about carefully given the dry climate, but flowering plants such as bougainvillea, oleander, hibiscus, and jasmine would probably flourish, their perfumes filling the harem building when the large garden doors were open.

A fountain, with water playing, would form the focal point in the centre of the area. The original has fallen to pieces beyond repair, so I think about commissioning a new one, perhaps with lions' heads as the water spouts, or maybe I need to find out what's the national animal here. Money, in Amahad, seems to be no object. Lying still, I imagine the perfume of flowers and the sound of water from the fountains filling my senses. Lost in my thoughts my eyes close. I start to drift off, my reason starting to get jumbled and soon make no sense at all.

CHAPTER 17
Kadar

A venue for hen parties? Whatever fucking next? As I sit at my desk reading the proposal put together by my sister-in-law, I'm not quite sure whether to laugh or cry. *Is this a joke, or is she serious?* I wonder. Considering her pitch, I idly tap my pen rhythmically against the cracked leather inlay of the old-fashioned piece of furniture which was my father's, and his father's before that. A cumbersome workspace for the modern world, but one which I can't dispose of or bring myself to replace, possibly because my subconscious thinks it might still hold some of their wisdom from the decades, or even centuries, of use. One thing for sure, I could feel the old emir turning in his grave at the thought of the harem being filled with screaming drunk women. Or then again, perhaps he wouldn't. Although he kept it in his pants while in his home country, I'd heard rumours that he was a horny old devil when abroad. But I don't want to dwell on that; he was my father after all.

East meets West. Instead of dismissing the idea out of hand, I begin to think seriously about it. Cara's proposal is well written and deserves proper consideration. She's tempting me with the well-known fact I want Amahad to be seen as a progressive, forward nation, and attracting foreign visitors here is one of my topmost aims. The tapping of my pen speeds up as I make a quick decision. I press the button, adding my electronic signature to approve Cara's request, and allow myself a grin. I can see how she thinks it would work.

Bringing tourists to Amahad. But therein lies a major problem. They won't fucking want to come if there's even a hint of any unrest in the country. My vision to make Amahad one of the most progressive of the Arab states is not looking too achievable at the moment. Still, we must plan for the future, and be confident the unrest will be contained—hopefully by the time the renovations to the harem are completed. The loud beep of the intercom interrupts my thoughts.

"Sheikh Nijad is here, Your Excellency."

"Thank you, Richard. Send him in."

I stand up to welcome my brother, noticing the drawn look on his face immediately. He seems tired, and his robes are dusty with sand. Apparently, he's come straight here from ▯alr▯▯, without stopping to change. Whatever it is must be important.

"Ni, sit. Refreshment?" I'm concerned about him. While I sit safely behind my desk to find a resolution for our issues, he's exposed on the front line, and the situation seems to be getting more dangerous by the day.

He grins as if it's the most welcome question anyone's asked him for a while and nods, "Could murder a beer."

I open the fridge behind my desk—an addition since my father's times—and extract two bottles. My two brothers and I had picked up certain habits in the West which we continue, discreetly, in our homeland. Using the bottle opener, I snap off the tops and pass one to him. He takes a long drink, apparently thirsty. I wait for him to finish and take a breath before I start to interrogate him.

"What's the latest?"

"We've got a fucking problem."

I arch my eyebrow; I would have thought we had more than one, but curb my impatience as to which is currently causing the most worry as he takes another gulp of beer, and wait for him to enlighten me.

"Abdul-Muhsi."

I breathe out a long sigh, resting my head down into my hands, drawing my fingers up and over my headdress and grimace. "What's he done now?" I dread hearing the latest about the man who's a constant thorn in my side.

"Disappeared."

"What?" For a second I wonder whether that could be good news.

Nijad quickly disillusions me, "He's up to something. Just don't know what yet. I've got Rais looking for him, but we think he's crossed the border and not just for a short visit." He slams his bottle down in disgust. I know his hatred for the rogue Sheikh is even greater than mine; at one time Muhsi had been very vocal in calling for Cara's execution.

Narrowing my eyes, I ask for the confirmation I don't want to hear. "Into Ezirad?"

Nijad nods, and I frown. Ezirad is not friendly to us. Being an underdeveloped country with poor leadership, they are responsible for the route via which jihadists enter into Amahad. Although I still believe Abdul-Muhsi's influence over the rest of the desert is weak, if he's teaming up with external forces we may have serious trouble ahead. Which, reading between the lines seems to be what Nijad appears to be suggesting. Following the Arab Spring, Syria, and the terror of ISIS no country is safe. Forewarned though is forearmed, and with our neighbour and ally, Alair, we're fighting the constant battle to keep the terrorists out. Abdul-Muhsi on the loose is not what I wanted to hear.

"Is it affecting the new oil field development?"

Nijad shakes his head. "Not at present. We're still in the stages of drawing up a production and development plan with the operator. Jasim's working with his counterpart from Alair. I understand plans for the pipeline are well underway, though."

Having discovered billions of barrels of oil under the sands of the Southern Desert not only do we need to extract it, but we also need to transport it to the coast for distribution. It's one hell of a project, which Jasim is directing, liaising with the major oil companies from his base in London. The oil field is mostly in Amahad with a good portion in Alair, but a small section is in Ezirad. The knowledge of the latter is a fact we're withholding at present.

"I can see problems, Ni. When we start laying the pipeline and constructing the wells, we'll need to guard all the workers, as well as the structures themselves. They'll be visible targets, and I don't want them to be easy ones."

"Hunter Wright is down there keeping an eye on what's

going on. Carter will assign more men from Grade A if we need them."

"Cara's hugging friend?" I bark a laugh, referring to Hunter and the intimacy with which he treats my sister-in-law.

Nijad grimaces, making me chuckle knowing he has to bite his tongue whenever the two old friends meet. Being possessive, my brother doesn't like anyone but family to get that close to his wife. Then my own eyes narrow, "Aiza said she had plans to visit. I knew there had to be something behind it. Well, she'll stay in the fucking palace, and he remains in the desert." I tell him, as the reason for my sister's sudden desire to return home falls into place.

"You noticed how they got on at my wedding, then?"

"I'm not blind, Nijad." I'm not at all happy, "She's too young to be interested in any man."

Nijad chuckles, "She's twenty-one, Kadar, I don't think she'd agree with that assumption." Then he frowns, "But even I don't like the thought of our little sister with the likes of Hunter. He's far too worldly for her."

For a moment I wonder just how much we do know of our little sister, and what she gets up to unchaperoned abroad. But that's a problem for another day. "Anyway," I return to the original subject, "Aiza won't be going anywhere near the desert," I reiterate, "It will be enough for us to ensure the protection of the foreign workers."

"I agree." Like me, Nijad's returned to the business at hand, "In this, most of the tribes are behind us and united. Once the oil fields are up and running, they stand to gain tremendous benefit—a return on the investment they initially made. That should apply to the Qaiquw tribe as well, so there's no reason for them to upset the apple cart. But Abdul-Muhsi is after more."

"My throne," I say, drily. Is this the start of an outright challenge, the coup I've been dreading? How many others he can raise behind him? And even if he's little support amongst the other tribes, if he's crossed over the border into Ezirad he might be returning with an army to convince people by force.

Nijad and I spend some time mulling over the situation, but the overriding issue is to locate Abdul-Muhsi and to find out what the hell he's up to. There's not a lot of advice I can offer my brother as he's already got the same plans in place that I would have suggested.

After we've talked it to death and we realise we're going round in circles, Nijad takes his leave to go and visit with his very pregnant wife. He'll be going back to the Desert City in the morning; his work is too important, taking precedence even over family. An insurrection is the last thing we need.

Left alone I realise how I'm lucky to have him by my side. Briefly, I muse that four years ago I'd never have believed he'd come back from his playboy lifestyle and make his home in his native country, let alone become such a valuable right-hand man to the emir.

Returning to my paperwork, I catch up with the backlog that has built up during the day. Most of my time is taken up with people calling or visiting, assuming I'll always have the solution to their problems as though I'm some divine being rather than just a man. Alongside the interruptions, there are also numerous emails to answer and, before I met with Nijad, a late meeting with Sadiq, our new Minister of Finance, also helped to set me behind. So it's close to midnight before I'm finally able to put down the documents and close my laptop, at last, feeling I've done enough and my conscience allows me to leave for the night. Just a typical day in the life of an emir.

As I stand, stretching my tired muscles, rolling my neck to try to get the knots out, I recall how weary my father would often look. After walking in his shoes for four months, I'm coming to understand him a little more. Everyone wants a piece of you; everyone depends on you, and there's nowhere to hide.

My legs are stiff with sitting for so long. Knowing I won't be able to switch off and sleep unless I do something, but too tired to hit the gym, I decide I'll just walk to stretch my legs.

I leave my office, my guards following at a discreet distance, tracking my progress through the palace. I can hear them in radio contact, passing their responsibility along as I walk from one section to the next. Despite the fact I'm in my official residence, security is, and will remain tight, at least until we find out what the insurgents are up to and can make a realistic assessment of the risk.

The palace of Al Qar'ah is vast, and I get sufficient exercise by just treading the ancient corridors, keeping to the interior so I won't faze my protection by walking in the dark outside. I pace through the modern areas, the seat of government, into the habitable parts, and then come to the more abandoned areas which have become disused over time. I'm deep in thought and not sure or caring where I'm walking to. My feet move automatically, one in front of the other, propelling me along. I might be walking in circles for all I know or care.

I didn't want this role. Although primed from birth to follow in my father's footsteps it's a burden that, in today's world, is outdated and outmoded. How can one man have responsibility for a whole country? Why should I have the responsibility for the life and death of my subjects? How can anything I do be without question, however ridiculous my decree? The country's so old fashioned I could proclaim the sky is pink, and anyone who disagreed with me would do so at the risk of losing their head! Every decision rests with me, and that weight I carry means I can have no personal life nor can I be ruled by any emotion other than a love for my country.

I'm expected to procreate in such a way as to produce another clone to be trained from birth to be an absolute monarch. *Fuck!* Who'd want to be me? Perhaps I should just turn it over to Abdul-Muhsi—at least he wants the job. Then I could leave, go where I want, be who I want. But no, I can't even fucking think about that. I love my country, my fellow Amahadians. I couldn't abdicate and leave them with a religious zealot ruling over them. But fuck me, sometimes I wish I could.

Suddenly I look up, recognising my wanderings have brought me to the oldest parts of the palace and the original Sultan's suite of rooms, uninhabited since my great-grandfather's time. My subconscious must have driven me here. I had, of course, recently been considering

Cara's proposal so that could have influenced the route I'd taken. Oh well, I've come this far; I might as well explore. Pausing, thinking back, I don't think I've been this far into the palace since I was a child playing hide and seek with my brothers.

My interest spiked, I move forward into the suite, now unfurnished and with only flaking gold leaf on the walls giving a remaining hint of its former glory. Sparing just a quick glance into the empty rooms, I head for the door at the end of the hallway, my memory reminding me that behind it is a hidden stairway. Coming up to it I stop and pause, imagining times past. Where it leads is the hub of the magic that Cara wishes to embrace in her plans, but for me, is heritage and custom I'm being asked to despoil. Although, perhaps, it's well past time to put that part of our history behind us.

I stand for a moment, staring at the discreet entrance, knowing if I enter through the small, inconspicuous door it will take me to the lookout point where in times past the Sultan would sit, looking down on his harem below deciding on which concubine he would call to his bed that night. Having made his choice, he would summon a eunuch to bring his favourite to him.

Lucky him! My destiny is to be tied to just one woman with nothing that passes for choice in the matter. I'll be selecting my life partner based on little more than looks and breeding.

Damn it! Everything that I am loathes the position I've been put in. But to keep the peace I need to prove myself as a stud able to produce sufficient progeny to continue my line. *But will selling myself achieve the desired outcome?* If I was in a sombre mood before, I'm in an even blacker one now. As I stand in the sultan's suite, surveying the empty rooms that once were filled with such luxury, I slowly shake my head. I'm expected to live in the past but move Amahad into its future. I'm not a man, merely a pawn.

A guard hovers behind me. Having lived with the presence of such security all of my life I don't generally notice that I'm not alone, but tonight I have the need for solitude. It could well have been that desire which has drawn me to the small doorway in the wall. Making a decision I enter, closing the door behind me. Tradition dictates I will not be followed here.

Suddenly it dawns on me that I've never actually seen this part of the palace before. Only the Ruler was ever allowed to see his concubines, so up to four months ago the rooms below belonged to my father as emir, except for that short period when he turned them over to Nijad. But now that I've inherited the position the harem is mine. Seriously, fucking seriously, I'm going to have to decree the harem deconsecrated, or whatever the right word is, to even allow the workmen to enter to do the renovations. Until then, the only man allowed inside is me. Quickly I decide to take advantage of the one place in the palace where I can be guaranteed the privacy that tonight I seek.

I walk the two steps down to the peephole. Fuck, Cara was right; it's a shambles down there. Everything is crumbling away. For a moment my conscience gives me a pang of guilt; was this where we incarcerated my sister-in-law for weeks? It's hardly habitable! Although we had managed to set up one of the rooms, so it was just about able to be lived in, we hadn't provided much in the way of comfort. I suppose, at that point, thinking her a thief, keeping her in luxury was far from our minds. But even so, what a depressing place; tapestries fading and crumbling, walls threatening to topple over, the central feature, the bathing pool, empty and cracked; dust covering everything. I can't imagine why Cara's so enamoured of the place.

Closing my eyes for a second, I imagine how it might have been in its heyday, the women sleeping below, babies crying; children restless in their sleep, all the female members of the family and concubines of the monarch. At least I'm only going to be responsible for the one wife; I suppose I should be grateful for that!

When the soft cry first reaches my ears, my initial thought is that my overworked mind is hallucinating, my tired brain summoning up sounds from a long forgotten era. But when the moaning comes again, I realise this is no dream, and the sound I'm hearing is far from a cry of pleasure, but instead, one of distress. This is no fantasy conjured up by fatigue; this is real. My eyes flick open, and I lean over, looking down, right below me and can hardly believe my eyes. There, illuminated by a beam of moonlight slanting in from the outside is a woman, lying on the bed in the only room furnished and fit to live in. My brow furrows and creases as I recognise the form of the person responsible for restoring the harem, the woman who had never been far from my thoughts, but who I hadn't seen since the day I'd brought her here, Zoe Baker.

But why the fuck is she here? Surely we've provided her

with suitable accommodation elsewhere in the palace? Cara didn't expect her to live in the harem, did she? But the question why she might be sleeping in a concubine's cubicle beneath me loses significance as her cries get louder and more tormented, and I watch as she begins to thrash against the sheets. Night terrors. I'm only too well aware of those. I need to wake her.

With some urgency, I carefully descend the crumbling steps of the hidden stairway and enter the harem, crossing the open space swiftly to be by her side. There's a lamp beside the bed, and I light it, hoping the illumination might be enough to disturb her dreams, but if anything, she writhes more desperately, her hands held up as though warding someone away. My hand goes out to touch her shoulder when I notice something and still with my arm hovering in mid-air. It's the first time I've seen her arms bare; she always wears long sleeves, and now I understand why, and the sight brings a muffled curse from my lips. Fuck, now I have the opportunity to examine her wrist, I see it in its full glory and realise how awkwardly the bones have fused. The injury can't have been that long ago as it still looks a little red and painful. Why hadn't she had it taken care of properly? But then I recall the bastard she was running from and have no need to look any further for the reason. It would have been too risky for her to register at a hospital.

Moving my gaze up her arms and body more evidence of his cruelty comes into sight. Distinct cigarette burns pepper her limbs, and there's a silver scar at the top of her shoulder looping round from the back. Gritting my teeth, I suspect if I turn her over I'll find whip marks marring her skin. What kind of a monster is St. John Davies to hurt a woman in this way? It was one thing to hear about it, quite another to see the permanent testament to his viciousness that she'll carry with her for the rest of her life. There and then I make a vow; he is a dead man. The timing and method can be determined later, but he's not going to live to do this to anyone else ever again. No wonder she's having a nightmare. She might have gotten away from the man, but it's evident he still has a hold over in her dreams. My gut clenches with pity.

In the few moments I'd been absorbing her visible injuries, her mental anguish has worsened. She tosses this way and that as though trying to evade something or someone. The sounds she's emitting make me squirm. A wave of emotion floods through me, an overwhelming desire to protect her, heal her and keep her close. To never let her be hurt again, even in her dreams.

Completely forgetting who and what I am, clearing my throat I call out to her, "Zoe." Disregarding my resolve to distance myself from her, I use her first name as I address her softly. She doesn't hear me. "Zoe!" I call louder, but she's deep in the grip of her dreams. Reaching out my hand I gently shake her shoulder. She stills, opens her eyes and screams, the sound echoing off the walls. Her arms start flailing. She catches me hard across the face, and I rear back. My movement causes her to freeze.

"I'm sorry, I'm sorry! I'll do better!" She's still lost in nightmare land. Her face is tight, her body shaking. She's terrified. "Please don't hurt me again!" Her eyes are open, wide with terror. As they flick back and forth, I realise she's waking and trying to understand where she is.

"It's me, Kadar. It's I who should apologise; I woke you. But you very having a bad dream." I speak calmly, quietly, trying to calm her, one hand ruefully rubbing my face where she struck me. "I heard you, and I knew I needed to wake you up. You're safe: you're in Amahad, far away from that bastard who hurt you." I keep speaking, letting the words roll over her as she gradually comes to her senses. "You're safe, habiti. I won't let anything happen to you." Fuck, why did that endearment roll off my tongue? My love? What am I thinking? I don't know how that slipped out, or where it came from. Resolving to keep a tighter hold on my words, I trust her grasp of Arabic is poor.

She stares blankly, but as I continue talking, using as gentle a voice as I can, she gradually begins to focus on me with recognition in her eyes. But my presence doesn't have the immediate calming effect that I had hoped. "What are you doing here?" Her voice is little above a whisper. If anything it seems I'm scaring her further. Her chest rises and falls as her breaths come in short pants, but whether caused by residual fears from her dream, or my presence, I'm not sure.

To calm her I decide to stick to the truth, "To be honest, I don't know. I needed a place to be alone. Matters weigh heavy on me; sleep evades me." In those few words, I've told her more than I'd admit to anyone else.

She scoots up the bed looking flustered and apologetic, "I'm sorry I stayed here. I didn't want to interrupt your solitude. If you can give me a minute to dress, I'll go and leave you alone. I didn't realise you came to the harem." She makes as if to get off the bed.

"No, stay. I'd like the company." I realise I don't want her to go; suddenly seclusion is the last thing on my mind. "I don't usually come here; in fact, it's the first time I've ever visited this part of the palace. I was looking over Cara's proposal earlier, and it must have stuck in my mind. I was just idly walking the corridors and ended up here. I have a lot on my plate, Zoe, it's overwhelming at times. I'd like someone to talk to. And perhaps you'd like to have someone to converse with too. That was one hell of a nightmare you were having." When she rests back against the cushions and pillows at the top of the bed, I take it as the invitation.

"May I?" I indicate that I, too, want to sit on the bed. It's the only piece of furniture in the small room. She hesitates, and then shifts over leaving enough room between us, so we're not going to touch. Her evasive action doesn't go unnoticed, and I realise she is scared at just the thought of me or probably any man, being close to her in an intimate situation. Glancing at her for a moment, I grow even more concerned. She's still breathing so rapidly I'm worried she's heading towards a panic attack. I take charge quickly. "Look at me, Zoe. Look. At. Me." I wait until I have her attention. "Breathe with me."

She gives a little shake of her head, not understanding.

"Watch me. Breathe as I do." Exaggerating my actions, I slowly take a deep breath in and hold it, then let it out. I do it again. She focuses on me now, and just as I intended, begins to imitate my actions. Gradually her breathing slows into a more regular rhythm, and I see some of the tension seep out of her.

I reach over to get her the glass of water on the table by the bed. She immediately flinches and throws her arm up to protect her face.

"Easy, easy!" I still, completely motionless, "I'm only getting you a drink." I wait until she nods, and then pass her the water. Gratefully she takes a sip, and then another. Finished, she passes the glass back to me.

"Better?" As she nods, I shake my head, "He put you through hell and back, didn't he, habiti?"

She looks down at herself as if only just realising she's dressed only in her underwear, noticing that her injuries and scars for once are in plain view. "I'm sorry," she repeats, her voice full of shame and regret. Her hand reaches out for the sheet and uses it to cover her body.

"You're fucking sorry?" I can't help rasping out. "What the fuck are *you* sorry for?"

She seems to shrink into herself, "It's not pretty, is it? I'm sorry you had to see it."

"Ye Gods! You're sorry *I* had to see it? Fuck that, Zoe. I'm devastated that *you* had to suffer like you have." I throw my headdress off onto the floor and feel my expression growing cold and fierce. "I'm going to kill him for what he's done to you."

She gasps in air, shocked, and reaches out her hand to my arm, "No, Kadar, you can't."

I stare at her blankly, "Yes, I can. When, where, I can't promise you that. But it will be done. I want to fix it, so you never need to be scared again."

"Why? Why would you even care?"

I start. Gazing intently into her eyes, realising that I have no fucking idea why vengeance for her wounds has become so imperative, or where this desire for revenge has come from. I only know I can't deny it. As I take in the vision in front of me, I start to understand. I'd tried to stay away, but I failed. I just can't resist; there's just something about this woman that calls to the man in me.

Her bed hair, which looks more attractive to me at the moment than that of someone freshly groomed, falls over her face, and I put out my hand to push it back. As she starts, I pause my hand in mid-air and then move it again. She stays still as I push the strands back, and I feel a small victory. *She let me touch her.* A stirring in my loins tells me I want to touch her a whole lot more. I realise I haven't answered her question. I decide to be honest with her, and with myself.

"I care, Zoe, I started to care the moment I met you. When you walked into my office wearing that ridiculous disguise I knew I had to help you. I assure you," I pause and chuckle, "I don't make a habit of employing someone with no name, no proof of identity or qualifications. I just knew I had to keep you safe." *And,* I add silently, what I could never admit aloud. *I wanted to keep you near me.*

"Kadar!" Shocked she shuffles over the bed, increasing the distance between us. "What exactly do you want from me?"

She's alone, she's almost naked, and she's in my harem. All at once I realise she's scared. And she's right to be. It would be so easy to ease my throbbing cock in her warm depths, to gain the release that I seem to need each time I see her. I turn my head away. Sitting up and leaning forwards I cup my chin in my hands, rubbing the stubble that indicates I'm in need of a shave while wondering what the fuck am I doing? Why am I even here? Why am I staying, talking to her? I can't use her; she's not a quick fuck, not a one-night stand. I could never do that to her. But I can't start a relationship either. Fuck, I've no option but to pick out my wife like selecting an item from a catalogue. I'm not like an ordinary man; however much I'd wish to be, I can't have a fling with her to see where it might take us. My future is mapped out.

Trying to keep a tight rein on myself, I offer her the little that I can, "I worry about you, I care about your safety. I want to be your friend. And I think you need one of those, habiti." That's the third time the endearment has come from my lips unbidden.

After a moment's silence, while she digests my words, I hear a deep sigh. "A friend would be nice, Kadar. I've not had a friend for a very long time. He stopped me seeing them, stopped me calling them." Her voice hardens, "He threatened to hurt any of my friends if I didn't stay in line, and he wasn't joking. One of my friends is in a wheelchair because of me." I hear the catch in her voice and don't need to turn around to see the tears in her eyes, but I do, and again I raise my hand to her face, and she lets me brush them away without hesitation.

"You did nothing to your friend, habiti. Whatever happened, that bastard was entirely responsible."

"But it was me who trusted him…"

I shake my head emphatically. "He played you. He knew exactly what he was doing."

"I don't trust anyone Kadar. I can't, not anymore. Because I can't trust my judgement. And I don't want to make friends, in case I put them in danger."

I swing my legs up onto the bed and pull myself up beside her. We're both sitting with our backs against the cushions, still with inches of bed between us. I put out my arm and put it behind her, my hand first hovering then settling gently on her shoulder, pleased, this time, she doesn't start or cringe. I pull her closer to me. "Well, I'm your friend, and you're not putting me in danger. Or anyone else here. St John-Davies doesn't know you're in Amahad, and he's not going to find out. Anyone who knows who and where you are, I trust with my life. So don't be afraid to make friends, Zoe." I'm pleased when she relaxes her head on my shoulder. "And what about Cara? You're getting along well with her, aren't you?"

"I like Cara," The pause tells me there's more to come, "But I envy her. She has everything I ever wanted, a loving husband, and she's going to have a baby."

"You'll have that one day." I take her hand and squeeze it. And then know I'm going to have to put her straight if she has any thought of having that with me. Taking a deep breath, I begin to bare my soul. "Zoe, I didn't expect to be the emir, not for another twenty years or more. I was going to take my time, find the wife I wanted, the person to be by my side when I eventually came into this role, but things haven't worked out the way I planned."

She listens intently as I continue, "It's not easy being the ruler. There are certain expectations on me. I need to keep this country together, and that means sacrificing my own hopes and dreams."

Now it's her turn to press her fingers to mine, giving me physical support. My head bows down to my chest, and I shake it gently before I continue, "The tribal leaders want a union between Amahad and one of the neighbouring states, or with one of their own tribes. They want me to enter into a political marriage to strengthen our ties for the good of the country. A union that they approve of." I swallow, and tell her the rest, "I have agreed."

She places her small hand under my chin, and gently turns my head to face her, "Your marriage will be an arranged one? When, Kadar?"

It's impossible to tell what she's thinking. "Soon. Oh, Zoe, I don't want to go through with it, but I haven't a choice. Unless I want to abdicate or risk civil war. Anything I can do to keep the peace in Amahad, I must do." I give a small grin, "I told you, I needed a friend, didn't I? I can't speak to anyone else about my feelings— not even my brothers. With everyone else, I keep up the front that I'm already married to my country, and would do anything for her."

A smile comes to her lips as she whispers, "I'm honoured, Kadar. And I'm here, whenever you want to talk."

Talk. I would be lying to her and myself if I said that is all I wanted from her, but it's all I can offer, and probably all she wants to give. She's just escaped from an abusive relationship, after all. But here I am, lying on a bed next to an desirable woman and my cock, luckily hidden by my robes, is throbbing, trying to insist I do something about it.

I let my eyes roam her body, barely concealed by the sheet she's covered it with. Unbidden the thought comes to me of how I'd like to see her bound in my ropes. Then, realising the dangerous direction my thoughts are taking, know I have to make a move and leave. Before temptation overwhelms me.

I allow myself one last touch to her beautiful face, "Zoe," I breathe.

CHAPTER 18
Zoe

Abruptly the emir pulls away from me, standing and walking to the end of the bed. He seems deep in thought, and I fiddle with the finely embroidered linen beneath my hands, wondering what he's thinking.

He gives a snorted laugh as though he mocking himself then turns back to me, holding out his hand's palms up. "I've nothing to offer you except my friendship and protection. But I'd like you to accept both." After staring at me for a moment, he continues and repeats, "Friendship, Zoe. That's all I want from you." He picks up his headdress from the floor where he threw it. "It's late—or early, whichever way you look at it. You need your rest. You should sleep now." Walking back to the bed, he leans over and gives me a chaste kiss on the top of my head. "In the morning I'll make sure the paperwork is completed so you can get workmen in and start the restorations. Anything you need doing, let me know and I will arrange it." He holds up his hand to stop my protest. "And if you want to speak to me, at any time, about anything, tell your guard, and we'll arrange it. I mean it, Zoe, there's no need for you to feel alone."

There's nothing I can do but to thank him.

He smiles, nods, and then gives me a courteous bow and

exits via the hidden stairway. My professional interest sparks. The Sultan's entrance!

For a moment I lie stunned, unable to believe the turn of events and my conversation with the emir. Suddenly I start to chuckle; realising Kadar had had no idea I would be sleeping in the harem tonight. *Shit, I hadn't planned on it myself.* Well, I certainly got the atmosphere I wanted to soak up. A hearty laugh breaks out of me as I wonder at the shock Kadar must have thought to have found a woman ready and waiting in his harem. I'd love to have seen his face before he had to wake me from the nightmare of my past. Idly I wonder about the coincidence of us both being drawn to this place tonight.

I giggle to myself. I never imagined the emir would pay a visit while I was asleep in his harem, Just like the Sultan with a concubine of old. *Huh!* I smile. But without the sex, of course, and however much his closeness made certain parts of me awaken and throb, I know now that's completely off the agenda. Kadar is an honourable man, his future is pre-ordained, and I'll have no part of it. But to have him as a friend? I can't help but be proud he feels able to confide in me.

The room seems full of the scent of sandalwood, the odour that I'll forever associate with him. He might have gone, but his presence still surrounds me. Tired, I soon fall back asleep, but Ethan doesn't return to haunt me. Somehow Kadar has banished him away.

＊＊＊＊

It's mid-morning when Cara visits the harem, proudly waving a document in her hand. It's in Arabic, so she interprets it for me. Kadar has already made good on his promise, and as emir has rescinded his rights to the harem. Although it means we can now engage workman to get going on the renovations, part of me is sad that Kadar no longer has his special place that he can truly call his own. Some of the magic already seems to have gone. Instead, it's replaced by his sister-in-law's enthusiasm. Cara's so upbeat and passionate about how the work can now proceed, that I soon get caught up with deciding where we're going to start first.

An hour or so later we've worked out a plan of action, and she leaves me alone. As I walk around with renewed purpose, noting what preparation needs to be done and making detailed notes for contractors to follow, I take a moment to enjoy the peace that will all too soon be shattered with the sounds of drills and hammering.

Writing up the specifications takes me the rest of the day. Asif brings me food so I can continue uninterrupted, and I warn him I'll be staying late this evening, wanting to get what I've started finished. Although I offer to find my own way back to my accommodation, no longer seeing the necessity for a full-time guard, Asif tells me he'll return later on and wait outside. I don't see the need, as Kadar has said, Ethan hasn't a clue where I am, and isn't going to find out. But the thought they're taking no chances with my safety is a comforting one.

I'm not planning on staying in the harem tonight, but the hours and minutes seem to go by so fast, and I've still not completed everything I wanted to do. Now we've got the go ahead I'm almost as impatient as Cara to contact contractors and start getting quotes. So I'm just wrapping up the final spec when the golden doors to the harem open. I glance up, expecting Asif be checking to see whether I'm ready to go, but instead find myself staring into the face of the emir.

"Kadar!" I'm genuinely pleased to see him.

"You're still hard at work, then?"

I wave my tablet at him, "Just finishing up. Once I've tidied my notes up Cara, and I will be able to begin the process to award contracts."

His eyes narrow, "You work too hard."

I laugh, "Work? Is that what this is? I'm enjoying myself too much, Kadar, to call it that."

Shaking his head, he comes across to me, "I wish I had your enthusiasm for everything I do."

"Hard day?" I feel sorry for him.

He studies me for a moment then, seeming to come to a decision, removes his headdress and lightly takes my arm, leading me across to the bed, the only place where we can sit in comfort. As if it's now become our custom, I sit on it and scoot up until I'm leaning against the headboard, then he does the same, placing himself beside me. When he reaches his arm over my shoulder, I have no qualms sitting forwards so he can place it behind me. I lean back against him, allowing myself to enjoy the comfort.

"I envy you, the work you're doing here. You'll be able to see it coming together, just as you planned."

"Huh!" I laugh, "I do hope it all goes to plan."

He gives a brief smile, then runs his hand over his face. "I have a strategy for Amahad, I want to modernise, to make sure all the population has access to good schools and medical facilities, but with so many obstacles in my way, it's hard to see how I'll be able to make it all come together."

"You see the pool, over there?" I point outside the cubicle and wait for his nod. "I envision a beautiful mosaic, but I don't have the skills to do it myself. I have to rely on the artisans we're employing to translate my vision into reality."

"You're saying that to achieve my ends I have to rely on other people?"

"I don't know enough to advise you, Kadar, but you can't do everything yourself."

"You're right, Zoe, but it's hard to delegate, to release control. But I'm trying. I'm taking the first steps."

For the next half hour, he tells me of his idea to put in place an elected government, almost bouncing ideas off of me about how it's going to work. I relax against him, proud he's sharing his hopes and dreams with me. *Zoe Baker, advisor to the emir, who would ever have thought it?*

Time's getting on, so soon he picks up his headdress, and takes his leave. I do likewise, finding the ever patient Asif waiting for me outside the golden doors. But I feel lighter than I have done for months as I make my way back to the little house I'm really starting to think of as home.

For the next couple of days, I'm run off my feet, showing potential contractors around and, with Asif's interpretation skills, explaining the work involved. It's hard and frustrating work. Some of the technical terms are beyond even Asif's quite large vocabulary, and miming is often required for me to explain the standards I wish them to follow. But at last, they seem satisfied and leave, ready to prepare their quotes. I'm hopeful work can begin within the next month.

With little more to do at the moment in the interior of the harem, I at last turn my thoughts to the garden. And that's where I am when Kadar finds me this evening, sitting on the edge of the broken fountain, lost in a daydream and enjoying the cooler air after the heat of the day, he approaches so quietly he startles me, and I almost fall off my perch.

Reaching out his strong hand, he steadies me, "Careful." His grin makes him look younger.

"Sorry, I was miles away." Standing up, I brush the dust from my clothes.

"No, sit. I just needed a break. It's pleasant out here." As he speaks, he looks around him, "You've got your work cut out for you here, too."

"It will soon come together. I'll be able to get my hands dirty; it's work I enjoy."

He pulls my left hand towards him and pushes up my sleeve. As he exposes my twisted wrist, I try to move it away. He doesn't let go, and instead, his fingers gently caress the scars. "Can you work like this?"

This time, I wrench it out of his grasp, "I assure you I'm perfectly able to do my job." I snap at him, my weakness not something I want to be reminded of.

A quick shake of his head shows I've misunderstood

him, "I'm not criticising you, Zoe, I'm concerned. I'd like to get a doctor to look at it for you."

"No, Kadar, you've done too much for me already. If I go through an operation, it might put me out of action for a while. I can cope, for now. Maybe it's something I'll look into later."

His eyes meet mine with a searching gaze, "I hate that you have that reminder of him."

I huff, "I've enough other mementos without that."

Another pointed look reminds me he saw them that first night in the harem. I relent, "I'll think about the offer, Kadar, just not right now."

Thankfully he leaves the subject alone, and we sit in comfortable silence for a while, listening to the birdsong as the colourful creatures flit around, preparing to settle for the night. The air is tinged with the perfume of the cultivated gardens just beyond the harem walls, making me impatient to start the planting here.

Before long, I pluck up the courage to ask something I've been wondering about. "Kadar, your bride, how will she be chosen for you? Have you any say in the matter?"

A quick glance, his eyebrows raised, shows me he didn't expect the question. For a moment I wonder whether he's going to answer, then, with a sigh and the now customary removal of his headdress which seems to signify he's the man, and not the emir, he starts to speak. As he tells me about the ball that's been arranged, that his advisors are compiling a list of likely candidates from whom he'll be expected to choose his mate for life, I find myself full of compassion for the man who's prepared to give up his happiness for the sake of his country. And I can't help a little voice inside me that wonders what I'd have to do to get myself on that list. Then I shake myself. *For fuck's sake, Zoe, there's no chance in hell of that, you haven't the right qualifications. If you weren't good enough for Ethan, you're a million miles away from being good enough for the emir.*

And in any event, lined up with a bevy of beauties, I wouldn't have a chance of being the one of his choice.

CHAPTER 19
Kadar

Darkness falls around us. I can't imagine what Zoe is thinking, but she's gone very quiet. Although I'm glad I explained about the ball, got it out there in the open and made clear where my duty lies, I'm sure that as a Western woman she finds it hard to understand. I only hope it doesn't change things between us as I'd miss being able to come and spend time with her.

I've always known my marriage would have to be the right one for my country, even when I'd expected to have a wider choice. So I've avoided getting involved with a woman for that reason; not wanting to raise expectations which couldn't be fulfilled, instead having brief liaisons in the BDSM clubs I frequent abroad. So to be able to sit and talk, to confide in someone, is a luxury for me. I'm drawn to Zoe, drawn to come and seek her out in this place I still, for the moment at least, am able to think of as mine. I enjoy just being with her, even in the moments when we just sit in silence, appreciating the peace of the harem, able to let my guard down around her. I find myself relishing every moment I can steal to be with her.

I can't deny my physical attraction to her, that it's the fullness in my loins which makes me come to the harem, as well as the desire to talk. But conversation will have to suffice, even while it's slowing killing me. I can't pretend we can ever be anything other than friends, however intense my desire I wish it could be more.

I'm attracted to her body, but I'm also charmed by everything about her. I've told her my secrets; now it's time for her to share those she keeps hidden.

Turning to face her I take her hand in mine, and gently squeeze it, "Zoe, I want to know what happened. Talk to me. Tell me how it started and how you got caught in St John-Davies' clutches. How did you meet him?"

She gives me a sharp look, and briefly I'm left wondering whether she's going to say anything at all. I won't push if she doesn't want to tell me, but I believe it will be beneficial for her to share, rather than to keep everything bottled up inside. I have my doubts she's ever told anyone the full story.

As I watch, a tear appears at the corner of her eye, and she almost angrily brushes it away. Then, once she starts, it all comes tumbling out.

"I was working for him, restoring a garden. He asked me out. Oh, he was the perfect gentleman. Handsome, sexy and wealthy. What more could a girl ask for?" she shudders disparagingly. "I was so stupid. I was swept off my feet—thought I'd found the love of my life. Especially when he asked me to move in with him. Now," she pauses to wipe away another tear, and shudders, "Now I believe it was the thought of the man and what he could offer me more than the man himself. I think I was in love with the idea, not with him. So what does that make me? Fatuous at the very least. Greedy? A fortune seeker?" She glances at me then pointedly looks down towards her dainty feet, "I didn't feel like that at the time; I convinced myself I liked him, thought I'd be able to love him. He didn't want to jump straight into bed with me, he said he wanted me for me, not my body. I thought that was sweet."

"That alone should have told you he was an idiot!" I don't know what made me interrupt her, but looking at the woman sitting beside me I can't believe how anyone could keep their hands off of her, seeing I was having such great difficulty myself.

She throws me a quick, timid smile, acknowledging the implied compliment, but I can see I've embarrassed her. "When at last we, er… were intimate it wasn't spectacular which I put it down to my inexperience." Another squint towards me as though to make sure I'm not offended by this level of detail, and then shrugs, "To be honest, it was much on a par with my previous encounters, so I didn't think anything was particularly wrong when the earth didn't move. But as time went on I realised the intimacy was for him, not me. And he soon started taking me when and where he wanted, whether I was ready or not."

I hadn't missed the point about her inexperience, but what was more important was his cruelty as I realise she's admitting he'd raped her, repeatedly. I see red and snarl, "Why didn't you leave?"

Instead of answering she looks out into the blackness now surrounding the gardens. I know there's nothing she can make out in the dark. Instead, she seems to be turning in on herself. Gentling my voice, stroking my fingers over the hand I'm still holding, I instruct her, "Talk to me."

With a sad little shake of her head, she continues, "I've never told anyone the whole story, Kadar. It makes me look like a first class idiot. I didn't even go into details with my best friend, Sophie."

"You are certainly not an idiot!" I'm unable to keep the bite of anger out of my voice. "Zoe, it might help to get it all off your chest. Let me share your burden. I promise nothing you can say to me with make me judgemental or change my view of you."

Whether it's the time of night, the magic of the harem, or my promise, but after a few seconds to gather her thoughts, she resumes her story. As I listened to her tell me how he started to destroy her self-respect and slowly began to control her life, I cursed quietly, remembering the clothes I'd bought her and her protest on the plane.

"Zoe, that's not what I wanted to do."

She puts her hand on mine; I relish the fact she's made contact, "Yes, you did, Kadar. You chose what you wanted me to wear."

I have to fix her misassumption, "I chose what I thought *you'd* like to wear, habiti. There would have been a very different selection if I'd only given you what I would like to see you in." I turn and wink at her. *Me, fucking winking? The effect this woman has on me!* "I asked a personal shopper to select appropriate clothing for the climate—I'm afraid I get very little time to go women's shopping."

I hear a little giggle, fuck, it's a beautiful sound, and I suspect she's picturing me walking around a department store choosing her lingerie. Shit! I shouldn't have thought of that; I turn a little to my side, so she doesn't see the physical evidence of the effect she's causing.

As she resumes her sorry tale I have to make great effort not to show my ever increasing anger as she proceeds to explain how he isolated her from her friends leaving her no one to turn to for support."

Her hand still touching mine, I slowly turn my palm so I can curl my fingers around hers. "What about your parents? Zo? Family?"

Her eyes open wide and she recoils away. "Don't call me Zo! That's what he called me!" She shudders in disgust, and I file that vital bit of information away, not wanting to upset her again.

But a weird feeling inside of me makes me want to come up with a name for her that is mine, and only mine, "Okay," I wait a second before adding, "Zee."

I'm the emir; I hold the fate of my nation in my hand, but I sit here, holding my breath as I wait for her reaction. When she turns to me with a small smile and a quick nod of her head, I feel like I've won the jackpot.

"I never knew my father; my parents didn't marry." She breathes in sharply, and pauses, throwing a quick glance my way to gauge my reaction. I remained impassive, whatever her background it's only served to make her the woman she is today. "Ethan hated that I was a bastard, and concocted a story for me to tell if anyone ever asked about my background."

"What about your mother?"

"Well, yes," she draws in a deep breath, "She's on husband number six now. She got a taste for matrimony when she didn't like being a single mum. We haven't been very close for years."

Again I clasp her hand tighter for a moment to show my support.

"Once I'd left home and got settled she went to live in the south of France—she enjoyed the heat and scenery, said it gave her inspiration for her artwork. So she wasn't nearby when things went bad. Ethan disapproved of her because of her number of marriages and dissuaded me from contacting her. We didn't have the mother and daughter relationship where we text or ring all the time in any event, but eventually he stopped me having any communication with her at all. The one time I disobeyed, I learned not to do it again the hard way."

"Habiti…"

"I can't believe how stupid I was!"

Seeing her anger directed in on herself, I have to put her right, "He was a con man and very good at it. You were his victim, and he played you. There's no need for you to feel guilty." At least the hatred that's burning inside me for the man who hurt her is causing my arousal to fade. "When did he start abusing you?"

She huffs a laugh, but there's no mirth in it. "Looking back, it began from day one. I tried to change my behaviour to what I thought he was looking for, but whatever I did was never good enough. I was always an outsider with his friends and the way he lived his life; we had nothing in common. As I couldn't conform, he made me feel ignorant."

I feel her growing tense, her fingernails digging into my

hand. I don't complain, not wanting to interrupt her.

"The first time he was violent it was because I dared to contradict him. He was so much more worldly than me; I used just to agree with whatever he said. We were dressing to go out; he said something; I disputed it. I got a fist in my stomach. I was so surprised I didn't know what to think. He ignored it, and I went along to the dinner with him as arranged just because I didn't know what else to do. It was a couple of weeks before he did anything else.

"When it got really bad, I did try to escape. I hadn't made any plans, just knew I had to get away. I waited until he'd left for work, and then I got in my car and drove. I went to see Sophie, and she greeted me like, well, a long lost friend." She smiles slightly at the memory, and then unbidden tears start to fall down her cheeks as she explained in gory detail just exactly what that fucking man had done to punish Zee from trying to escape. He'd put her friend in a wheelchair.

She starts crying in earnest, and to my surprise shifts over towards me, "Kadar, my best friend, is out there, disabled for life and it's all my fault! And I don't even know how she's doing!" I put my arm around her, hugging her close. It's a non-sexual contact; we can both feel that, and something she badly needs at this point.

"Does she need protection now?" I'll do anything I can to take away her pain.

"I don't know!" The frustration is pouring out of her. "When I finally escaped, I met a man who helped me, and I desperately need to discover whether Ethan got to him too. But, there was this mountain of a man, and Josh—the one who helped me—sent him to make sure Sophie was okay. And then there's Ida as well who sheltered me. I need to find out, Kadar, but I don't know how! I worry every day that he might be hurting someone close to me to get me back. I don't know how to find out if they're safe!" she ends on a wail.

I pull her even tighter into me. "I do," I tell her firmly, a plan already forming in my mind, "Tomorrow you give me all the details I need to get them traced, and we'll find out. Your mother, too. You'll be able to talk to them very soon. I promise you. And if they need protection then I'll arrange it." With my free hand, I tilt her face up, forcing her to look into my eyes. "You're not alone now, habiti. Lean on me."

CHAPTER 20
Zoe

You're not alone! Lean on me! I go so still, for a moment. Letting out the breath, I hadn't even realised I'd been holding as a long sigh, I hear his words echoing through me. I'm no longer the innocent girl who takes things at face value.

"Why would you want to help me? You've given me a job, brought me out of Ethan's reach. Why go out of your way to do more?" I know I sound ungrateful and suspicious, but it's important to protect myself better than I did last time. Ethan seemed so plausible at first, so excellent at acting a role he should have had an actor's Union card. Why should Kadar be any different?

I shudder. I can't deny my physical attraction to the emir, that his closeness arouses me, but his dominance scares me. The talks we've had here, in the harem, have brought us closer as friends, but if I accept any more of his help, then I'll become dependent on another man. And what might he ask of me in return?

It's as if he's able to read me, as I go to pull away he holds me a second longer and then releases me. "No strings, Zee. I promise you."

I can't believe him, can I? All the damage Ethan caused to my self-esteem no longer allows me to take anything at face value. "Kadar!" The plea is wrenched from me, "Be honest with me. What do you want from me?"

"Be honest? You want me to be honest?" The moon has risen so I can see his features clearly; his face twists as though he's tortured. He drags his hand over his shortly cropped hair. *I wish I could do that!*

"You want honesty? Zee, I'm trying to be honourable here. I've told you my situation, I can't take this any further, it's not fair to start anything with you when I've got commitments to fulfil. But honestly? Zee, you're a beautiful woman. No," he shakes his head at my quick denial, "Believe it's the truth. You're beautiful, inside and out. It's so fucking hard to control myself around you when all I want to do is to hold you, touch you, kiss you. The things I want to do to you." Now he puts both hands on his head and sweeps them down. "Fuck, I don't even know if you have the same feelings for me, and I don't want to fucking know. The only principled thing I can offer you is my friendship. And friends look after each other. Let me help you, Zee. Let me in. In some small way, in the only way I can, let me be part of your life."

* * * *

Two days have passed since that night in the harem and Kadar's impassioned declaration. Forty-eight hours where I've tried to come to terms with the fact that Kadar admitted he wants me as much as I want him. And the unfairness of it all that there is, even if I could summon up the courage, there's nothing we can do about it. I've taken to leaving the harem early each evening, not sure what to say to him if he tries to see me again, and I believe he's feeling awkward to as neither does he seek me out. He's offered me friendship, but it's only a cloak, and underneath both of us want more than that.

To avoid meeting him, I wrote the information he'd requested on my friends and mother in a note Asif promised to deliver. I couldn't trust myself to give it to him personally. If I see him, now knowing how he feels, it would be all too easy to do something I might regret. So I spend my time immersed in the details of the restoration, wanting to create something to the best of my ability as a substitute for my affection. When I'm long gone, something will be left of me here in his palace. Part of myself.

I sit so engrossed in sketching out my latest ideas for the harem garden that when Asif appears with the summons to the emir's office, it comes as a surprise. My gut clenches at the thought of seeing Kadar again, seeing the man I'm having great difficulty putting out of my mind. But an invitation from the emir is impossible to ignore. And the thought of meeting him in his official office, away from our special place is daunting.

In the magical atmosphere of the harem anything seems possible, but in the cold light of day, I wonder how I could even think of accepting something even as simple as an innocent friendship from such a great man. He's got a whole country to run; he's no time to be my friend. Thanks to Ethan I'm used to mingling with moneyed people and the rich and famous, but I never fitted into that world, my social ineptitude always an opportunity for 'correction.' Kadar is royalty, and that's a whole different level again. As I walk the corridors almost with trepidation, I become nervous. *Why has he asked to see me?*

The emir's assistant rises as Asif brings me to the antechamber. With a smile, I recognise Richard, the man I'd met at the embassy in London. Having acknowledged my presence with a nod, Richard then goes over to knock on a large ornate door, opens it, and then waves me straight in and makes a brief introduction. "Zoe Baker, Your Excellency!"

Kadar steps forward and takes my hands in his, "Welcome, Zoe. Come in and have a seat." He uses my proper name, not the pet name he gave me. It's a greeting for a friend and appropriate for a formal meeting. With those words and the welcoming expression on his face he simultaneously puts me at ease while causing my heart to beat faster. I'd almost convinced myself I could ignore the effect he had on me. I was wrong.

As he leads me over to a conference table next to the windows, I notice there's already a man sitting there. I look quizzically at Kadar, waiting for an introduction. He doesn't disappoint.

"This is Zoe Baker," Kadar addresses the stranger before turning to me, "And Zoe, let me introduce you to Ben Carter. He's the senior partner of Grade A Security based in England."

The man introduced as Ben gets to his feet and reaches out his hand. As I shake it, I realise this must be Sean's boss. His grip is firm, his hand dry and when I glance at his face I see a confident, handsome man in his early forties. He releases my hand but cocks his head to one side as though assessing me.

"Come, let us sit. Ben, would you like to update Zoe on what you've discovered?" Kadar interrupts our greeting.

The conference table is large, but the three of us just use one end. It's comfortable as there's sufficient space between us so as not to be cramped, but on the other hand, intimate enough for a serious conversation. Kadar sits at the head with Ben opposite him. I watch as the man from Grade A opens his laptop, taking a moment to log into his systems before he starts to speak, first clearing his throat with a small cough.

His eyes flick towards Kadar, then back to his screen, finally settling on me. "After you left St John-Davies, Zoe, all hell broke loose. You covered your tracks extremely well, and I must say I'm very impressed. I think you could teach my people a thing or two about how keeping a low profile."

I shrug, brushing off the compliment which I'm certain is an exaggeration. "It was simply a matter of survival. And by then I knew what resources Ethan has at his disposal. After my first attempt, he'd boast and list the various ways he could have caught up with me. Unwittingly he helped me to escape by telling me what to avoid."

Ben nods, "Know thy enemy, as they say. It obviously worked for you, Zoe. He's a very powerful man, with powerful connections. And heaven knows the systems he's able to hack into as his company is one of the primary security system suppliers in the UK."

"That's why I avoided CCTV cameras like the plague."

"You did well." He smiles at me appreciatively, but I don't take it as praise. If he'd caught up with me, I knew Ethan wouldn't risk me running a third time, but still his approval gives me a warm feeling.

He glances at me curiously, "Did Ethan ever mention any previous girlfriend to you, Zoe?" As he asks the question, he calls up something on his laptop.

I think for a moment, my brow creasing. "No, in fact, we avoided the subject of any prior relationships. Neither of us were virgins. I suppose I didn't want to know, and neither did he."

Ben turns the laptop around to face me. Kadar leans across so he can see it too. On the screen is a picture of a pretty girl, not unlike myself. She has blonde hair, nearly the same shade but slightly longer than mine and her complexion is also fair. Her eyes are blue, just like my own. She's smiling at the camera as if she's happy to be having her photo taken. I raise my eyebrows, quizzically.

"Her name was Clara Fowler," Ben answers the question I was about to ask.

"Was?" Kadar interjects, quicker than I at catching onto the past tense Ben had used.

"I'm afraid so. Two years ago she was found dead in a canal. I'm sorry to say there's evidence she'd been subjected to some fairly substantial abuse over a period of time." He pauses for a moment, wiping his hand across his eyes as if it was hard for him to relay the details.

"There's more, isn't there?" I'm not sure I want to hear it but feel I need to.

"Yes, Zoe, there is. It looks like she was pregnant at the time of her death, and a brutal, amateur abortion procedure had been performed, certainly not by any qualified medical professional, presumably to remove any evidence of DNA. The evidence points to that being the cause of death. She bled out."

I gasp and cover my mouth. As I shudder Kadar reaches over and puts a comforting hand on my arm. He glares at Ben, "Fuck, Ben! And you're telling us this, why?"

"Because before Zoe, Clara was known to be Ethan's live in girlfriend for some months before her disappearance."

"Surely that made him a suspect in her death?" Kadar asks with a perplexed his expression.

Trying hard to get the circumstances of Clara's demise out of my mind, I give a snort of mirthless laughter. "Ethan's Teflon coated and can wriggle out of anything, Kadar."

Ben dips his head, showing he agrees. "What Zoe says is true. In fact, all of the evidence, which was probably planted, suggests she had left him, he says amicably, a couple of months before her death. In truth, she appeared to disappear off the face of the earth. No friends or family had seen her, and likewise, all of Ethan's household staff denied her being in his mansion during that period."

"All the staff except Hargreaves go home at night. And that mansion's so massive she could have been hidden away from them by day. There's a whole wing that's closed up and unused."

"Who's Hargreaves?"

I answer Kadar, "Ethan's driver come bodyguard. And a sadistic bastard."

"He touched you?" The question comes out as a growl.

"Oh yes," I look at him pleadingly; I don't want to say more. My mind is racing over something I remember only too well, making me realise I escaped only just in time. The last time Ethan had taken me he hadn't worn a condom. Was that because he didn't care if I got pregnant too? Because my days were already numbered? I grow cold, and a shiver runs down my spine.

"What does Grade A think happened?" Kadar directs the question to Ben, but dark eyes rest on me, at first steely then softening. He understands that some of the details are still too hard to bring into the open, particularly in front of a stranger. He gets back to the point, turning his attention back to Ben.

With a sigh, Ben continues, "All conjecture, of course, but a plausible explanation, given the man in question, is that Clara was treated like Zoe, gradually isolated from friends and family, and then abused. But in her case, she must have fallen pregnant. Now a man like Ethan wouldn't want that—a child from a temporary lover who would have a legitimate claim to his estate. Our assumption is he hid her away somewhere. It wouldn't have been difficult for a man of his means to do, and as you say, Zoe, it could even have been in his house. God knows what she went through while he was having his fun with her. Until she died."

"Fun? *Fun?*" Kadar gets to his feet; his hand slashes through the air in disgust. "For fuck's sake, why is this man still breathing? If he were on Amahadian soil, he'd be worm food by now." He turns away, mumbling to himself, "For fuck's sake, this is outrageous."

"I've told both of you this because you mustn't underestimate him."

"I think Zoe already knew that!" Kadar sounds angry; he throws a furious look at the man from Grade A. "Was it necessary to go into details?"

Ben is unrepentant, "Yes, I believe it was, for two reasons. Firstly, Zoe has to understand that Ethan will not rest until he finds her, he's not a man who likes loose ends, and doesn't like anyone to beat him. And secondly, she's right to be worried about her friends, and her mother. She must continue to have no contact with them. At all."

A cry escapes my lips, even though I tried to suppress it, drawing the attention of the two men. "But I need to know my mother's okay. And Sophie. Oh my God, what's happened to them? If Ethan's that desperate and dangerous, he'll have gone after them trying to get information about me. What am I going to do?" My hands go to my face, rubbing and pushing at my cheeks in my frustration. Had I been selfish running away? Had I just caused trouble for those close to me? "And what about the mechanic, Josh? He *helped* me! And Ida!"

I feel Kadar move behind me, as he leans over, puts his hands lightly on my shoulders, and begins to massage my neck. "What news have you got for her?" Although he's comforting me, his attention is still on the other man. I lean into his touch, welcoming it, making me realise that we had indeed crossed a bridge that night in the harem.

Ben ignores the over-familiar actions of the Amahadian ruler, instead again consulting his laptop. "As soon as you gave me the details I got a team onto it." He glances over to me, "You've no need to worry. Your mother is well. St John-Davies is having her watched, of course, but we managed to get a message through to her when she visited her solicitor's office letting her know you were safe. She didn't want to know where you are, Zoe. Ethan has already paid her a couple of visits, and made threats against her and her husband, but in the end, he had to accept she had nothing to tell him. I'm sure he'll keep an eye on her, though; he'll suspect you won't be able to resist making contact with her sooner or later, so you have to continue to avoid doing that for now. Oh, and we're keeping a close eye on Ida, but apparently, the message got successfully delivered that she didn't want you to tell her where you were going, so it looks like she's fallen off his radar. Ethan might be dangerous, but he's not stupid. He won't waste time on anything if it doesn't help further his cause. And in this case, that's to find you."

Even though I try to stay one hundred percent tuned into the conversation, a niggling thought at the back of my mind questions why my mother visited a solicitor. *She couldn't be divorcing number six, could she?* I shut down that notion and give all my concentration back to the main topic. "It's already been months since I left him, Ben. Surely he must give up soon?"

He shakes his head, grimly, "He's a tenacious bastard. It will be a very long time if ever before he lets this go. It's become a game with him, and he doesn't like to lose." He stares at the screen in front of him, "Now, your friend Sophie has disappeared."

"*What?*" I yell, interpreting his words at their very worst.

"What the fuck, Ben?" Kadar is angry on my behalf.

Ben looks sheepish, "Sorry, sorry." He holds up his hand, "I didn't mean it that way. She's perfectly safe. Sean went to the garage and met Josh. It seems that the mechanic didn't raise any red flags for Ethan, so he didn't get a visit. But his colleague, a Mr Adam Horseman, went to check on Sophie the minute he understood what they might be dealing with." Ben's eyes narrow, and his features manage to combine to express a strange mixture of sympathy and anger. "It was apparent from the state of you when you arrived at the garage that morning how serious the situation was."

I feel, as well as hear, Kadar growl behind me.

"Go on…" It seems there is still more of Sophie's story to be told.

"Mr Horseman offered Sophie his personal protection, and she accepted it. Luckily he was with her when Hargreaves paid her a visit. He made it clear he didn't believe that she was ignorant about your escape, and just as obvious he would be returning, presumably hoping he'd find her alone. Horseman has contacts in the States and persuaded Sophie to go with him for an extended visit. He believed his 'friends' would be more than a match for Ethan."

"And Sophie went with him?" It didn't seem credible that Sophie would go off with a perfect stranger. Sure I'd met Horse, but only for a moment. But truthfully I knew nothing about him. And does he really know what he's up against? "How can he keep her safe? Ethan can track people anywhere." I'm still worried for her.

But there's a strange twinkle in his eye as Ben rushes to reassure me, "Horseman's friends are an outlaw biker club, well used to evading authority. They'll give Ethan a run for his money. Frankly, I think she's probably in the safest place possible."

"What? Bikers?" My voice comes out as a high squeak. "But she's in a wheelchair!" I give a gasp and shake my head, but my face widens in a smile. The Sophie I knew before her accident would have risen to the challenge and would have loved every minute of a new adventure. But how would she be coping after the hit and run that had taken the use of her legs from her? I longed to be able to contact her but accepted I had no chance of being able to catch up with my friend. But oh, the minute I could I was going to be on that phone, and I'm so looking forward to *that* conversation. Then I felt my eyes prick with tears. Would this ever be over? Ethan won't give up; even Ben had confirmed that.

Kadar retakes his seat, and I mourn the loss of his touch. "So what do we do about St John-Davies? We've got Zoe here, scared out of her mind, her friend in another country and her mother who's under twenty-four-hour guard. We have to stop this bastard, and I can only think there's one way of doing that. He needs to be removed permanently from the equation."

My eyes flick to Kadar in shock. Is he saying what I think he is? Okay, so he'd said it in the heat of the moment in the harem, but here in the cold light of day it sounds like he's serious about it. Kadar is the ruler of a country surely he should abide by the law? Then again, here in Amahad, he *is* the law. And why should it bother me? Ethan would kill me as easily as swatting a fly. Surprised I'm condoning murder, I start thinking a permanent solution sounds very attractive.

"I agree. And I've been working on a plan." Ben's eyes flick to me, and his raised eyebrows ask the emir a silent question. It's clear he's suggesting I'm not made privy to his plan.

"I deserve to know," I interrupt any effort to remove me from the conversation, "You praised me for being able to evade Ethan, but that was because I had the knowledge to do so. I won't be kept in the dark now. It's my life you're going to be discussing. Don't shut me out."

At my assertion, I'm briefly the object of Kadar's stern gaze, but turning his attention back to Ben he nods, slowly. "What's your proposal?"

After another glance in my direction, followed by a quick conciliatory smile, Ben continues, "We can't do anything while he's in England. Taking a man out, particularly someone at his level of society would be extremely difficult. He's too well protected. We need him somewhere where we have total control." Ben's voice has changed, it's dropped a level, and has become cold. Even if I'd misunderstood their intentions earlier, the tone he's using now would spell out they are seriously planning to take a man's life.

"Somewhere the ruler is absolute monarch?" Kadar

catches on fast; I'm a couple of seconds behind him.

I realise the implications of what he's suggesting, "You want him to come here?" I've felt safe in this Arab state, and the thought of Ethan coming to destroy my newfound peace makes my stomach start to churn. No, I don't agree with this plan. I'd rather not be on the same planet as the man who abused me, let alone in the same country.

Ben throws me a look of sympathy, but my uneasiness is, of course, not going to make him alter his plan. "Yes, Zoe. We intend to let slip that you are here." At my gasp, he reaches over and takes my hand, squeezing it for reassurance, "We will not put you in any danger; I promise you that. You'll be well protected and kept out of his reach. We can 'disappear' him in Amahad, and hopefully, this sidekick Hargreaves with him." His eyes go from me to Kadar, "This is not the way Grade A normally does business, but in this circumstance, St John-Davies is like a rabid dog and there's only one way to deal with him. He needs to be put down."

Kadar's eyes are on me for a moment, and then turn back to the man from Grade A. "Zoe's safety is not to be put in question, Ben. We need to have a detailed plan before we leak news of her presence here, and it must be foolproof. I'm not having her safety compromised in any way. I promise you, Zoe, you'll never even have to clap eyes on this bastard, and Ben, you need to assure me you can guarantee that before we go ahead." Kadar has used a voice I've not heard from him before. It's full of authority, and it reminds me he is a monarch, head of his country, and used to being obeyed. And it reassures me he'll do everything he can to keep me out of harm's way.

As Ben nods his response, the emir's face turns thoughtful; his features tightening, and there's a dark glint in his eyes which sends a shiver down my spine. "It's always such a shame when a foreign national has an unfortunate accident on our unforgiving sands." His voice is cold, hard.

Ben's reply is a chilling laugh, "I'm sure we can arrange something. I'll get back to England and get the wheels turning."

"I'd like Jon Tharpe to be involved if that's possible?" Before receiving an answer, Kadar turns to me. "Jon's provided bodyguard services for us for many years now."

The senior partner of Grade A Security shakes his head. "I'll get you a good team together, Kadar, but as I've said before, right now I'd rather leave Jon directing the operation from the office. He wants to stay close to Mia; she's having a bit of a hard time of it. They're trying for another baby, so Jon wants to stay close by unless there's an essential reason for him to leave. But of course she's worried she might never be able to carry a baby to term, and of course, that stress doesn't help."

"I'm sorry to hear that." Kadar sounds genuine, "I'd hoped she would have been on the road to recovery by now."

"The miscarriage has started up her flashbacks again, and she can't seem to get things out of her head. Jon's been taking her to the club to see whether he can get her mind to quieten."

The ruler of Amahad nods his head, "He's a good

Dominant. I saw Mia under his whip when I was in the dungeon last."

"Yes, the club seems to help her, gradually he's pushing her boundaries, and she's responding well. And of course, we all enjoy a good demonstration from a whip master."

"Yes, he's impressive with a single tail, he was using an eight-footer when I last saw him. I'd like to have the time to ask him for lessons."

"Perhaps you should offer to reciprocate with Shibari tuition. The way you bound Diamond with your rope last month was apparently quite something. People are still talking about it in the club. Perhaps you can do another demonstration next time you're in the dungeon?"

They seem to have forgotten I'm sitting here, and my mouth falls open at their discussion. *Oh my fucking God! Dungeon? Whip? Rope? Binding? Christ Almighty!* I stare at Kadar as if I'm watching him turn into a monster in front of my eyes. They must be talking about the club Sean had told me about that morning in Manchester. The fucking BDSM club. And right in front of me, Kadar has confirmed he's a member. And so's Ben? How can I depend on them to save me when they use the same tools as Ethan? They're as bad as him! Shit! Just when I was starting to believe Kadar was different from Ethan. He's not, he's the same!

My mind has put two and two together at lightning speed as the two men talk, ignoring my presence continuing their conversation about a woman whipped as though it's a normal occurrence. And how the fucking hell is that supposed to help her? Memories of Ethan's playroom come back to me as though a sledgehammer hits me, and the scars on my back start to sting. *Has Kadar got a playroom of his own, here in the palace?* Suddenly I recall the exact words he'd said to me in the harem, *'the things I want to do to you'.* And I thought he'd been talking about making love to me! No, he was obviously talking about something very different.

I have to get out of here. But where the fuck can I go? I can't be alone with Kadar ever again; that's a certainty. Why the frigging hell did I ever think I could trust him?

I stand up so quickly my chair falls over, shocking the men and reminding them I was there. "I'm sorry," I start to stutter out, as two sets of eyes land on me. "I've got to get back to work. I'll leave you to continue your discussions."

They stand, Kadar looks so stunned he doesn't make a move to stop me. Trying to maintain some dignity and not just bolt for the exit I manage to walk almost normally over to the office door. I open it, step through, and close it, leaning my back against the wood, breathing hard in relief at my escape. But I can't flee the vision in my head so easily; Kadar standing over me, dominant and demanding, a whip in his hand. What frightens me most is that the thought is bizarrely sending tingles down my spine, and the sparks inside of me are not of fear, but *arousal.* I'm a fucking freak! Do I want to be abused again? Is there something warped inside of me that desires to be mistreated?

Opening my eyes, only to see Richard looking at me in bemusement, I realise what a sight I must be, chest heaving, using the door as support. Pulling myself together, I step away from the doorway and quickly exit the royal office, almost running through the corridors in my desperation to return to the sanctuary of the harem without sparing a thought for poor Asif trailing behind me.

CHAPTER 21
Kadar

What the fuck? Something upset Zoe, something that made her turn tail and run as though the demons of hell were after her. What the fuck was it? Why did she leave so abruptly? As emir, I'm not used to such a show of rudeness, but I was so startled to see her get up and run like a spooked horse, I was unable to react and stop her in time. Playing back the last parts of my conversation with Ben, it hits me like a bolt of lightning that talking about whips and bondage was not perhaps the best idea around an abused woman. Fuck! *How could I have been so stupid?*

I've plainly lost concentration and barely notice as Ben, diplomatically hiding his surprise, wraps up our conversation smartly and takes his leave. Left alone I sit with my hands steepled in front of me, wondering what the hell I can do to make this right? Everything I am tells me to go to the woman, to comfort her and explain, but how the fuck am I going to do that? She doesn't even understand herself. It's easy to see she's submissive and is crying out for a Dominant's control, but it's all got warped in her head because of that bastard, Ethan. Seeing her beat herself up, and take the blame for getting involved with that cruel man breaks my fucking heart.

Tapping my fingers on the table, I try to come up with a

plan to get her to trust me again. Two nights ago she confided in me and allowed me to see her fragility. Though she won't understand, I know she needs to relinquish her tightly held control. As it is, she's unable to let go of her fears and is as tense as an overwound clock. Ethan still retains power over her life, and will continue to have it even after he's dead unless someone helps her.

I cancel my next meeting, unwilling to waste time discussing the fiasco in the southern desert when I can do nothing at all about it, justifying my action by thinking Nijad and my army generals know precisely what they're doing without the input of my two penny's worth. Instead, I find myself going to the harem with the hope to be able to do something that only I can. But I leave knowing it's going to be hard to get her to listen to me, let alone explain my conversation with Ben. How could I have got so carried away and forgotten she was there? And how do I now explain to an abused woman the dynamics of a Dominant's relationship with his sub? Fuck it; I'm going to have my work cut out here!

Still not clear in my mind exactly how I'm going to approach her, I enter via the old Sultans' entrance, just as on that first night when I so unexpectedly found her in the harem. But this time I don't find Zee alone, and keyed up as I am, a few seconds later I'm incredibly grateful that I made no noise that would have signalled my entry.

Cara is with her. Believing there's no one else around, they are talking at a normal volume, and their voices come across to me clearly. And the first few words I catch inform me their discussion is fascinating and quite possibly paving my way for the conversation I want to have with Zee. I may be emir, but I'm not beneath hiding in a doorway out of sight, so I don't interrupt them.

"So I'm right, Kadar is a Dominant?" Zoe's voice comes out as a high-pitched squeak.

"Oh, sweetie. They all are. Kadar, Nijad, and Jasim. Jasim runs an exclusive BDSM club in London."

"Nijad? Nijad's a Dom? Is he… is he like that with you?"

I presume Cara's nodded or given some other such non-verbal answer when Zoe continues, "You let Nijad hit you?" I smile, as her voice gets even higher, knowing my sister-in-law won't want to let that go.

Cara laughs. "Hit me? God no! Never! Well, not in the way you're thinking."

"But you can't be a submissive; you're too clever and independent!"

I shake my head wishing I could correct that misconception. I also long to be able to peer around the corner to see their faces, but for now, I have to be content with staying hidden. How's Cara going to explain it to Zee? Unwittingly, it seems she's doing exactly what I came here to do. Putting things into perspective.

"Of course, I'm his sub, and he's my Dom, as well as my husband. See, I'm wearing his collar."

"I don't understand." Zee almost wails.

"Sweetie, being clever or independent has nothing to with being submissive. I let Nijad have control in the bedroom, but in most other areas of life we're equals. Being a good Dominant he knows what I need, and when I need it."

"Ethan used to hit me."

"Ethan was a fucking prick. He took all your control away from you. A Dom/sub relationship is entirely different. The sub has all the control."

"I've heard that, but I still don't understand it. How is it possible? When the man's so much stronger? Physically, I mean."

"It's a relationship built on trust. Did you trust Ethan?"

"Until he started hurting me, yes."

"Really?" Cara's voice rises at the end of the word, plainly making it a question. "Did he always have your best interests in mind?"

"Well," there's a pause, "He was helping me fit into his world."

`"I think you have your answer there. He was looking out for himself, not for you. A good Dom always takes care of the sub's needs, not the other way around. It seems you took Ethan's needs and made them your own. And when he started abusing you, did you ask him to stop?"

"Ask him? *Ask* him?" Zoe's voice sounds frantic. "I frigging begged and pleaded with him. It made him worse. He enjoyed it when he got me to the point when I couldn't take any more, and even then he wouldn't stop."

"I trust Nijad with to know just what I need, and to give it to me. I trust him with my life, and with the life of my child." Cara's voice softens, and I can hear the deep love she has for my brother coming through the words and it makes me smile. If only I could imagine having that kind of relationship one day, but the chances of a second arranged marriage in our family being such a success are slim to nothing. "If Ni ever does anything I don't like, all I need to do is use my safeword, and he'll stop immediately," Cara continues.

"I can't imagine ever trusting a man like that."

"After everything you've been through I'm not surprised, sweetie. But I'll tell you this; you would be able to trust Kadar. Ethan was a domineering bully. He just wanted to hurt you to get his kicks, there was no power exchange between you, you had no way of stopping him. The difference is for example, if in the unlikely situation Nijad ever went too far and did something to that made me uncomfortable, it would be in my control to bring it to an end. A sexual Dominant is entirely different from a sadistic man like Ethan; a Dom gets his thrills by giving you pleasure. And believe me, the pleasure's so intense you wouldn't credit it." I hear her sigh, "It's addictive."

There's another slight pause before Zee says anything else, and I'm starting to think about revealing my presence when her next words shock me to the core.

"I've never thought much of sex. It always seems one sided. At best it's awkward and irritating, and at worst, well, it's painful."

The dismissive confession from Zoe makes me sad.

"You mean he took his pleasure but gave you none? You didn't orgasm?" Cara asks the question I suddenly want to know the answer too, but she's more frank, more direct than I would have been.

There's a short period of silence before she replies, and then her voice is so quiet I can hardly hear it. "No. But that's probably down to me. I've never enjoyed sex with anyone. It was just something to get over and done with as quickly as possible. I know I'm different to other women, I just don't react the right way."

"Oh! God no! No, sweetie, that's not your fault. You've not been with the right man is all. A man who takes care of your needs before his own. A man who makes sure that you're enjoying yourself. Just lying back and thinking of England went out with the Victorians. You just have to find yourself a real man. And if Kadar is the same as his brother in that department you couldn't go far wrong trusting yourself to him."

Cara's perhaps being too candid now and I find myself in two minds about staying. I grow embarrassed as I listen to a conversation I have no business overhearing particularly now they've started discussing my sexual performance, of which Cara obviously has no first-hand knowledge. But the thought that there's potentially so much I can teach Zee has my cock hardening like a stone. Apparently, it wasn't just Ethan, but her other lovers who were also selfish pricks! It's high time she found a man who could teach her what intimacy between a man and a woman should be all about. Although I know eavesdroppers are never supposed to hear anything good about themselves, I decide to stay put. My conscience pricks as I acknowledge I'm listening to a very private conversation.

"And you care about Kadar, don't you?" Cara continues talking; her voice becomes teasing.

"What? No! Of course, not!"

"Be honest, Zoe. Why did you run when you thought he was a Dominant?"

I smile to myself; Cara's made a good point.

"I, er… He's so powerful; he's the emir."

"Okay, he's the emir, what power does that give him over you? Only the authority of an employer. If you weren't a little attracted to him, Zoe, you wouldn't be bothered where his sexual inclinations lay. The fact you ran, when you heard he might be something more than you think you could handle, speaks volumes."

There's a pause, and then a little voice speaks. "Am I that transparent?"

Cara laughs. "It's not only Doms who can read people. I had an inkling you and Kadar would get on from the first time I spoke to you on the phone, it was part of the reason I set up the interview with him, and it worked, didn't it? He gave you his protection. But, hey, listen, Zoe, Ethan treated you like shit, but it's time to take your life back. You're clearly attracted to Kadar, and I think he'd be the right man to help you."

"He's the emir." I hear the frustration in her voice, "And he's told me, his marriage is being arranged as we speak." She seems hung up on my title, and not for the first time I curse my destiny and that I have so little time of freedom remaining.

"Pah! He knows exactly what I think about that. I've tried to persuade him to cancel the whole thing, but of course, he won't." After expressing her vexation, Cara heaves a deep sigh, "Okay, so his life is unfortunately mapped out for him. I'd hoped meeting you would get him to change his mind, but no. So you can't pin your hopes on anything permanent. But what you should think about is that Dominants like Kadar like to fix damaged subs, and you, honey, are definitely damaged. I'll tell you something that perhaps I shouldn't. I can see Kadar is attracted to you. He's done so much, put himself out for you. And he plans to kill the man who hurt you. He's never acted this way before, never shown any particular interest in a woman. He likes you, Zoe, and I have a feeling he would jump at the chance to have you as his sub. If only for the short time he has left before that darn wedding. And that could help you to start healing, and begin to trust the male sex again."

As Cara's words sink in, I have to wonder what the fuck was that all about? She knew Zoe and I would get on before we'd even met? Had that interview been a setup? I knew there had been something behind it at the time. But Cara's barking up the wrong tree if she thinks there's a chance I can cancel my marriage. I have to go ahead with it as part of the bargain I made with the sheikhs. However much she's argued it with me—and I've considered every argument she's put forward, and I agree with many of her points—the stark truth of the matter is, for the good of Amahad I have no option but to go along with the farce. And as she's stated, I've very little time remaining before I'm hitched to another wagon.

It shocks me more how Cara's able to read me so easily, but I suppose I've given myself away. She's right; I've never done so much for a woman before. That doesn't mean I won't be suggesting to Nijad that a spanking might be in order for gossiping about the emir. There's quiet for a few moments, and I gather Zee's considering what Cara's telling her. I become very interested in what she's going to say next.

"I hear what you say, but I can't believe he would even want to help me. He's said we can only be friends. And I'm not ready to take it further, I couldn't!" Zoe's voice sounds desperate and high. "He's all but promised to another. And though you keep saying it, *I'm NOT submissive!* Fuck, Cara! How on earth did we get onto this topic?"

"Because you ran away when you found out the kind of things he was into, it frightened you. And you wouldn't have been scared if you didn't have feelings for him. Friends laugh off one another's kinks."

Zoe's almost whining as she protests once more. "But Cara, you've told me he's a Dominant. I AM NOT A SUB!"

"Yes. You. Are!" comes the definite response, leaving no room for argument. "And when you find the right person you'll let him have control. Remember, you'll be giving it, a Dominant doesn't take it from you. I still think you should let Kadar show you what I'm talking about. Let a man you care about show you about submission."

As I round the corner bringing myself into their sight Zoe's eyes widen, and I watch her face flush red with embarrassment seconds before she covers her cheeks with her hands. Her mouth is open in a wide O. Cara hasn't seen me yet, so I sneak up behind her and whisper softly into her ear. "Quack!" The illusion to her waddling was a dangerous joke for me to make, having got me in trouble before. But I can't resist, at eight months pregnant, how she walks really does remind me of a plump duck and in my more relaxed moments, I love to tease her.

"Shit! Kadar! Jesus H Christ, you made me jump! Do you want to bring on the birth early?" she swings around and slaps me on the arm. Violence against the emir's person was a punishable offence in my father's day, but I love Cara as though she was a sister of my blood, and she's allowed far more liberties than other people.

I pull her into me and give her a hug and a peck on the cheek. "I think Ni would thank me if I did." I know my brother's anxious to see his first child make its safe entry into the world.

"Mmm. Actually, I wouldn't mind either. Want to try sneaking up again?" I love the way she laughs at me; never letting me take myself too seriously. Then, pulling out of my arms, her eyes narrow in suspicion, "Just how long have you been standing there?"

I smirk. "Long enough to tell Zee my answer," I pause, directing a long look at the woman in question, "I'd be delighted to show her how pleasurable it could be to submit to a man."

"No!" An anguished shout.

But a tinkling laugh draws my attention back to Cara as she tells us, "I think that's my cue to leave!" Then, adding nothing else, Cara leaves the harem as elegantly as the mother of a rather large unborn child can, and leaves me alone with Zoe.

I watch her look this way and that as if trying to find an escape route, trying to conjure up any excuse to leave.

"Er, I've got to be going as well…" she turns, and fuck it; she's literally running for the door.

"Zee! Stop!" I use my most dominant voice which halts her in her tracks. As she waits frozen, her back towards me, I command, "Come to me."

She hesitates, but I repeat the order and as if I've got her on an invisible string, she rotates, and her feet move in my direction, walking mechanically, like an animated doll. She halts a couple of feet away from me, her face furrowed in consternation.

"Talk to me," I demand. I watch as she swallows a few times.

"How long were you listening?" I hear a tremor in her almost inaudible voice, and her eyes can't hold mine. She looks like she's replaying the conversation in her head.

"Long enough," I admit, folding my arms and looking at her thoughtfully. "You feel the same attraction to me as I do to you, don't you, Zee?" Is she going to come clean and confess? Or try to wriggle her way out of it.

There's a long pregnant pause before she answers, and then I can only just hear the whispered denial, "No." But her face is still flushed, her eyes open wide, and her pupils are dilated.

I study her, as a Dominant I've learned to read people well. She's not telling the truth, but only because she's scared. And underlying that, there's something she can't quite conceal, she's excited and intrigued. But first I've got to make a few things clear.

I take a step towards her, wanting to reduce the physical distance between us. She shuffles back. "Habiti, we've had a lot of conversations here in the harem. This one's no different. Just relax." I can almost hear her heart frantically beating, her breathing erratic. I decide to lay it on the line for her, "I'm a Dominant, Zee, I was born that way, it's in my nature. Shush!" She's about to speak, so I hold up my hand silently asking her to let me finish. "I take charge. I need to be in control. And I have an inbuilt desire to protect and nurture. I've been doing this a very long time, and it's true, when I have a submissive, I like to push her to her limits, whatever they are, to achieve her utmost pleasure."

"So that's how you could condone what Ethan did to me? Push me to endure more than I ever thought I could?"

She's shrinking into herself, as though remembering the pain. I rush to correct her, "Limits are what you, as a sub would set, habiti. And I appreciate yours would be set at a very low threshold. I would certainly push them, but not walk all over them. I'd drive you to enjoy the pleasure your body was made for. What St John-Davies did was abuse, pure and simple, he had no regard for what you liked and what you didn't. You might not know this, but he was, at one time, a member of Jasim's club, Club Tiacapan."

She nods her head, "Sean told me he was banned. But the fact he was there, means he is a Dom, doesn't it?"

Shaking my head emphatically, I put her right, "No, not in any sense of the word. He was banned from the club, permanently, and as a result, from most other clubs which have anything like a selection procedure, both in the UK and abroad. To protect other subs, something like that isn't kept quiet."

"What did he do?"

I don't want to tell her too much, "He went too far. It was my brother, Nijad, who'd gone to the club that night and who was first on the scene and stopped him. He ignored a sub's safeword." In fact, while whipping the woman he ignored it three times, and she'd ended up needing stitches. Once I'd connected the names I'd reminded myself of the details. She's silent, and I let her digest that information.

"Ethan had a playroom—I called it my torture room. It had all the equipment, spanking benches, a St Andrew's cross…"

"Because he couldn't play anywhere else by then, habiti. But just because he had the equipment, that doesn't make him a Dom. You didn't have a safeword, did you?"

She shakes her head then tells me, "Whether I did or not is beside the point. Kadar, what's important here is that I accept you're a Dom, and maybe you're right, Ethan wasn't, but the fact of the matter is, I'm definitely not a sub."

I move forwards again, and as though we're in a dance she takes a pace back, bringing her up against a wall. There's nowhere left for her to go. When she realises, her eyes flick up to mine in panic. "Relax, habiti; we're just talking," I remind her then wait until her breathing again starts to even out. At the moment I avoid touching her, content to let my voice do the work. I deepen my tone.

"You've never had a man who wants only to pleasure you, have you, habiti? You've only had vanilla sex before. Perhaps they got you aroused, perhaps not, but when they took you, they fucked you until they came. Did you pretend, Zee? Did you fake your orgasm?"

Her face flushes bright red, and I know my words hit the mark.

"Did you lie and tell them how wonderful it was?" Her eyes look down, proving again I'm right on target. Putting my finger under her chin, I gently force her to raise her head, so she's staring at me, "A Dom would never be fooled, a Dom would be looking to every reaction of their sub's beautiful body and would know exactly the point she reached her peak. She wouldn't have to pretend." I haven't taken my hand away, so I move it up, and gently caress her cheek. "A Dom would know if his sub was aroused, and would see her erect nipples," I glance down, and don't bother hiding my grin as I see hers peaking through the top she's wearing, "By the flush on her face," my fingers stroke her burning flesh, "Her heart rate would speed up, her breathing would become fast…"

"That would be from fear." She tries to deflect me, "I don't want a Dom. I am *not* a sub."

"What if I touched you in all the right places; used my tongue and my hands on your sweet body, aroused you to levels you've never known before, and then, as your Dom, ordered you to come?"

I can smell her arousal from here, but she still denies it. "I'm not taking orders from any man, ever again." Challenge flashes in her eyes, "If, and it's a big *if*, I ever want a man in my life again, he's not going to have any control over me."

"Then you're destined to be disappointed, habiti." Sadly, I shake my head, "In your bed, you need someone to take charge, someone who knows your body as well, if not better than you know it yourself. Someone who knows what you need to reach the pinnacle of pleasure." Pushing forwards again, I trap her against the wall, then place my hands either side of her head on the brickwork behind her. "Just say 'red' if it gets too much."

"Kadar, what are you doing? I said I don't want this. Please let me go."

But every physical reaction of her body is telling me something different from her words. Her pupils are so enlarged her eyes appear as dark as my own, her breath is erratic, and she's making no effort to escape me. I know if I placed my hand in her underwear she would be drenched. She must know it too, and that she's lying to me.

"Just let me take charge, habiti. Trust me."

"You want to have sex with me?" The tone of her voice makes it sound as though she expects me to take her simply for my pleasure. Has she genuinely never enjoyed any aspect of sexual intercourse?

My glare stops her from going there; going to that place where I would never, ever go. Never have I, nor ever will I, take a woman by force. I school my features to show calmness I don't feel as I seek to reassure her, "No, Zoe, I'm not going to have sex with you. In fact, I'm not even going to take off my clothes. But I am to show you how much pleasure you can find when you let a Dom take charge."

She doesn't understand. Her fluttering hands showing her confusion. "But sex is about the man; you have needs." Her eyes meet mine but only for a brief moment, "I don't understand what you're saying. Isn't having sex what being a Dominant is all about? Having a sub to serve you, so you can take what you want? Sex without the obligations of a relationship?" Now she turns her head away, biting her lip so I can see something else is worrying her, "I don't turn you on, do I?"

When she at last voices her concern, I'm astounded, "The fuck, Zee? I've been rock hard since the day I met you. You turn me on, habiti, like no one ever before." I rub my hand over my brow, frustrated that I can't get through to her. Sighing, I try again, "Zee, I've known my destiny since my birth. I've gone through many long periods of self-enforced abstinence as I don't play on my own fucking doorstep. When I'm out of the country, yes, I admit I do, but at home? I have a reputation to uphold so I assure you I can control myself. That I don't need to have sex with you, doesn't mean I don't fucking want to."

"So your reputation would be tarnished if we sleep together? So we can't do anything?" She sounds almost hopeful as though she's found a way out of this.

I laugh, keeping my voice soft and gentle, "I'll not be taking you to my bed, Zee. You're right; that option is not open to me; but here, in the harem? Whatever we do, no one need know."

Now she looks panicked, "What, what are you suggesting we do?"

I grin, "I'm going to show you how gratifying it can be to submit to your Dom."

Her tongue comes out to lick her lips. I can read her like a book. Her body, clearly showing her arousal, is at odds with her brain, which is telling her to run. I decide the time for discussion is over; it's time to take control. "Do you know why I followed you here? Why I came to the harem?" After her eyes open wide and she gives a little shake of her head, I continue. "I was angry, little one." My voice grows stern, "You left my office without explanation, without giving me a chance to talk through what had concerned you."

"I, er, I'm sorry. I thought the conversation was over, that you were just catching up with Ben." The words fall out one after the other. Again she's lying to me, and the blush that reappears on her cheeks shows me she knows exactly what she's doing.

Sadly, I shake my head, letting her know her excuses don't wash with me. "You got scared when you realised I was a sexual Dominant, Zee. Don't deny that was what upset you, but along with your fear, I think it excited you too. Don't keep fighting it, Zee, let me show you what it can be like if you just accept your submissive leanings. Give yourself to me, trust me to know what you need."

Taking a step back I bring my arms down, so she's no longer trapped, and hold out my hand. "Come." I wait for her to take her first metaphorical step in accepting me as her Dom. Holding my breath in anticipation and hope, wanting to feel her small palm touch my own. She hesitates, and then does exactly that. I give her fingers a gentle squeeze, showing my appreciation.

"Eyes on me."

She was looking down at our joined hands but now lifts her eyes to meet mine. "Communication is vital between in a D/s relationship Zee. You should have waited and talked to me, not just run away. You displeased me. There should be a consequence to that, but this time, I'll let it go." When I mention my displeasure, her gaze dropped to the floor. When I say there's a consequence, she looks back at me again, her fear plain to see.

"You know about safewords?" I need to make her understand that she holds the power to stop this, at any time, so want to ensure she knows the tools at her disposal.

"Only from what Cara said, and Sean mentioned it before." Her voice shakes.

I quell the heat that rises through me as I wonder how the fuck safewords had come up in conversation with Sean and am proud when I'm able to continue with an even voice, "The only word you need to know for now is 'Red.' As soon as you say that I will stop whatever I'm doing." There's no point asking her to trust me; I've still to demonstrate I'm worthy of that.

"What *are* you going to do?" Her voice is breathy, still scared, but there's more than a hint of arousal in it. The thought of my domination turns her on, however much she doesn't want to admit to it.

Knowing helping Zee overcome her fears is at this moment more important than any of the business waiting for me in my office, I explain to her, "I'm going to show you what it is that you've been missing." I take a deep breath before I continue. "Unless you say your safeword out I'm going to take you over to the bed, and show you the beauty of submission."

Her eyes open wide.

I stare at him. He's asking too much of me. He wants me to submit to him? "I don't think so," I tell him emphatically, so there's no room for any misunderstanding then suck in my cheeks, trying to get enough moisture to swallow as concern has made my mouth dry. "Don't you think Ethan made me submit to him?" Tears come to my eyes as I remember, "In his playroom, he used to tie me up and hit me with his hand, paddles… canes. He used to have Hargreaves whip me while he stood by and watched! I know enough that I don't want to go through any of that again." I turn away from him, "Been there, done that, got the T-shirt thank you very much. If that's what being a sub is all about I don't want to know!"

Kadar takes a step towards me; his hand held out in invitation. His eyes have gone so dark it's impossible to read what he's thinking. "Trust me to show you something different, Zee. Trust me to take care of you. What I'm about to do is for you, not me." He frowns, and a vicious look comes over him, "I do not get my kicks from hurting women. Ethan is not a man; he's an animal. And he's *not* a Dom."

How can giving a man control be for me? I shake my head in bemusement. It's not that I truly believe Kadar wants to hurt me, and I know some women like giving men their power. But experience has taught me it's not something I'd do voluntarily. But I can't deny his closeness, this discussion, is having a physical effect on me. I feel wet down below, and the throbbing between my legs is more intense than I've ever known before. If I'm honest, just talking to Kadar has made me feel more turned on than anything I've experienced in bed with any other man. Ethan never talked about what he was going to do to me; he just did it. The fact that Kadar's telling me, giving me a choice, is different. I can't understand my reaction to him, how my own body's response is betraying me. And darn it, that look on his face, the gleam in his eyes. He knows exactly the effect he's having on me.

Can I believe he'd be so selfless as to expect nothing in return? Surely he'll want me to take care of his needs in some way? All men do. I turn away from him, thinking of my previous experiences. Men touch women only as a sure fire way to get their release.

Now fear takes hold, swinging around, I attack him verbally, "You want something from this. You have to, and I'm not prepared to let you use me, Kadar. I can't do that again." I can feel my private regions clenching as though to repel an intruder. Sex and pain are interlinked in my head, and not in any pleasurable way, men have only ever used me before. Ethan was by far the worst, but in my admittedly limited experience, the others I'd been with had also been selfish. Rapidly my arousal fades as I realise the consequences of giving in to him. *I'm not going to be a victim again.*

"I'm not asking, not demanding, anything of you, Zee. My fulfilment will be seeing you satisfied and happy. I can't, and won't ask for anything more." He wipes his hand over his face, then stands back, one arm cupping the elbow of his other, and the palm of that one supporting his chin. "I'm not free to give you anything else of myself; my future is already written as you know. I can make no promises, have nothing to offer beyond helping you understand yourself, your wants and needs. I want to help you come to terms with what happened to you, to accept it wasn't your fault, and to assist you to move on. I want to show you another side of Dominance. The right side." His gaze is intent, his voice deep and authoritative, and I feel a shiver of delight down my spine. "This is all for you, Zee. I will take nothing from you."

I stare at him, this dark, formidable Sheikh, who's asking me to put my faith in him; to give him the trust that Ethan destroyed? Suddenly it's as though a light bulb switches on in my head. If I keep harping back to my experiences with Ethan, if I refuse to move forward, am I letting him still control my life? Should I take this chance and jump into the unknown? Swallowing rapidly, I ask, still undecided, "I say red, and you'll stop?"

"At any time." The promise and assurance in his voice are evident. I don't know why he's doing this for me; he is the ruler of a country; he could have any woman he wants. But he desires me. He's made that clear. And I want him, or at least, what he can offer me. So it all comes down to whether I can trust him or not.

He has given me his word; as ultimate ruler, his word

must surely count for something? He has to be trustworthy, doesn't he? *But Ethan ruled a company* a voice inside reminds me. *Having absolute control doesn't equal being honest or honourable.*

He waits patiently. Not pushing, not pressurising. I'm sure as emir he has something pressing he needs to do somewhere else. But unlike Ethan, who would come home for a quickie between meetings, setting a time limit that provided sufficient time only for his pleasure, Kadar's not looking at his watch or showing any signs of impatience or agitation.

Can I do this? Or looking at it another way, can I afford to throw away this chance? I might never have such an opportunity again, a man, focused solely on my needs. Suddenly I decide to take a leap of faith. "O… kay." My voice is hoarse, my fear shining through. Panic only seconds away.

For a moment he makes no move, only his eyes flick over me, assessing me. Then, once again, he holds out his hand, and at that invitation, I reach out mine to take it.

I pull back immediately. With just that brief touch, I felt sparks fly like an electric shock. Throwing a quick glance up at his face, I see his eyes flash in recognition of whatever had passed between us. He felt it too but is the first to recover and react. His large hand comes out again and encircles mine firmly, this time giving me no chance to withdraw. For a moment we stand there, acknowledging our connection. My arousal, which had receded as the memories of Ethan swamped my brain, returns with a vengeance. With a cautious nod I give my permission to proceed.

As if he'd been waiting for that signal, Kadar gently leads me over to the bed. He lets go of my hand and points, "Lie down, on your back, Zee. Put your hands above your head." He waits.

I stagger backwards, "Red!" I cry out, my fear overcoming me.

Immediately he stills, and I flinch, waiting for the blow, my reward for my disobedience. It doesn't come. Instead, he gathers his robe around him, bows his head, and starts to walk to the secret staircase, ready to take his leave. I'm drawing breath into my lungs as rapidly as I can; my heart is beating fast, too fast. *But I don't want him to go.*

"Stop! Wait!" I run and grasp his arm. He turns his stern face towards me; I see the disappointment in his eyes, and something else, despair as though he's failed. "Please, I'm sorry. I panicked." He stills, and looks at me, considering. Something hits me as forceful as a blow from his hand. *He stopped. When I said the safeword, he stopped. Everything.* All of a sudden, I realise maybe I can take that next step, maybe only a tiny one for now, but at least it's in the right direction. "Kadar, you stopped. You did what you said you would do. I can't go all the way and say that I completely trust you. But what's different is that I am starting to have faith in you. I might not get there today, but I'm willing to give this a try. I didn't think I could even go this far, but when you stopped, well, you didn't force me. Or punish me." I take a deep breath, trying consciously to slow the rapid beating of my heart. "Please, please..."

"Come." He takes my hand again and says no more as he leads me back to where we were, I wait for further instruction, he doesn't hesitate, "Lower yourself onto the bed."

Shit! Can I do this? Can I voluntarily get into the position that Ethan forced me into so often, vulnerable and open to him? But Kadar is right. To exorcise my demons maybe, I need to face them. To create new memories that will chase out the old. I close my eyes and gather my resolve. I lay myself down, on my back.

Kadar had hit the nail on the head about my previous sexual encounters. And yes, I did pretend I was as satisfied as my partner, though in reality, glad to have got the messy bit over so we could cuddle and go to sleep. I'm starting to suspect it won't be that way with the emir.

His coarse, strong hands take my arms and manoeuvre them above my head, pressing gently on my fingers, so I hold onto the bars of the headboard. I wait for him to cover me, trap my legs in his, to restrain me my hands with his, but he does neither. With embarrassment, I feel him push my silk trousers down past my hips, and then he pushes up my tunic, and unclips my bra, exposing my breasts. Gentle hands cover them and caress them then, before alarm has a chance to emerge, his gorgeous head is there, mouthing and laving one of my already erect nipples. I push my body up into him, and hear him chuckle in response. A zing of pleasure goes straight to my clit. Alternating with his hand and mouth, he gives both nipples the same treatment until I writhe and think of nothing but the complete pleasure he's giving me. And I want more.

"Beautiful, absolutely fucking beautiful." He lifts his head and admires his handiwork. Glancing down at myself, I see my nipples red and peaking harder than I've ever seen them. For a second his eyes meet mine, then, keeping his gaze locked on me, he moves further down my body, and pauses, his fingertips touching the elastic of my plain, everyday knickers. "I want these off." It's a statement, but I know he's asking my permission.

I've gone so far I can't turn back now, "Yes." A quiver runs through me, part hating the fact I'll be so exposed to him, but also in anticipation of what he's going to do.

He lifts me slightly so he can slip my underwear down my legs and then before the seed of a panic attack can take root, he gently starts rubbing his palm across exposed skin of my stomach. The motion, although not overtly sexual, seems to communicate directly with that significant bundle of nerves between my legs, making them pulsate.

"Never run from me again, habiti, not without speaking to me. I want you to remember this, Zee. Remember the importance of communication. It's important between friends and vital between a Dom and his sub. Keep your hands above your head." I hadn't realised I'd started to remove them, but immediately I follow his instruction the warmth of his hand descends, the motion circling as he moves closer to the centre of me. My body flinches, as the memory of Ethan touching me, forcing his fingers or his cock inside my dry channel, comes to me. I tense, waiting for the pain, but his hands avoid that part of me, moving down, massaging my legs.

"Relax, habiti; I'm not going to hurt you."

"I'm sorry…"

"Shush," he stops me, "Just feel my touch, don't think

about anything else. There's no room for a third person here. Let go of any thoughts of anyone else touching you."

It's difficult, the last time a man to intimately touch me was Ethan, and he'd been so rough.

I feel him kneel on the bed, gently moving my legs apart. I try to resist, fighting to keep my legs tight together.

"Has anyone ever licked your sweet pussy, habiti?"

"No!" I gasp out, now desperate to close my legs. The dirty words coming from his mouth while unnerving, excite me and even though his strong hands are holding me apart, open and ready for him, saying my safeword is the furthest thing from my mind. The throbbing intensifies and with mortification, I feel myself getting so wet I must be staining the bed. He can't really be suggesting he's going to do *that*, can he? No man has ever done that before, and while my mind can't understand how I'll like it, my body has other ideas. Automatically I begin wriggling as I try to find some relief. I hear a chuckle, and his hands still me.

Then, his head lowers, and at first his warm breath is the only thing that touches me, but that gentle caress of air is enough to have me arching off the bed. Another chuckle, I feel the vibration, "Be still, habiti, just enjoy." And then his tongue is licking me *there*, swiping from the opening of my channel to that oh, so sensitive place where all the nerves congregate. He works his mouth around, licking, sucking; his tongue spearing inside of me.

"Hmm, I suspected you would taste good, but I never dreamed how sweet you'd be. I could get addicted to this; I can't get enough, habiti. You're so wet for me. You're dripping."

I shiver at his words; they make me embarrassed, but also turn me on as much as his talented mouth. *I can't believe he's doing this.* My hands grip the headboard as hard as they can as the feelings he incites take me beyond any conscious control. All thoughts have gone; I can't think of anything but the pleasure he's bringing me. I feel his teeth close on that nerve bundle, a sharp bite to my clit that does nothing but shoot my level of arousal up to a seemingly impossible level.

But he pulls away before I find my release, and I can't prevent the moan of frustration, but the touch of his fingers, swiping through the wetness between my legs, reassures me he's not finished yet. His mouth returns to my source of pleasure, and his tongue circles. I try to rise into him, try to get him to apply more pressure just where I need it, but he pins me down, restraining me. I'm getting frustrated. *But I'm not scared.*

"Shush. Trust me. Take what I'm giving you. I know what you need."

Nobody else ever bloody well has. I think the words to myself. *No one* has ever known what I needed. But the sensations I'm feeling are already a million times stronger than any, even my battery operated friend, has given me. Safeword out? *Like hell, I will.* I groan, he laughs softly. I beg, "Please."

He slips a finger inside me; it slides in easily as I'm so wet for him, and his mouth now starts to suck. I try to squirm, but he holds me tight. I pull up against him, anything to get me to release. I'm so ready to come; I just need something more, him to move. He slips another finger inside me, gently stretching me, and I feel his fingers curling around as if he's trying to reach my clit from the inside.

"Please," I gasp out again.

He chuckles, the sound waves oscillating across my clit, almost making me explode on the spot but he lifts his head before I quite reach it. "Ask me to let you come in my mouth, little one. Ask me."

I can't ask him that! It's too dirty. But he waits, hovering just above where I need him, his warm breath invoking spikes of arousal that are almost painful and not quite enough to let me go over the top. Feeling like a coiled spring, I summon up the courage and to rasp out the only words that will apparently make him take mercy on me, "Please, Kadar, let me come in your mouth."

Suddenly there's pressure inside from his fingers, his tongue presses on my clit and then there's a sharp nip of his teeth. I can't take a breath, the sensations build and overwhelm me, I can't take it, I can't stand this volcanic feeling inside of me.

"Come for me." His dominant voice commands and my body obeys the demand of its master.

With a scream I let everything go, I reach the top, then explode, the feeling, so intense everything goes black for a few seconds, then I come back to my senses, mortified. His strong arms surround me, lifting me up, so I straddle him, and I collapse onto him, hugging him tightly, unable to fight back the tears which stream down from my eyes. No one has ever done anything like this for me before. I'm still sobbing, but sitting on him I can feel the hard evidence of his arousal and also very aware of the wetness beneath me, soaking into his robes. Scrunching up my face, I gaze up at him, ready to give my stuttered apology. But he's smiling at me, a depth of warmth in his face I never expected to see. Putting one hand behind my head, he pulls me to him and kisses me deeply, taking complete charge, dominating me, holding me in place to plunder my mouth at his will. I taste myself on him and love it. I've no thoughts of pulling away, so desire to escape. He *owns* me with that kiss.

It's a long time before he releases me and pulls away with a satisfied smile on his face. "I think you liked that," he says, amusement in his eyes. "Fuck, habiti, that was the best feeling in all the world."

"I've never…I'm sorry…I…" My face glows; I can feel the heat.

He studies me, and he knows what I'm trying to say. "You came, habiti, it's good." His dark eyes glow now, with satisfaction as though he'd ejaculated himself. He smiles down at me, "You see, Zee, letting me take charge didn't take anything from you at all."

I can't speak; I just nod my agreement. I'm amazed and still dazed that he's taken nothing for himself. As my breathing gets back to normal, I shift and pull myself up into a sitting position.

He glances down at himself where I've stained his robes, and his face grows rueful, "I'd happily wear your essence as a badge all day, but I've got a meeting with the finance minister, er, in…" he lifts his arm, shrugs back his sleeve and consults his watch, "Er, in less than an hour. I think I'd better change first." He laughs gently, the sound soothing me. He presses his lips to my forehead in a gentle kiss.

"Never walk out on me again. We talk. About everything. I don't want there to be misunderstandings between us. If something worries you, we'll talk about it." He repeats his previous instructions.

Sitting on him as I am, I can't miss the hardness beneath me, but he seems true to his promise. This was all for me, and he wants nothing in return. Starting to trust him, I feel some of my old cheekiness come back. "Well, if that's the punishment I'm going to get…"

"Wench!" He stops me with another kiss, this time, a chaste brush of his mouth against mine. Then he pulls me into his hard, muscled chest, his arms encircling my back. I feel so safe and secure I never want to leave, and I have to force myself to remember this is all he can offer me. A chance to show me that I have control, that I could trust a dominant man who doesn't use his strength against me, who respects my limits. As I relax in his arms, my fingers clutch at his robes. I could fall for this man.

As quickly as I achieved an endorphin high, everything suddenly crashes down on me. My legs still feel shaky as I pull myself away, his arms releasing me as soon as I start to move. I stand and turn away, and as discreetly as I can rearrange my clothing. It doesn't help that my foot catches in the hem of my trousers, I stagger momentarily, almost falling back against him, but a strong arm reaches out to steady me. He doesn't comment.

Once dressed and my armour restored, I feel more confident, "You should leave now," I mumble. I don't know how to end this encounter. The swishing of his robes behind me tells me, Kadar, too, has got to his feet. His arms encompass me once again, but his hold is light, so I don't feel trapped.

"Thank you."

"For what?" I'm puzzled; I've given him nothing. He's leaving here unsatisfied; I can see the evidence of that.

"The gift of your submission." He turns me to face him, putting a finger under my chin, so I'm forced to look into his face. His features are relaxed, showing none of the tension or discomfort I assume his hard erection would be giving him. He looks genuinely grateful.

"I don't understand." I wave in the general direction of his genitals.

Giving a wry smile, he tells me, "I don't need any more satisfaction. A man learns to deal with such discomfort early in their lives. You gave me a gift today. And, for a while, made me forget the pressures of being the emir. I thank you for that, habiti. But now I must leave you." He hasn't released my chin, so I don't miss the hardening of his features as he prepares to return to work. "We'll talk soon, Zee." He pulls back from me a little. "This is all I can give you, you know that, don't you? I can only give you a taste of what you can find with the right man. You are submissive, and you need to embrace and explore that."

I give him a nod to show I understand, his future is mapped out for him, and there's no place for me in it. With a final squeeze he turns, and I watch him leave the harem.

Wow! My legs are still shaking from the aftermath of that

tremendous orgasm, the first that any man has given me. I sink onto the bed, putting my head in my hands, trying to sort out all the conflicting thoughts and feelings that flit through my head, making it spin. In one morning Kadar has forced me to rethink my opinion of the male sex, and of what Dominance and submission might mean. I can't believe he left the harem without taking anything from me. I'd been convinced I'd end the morning with him inside me, and I'm not sure I'd be ready for that. But his demonstration of what a sexual Domination could be like, well, that was certainly was something else. Rubbing my tired eyes, I admit to myself that I wouldn't say no to exploring it a little further. *With Kadar, only with Kadar.* I couldn't imagine trusting another man.

Nevertheless, I must remember to keep my feet very firmly on the ground. There's no future in getting attached to the emir; he's made that very clear. Closing my eyes, I relive every moment of our encounter, trying to commit it to memory to sustain me for the future.

CHAPTER 23
Kadar

Having changed into fresh robes, I return to my office just in time for my meeting with Sadiq. Although I try to concentrate on the information he's providing, I find it difficult to keep my mind on track. Zee's submission almost blew my mind. I'd taken things much further than I thought I'd go, having visited the harem simply to have a candid discussion. But after hearing the girls' conversation my plans had been blown out of the water, and at last, I'd had to admit the attraction I've been trying so hard to conceal from myself as well as from her.

With a concerted effort, I force myself to compartmentalise this morning's events, locking them away in my mind and turning the key. Once done, I turn my attention to the spreadsheet in front of me and afford my Minister of Finance the courtesy of actually listening to him. Zee had given me the gift of letting me forget my role and who I am for just a short time, but now it's back to the business of running the country.

The meeting's a routine one. I go through the last month's figures with Sadiq for the next hour and, after concluding that the financial health of the country is in a favourable situation—mostly attributable to the new fund manager Cara had appointed—we wrap up the meeting. As Sadiq bows and takes his leave, I relax back in my chair, allowing myself the novel luxury of a moment to myself, and use it to think about the situation with Zee and her abusive ex. But it's not long before I'm interrupted by the door opening, and Nijad enters without waiting for permission.

The fact my brother feels he can just walk into my office is just another example how protocol has relaxed since I've become emir. I've also tried to stop the deep bowing and obeisance of my palace staff, but there I haven't been so successful. *Baby steps*, I tell myself, *baby steps*. Bringing a country like Amahad into the twenty-first century is something to be done in stages.

"What can I do for you, Nijad?" I sigh as I greet him, trying to hide my exasperation. This morning's very pleasant interlude with Zee has set me behind.

"Cara told me that you visited the harem." My brother crosses the room and without invitation, takes a seat across from my large desk, and positions himself so he can see me without my computer screen being in the way. The only change from when my father occupied this office is the technology that now invades the ruler's domain.

"So?" My tone queries why that should be a subject of interest for him.

Nijad looks at me carefully. It's strange that I've now become so much closer to my youngest brother. Even when often he might say things, I don't particularly want to hear.

"Well? If all you want is to stare at me, I'll give you a photograph." I say gruffly, impatient as I wait for him to speak.

"What is this woman to you?" His piercing dark eyes are fixed on mine.

I'm not prepared to answer that question. Not because I don't want to, but because I can't. So I'm honest in my reply, "You want the truth? I've no idea. But don't worry, brother. I know what she can't be."

He nods, dipping his head up and down slowly, as he reaches his own conclusion, "The last fling before your marriage?"

"If I wanted a fling, as you call it, I'd have taken a trip abroad."

"So she's more than that?"

I wonder how much I should disclose. Maybe sharing my thoughts would help me get a better handle on them. With a sigh, I begin, "There's something about her, Ni. From the moment I met her, there was an attraction. Even before I knew what had happened in her past. Something about her called out to me."

"And is this attraction mutual?" His brow furrows as he thinks about what I've said. Only a few words, but a window into the type of thoughts he knows I've never had before.

"I believe so." Standing, I walk across to the floor to ceiling windows that form the outer wall of my office. I look out but don't see the beautiful landscaped gardens. Instead, I see Zee's face as she screamed out her release. Quickly pushing that vision away, I resume, "She can't trust easily. She's attracted to me, yes, but fighting it. That bastard broke her. He fucking destroyed her."

"What are you going to do about it?"

It might not be the answer to the question he's really

asking, but there's no doubt in my head what I want to so next, "I'm going to kill him."

"No, you're not." It appears I've shocked him as Nijad stands, his stance warrior like, "You can't get your hands dirty like that, brother. Killing him will be murder."

"No," I snarl, "It would be a warranted execution."

When he continues I realise he's not shocked by the act, but by the suggestion of the perpetrator. "But not a sentence personally carried out by the emir. You must distance yourself, Kadar, and you can't leave the country at this time." Nijad rips off his headdress and throws it on a chair before coming to stand by me, shoulder-length hair flowing free. His action demonstrating we're in no formal setting. I follow suit, and then run my fingers through the bristles of my shorn hair. He stares at me. "If you are anywhere in the vicinity when St John-Davies dies you run the risk of exposure. Especially if word of your relationship with that woman becomes known."

"She's not *that woman!* She's got a name."

He smirks at me. "I knew you had feelings for her."

"Fuck you!" Then I grin; he's caught me out, but now he realises how much she means to me, I know I'll be able to rely on his help. I get back to the conversation. "Ben Carter thinks we should lure him to Amahad; leak that she's here. He's working on a plan of action as we speak."

Nijad waves to the comfortable couches, conducive to an intimate conversation. I follow him over, and we take our seats.

"It's a better idea than you going to him. But will he come?"

I shrug. "With Zoe as bait, I think there's a good chance."

"Would he come alone? Or would he have his private army with him?"

I lean back and cross my arms. "I don't believe St John-Davies will want to advertise his presence here. If anyone, he'll probably come with Hargreaves, his sidekick and bodyguard, from what Zee has told me, there's probably no one else he trusts so implicitly. Not if his aim is to kidnap her and take her back."

"He might simply kill her."

"That will probably be his end game, but I think he'll want his fun with her first." My teeth clench at the thought of what he might do.

My brother's expression is a mirror of mine, "We can't allow him near her," he says, then offers his soldier's opinion, "He might give up on his playtime if we push him into a corner leaving him no option other than to kill her. We need to act very carefully on this and keep her well out of his way. It would be too risky for her to be in the same vicinity."

I agree, but as I uncross my arms and open my hands palms up I show him I've not thought through how this might play out.

"Take her to the desert city, secretly."

Nijad's unexpected suggestion stumps me, "Why?"

"Let him think she's here in the capital, but in reality, she'll be safe in ?alr??. And, brother, it's a good time for you to meet the desert sheikhs in situ to discuss your plans for a representative government. So you can have a legitimate reason to be out of the way too, with a cast iron alibi nobody could question." He breaks off, looks at me, and grins, "Part of the harem at my palace has been, er, adapted, but the gardens remain. It's in a far better state than the one Zoe is renovating. Let her go there as research for her work here, to get some ideas. It will just be a coincidence that you're both flying out there at the same time."

I'm emir, but I find myself spluttering, "You're suggesting I take Zee to *your* harem?"

"Why not?" Nijad sounds very amused.

"Because you've turned it into a Dom's Dungeon!"

"Exactly!"

His one-word answer silences me. I stand quickly, sweeping my robes around me I start pacing the room, my thoughts whirling a dozen a minute. I turn on him. "But if I'm there, and Ethan comes here…"

"I'll deal with him. Far better, that you're out of the way. You can't afford to get mixed up in something like this, Kadar. Fuck, you're the emir! You need to stay whiter than white."

I can do nothing but appreciate my brother's offer, even though I wanted to deal with the prick myself. But there's something I don't like the idea. "I can't let you do that. It's too risky, Nijad."

"Bollocks!" Nijad's fist hits the table. "Give me some fucking credit! Ben Carter's on board, have some faith in us. You think I haven't killed before?"

I suppose it's in an older brother's psyche to want to protect his younger sibling, but as I turn, I see Nijad properly for perhaps the first time in years. I've become so accustomed to his permanent limp that I hardly notice it anymore, but I can't forget his life-changing injury was received in service to our country. The many successful campaigns he's led to keep jihadists from crossing our borders mean his military experience is far more extensive than mine. I'd done the requisite time in the army, of course, but after that my focus turned to diplomacy and government. Now, perhaps it's time to admit that Nijad's skills in that area far outweigh my own. Especially those he's honed when fighting alongside the desert sheikhs where life is precarious, and retribution swift.

I return to the seating area. "The idea has some merit. But I'd want to be kept informed and in the loop with your plans."

Nijad rises and clasps my hands in his. "You can trust me, brother. And don't forget I had my own reasons to hate the man."

I put my arm around him and draw him close. Although I'd have preferred to see St John-Davies' lifeblood seep out of him with my own eyes, being able to protect Zee and keep her safe is more important to me. And I can depend on Nijad. He'll get this unpleasant task done, in the same competent way he does everything else.

* * * *

Just a day later and the plan starts to take shape. I meet with Ben and Nijad in my office.

"Will Richard help us?" Ben leans forwards, hoping for the right answer.

"He's been with me for years; I'd trust him with my life." I bark a laugh, "He knows nearly all my secrets, and he's known Zoe's identity since the day I first met her."

Nijad nods, "I think the idea has merit. Richard heralds from England, and it wouldn't be thought unlikely he keeps up with the news from the UK. He'll be well aware of the missing Zoe Baker and the huge fucking incentive on offer for news of her whereabouts. I don't think St John-Davies would be suspicious if even a senior palace employee decided to line his pockets in this way."

Ben's obviously in agreement, "We'll ask him to ring the hotline number and lay claim to the reward. Give him instructions to tell them that she is here in Amahad, in Al Qur'ah, working in the palace.

"You sure he'll come?" The plan hinges on St John-Davies personally taking the bait rather than sending his men.

A smirk comes over Ben's face, "I'd lay down good money that St John-Davies will come himself. The kind of man he is, he'd be unable to resist tormenting his prey."

"Richard will have instructions to leak that Zoe is simply an employee. We want to keep any suspicion of the ruling family's interest in her well-hidden." Nijad takes over, "From the information that will be given to him, St John-Davies will surmise she's a woman on her own, working in a foreign country, isolated, and without protection. Hopefully, what your assistant divulges will lead him to believe he has an easy target: a woman who has relaxed her guard, thinking she had escaped his clutches, being so very far away from home."

"How will you take him?"

"St John-Davies is a major player in the security game," Nijad starts with an evil grin, "It wouldn't be any surprise that, as the government of Amahad, we would be well aware of such a prestigious person paying the country a visit, so I, on your behalf, Kadar, would invite him to the palace for a diplomatic evening. How it will play out after that would be finalised once the size of his entourage is known."

"I'll be dealing with that sadistic bastard Hargreaves if he comes along," Ben explains, and by the glint in his eyes, I suspect he's looking forward to it. "But are you certain your man can play his part? If he arouses suspicion, St John-Davies might suspect he'll be walking into a trap."

Standing I pace the room, deep in thought. The plan hinges on my assistant being credible enough to attract St John-Davies here. If I didn't trust him as much as I did, Richard could be the weak link in the chain. But I know him well and trust him implicitly, so I have absolutely no concern assuring Nijad and Ben Carter that Richard would play his part credibly and with utmost conviction.

I don't hear from Kadar the next day which disappoints me, even though I'm in no position to make demands on him. I miss him, but can't stop thinking about him, the incredible intimacy between us repeating in my head on a loop. *At last, I know what Sophie had been on about. And understand now how that kind of pleasure could be addictive!*

My feelings for Kadar are mixed and muddled up, and more than I should allow myself. Sometimes I want to see him more than I want my next breath, and then I become scared, frightened by the depth of my growing trust in him. I could easily get too personally invested in this incredible man. Although I try to place any thoughts of the intimacy that had occurred between us firmly out of my mind and attempt to accept it for what it was—a demonstration of the D/s dynamic—I still can't stop my traitorous mind from wishing it could be something more.

Even as I remind myself there can be no future with the emir and try and get thoughts of a repeat performance behind me; I still *need* to see him if only to find out what their plans for Ethan are. The idea that my tormentor will be coming to this country—that he'll be so close to finding me—is terrifying. To keep my sanity, I have to understand how they propose to keep me safe.

I know I should trust Kadar and Ben's team to know what they're doing, but I can't get rid of the nagging seed of fear starting to grow in the back of my head. Ethan has ways to see all, to know all. Can they really trump him?

When the harem doors open mid-morning on the second day after he'd taken me to such incredible heights, and Kadar enters, I'm not sure how to greet him. I have the compulsion to run into his arms, but force myself to remember I don't, and can't have, the right to initiate such intimacy, and instead plant a polite smile on my face.

But my attempt to distance myself is destroyed with his short, one word greeting. "Habiti."

As he walks towards me I feel awkward. What do you say to a man who's had his mouth on, and hand in your private parts? And with whom you've discussed the murder of your ex? At the intensity of his expression my welcoming smile fades, and I turn away in a flush of embarrassment, not knowing how I should respond.

But I shouldn't have worried, he's a Dom and doesn't leave me floundering for long.

"Look at me!" Immediately taking charge, his command draws my eyes to his, and what I see there warms me. Reaching me, he lowers his head and presses his lips to mine. I feel an almost not there whisper across my mouth that makes me want more. I can't help it, I press up against him, and as if he is waiting for that signal he flicks out his tongue, forcing me to open for him. Our mouths mash against each other, tongues and teeth clashing with a sudden insane violence. He tastes of coffee and something that's uniquely him. With a groan I stand on my tiptoes at the same time as he supports me, taking my weight and pulling me up close against him. I feel his hardness against me, and my responding readiness as sparks are igniting deep inside me making my stomach clench, sending shock waves down to my pussy. I moan into his mouth, and he groans in return. All at once I realise I have to stop lying to myself. I want more from this man than he can ever give. Then the realisation he'll soon be a married man cuts through me like a knife and I force myself to pull away before we can make a mistake,.

"I'm sorry." I gasp.

"No, don't apologise. Fuck, Zee. If anyone's to blame, it's me. The moment I saw you…" Kadar turns his head away. His arms are still holding me, but at a distance. When he looks back, his eyes are hooded, "You unman me, Zee." Gently he brushes his hand down the side of my face, his expression one of immense regret. "I've nothing to offer you; you know that. And there's no mileage in wishing things were different." He stares into my eyes compelling me to understand and then nods when he sees that, albeit sadly, I do.

Taking my hand, he leads me out into the neglected and desolate garden of the harem. The sun is beating down, hot and furious, but we find some shade under a dying palm tree. Wanting to change the subject to something far less dangerous I wave my hand around, indicating our surroundings, the crumbling walls, the dead wood of long ago plants. "I can't wait to get started on this, Kadar."

A brief nod of his head shows he appreciates the new direction of the conversation, "What are your plans?"

"With Cara's help, we're taking on some local craftsmen. They'll rebuild the walls, and once the raised beds are in place and the paths repaired I'll get people in to do the plantings. I've been researching the best varieties, the ones most likely to survive here. Of course, we'll also have to fix the irrigation systems." I look out over the harem grounds, in my mind's eye seeing greenery and bright colours instead of the greys and browns that now surround us.

We sit in silence for a moment, and then Kadar takes my hand in his and pulls me in against his shoulder. "Zee, as emir the people expect me to be married, and are anticipating I'll soon produce an heir. Only within very limited boundaries have I any choice in who my wife will be."

I sigh, softly, "It's okay, Kadar, I don't hold out any hope that things could be different. I'm not ready for a relationship with a man yet, and might never be. So even if you were free, this wouldn't be going anywhere." As the words leave my lips, I wonder how much of what I've said is a lie.

"Don't cut yourself off like that!" he sounds angry. "Don't allow that man to ruin the whole of your life. You gave him a year and a half, don't give him anymore." He gives me a gentle shake, "There's a man out there waiting for you, someone who will love you as you deserve. Someone who would give their life for your's." He pulls me into him again, and I feel his lips touch my hair, "I just can't be that man, Zee. Whatever my feelings are. If things were different, though…"

As his voice trails off, I wonder why he's telling me this now. I mean, I already know that even if his wedding wasn't already being arranged, a nobody from Surrey is never going to end up marrying a Sheikh, particularly when he's also the ruler of a whole damn country!

"I'm giving you my protection, Zee. That's all I can offer you. I'll do everything to keep you safe." Then, before I can say anything, he continues and answers my unspoken question, "Zee, the information that you're here in Amahad will be leaked tomorrow." He pauses, waiting for my reaction.

I pull away and stand up, shivering as though someone's just walked over my grave. I knew it was coming, but that doesn't stop the bombshell he's just dropped scaring the wits out of me. I'd felt so much relief being on a different continent, so far away and so out of his reach. I'd been happier than I'd ever been, working here, enjoying my new life. And now Ethan's virtually been invited in to destroy it all over again. He's going to be too close to me. *What if their plan fails?* I feel a hand touch my shoulder.

"You can't hide forever. We need to deal with this, so you can get your life together and move on. You shouldn't be living like this."

Like this? Move on? "You want me to leave Amahad?" His words wound me.

"Never in a million years. But I need you to feel free to do so."

I trail my hand over an ancient twisted vine. The plant is

long dead, and my heart feels much the same. Even if I could return to the UK, I'm not sure I'd want to. But I'm also not sure I can stay here and watch Kadar with his new wife, especially now I know exactly what pleasures he can give her. I shake my head as if I can rid myself of the vision of him in bed with another woman that's entered my head, and try to concentrate on the other things he's said.

I know he's right before I can make any decisions about my future Ethan has to be dealt with. "So, tell me. Exactly what's the plan?"

He's beside me again. "Cards on the table time, Zee. In six weeks' time, there's going to be a ball, here, in the palace. The occasion when I'm expected to make my choice of bride."

Smothering my gasp, I force myself to remain impassive and not let my face betray my anguish. I knew it was going to happen, I just hadn't appreciated how little time we had. Somehow I'd convinced myself it was a long way in the future; now it appears he's counting down the weeks. It seems a barbaric way of doing things, a crude system to choose a mate for life. Mind you; I thought I'd fallen in love with the perfect man and look how wrong I'd turned out to be. Who am I to say that his way is any worse?

After giving me a minute to digest his revelation he continues. "We've got a month to get your life back on track, Zee. That's a month to deal with Ethan and to restore your trust. So I'm taking you to the desert city, to [illegible]alm[illegible], to Nijad's palace."

That was unexpected. "What? Why?"

He stops my questions by placing his finger over my lips,

"I don't want you anywhere near St John-Davies. He'll be lured here, to the capital where Nijad and Carter will deal with him. You'll be safe with me in the Desert City."

"But your reputation? How can you explain why you're taking me there? Surely you can't afford any rumours with the meat market so close." I cover my mouth with my hand immediately realising how rude I've been and the assumption that I jumped to. "I'm sorry…"

"Don't be." He gives a self-deprecating grin, "I feel much the same way. But Zee, I've known my destiny from the time I came to rule. I accept it. I might not like it, had hoped it would be otherwise, but I can't change it. Though, perhaps especially now I wish that I could." He gives me no chance to process that rather strange last comment as he continues immediately, "And I have a legitimate excuse to go to the desert city. I need to meet with the tribal leaders to discuss the way forward for Amahad. Something I've been putting off for too long. *I* need to go. And the harem at the Palace of Palms is in a far better state that this one, the gardens are all intact and traditionally laid out. I thought it would be good research for you to see what you might try to accomplish here."

It was a good cover story for getting me away at the same time as the emir, and there was no way in hell I want to come face to face with Ethan. But something rankled, making me ask, "The harem?" I purse my lips. "Cara mentioned something about that."

"Did she now?" Kadar's face is full of amusement, "What did she say?"

Tilting my head to one side I try to remember. "Not a

lot, just that it had already been renovated."

Now he laughs. "Yes, it has. And I'd be interested to see your reaction. And I'll be seeing that soon enough—we're leaving this afternoon. Can you be packed and ready to go by two o'clock?"

"That quickly?"

"Yes. The information will be released to St John-Davies in the morning, and I want you a long way away from here before then. I won't take any risks with your safety, Zee."

His conviction and the promise which seems to come from his heart elicit my confirmation of my readiness. After I've assured him there's no issue with being prepared by the appointed time, he takes his leave. I realise neither of us had alluded further to that devastating kiss. My hand touches my lips, as I remember his caress and again recall the intimacy between us two days ago when, for the first time in my life, a man had touched me without taking anything for himself. His selflessness is astounding. Then I feel as though I'm being stabbed me through the heart when I realise I'd at least like to be able to have more time to explore what we could be together.

But he's giving me one month out of his last six weeks of freedom! There must be a devil sitting on my shoulder, whispering into my ear as I consider taking a chance on a man for the first time since Ethan had stormed into my life. Kadar can't enslave me in the way that Ethan did; he hasn't got time; he's promised to another. But as he won't even meet his prospective bride until the ball, I wouldn't be encroaching on another woman's ground if I enjoyed this time with him now, would I? What if I have the opportunity to play the role of his sub again if we get a chance to be alone together in the desert city? What if he shows me those things women should enjoy, and that I've been missing out on? The things my friend Sophie so clearly revelled in.

The thought of my friend is sobering and brings me back to the reality of my situation. My tremendously bad taste in men not only led to my abusive existence but caused harm to the people I love.

I rub my hand over my lips as if to remove any lingering taste of Kadar from my mouth, and stamp down on the residual fluttering of my heart to remove his presence there. To get involved with such a man, even temporarily, would be a grave mistake.

CHAPTER 25
Kadar

For fuck's sake, what made me kiss her like that? Her lips against mine, her tongue in my mouth and her unique taste has left my cock rock hard. If she'd pressed up against me any longer, I would have come on the spot. *What am I, a fucking schoolboy, experiencing his first crush?* As I walk through the corridors, back to my office to make the final arrangements for my absence from the palace, I can still smell her on my clothes, her sweet perfume which is all her, not something that's come out of a bottle. Never have I felt this way about a woman before.

Never have I felt so unable to divorce myself from getting attached. I've had plenty of liaisons, but that's all they've been—opportunities to scratch my itch. And I've not even had my cock in this woman, yet I feel more emotionally invested in her than I've ever done with any other before. Is it that's she's lost all faith in men, and that I, as a Dom, desire to mend her? To restore her to the confident woman I'm sure she was before St John-Davies got his claws into her? Whatever the reason is, I have to try to keep some distance between us. I can't let her have the slightest inkling of the depth of my feelings. I need to keep reminding myself, and her, that in a month and a half I'll be committed to my bride. A bride with the right credentials and the approval of the country to be my wife.

But even once back in my domain, I go through the motions of my labour with visions of a cute blond refusing to get out of my head. I work on autopilot, as I hand the reins of the country temporarily over into Nijad's care, and the memory of her beautiful eyes makes it difficult to concentrate when Richard updates me on the relevant information I'll need in ?aln?? The reports on the success my assistant's had with setting up meetings on such short notice with the Sheikhs of the southern desert nearly go over my head.

I have to force myself to pay attention when he relates their reaction to the summons—the majority seem to appreciate the honour that their emir is going to them, instead of commanding their presence in the capital. Except for some, of course, who see it as weakness. I sigh deeply when he tells me this, remembering my father's much harsher regime and that he was probably the more respected for it. Educated in the West, I find it impossible to continue to rule in his autocratic way, even if it's what some of the desert sheikhs seem to expect. Although I must make changes slowly, they will need to accept the old emir is gone. And that Amahad *will* be dragged, albeit kicking and screaming, into the twenty-first century.

At last free from my duties, precisely at two o'clock, I go to the helipad where Zee is ready waiting for me, a tatty looking rucksack by her side. That she's making a small show of independence by not using the expensive luggage I bought for her makes me give a small smile. I don't miss the slight challenge in her eyes, or the touch of fear, as the guard lifts her scruffy bag into the luggage compartment and inwardly curse, knowing she would have received a rebuke for even that small rebellion in the past.

To ease her worries, I make no comment, and simply help her into one of the rear seats in four-seater helicopter and assist her with her harness, explaining how she can use the headset to communicate. She's nervous, and I don't need to hear her words telling me this is her first flight in a helicopter, I can see that for myself. So I reassure her that the craft is regularly serviced and perfectly airworthy, adding that all precautions have been taken against sabotage as I explain she's got no need to worry. Then I get into the front passenger seat. Generally, I'd prefer to fly myself, but with the troubles we've been having recently, and the threats which seem to hang in the air, an extra armed man on board could be helpful. The pilot enters the craft but doesn't start the engine.

"What are we waiting for, Kadar?" Zoe asks, curiously, fidgeting at the delay.

My answer isn't verbal; I just wave towards the palace entrance. There, hurrying across towards us is the close protection officer she knows all too well. Sean Cooper. I feel a stab of envy at the broad, welcoming smile she directs at him, and the gasp of pleasure that I hear escaping her lips. For a second, I wonder whether it was such a good idea to accept Ben's proposal that she has this additional protection detail with St John-Davies coming to the country, or at least should have insisted on the innocuous Harry.

As an unexpected and unworthy bolt of jealousy hits me,

I fight to keep any betraying expression from my face while I study the man running across the tarmac. Sean's free and single, and unlike me has no prior commitments, and Zee seems overly pleased to see him. As he takes the seat beside her, the alien feeling of envy deepens, particularly when I glance behind as the rotors start to turn above us, and see Sean takes Zoe's hand in his, holding it tight, picking up on her nervousness and providing her with the comfort I don't dare give her publicly myself.

My feelings of resentment don't dissipate during the two-hour journey. Although they make sure to include me in the conversation, I'd like to have been the one pointing out the herd of desert ibex we fly over, the graceful animals picking up their heels and taking flight at the sound of the rotors spinning in the air. I'd like to have been discussing her progress and plans for the harem, as well as updating her on what's happening in her homeland. Not that I'm excluded from doing any of this, but it was rash enough for me to take the same flight as her, let alone, in front of the pilot, give the impression it was for anything other than expediency and a desire to reduce our carbon footprint.

It's with an intense feeling of relief that we arrive and touch down on the helipad to the rear of the Palace of ?alr??, the building neither as large or grand as the Palace of Amahad, but still impressive nonetheless. The air is hotter and drier here. In the capital citizens can feel the benefits from the sea breeze; in the heart of the desert there is nothing but unrelenting sand and shimmering heat in all directions.

?alr?? is situated on what was once a busy caravan route

across ancient Arabia, and built up to service the needs of the travellers. Over millenia, it has remained a focal point for the desert tribes. Originally a Sultan reigned in the palace, but the unification of Amahad in my grandfather's time negated the need for the southern tribes to have a separate ruler. Palma, however, still houses the government offices looking after the particular requirements of this region, and is now expanding to house the administration responsible for the development of the oilfield in the desert. As the focal point in the desert, it's the ideal place for me to meet with the sheikhs.

Once we've landed and exited the helicopter, I quickly usher Zoe and Sean into the palace before they start to overheat. Even I find the air unusually hot, and I was born to it. Knowing the climate of their home country well, I can understand how oppressive and uncomfortable they'll find it, but once in the palace, the air is cooler. The older parts kept to a tolerable temperature by massive ancient fans in the ceilings and the newer or more recently renovated areas by modern air conditioning.

Although my visit was a last minute arrangement, that hasn't stopped a welcoming committee from being hastily assembled to acknowledge the honour of their emir paying a visit to the region. To avoid Zoe and Sean being caught up in the pomp and ceremony, which I have every expectation will be more tedious than enjoyable, I send them on ahead to the living quarters and the accommodation that has been made ready for them. The sight of them walking off together—Sean's hand resting low down on Zee's back—does nothing to pacify the green-eyed monster within me. Nor does the knowledge that they'll be sharing the guest suite adjacent to the royal chambers, usually occupied by Nijad and which today will have been assigned to me. I tell myself their suite has three separate bedrooms, adding the mental reminder Sean would be unable to do his job if he didn't remain nearby. But the pang of jealousy is hard to dismiss.

In the end, it's well into the evening by the time I'm done with formalities. Five of the ten desert sheikhs were in attendance, Sheikhs Rais, Ghalib, Jibran, Sofian, and Wahid. Of the absentees, three were concerning. I hadn't expected to see Abdul-Muhsi of course, and have to admit part of me was relieved by his absence. But it worried me that Fadi and Tamir hadn't put in an appearance. Their camps are indeed the closest to the desert city, and thus their absence surely a deliberate snub. Khalaf and Nazmi, who are based further away, had at least sent apologies for their not being here, so I can't immediately interpret the fact they haven't turned up as a sign of their lack of support.

Once I'd become resigned to the disappointing empty spaces around the table, I found it extremely useful getting the five attending sheikhs together and made a mental note to thank Richard for his foresight in arranging our first meeting in an informal setting. The conversation at dinner had been enlightening. Being able to introduce my plans for a democratic form of government in a casual way meant we'd had some serious discussion, with my proposal receiving a cautious welcome by those present. With the expected caveats, of course, which include ensuring sufficient sway is given to the desert tribes. We'd ended by drawing up a rough agenda for our meetings in the following days. All in all a very productive evening.

But the few hours of being a politician, ensuring every single word uttered from my lips was censored and diplomatic, had been draining, and when I eventually make my way to the royal suite I'm more than ready for some form relaxation. The trouble is, my preferred way of relieving my stress would be to sink my cock deep into, what I now know is, the very tight pussy of a petite blonde who happens to be staying in the suite next to mine. And that is just not going to happen. My brain knows it, but my body hasn't got the message as I harden at the thought of the woman so close and yet so far, my cock pushing against the material of my desert robes. Then I remember Sean is sharing her suite, and the idea of another man being so near to her makes me want to hit something. My fists clench by my sides, as I try to control the unreasonable feelings inside of me. If she wants Sean, I should let her have him. I have no right to her; I cannot claim her as mine.

As I near my brother's rooms, two servants exit the royal suite, evidently having turned down my bed for the night. I acknowledge their bows while noting the extent of their obeisance is so great, they almost end up folded to the floor. Such behaviour is common in the capital's Palace of Amahad; my father had insisted on the strict protocol in any royal residence. But here, in the desert city, Nijad's informed me he'd almost entirely stamped the habit out, requiring nothing more than a verbal greeting or at most a slight dipping of the head as a mark of respect. *Hmm, perhaps these two haven't got the memo.* Or maybe Nijad has been exaggerating the extent of the reforms he'd accomplished. But I have to admit, I haven't been in the Palace of [illegible]alm[illegible] for some time and have no up-to-date knowledge of the servants here.

Their greeting reminds me of how I'm trying gradually to change the formalities in the main palace. My father encouraged the traditional practice of excess deference which has been afforded to me since birth. I see no need for it, but it's hard to stamp out old habits. The behaviour of the two servants I've just seen makes me resolve to try harder. In this day and age such exaggerated signs of respect are out of date.

As I walk into the royal suite, I think over the whole of the passage I've taken from the formal dining room to this point and realise not once had Nijad's boasted reforms been in evidence. Each guard, each servant, had greeted me in the old fashioned way. Why? Had they reverted to their traditional behaviour because I'm the emir? It's possible. Something is niggling at me, but having spent the last few hours negotiating and fighting to keep my wits about me to avoid stepping on any overly sensitive metaphorical toes, my brain refuses to fire on all cylinders. So I store the observation away in the back of my mind if only to tease Nijad about it on my return to Al Qur'ah.

Entering the royal bedroom, I throw off my robes and headdress and pull on a pair of jeans and a T-shirt, no longer wanting to feel like the ruler. As I change, I feel the shackles of state fall from me, and I'm just a man again. An average, hot-blooded man with a dick still twitching at the thought of the woman next door. Giving myself a mental shake I return to the suite's sitting room, and sprawl on the luxurious cushions spread around a low table, staring at the jug containing a fruit drink set on it. There's no alcohol in the southern desert—even in the palace—a fact I currently resent with a vengeance. *If there was a time I needed a fucking drink, this is most definitely it.*

I stare at the offending carafe for a long moment before slashing my arm forward and sweeping it off the table, uncaring that it's smashed or that the liquid soaks into the expensive antique carpet. Lithely unfolding myself, I get to my feet, my fists tight by my sides, tension rolling off me in waves. There is no way I can relax tonight, not on my own. The longing, the yearning, comes over me like a wave. *Fuck it! I have to see Zee.* My desert blood rises through me, and I move like a warrior about to stalk his prey. *I want her. I'm going to have her.*

All common sense leaves me as I exit the royal rooms. I'm no longer the emir; I'm an aroused man going after my mate. With no hesitation I knock loudly on the door of the guest suite, and when Sean answers I brush past him with little more than a nod, zoning in on my quarry.

She's standing at the door of her room, already dressed for bed in a negligee and light silk robe. Her blond hair is just long enough to touch the swell of her gorgeous breasts. One long slender leg pokes out through the soft flowing wrap, and the way her belt is cinched shows off her shapely narrow waist emphasising the swell of her ample womanly hips. I swallow, already uncomfortable in my tight jeans.

Having feasted on her body my gaze rises to her face. She's startled, her eyes open wide as though she's having trouble recognising me probably as she's never seen me dressed so casually before. Her blush and the way her tongue comes out to lick her lips tell me she is not unaffected by the sight. The air is tinged with her arousal, but I stay where I am, retaining just sufficient control to prevent me rushing and falling on her like an animal. I'm not blind to the hint of uncertainty in her eyes.

"I want you." It's all I can stammer out; proud I'm able to form words at all.

"This is not a good idea, Your Excellency," Sean stands close behind me, his voice full of contained anger as he uses my title to remind me who I am.

I swing round to face him. "No! Tonight I'm not the emir; I'm merely a man. And you don't stand in the way of a man who wants his woman." The bodyguard doesn't budge. Does he not realise how dangerous it is for him to obstruct me from the object of my very deep desires? "Leave us!"

"No." He steps closer to me, his posture threatening, "I don't care who you are; Zoe's not ready for this."

"Zee," I turn my back on him and look her straight in the eye, "I can't promise you a future. But fuck I need you. I *need* you tonight. In my bed."

Her eyes flick between us, confused, scared at the animosity in the air and taken aback by my demand. But she's not retreating. Does she realise the way she's pulling back her shoulders is causing her already erect nipples to poke against the thin silk of her clothing? Is she aware her slight movement has caused her robe to part, showing bare flesh up to her thigh?

"Zoe, he's not going to touch you while I'm here," Sean states adamantly. He's going to get hurt if he keeps this up.

Her attention is caught momentarily by her protector, but it's back on me within seconds. "Kadar…"

I don't let her finish, "Sleep with me, habiti. Come with me now." I hold out my hand to her.

Sean starts at the endearment and throws me a strange look, but he's not giving in, "Kadar!" It's a shout that makes me turn back to him.

"What?" I snarl. I'm fast running out of patience, and he's going to find himself decked in a moment.

"She's going nowhere. You think I'm going to let her go out of here with you into your suite? Into the *dungeon?*"

I hear a gasp; Zoe's covering her mouth. When she takes her hand away, her eyes are even wider, her face full of shock. "Dungeon?"

"Yeah, sweetheart. Nijad's converted part of the harem into a Dom's Dungeon, and the entrance is via the royal suite." Sean explains to her, not too helpfully in my opinion. I wasn't even thinking of taking her there tonight.

She starts backing into her room then pauses her retreat. "You brought me here to take me into a *dungeon?* That's the alterations you were telling me about?"

Before I answer, I study her face. Fuck me; she's scared, yes, but there's also an element of curiosity there. I try to calm myself, holding out my hands palms open upwards to signal my sincerity. "A lot of the harem is still intact, and as I told you, the gardens are magnificent. Yes, a portion of it's been converted into a fully equipped dungeon which Nijad and Cara use, or used to use, it's a bit, er… awkward at the moment given her condition." My reference to my sister-in-law's advanced state of pregnancy brings a fleeting smile to her face, but it quickly disappears. I shake my head, "I'd love to take you to the dungeon, habiti, but tonight I have no intention to do so. It's not the reason you're here. We expect St John-Davies to arrive in Al Qur'ah in the next few days, and I've brought you here to the desert palace to keep you safe."

She holds her position, giving no more ground. "Why, why are you here now then?" Her soft voice trembles, but I can hear the intrigue there. Her apprehension that had appeared at the mention of the dungeon dissipates and a slight flush reddens the tops of her breasts visible beneath the robe. As I watch her intently, her eyes can no longer meet mine, but as she drops them, she makes a reciprocal inspection of my body, of my very visible throbbing desire for her straining at the zip on my jeans. *Fuck, I'm going to get marks embedded there if I don't release my cock soon.* She doesn't miss it, and I don't overlook her crossing her legs, moving as though she's trying to ease some discomfort. I realise I can read her like a book. She wants me as much as I want her.

Sean's a Dom; he doesn't miss the signals she's giving out either. I hear him clear his throat behind us, and suddenly I realise that I was right to be jealous, he has feelings for her too, more than he should have as her bodyguard. But it's me she's looking at, not him. It's me she's devouring with her eyes.

He draws our attention with a cough, and his words signify his surrender, but his tone carries a warning, "It's up to Zoe. If Zoe wants you, then you stay here. You're not taking her to your suite, Kadar. I'll be right here in the next room, and if I hear her cry out or scream I'll be straight in. If you scare her or hurt her, I can't promise you'll walk out of here alive, Kadar. Emir or not."

"I hear you. But make sure you don't misinterpret any cries or screams. Any sound you hear will be of pleasure, not pain. And I don't want to die because I've pleased my woman. And don't underestimate my skill, Sean. You might be the one leaving in a box."

"Stop it!"

Zoe looks at us with a frown on her face as though she's separating kids on a playground, and for a second, I see her giving our children a dressing down. *What. The. Fuck? Children?* I shake my head to clear the vision. I have to focus on tonight. This one night that I can give her.

"Kadar, I want you. But I'm not ready for this, for you." The admission passes her lips as a whisper, and she gazes down at her feet.

Moving towards her I close the distance between us and put my fingers under her chin, tilting her face up until she can't avoid my eyes, "Trust me, Zee. I won't take more from you that what you wish to gift me. I'll give you control, Zee. I won't hold you, force you or even undress you. You take it all at your pace. And if you can't continue, you stop. If I scare you or frighten you, scream your safeword and Sean will come running. And if I do scare or frighten you, I'll deserve whatever he wants to dish out." I lower my hand, dropping it down to my side, keeping my palms flat against me, offering no threat or pressure. It's hard to maintain a relaxed stance with blood pumping so strongly through my veins. I feel lightheaded with passion, but I'm not going to force myself upon her. I'd never do that to any woman.

I almost feel Sean relax behind me, as though he realises that he has lost. Like I'm offering her control, he's got to accept her choice.

How long we stand there, I'm not sure, but we both give her the space she needs to make her decision. Suddenly she looks up, her gaze flicking from me to her bodyguard, then back to me again. She nods, slowly. "Kadar, make Ethan go away."

As she steps to one side, inviting me into her room, I understand the meaning underlying her words. She wants me to take away the memories of him away, to replace them with something new. To show her how good a real man can make her feel. It's a heavy responsibility, but one I feel confident I can carry. As I follow her into the room, I close the door firmly behind me.

When I came to the door of my room and saw Kadar dressed in those tight-fitting jeans and a T-shirt that hugs him so closely, doing nothing to hide the hard body beneath, exposing his arms, so muscular and powerful, I felt an immediate rush of arousal soaking my underwear. His posture, his expression, everything about him emphasises his aura of strength and dominance that comes not only from his inherited role but uniquely from the man inside. He's so tall, towering over me. This man wouldn't need a Hargreaves to hold me down for him to hurt me; he could control me with one hand. I should have shut my door, shut him out. Run and hidden or taken Sean up on his offer of protection. But something stops me; a feeling of desire that fights to counteract my fear. *Could I have him just this once?*

I listen to the angry words being tossed around between the two men, but my focus is on the emir. No, not the ruler of Amahad, but just a man. A hot-blooded man who so very obviously wants me.

I'd spent time with Sean today, enjoying catching up with him, hearing about what was going on back home and unable to deny there was a bubbling attraction between us, at least from his side. His seductive glances, his suggestive comments made me giggle but elicited no other physical response. By contrast, as soon as I saw Kadar again my body immediately awakened, need flooding through me, letting me know my bodyguard couldn't hold a candle to Kadar. Sean is a decent person, and I'm not blind to nor feel threatened by his overt flirtation. He isn't a man for a happily ever after, nor will he ever be, until he makes up his mind about what he's looking for.

On the other hand, there's no chance of a happy ending with Kadar. He has commitments on him; obligations for a whole nation. But however much I try to ignore my feelings, I can't stop me from wanting him or needing him to ease this ache inside me, wanting to experience, even if for just one time, what it would be like to be in his arms. Instinctively I know it would be like nothing I've ever known before. I'd never wanted any man so much. But I'm too scared to follow through.

Too afraid, that is until he says he'll give me all control and an out if it gets too much. I just use my safeword, and he'll stop, or Sean will come to my rescue if he doesn't. No comparison to the circumstances where Ethan tortured me in his playroom, with no one to come to the rescue. *What have I got to lose? Can I summon enough courage to do this?* There's no doubt he wants me, this virile man standing in front of me. Could he make the bad memories go away? No pain, only pleasure. Would I be a fool to turn him down?

While different thoughts battle in my head, he stares at me, the intensity of his gaze making me uncomfortable, making me squirm. I shift my legs to try and ease the ache between them, but I can find no relief. My arousal must short circuit my brain as I find the words coming out of my mouth, "Kadar, make Ethan go away."

He wastes no time, coming forwards, making me retreat into my room as he shuts the door firmly him. Despite his assurances, a sudden wave of anxiety turns my anticipation into fear. Scared he's going to be rough—to grab me, to strip me, to force me—I can't get my breath, can't get the oxygen I need into my lungs. He moves closer.

"Eyes on me." His dominant tone imposes itself through my scattered thoughts, and I can do nothing but obey. He takes my hand and puts it against his chest so I can feel his heart beating. "Breathe with me. In, out, deep breath in, and out," he instructs me. I try to mimic his movements, concentrating on the hard muscles of his upper body beneath my hands as they rise and fall with each intake of breath. Gradually my breathing calms, my panic attack dissipating. My eyes are still fixed on his as he asks me, "You remember your safeword?"

I confirm it by nodding.

"Verbal answer, habiti. Talk to me," he reminds me.

"Yes. Red," my voice comes out only just above a whisper.

"If you use it I'll stop immediately, as I did in the harem. Nothing will happen here tonight that you don't want to take place. And, for just this one night, nothing which you don't control." His dark eyes examine me, and what he sees seems to satisfy him. "Now, tell me what you want to do. Or better still, what you want me to do."

Reading the sincerity in his beautiful dark eyes, I feel

uncertain. He's offering me the moon, but I'm not sure what to do with it. "I don't know how to do this," I tell him hesitantly, honestly, and then give a soft disparaging laugh, "I'm like a child given loose rein in a sweet shop. I don't know where to start."

"Do you want me to take my clothes off?"

His helpful offer surprises me. I was always naked first with Ethan; the fact I was unclothed while he was still dressed immediately increased his power over me. He'd used it as a form of humiliation, particularly when he made me strip in front of Hargreaves. So I'm amazed at the suggestion. I don't take long to think about it.

Do I want Kadar to get naked for me? *Shit, yes! The heck I do.* The thought sends a delicious shiver through me. To see his glorious body in all its glory? To discover what he's kept hidden under his robes? I'd be a fool to miss such an opportunity. I raise and lower my head, then remembering his instruction. "Yes, please strip, Kadar."

I'm all but salivating as I watch him reach behind his neck and pull off his T-shirt in one smooth move. Feasting my eyes on his now bare chest, I notice some old scarring over his abs that proves he's a warrior prince, no stranger to violence. He pauses, as though making sure I'm comfortable with his semi-nakedness. Eagerly I motion for him to continue, hardly daring to speak.

His hands move to the button of his jeans, and he flicks it open, his chest almost bare of hair except for the dark trail leading down and disappearing into his waistband. Slowly he reveals more as he lowers his zip. He's gone commando, and as he tucks in his thumbs and starts pushing the denim down off his hips nothing is hidden from my sight. I take an audible breath as his full length jumps free of the confines of his jeans. His cock is long and thick, much bigger than Ethan and I feel afraid that he'll be too much for me.

He notices my concern and puts out his hand to touch my arm. "We need do nothing you don't want to do," he confirms again. His voice is soft, seductive. "Remember, you're the one in the driving seat, and you can keep your foot over the brake." He continues removing the rest of his clothing, his bare feet stepping out of the sandals he's wearing.

Now this glorious specimen of manhood is standing completely naked, and right now, I have absolutely no idea know what to do with it. But there's no way I'm going to waste this opportunity, so I think of something fast. Rapidly swallowing down the excess moisture in my mouth triggered by this vision in front of me, I summon up the nerve to give my first instruction.

"Lie on the bed." With no hesitation he obeys me, lying on his back, his legs stretched out in a V that leaves nothing to my imagination, his hands clasped behind his head. His cock springs up, bobbing against his stomach as if it's a creature in its own right, and his balls hang heavy below. I've never taken the time to look at a man's body before, never felt I'd wanted to. But Kadar is something my eyes happily feast on.

His body isn't soft like a woman's; there's no femininity about him at all. He's all man, hard and firm, without an ounce of fat on him. His skin smooth, a delicious olive colour like a rich all over tan. As he lies still, unmoving, a giggle escapes caused partly by my nervousness, and also by the impulsive naughty thought that's slipped into my mind, "Are there handcuffs in the dungeon, Kadar? I could tie you to the bed."

"Probably, but no." As I raise my eyebrows, at the seriousness of his tone, he continues, "I want you to trust me, habiti. Tonight is about me giving you control, not you taking it and leaving me no choice. It is my wish that you explore me, do what you want with me. Use me as you feel fit and trust me to allow you to do so. Tonight isn't about Dominance and submission."

Although it had been an impish suggestion and I hadn't meant it, I realise I'd feel safer if I was able to tie him down. As I can't, all I can do is have faith that he's a man of his word. So nervously, I rely on my words to restrain him.

"Keep your hands behind your head."

He nods, acknowledging my request, and I gaze at the perfection laid out in front of me like a starving man at a banquet. But tonight's about more than just looking, and everything I do is up to me. Taking a deep fortifying breath and with one last sweep of my eyes from head to toe, I move towards him.

I start by kneeling beside his head and hesitantly bring my lips down to his. He opens for me, and I press into his mouth, our tongues dancing together. I love the taste of this man and already know I've become hooked. After our lips and tongues mash together for a minute, I pull my mouth away, but even that short break is too much, and I have to go back to sample him again, unable to resist bringing my head back down and stealing a kiss from his lips a second time. Ethan's kisses were all about him, taking, not giving, and then he'd ceased kissing me at all when he stopped pretending. And the few men before him weren't much better, seeing it as something to get out of the way before moving on to the main event. With Kadar, the kiss is foreplay all by itself. He starts thrusting his tongue deep between my lips—mimicking what I know he'd like to do with other parts of our bodies—and I start to squirm as tingling sensations assault me.

His body is tense; I'd have to be blind not to see he's fully aroused, the intimacy of our kiss affecting him as much as me. I draw back panting, and see by the dilation in his eyes and the rise and fall of his chest that the joining of our mouths has made him impatient to continue. For a brief moment, I'm scared he might take over, might become exasperated with my insecurity and slow pace. But apart from his heavy breathing he makes no move. Sitting back on my heels, I know it's up to me to make the next move. Before I allow myself to hesitate or reconsider, I shrug off my robe and pull my negligee up over my head. Apart from my underwear, I'm now as naked as the man beneath me.

His sharp intake of breath shows me his appreciation. As he eyes my breasts greedily, I take the hint and lean forwards, so my nipple rubs over his lips. I tense, waiting for the vicious bite. As he opens and mouths me, it's all I can do to control my fear and resist pulling away, waiting for his strong arms to come down and trap me. But true to his word his hands stay locked behind his head, and he uses only the tools at his disposal. As his tongue licks around the aureole and flicks over my nipple, a jolt goes straight down to my centre, and I can't hold back a moan. I'm desperate for attention on the other nipple, so I move further over him so he can lave that one too. I moan again, louder, as I wonder whether it's possible to come from his caresses on my nipples alone. I indulge myself a little longer, letting him suckle one breast and then the other. It's even better than that time in the harem, and I want more.

At last, I sit up and run my fingers down his body, tracing the scars, and then follow the darkening trail down to his impressive cock. He hisses air in through his teeth as my hand wanders lower.

"Can I touch you?" I ask him, half scared, half impatient to know what he feels like.

"Yes."

His gruff one-word permission seems all he can stammer out as I reach out, taking that impressive part of him in my hand. He's so wide my fingers can't reach around him. His cock feels velvety but as solid as steel. A drop of pre-cum glistens at the tip, and I can't wait to taste him. I collect the moisture on my fingertip and take it into my mouth, sucking on my finger.

He hisses again and gasps out, "You're killing me here!"

It's not my desire to torture him, but this is my time, and I've no wish to be hurried. I move so I kneel between his legs and take him in both hands, rubbing my hands gently up and down.

"You can touch me harder," he suggests, the words whistling through his teeth. "I won't break."

Acting only on instinct, I put my hands inside my underwear, wiping my fingers from my opening to my clit, collecting my juices and then use it to lubricate my palms as I continue to pay his cock the attention I want to. I stroke my now slick hands up and down his throbbing dick, able to feel the veins pulsing. Bending over I take the head into my mouth and gently caress him with my tongue, getting even more turned on by the combination of both our tastes. Then I take him in as deep as I can, feeling his width stretching my jaw open wide. It's the first time I've done this voluntarily without being forced; the first time I've used the skills I was compelled to learn to avoid the punishment I'd earn if I refused or gagged. It's the first time I've ever enjoyed it.

"Fuck, Zee!" He shouts.

CHAPTER 27
Kadar

I can't believe she just did that! Does she know how sexy that was? Fucking hell! I'm going to come all over her hands in a moment; she's no idea how close I am to shooting my load. *Fuck! Fuck! FUCK! Think of something different; name all the horses in the palace stables, list all the legal steps to change Amahad into a democracy, anything to take my mind of what her incredible fucking hands are doing to me.*

And then she leans forwards and takes me into her mouth, taking me in as deep as she can. She's fucking skilled at this. I'm a big man, but she suppresses her gag reflex, breathing in through her nose. Then I remember the reason why she's so good, and it chills me, suppressing my immediate urge to come.

"Habiti, you don't need to do that." It kills me to stop her, but I suspect she was forced to do it in the past. How can it hold pleasure for her?

She pulls back, releasing me so she can talk, "But tonight is about doing what I want, when I want it, Kadar. And I want to do this. You're not making me." She has a cheeky expression on her flushed face; she's enjoying being the one in charge.

And there's the difference. As I had expected, she's more

confident in control. And just for this once I'll let her have it. It's killing the Dom in me not to grab her, turn her over and thrust into her as deep as I can go, to direct the pace of our joining. On the other hand, the man in me is eager to see where and just how far she will go. Behind my head, my fingers are locked so tightly together I cut off my blood flow as I struggle to let her proceed at her pace. Fuck, this isn't easy for me; I'm denying my very nature. I pant as she continues to experiment, licking around the head, her tongue gently exploring the slit before she deep throats me again. I feel my balls tighten; if she's not careful, I'm going to shoot my load into her mouth.

"Habiti, stop. I'm going to come."

She heeds my warning and pulls back, sitting back on her heels, her hand wiping across her mouth, her tongue flicking out over her lips. It's the sexiest thing I've ever seen.

"I want you inside me," she whispers.

Oh, fuck yes! The words I've been dying to hear. Again I fight my inclinations as I struggle to make my words a suggestion and not a command, "Straddle me then. Take as much, or as little of me, as you want."

After slipping off her delicate underwear, she shuffles up the bed until her knees are on either side of my waist, and takes hold of my cock again in her tiny hands; it's such a beautiful sight it takes my breath away. I have a brief moment of concern, my size worrying me—it looks so large in comparison to her, my broad frame making her stretch her hips wide across my body. I don't want to hurt her or cause her discomfort, but I can do nothing to help.

She's wet enough, though; I can see her arousal glistening from here, and I can smell her too, such a glorious perfume that's exclusively hers. As my cock twitches and jumps in her hands, I don't think I've ever been this hard in my life.

She hovers over me as though unsure. Again I fight with myself, forcing myself to fulfil my promise, letting her take this at her pace. It takes everything I have to restrain my hands from touching her lovely breasts. I know I could help her—if she let me move I'd be able to give her more stimulation—but this is her show, I promised her that.

I remember to inhale, but hold the air in my lungs when she positions herself over me and gently wipes the head of my cock over her slit, her pussy juices providing the much-needed lubrication. And then she lets herself drop onto me, taking me so torturously slowly inside of her. Her eyes close, and her face grimaces at the stretch and burn she must be feeling. It's been a while since she had a cock inside her, and without boasting, I know I'm a big man, and I doubt she's ever had someone the size of me.

She's so tight! I encourage her with small thrusts, aimed just to consolidate the distance she's already taken inside her delicious pussy, leaving the decision up to her how much more she can handle. I don't know whether she'll be able to take all of me, but just as I wonder if she'll stop, this determined woman again amazes me as she slowly, but surely, sinks down until she's enveloped every inch.

"Kadar!" she gasps out, her head thrown back, her eyes half closed and her breath coming in pants.

I can't help it. Without conscious thought or direction, my hands move down, and I place them either side of her hips. She doesn't flinch, doesn't start away as if she knows she needs my aid. I use my strength to help her to rise off me, and then bring her back down again gently, so I don't hurt or frighten her. My hands might be doing the work, but I let her control the pace.

She clenches her pussy, and like a schoolboy, I know I'm not going to be able to last long. Her eyes close, her mouth opens, and she moans, a sound that triggers even more blood to race to my cock, its fullness almost painful now. She starts to twist her hips in untutored movements, her brow creasing in frustration, so I speed up, thrusting deeper and harder inside her. Her moans of pleasure come faster now until they combine into one long keen that both incites and encourages me. I'm getting so close, but she's not quite there yet so using one hand I rub her clit. It doesn't take much to get her to the edge, and soon her body freezes, tightens and strangles my cock with her internal muscles as she comes with a violence that astounds even me. It's the most glorious feeling I've ever felt, and there's absolutely no way I can hold back; her orgasm triggers something primeval in me. I come and come and come, my cum shooting up into her. Shooting up her tight passage, through her cervix and straight into her womb! *Fuck!* I freeze. *We didn't use a condom!*

As her muscles relax she collapses over my body, worn out from her release. I bring my arms around her, my hand gently caressing her back. I feel completely and utterly drained. She's taken every drop I had to give and therein lies the problem. *Is she protected?*

There can be no future for us. In little more than a month, I will be selecting my bride. Then there'll be a short engagement, of sufficient length to satisfy society and enough time to arrange a state wedding, after which I'll be taking a stranger to my bed.

What the fuck made me give into my baser instincts tonight? All my life I've taken strict precautions in all my liaisons. I'm not an ordinary man who can afford to make mistakes, particularly one of this magnitude. But I simply had to have Zoe, even if it was just for a few hours and the thought of using a condom never entered my head. She's become my weakness, sapping my strength of mind and wiping all rational thought away. What will be the result of my fucking selfish indiscretion if she's not protected? Shit, how could I ask her to have an abortion? How could I ask a woman kill a child of my blood before it even has a chance to grow? A pregnancy would be disastrous; any male child resulting from my stupidity tonight would be the heir to the throne of Amahad. An heir, completely unacceptable to the majority of my country's population.

I could abdicate. The option is not unattractive. It's so wearing, trying to keep the balance between the cultured cities of our country and the primitive tribes. I'm exhausted beyond belief at the end of each day from having to prove myself. If I gave it all up, Jasim would be next in line. *Shit, how can I expect the part owner of a fucking BDSM club to run a fucking country?* There's no way I could put that on him nor would he want it. And if not Jasim, then there's Nijad. But how could I live with myself if I transferred this weighty burden on the shoulders of my youngest brother knowing, in all probability, it would slowly kill him?

My hand slides against the softness of her unmarred skin broken with the raised reminders where St John-Davies had so cruelly whipped her. I never believed I would love a woman more than I love my country, but I have suspicions that could well be the outcome if I'm around Zoe much longer. I can't put myself, or her, in this position again and hope to Allah there'll be no price to pay for my indiscretion tonight. Since I was born, I've dedicated my life to Amahad—a love/hate relationship, but a commitment for life. I can't abdicate. Zee can't be my wife. She can't possibly be pregnant.

But what if she is? What the fuck would I do?

I have to know. If she gives me the right answer I won't have to spend the next few weeks torturing myself.

"Zoe," I can't use my pet name for her, not for this question, it's too important. I grasp her arms, pulling her up above me to make sure I have her attention. "We didn't use a condom. Are you using protection?"

CHAPTER 28

Zoe

Gasping for breath, my heart's beating so furiously I'm worried it's going to jump out of my chest. There's a rushing sound through my head as blood pumps frantically through my veins. It's the first time I've ever come while having sex with a man. The first time in my whole frigging life! Was it because I was in control? Or because I've at last met a man who cares for my pleasure as much as his own? When I was so close, he knew, helped me over the edge, making sure I had my release before he took his own. *Is this what it's supposed to be like? Is this what I've been missing?*

As my frenzied heartbeat begins to slow and my breathing returns to normal, I feel sated and satisfied and realise this is what my Sophie used to talk about. *Heaven help me; I don't think I'm ever going to recover!*

I feel his cock softening inside me while I rest in the comfort of his arms, the soft touch of his hands soothingly running up and down my back. Kadar, the emir of Amahad, but tonight just a man caring for his woman. He let me be in charge, but I knew how difficult that had been for him. I hadn't missed the tension rolling off of him as he itched to take back control. He knew just what I needed, and he gave it to me. And that's exactly what Cara had told me a Dom should do for his sub.

But he's no ordinary man or Dom, and I can't be either his woman or his sub. I know I can't continue exploring with Kadar. I've got to lock this memory away, stamp on my fast growing feelings for the man lying beneath me and force myself to remember in just a short time he'll choose his wife and marry for expediency, for his country.

I have to distance myself, seeing him, being around him, will be too much temptation, and more time in his arms will only make me fall harder. I have to build a wall around myself to protect my feelings, though I suspect I'm already in too deep and it's going to hurt to pull away. Tonight has shown me a side of intimacy that I never believed could exist between a man and a woman outside of the pages of a romance novel, but I mustn't mistake the beating of my heart for anything other than recovery from exertion. There couldn't be a man more unattainable for me to fall for.

This night is one to be stored as a beautiful memory; tomorrow I'll end this. Stop it before it goes any further, and before my heart gets broken, thrusting back down the thought that even now it might be too late. Giving in to the temptation to have more nights like this, to explore what sex could be like with Kadar in control, to trust him to show me his way of loving, would only make the eventual and unavoidable end worse. The only thing I could ever be is a mistress, and I'm not a woman who'd even contemplate that. There can be no future for us, and no good will come of delaying the pain.

Neither of us seems to want or have the energy to move. His heart beats in time with mine, echoing through my head as I lay with my head on his chest. His cock softens inside me and slips out, a trickle of liquid following. *We didn't use a condom.*

I try not to tense, not to give myself away as horror flits through my mind, hurtling me back to the last time Ethan raped me. But just as quickly I realise on this occasion the omission hadn't been a calculated action on Kadar's part, unlike the probability that Ethan's had. In his position, this wasn't the kind of risk he would consciously take. It's more my fault than his—I was the one in control, *I* was the one who didn't even consider protection—he probably assumed I'm on the pill.

Where am I in my cycle? Shit—I don't even know whether it's a safe time or not, the stress of the last few months has meant I've not been exactly regular. *What if I am pregnant?* Quickly I run through my options, remembering how I took immediate steps to remedy the situation by making sure Ethan's evil seed couldn't grow, and it hits me I don't feel the same urgency now. As Kadar's arms gently stroke my back, and his lips lovingly nuzzle my neck, I bite back a sob of despair.

I'm neither stupid nor blind to the devastating implications of me carrying Kadar's baby, not just to me, but to him and his country. If I'm pregnant, and I do nothing to prevent his baby being born, it could potentially lead to a civil war. His first born, a child with a commoner's blood. But already my feelings for Kadar run so deep; I doubt I could even contemplate ending a life we had created between us, despite the immeasurable problems that would follow.

Forcing myself not to panic, I realise my worries are almost certainly for nothing; we'd have to be extremely unlucky to have such a result from just one encounter. The greater likelihood is I'm not pregnant, so there's no point worrying about something that will probably never happen. And if any decision is to be made, it can be left until I know for sure. There's one thing for certain; I won't use this to trap him, I can't, the penalties on everyone would be too severe. If I am carrying his child, I'll need to protect the man behind the throne, and the Emir of Amahad must never, ever know.

"Zoe, we didn't use a condom. Are you using protection?"

Kadar's tersely spoken words let me know his thoughts have been running along the same track as mine. So I lie to him, hiding my face in his chest, shrouding the betrayal in my eyes, "No need to worry, Kadar. I'm safe."

I forgive myself for telling him this falsehood. The truth and its possible result potentially have the power to destroy him. As I feel, as well as hear, his sigh of relief, I know the huge lie I've told was the right thing to say. I don't want him concerned about something which is only a vague possibility.

He turns me, so I lie on my side facing away from him. His hold tightens as he nuzzles my neck and kisses my hair. Slowly his embrace loosens, and his breathing slows and I realise he's asleep. Vowing I'll only allow myself this one night to lie beside him, to enjoy his strong arms wrapped around me keeping me safe, I struggle to stay awake, not wanting to waste a moment of our closeness. I inhale the scent of sandalwood, man, and sex, listen to the soft sounds he makes in his sleep, storing up memories to comfort me in times to come and try to keep the guilt away.

If I'm pregnant, this man will never know his child. I'll have stolen something from him, but only so he can live out his preordained life. Silent tears roll down my cheeks as I think of the implications if indeed I'm left with a memento of this night. But however hard it will be to keep such a secret from Kadar, however much it could hurt him if he ever discovers the truth, the alternative would be so much worse. I hope and pray this night doesn't bear fruit, and it hardens my resolve not to repeat this intimacy. Once we might get away with, but we can't take the risk again.

The next morning I wake alone, tracks of dried tears on my face. Sometime during the night Kadar must have gathered his clothing and left without disturbing me, presumably to avoid the walk of shame as the daylight hours arrived. *Or was it that he didn't know what to say to me today?* Though the thought hurts me, it also comforts me. I don't relish the idea of the conversation ahead if he wants a repeat performance. I definitely can't allow that to happen. I lied to him once; I will not lie to him again.

Glancing at the bedside clock, I'm surprised to see I've overslept, and it's already the middle of the morning! Taking my time, I shower, dress, and fiddle around doing my hair until at last, I pluck up sufficient nerve to walk out of my bedroom. As I expected, Sean is waiting for me. And I have no bloody clue what to say to him.

He gets up as I enter the sitting room area, and comes

across to me, looking deep into my face, his hand coming up to cup my chin, turning my face up so he can see into my eyes. "You okay?"

His gently asked question almost makes my tears start once more. I nod slowly in answer.

"Zoe, Kadar has…"

Lifting my hand, I put my fingers against his lips. "Sean, it ends now. Whatever 'it' is. I have to let him go. I know that. For both our sakes."

Under his scrutiny my eyes drop to the floor. He leans down, placing a kiss on my head, and his arms come around me. I lean into him, for once needing this contact. "You know, I wished it was me?"

I realise that and have no answer for him. I don't want to cause anyone pain, and yet I'm hurting two men.

"But I'm glad someone was there for you. I just wish you'd found someone else, someone who could offer you something long term. But that wouldn't have been me, either, we both know that." He pulls back a little way, a smile turning up one corner of his mouth, "You sounded like you were having a good time, though!"

I gasp with embarrassment, mortified he heard us. He laughs, his joke carrying no malice, and he doesn't take advantage of my humiliation, simply changes the subject, telling me, "He wants you to breakfast with him. He asked me to let you know."

I hadn't realised how hard this would be, just the thought of being alone with Kadar again would be too great a threat to my resolve. My eyes flick around the room and settle on a pad of writing paper conveniently left on a sideboard. Pulling away from Sean I go over, pick up the pen lying beside it. Closing my eyes for a second, I compose in my head what I need to say before committing it to writing.

Once I've finished my note, I fold it, put it in an envelope, seal it and hand it to Sean. "Sean, will you take this to him, please?"

Without me having to explain he understands, taking my letter with a quick nod, and, after throwing me a look filled with sadness and sympathy, he leaves the room to deliver my message.

I stare at the closed door, and my hand comes to rest on my stomach. *No! I can't be pregnant, and I won't worry about it. Fate wouldn't be that unkind to me!*

CHAPTER 29
Kadar

Expecting to see Zoe, I'd arranged a breakfast buffet that lies on the table waiting for her to share it with me. But instead, it's Sean who enters the royal suite, his face carefully schooled, masking his thoughts. Without ceremony, he hands me an envelope, and my heart misses a beat as the implication of him entering alone suggests what it probably contains. Calling on all my diplomatic training I keep my expression casual and relaxed as I slit it open taking out the note inside. I read the contents, once and then again.

"Is she okay?" I put my hand to head and touch my fingers to my brow, realising how much it must have cost her to write the words.

"Yes, but she's made her decision. I don't know what she's written, but I believe I can guess. You've got to respect her wishes, Kadar."

He's not gloating; he even sounds sympathetic. "I know. She's made that very clear." I stand, my eyes closed, as the memory of my cock buried deep inside her assails me, together with the realisation that I'll never be so close to her again. I'll spend my life reliving that one glorious night we spent together; the night I connected with a woman on far more than just a physical plane.

The smell of the cooling food mocks me. *She's doing the right thing, what I should have instigated but didn't have the courage to do.* I've already memorised the contents of her short, but to the point, note. She doesn't want to see me again. At all. She'll only stay in Amahad if I keep my distance. At that moment I'd give just about anything not to be the emir, not to have my future wasn't mapped out and planned, so I could live my life with this woman by my side. Somewhere in the time from our first meeting in London to that night I saw her in the harem; she'd inveigled herself into my psyche, melting my ice cold heart. The thought of never seeing her, talking to her again, tears me in two. And that makes me realise she's right. It would only be worse for both of us if I went against her wishes and saw her again, even in the company of others, it would only be delaying the inevitable. And if she has feelings half as deep as my own, she'll be hurting too.

I realise Sean's waiting for me to speak. "I'll complete my meetings with the sheikhs, and then I'll return to the capital. She should be safe here; St John-Davies thinks she's in Al Qar'ah. Once we've dealt with him, she can return and continue her work. Or leave and go back to England, if that's what she prefers to do. Can you tell her that, Sean?"

The unlikely looking bodyguard slowly nods, understanding in his eyes. "I'll keep her safe, Kadar."

I know he will. He'll take care of Zee for me; I can trust him on that.

After the door closes behind Sean, I allow myself a few moments to grieve my loss, trying to convince myself it couldn't have worked any other way. She's only pre-empted the clean break that I would have to have asked for myself. Then I stand, pulling my back straight and once again putting on my headdress and gold agal—the symbol of my office—mentally girding myself for the meetings ahead. I'm back in control. Only the slight trembling of my hands betrays me; getting Zee out of my head might be an impossible task.

The guard outside my suite is sloppily dressed; his uniform unbuttoned at the neck. He yawns widely as I open my door, a sense of boredom rolling off of him. It crosses my mind that Nijad can't know how much standards are dropping in his absence and I'll need to enlighten him on my return. Any royal guard is also a member of our elite troops and as such should be sharp and disciplined. This man is anything but! The guard becomes aware of my critical scrutiny and belatedly stands to attention. I can't leave it like this—the state of my guards reflects on me.

"Zarr hatta satrat w ta'annaq nafsak!" Angrily, I tell him to button up his tunic and smarten himself up.

As I bark out my instruction he obeys, and then rasps out a sullen apology. Something makes me note the coarse dialect he uses, filing it away in the back of my mind to think about later. His behaviour has made me wary, but for now, disregard the niggling worry. Maybe I'll have to have him removed from guard duty, but his insubordination gets drowned in the mire of everything else going through my head and the disrespect shown by a guard pales into insignificance.

I'm late for our noon meeting, so can't afford to tarry. Winding my way through the corridors, eventually, I come to the staterooms on the ground floor where the five desert sheikhs are already assembled and waiting for me. The guard opens the door and then, at my instruction, steps back to wait outside. None of the sheikhs have attendants with them; what we're about to discuss today is not for other ears. Though I know all will have brought their soldiers and warriors with them, their men will remain in their camps set up outside the city walls, as evidenced by the camp fires I saw burning last night.

The ritual of coffee, the hospitality I offer my guests, begins. I raise my cup wondering who is friend or foe, who's already on side, and who still needs to be persuaded. I'm hopeful all the five who responded to my call are willing to work with me, but it would be wrong to assume anything and not to proceed with caution. Conscious that just one badly worded sentence could start a war, I allow one final thought about the woman who was in my bed last night, and then put her out of my mind. I need all my wits about me today and can allow no distractions.

I lift my head stretching my neck and then lower it, turning to survey the room. Sheikh Rais sits on my right, and he nods at me. He has already been helping to smooth the way with the other desert sheikhs. Rais's support, I have no doubts about.

Looking to my left, I take in Sheikh Ghalib, another who's less bloodthirsty than some of the rest. He's the oldest of those assembled today, but does wisdom come with age? Sheikhs Sofian and Wahid are relatively unknown to me, but I've not heard anything but good about their tribes, and there's nothing in any report I'd been given to suggest they are not supportive of my rule, or that they harbour dissidents within their peoples. Sheikh Jibran, though, I pause my recognisance of those assembled as I consider him, trying hard to read his body language. He's a cousin of Abdul-Muhsi, and if nothing else that makes me wary. Can I rely on him? Or could he be here as a spy?

Coffee cups drained, refilled with the thick syrupy liquid, and then emptied once more I rap hard on the table, drawing the attention of the five sheikhs. The meeting is now underway.

I commence proceedings by thanking them for attending today and passing around the agenda. The first item is the discussion of the jihadists crossing the border into Amahad from Erizad, a country we, unfortunately, have poor relations with and it's from there that the terrorists try to cross over into our land. Our reliance on foreign monies coming into Amahad means that we cannot allow ourselves to be infiltrated in a similar way as other Arab countries have suffered. We must protect the southern border, and I need the support of these sheikhs to accomplish that.

I begin hearing the reports from the assembled tribal leaders, increasingly feeling like a weight is being lifted off me as it appears, while we're not always successful watching every mile of the boundary with Erizad, any jihadists that have crossed over have been picked up and dealt with—viscously and permanently, their bodies placed at prominent border crossing points. It may be a primitive way of dealing with our enemies, but it's efficient, and I'm certainly not going to complain about the methods employed as long as we keep under the radar of certain international organisations. In truth, the vigour with which the invaders have been dispatched pleases me. In this, at least, these sheikhs are on my side.

Sheikh Ghalib indicates he wishes to speak, and I gesture, offering him the floor. But before he can open his mouth, the deafening sound of a massive explosion rocks the palace, making the very fabric of the building shake around us. For a split second, we all sit stunned, then stand as one, preparing to take defensive action, immediately assessing that the bomb, or whatever it was, while not in our vicinity, doesn't mean we, ourselves, are not the intended targets. Outside the window I see dust billowing around, then my eyes narrow in suspicion as I view the sheikhs standing around the table, trying to see if one of them doesn't seem as surprised as the rest, my gaze pausing notably on Jibran. But he, as well as all the others, appear to be in the same state of shock as I.

I open my mouth to speak when the door bursts open and the untidy looking guard enters with an automatic rifle in his hands. He holds it steady, his eyes scanning the room. I inwardly curse, berating myself for my stupidity and wishing I'd followed up on my suspicions earlier. This man is no member of the Royal Guard.

"Sit!" he barks out. The gun swings side to side, incorporating all of us in its range, the threat explicit. We've nothing to defend ourselves with. History counselling caution due to the volatility of the desert sheikhs, meetings between them had a strict no weapons rule, and all had subjected to a pat down from the guards before entering the room.

But before I have time to react to the threat, as if in a blur of movement a knife flies across the room, ending up embedded in the chest of the guard. With an expression of surprise, he drops the rifle, clasping his hands to the blade in his body, falling to the ground. My doubts about Jibran's loyalty disappear, and for once I'm glad my soldiers must have failed in their duty, and he'd managed to sneak a weapon into the room.

But *were* they my men? Recognition of the dialect that I'd picked up on earlier hits me, and I curse myself for not putting more emphasis on it at the time. Although, admittedly, on its own that would have no relevance as the Royal Guards are drawn from all tribes, and it wouldn't have been strange to find some coming from the Qaiquw. But now, with the evidence in front of my eyes, I realise the felled man must be one of Abdul-Muhsi's extremist followers.

Released from my frozen pose I go and kneel beside him; Rais has reacted quicker than me and has the rifle in his hands, the barrel pointed at the man in the throes of dying at my feet. Jibran's aim was true. Blood pours from his wound and his mouth. I grab him roughly. "What is this?"

The fanatical look in eyes fast glazing over makes me go cold. "You're dead, Kadar. And your English whore will get what she deserves." His voice is only just audible through the gurgling from his lungs.

"Who's your leader?" I shake him, trying to get confirmation that Abdul-Muhsi's behind this, but it's too late, and he's gone.

All the sheikhs are on their phones. Rais locks the door, and I place a call to Nijad. I ask my question tersely and receive his quick assurance he'll investigate. I look around at my companions, throwing a nod of sincere appreciation towards Jibran.

"The English whore?" Rais raises his eyebrows at me as he finishes his call summoning his men to the palace.

"An employee," I tell him while wondering why the fuck she's been included in this, unaware I'm giving away more than I want to with the blatant admission I'd known immediately who the guard had been referring to. I ignore the questioning look he throws me; now is not the time for explanations.

It's only moments before Nijad rings back with the information that chills me. I listen to him explain. "Who?" I ask him, curtly, "Who is the fucking traitor?" When he tells me the answer, I'm shocked, reaching out my hand to the table as though I need the support. Unable to believe how it could be true, but having to accept the veracity of what my brother said. It was Richard. Richard, my most trusted assistant. The man who's worked by my side for years. The man who knows almost every secret. Richard, who has betrayed me. Curtly, I leave Nijad with a request to find out as much information as he can and when I end the call turn to let the others here my disturbing news.

"The Royal Guard were given instructions they were not needed in the palace, but instead required urgently at one of the border points. The direction came from my office, so was immediately obeyed. I regret my assistant has turned against me." I pause for a second, betrayal like a physical pain in my gut. *Why, Richard, why?* I clear my throat and continue. "Any guards remaining in the palace should be treated as enemies of the state." I manage to keep my emotions and the betrayal out of my voice.

"They want to kill us." Sofian sums up what we all know, "You, and your supporters, Kadar."

The sound of shots come from outside, but not directed at us; it would appear the insurgents believe we're safely under guard. I nod to my fellow leaders. We are all sheikhs, protected daily by our soldiers and trusted men. Yet none of us are strangers to violence or have forgotten our military training. Albeit, for some like Ghalib, that might have been a long time ago. Whatever's going on, our enemy has underestimated their ruling sheikhs by sending just one man to control us. We're no fat-bellied sloths lounging around on thrones. We're warriors, taking pride in honing our fighting skills and keeping fit. With these men beside me, we have a chance to get out of this. If I doubted any before, I have no such concerns now. These men are with me, united by a common foe. As I unlock the door, they take their places behind me, ready to proceed with stealth, needing no further direction.

Rapidly I consider the layout of the palace, cursing I don't know it as well as I do that in Al Qur'ah. I hadn't heard any gunshots or sound from the direction of the staterooms and assume whoever's attacking the palace continues to think we're confined and controlled. My quickly formed plan is to get to the armoury, and once suitably equipped, find out what the fuck is going on.

The English whore. *What has Richard done?* It hasn't escaped me that he must have betrayed Zoe to St John-Davies and is probably now a million fucking pounds richer. And that means she's now in very real danger. I have to get to her, but first I need to know who, exactly, is currently in control of this palace. The only thing for certain is that at this moment is that it certainly isn't me.

Reaching the armoury without a problem, I pass out guns and ammunition with just one thought in my head. Before I lose my mind with worry, I need to find Zoe, to discover whether she's alive and indeed, still in the palace. And to do that, the sheikhs and I need to split up. Begging a favour of Rais, who I know has better knowledge of this palace, I ask him to take Sofian with him and go to the harem gardens to try to locate Zee and Sean knowing that's where they were headed today. Both sheikhs waste no time agreeing to my request. In my gut, I already fear they're on a fool's errand.

CHAPTER 30
Zoe

I'm determined not to ask Sean what Kadar's reaction was to my note—I didn't have to, I could imagine it. I'd put my decision in the strongest possible terms, leaving him no room for doubt or manoeuvre. Now I need to forget him, to leave behind useless dreams, to throw myself into my work. My intention is to do what I'm officially here in the desert city for; to visit the harem gardens.

Seeing the layout, cataloguing the types of plants and how the irrigation system works will give me ideas for the harem in the Palace of Amahad, and that's what I need to concentrate on now, to bury myself in restoration details and forget my night with the emir.

The day is hot, so I dress in light blue Capris and a white long-sleeved blouse. Although I've become used to wearing the Amahadian clothing that Kadar provided for me and which, undeniably, is far better suited to this climate, wearing European clothes mentally helps me distance myself from him as far as possible. I get a sense of my old self back as I dress in practical but modest and familiar clothing. I'm here to do a job; that's all.

Trying to regain my excitement for the project I speak as enthusiastically as I can, "I want to go the harem gardens." I stand up straight, and look up to Sean's eyes.

He recognises my determination for exactly what it is—a cover-up for my pain. "Now?"

I allow him to make his appraisal of how I'm coping, and steadily return his gaze. All tears have been wiped from my eyes, and my mouth is set. When he nods, recognising the fortitude on my face, I reply, "Now's as good a time as any." Without wasting time, I put on my wide-brimmed hat and collect my sunglasses from my bag. In my other hand, I hold my IPad for taking notes, and to photograph anything of particular interest.

It only takes him a moment to rifle through his bag and extract a baseball hat and what looks like expensive Ray-bans. "Let's go explore these gardens then." I follow him out of the suite, my short legs having trouble keeping up with his far longer ones.

At the end of the corridor is a surly looking servant. I've been surprised at the hint of hostility that seems to exude off the resident staff, certainly not what Cara led me to expect. She'd spoken in glowing terms of Lamis, her personal maid who'd stayed in the Palace of Palms, and who she'd asked to look after me during my visit. But I hadn't seen anything of her at all, or anyone who acted like I expected a maid would. Was it because we're Caucasian? I really couldn't believe there'd be such discrimination here, especially since Cara is white British herself, and she'd led me to believe she'd been welcomed with open arms. But some of the expressions on the faces of the staff actually make me shudder. And now I'm without the protection of Kadar, it unnerves me.

But at least I have Sean with me. I couldn't be more

grateful for that, especially when, in perfect Amahadian, he asks the servant for directions and ends up persuading him to be our guide. We follow him through the maze of corridors until eventually, we came to the harem. Part of which was boarded up and, as I now know, behind the boards is a Dom's Dungeon. As there's no entrance to it from here, I won't have to curb my curiosity. The only entrance is from the Royal Suite, and I feel a shiver for entirely different reasons, thinking how fiercely Nijad and Cara protect their privacy, wondering just what they might get up to in the partitioned off half of the harem. I can't stop my traitorous mind from speculating what it would have been like if I'd had the nerve to play with Kadar there. I force that thought out of my head as quickly as I can.

Bringing myself back to the business in hand, I start by looking around, soaking up the atmosphere. The unaltered half of the harem is in much better repair than the one in the Capital's palace. There's a mosaic on the floor that gives me an idea of how the ruined one in Al Qur'ah might look once repaired. But it's the gardens that capture my interest, and I move forwards trying to recognise and mentally catalogue the plants growing here. There are fruit trees, oranges and lemons, and immediately I imagine where I would place them in the garden I'm going to restore. Sean patiently walks around with me, pointing out where the irrigation channels run. He's a typical man, more interested in technology than plants. He wanders away to see how the water gets into the garden as I continue to make my rounds, drawing and sketching the layout so I can have something to refer to later.

I lose all sense of time; the garden is peaceful and soothing. The sun beats down, but there's sufficient shade to sit and cool off for a while. The fountain plays, and soon I can't resist slipping off my sandals and dipping my toes into the refreshing water. As I relax, I study my surroundings. Walls that must be twenty feet high enclose the harem, and there was once a massive arched doorway to the outside that has been bricked in. Perhaps, at some point, the resident Sultan wanted to ensure his women were kept secure and safe. *Or, didn't want them to escape.* My mind starts wandering off on a tangent, thinking of the women who lived here. Were they here by choice? Or were they forced? What did they think of being held at the whim of the Sultan, having to vy for his attention and to become his favourite?

Visions of semi-naked women relaxing round the pool, spending all their days pampering and being pampered fill my head when suddenly there's a deafening explosion, making me jump out of my skin. To my utter astonishment, the bricked in archway slowly disappears from view, stones and mortar crumbling down as if in slow motion, the whole gateway gradually becoming concealed in a cloud of dust and smoke. I just stand there, transfixed by the image in front of me that my brain can't quite compute, my mouth gaping open in shock when Sean, having recovered faster, wastes no time rushing over, grabs my hand, and drags me through the gardens and back into the harem. We reach the door that leads back into the palace. Sean turns the handle, but it's stuck and won't move. He gives it another try, but it won't budge. Realising we're locked in he uses his karate-type kick to seek to break the lock but the thick stubborn wood has no give at all. Glancing at each other, I can see we share the same concerns. Neither of us would be daft enough to run towards the gaping hole in the harem walls not wanting to meet whoever's on the other side. If we can't get out this way, we're trapped.

"What's happening?" I gasp out. Probably too loudly, as my ears are still ringing.

He shakes his head, "I don't know. It's likely to be an attack on Kadar. It's the first time he's visited the desert since he became emir, too much of a coincidence to be anything else. Christ, we hadn't factored that in!" I can only just make out what he's saying.

"But why blow the harem walls?" I don't expect him to have an answer; I think I'm just talking for the sake of it. I'm scared.

"I don't know—they might think this is an unguarded entrance into the palace, or perhaps they just saw a weakness they could exploit? Whatever, we've got to lay low." He looks around the furnishings of the harem and pulls me over where there's a day bed with curtains behind it. He pushes me until the fancy drapes hide us from sight. "Whoever it is won't know we're here. Hopefully, they'll just want to get into the main part. Keep your head down and be quiet. We should be safe."

"But why's the door to the palace locked?" I try to swallow, but my mouth has gone dry.

He shrugs, "I don't know." But the look he throws me is

full of worry. "It could be that someone inside has acted quickly to try to prevent them getting into the palace that way."

I notice he's already got a gun ready in his hand; a sign he's taking the situation very seriously. He looks out through a gap in the curtains, ready to spot any trouble before it gets to us. I don't want to think about it, but we're hemmed in here, between God knows who presumably even now clambering over the rubble and entering the harem garden, and that damn bolted door into the palace proper. Was he right someone inside was diligently protecting the palace from anyone coming in via the harem? Or were we trapped here on purpose? Were we, or more particularly, was *I* the target? My heart almost stops in my chest as I get that dreaded feeling in my gut. *Ethan.* Ethan's at the bottom of this I'm certain. I pray that I'm wrong, but I've always thought it was dangerous to entice him to Amahad.

We hear the sound of pounding footsteps; I try to count how many there are, but can't make it out. Half-a-dozen at least. But they are not running for the entrance; they're systematically searching the harem. I was right to be scared. Trying not to panic or even breathe in an attempt not to expose our hiding place, I edge closer to Sean, and he puts his free arm around me. The people hunting us shout at each other in a language that I don't understand. Sean does, I can tell by the way he freezes when someone shouts a particular sentence. I can't ask him what they are saying; I have to stay silent. But the footsteps keep getting nearer; whoever they are, they are close to finding us.

Suddenly a heavily accented voice rings out, "Come out, Miss Baker. We know you are in here. There is no escape. Come out now, and you will not be hurt."

My heart slams in my chest, and for once I take no pleasure in being proved right. They are after me. *Oh shit! He's found me!* The only comfort I can take is that I can't hear either Ethan or Hargreaves voices. Maybe there's a little time left, another opportunity to escape before I meet my fate. Sean squeezes me. As I crane my neck to look up at him, I can almost hear the wheels turning in his head. He bends down and whispers in my ear, "There are too many for me to fight. We have to assume they are armed. If I get a shot off it's likely to start a gunfight, and I don't like the odds, I won't be able to protect you." Lowering himself into a crouch, he slips his gun into his ankle holster that I hadn't even been aware he was wearing. He touches his lips briefly to my forehead as if trying to imbibe me with some of his strength. Then, placing his body in front of me as a shield, he leads me forwards.

A heavily armed Arab man in traditional clothing stands on the other side of the curtains. Even though I know nothing about guns, I recognise the shape of an automatic rifle from having seen them in films. It's a serious piece of armoury; this man means business. I'd underestimated the number, as well. There are around a dozen men, all in robes, all carrying weapons. Apart from guns, they have ugly looking scimitars in their belts that do not look ornamental at all. *But there's no sign of Ethan or Hargreaves.*

"Zoe Baker, the English whore." The man who's the

obvious leader speaks then spits on the ground.

I swallow sharply at his manner of address but am wise enough not to say anything, taking my lead from Sean who remains quiet, though I felt him tense at the name given to me. I examine the man holding us at gunpoint. He looks around fiftyish and has a paunch which makes his belt sit up over his waist. He has a deep scar from the corner of his eye to his mouth making him look cruel and fierce, and he's regarding me with a distinct expression of distaste. Then he switches his attention to my companion.

"Who are you?" He waves his gun as if trying to encourage a response.

Instead of the deep, authoritative voice, I've got used to with the bodyguard from Grade A; Sean answers in a high pitched squeaky voice, "I'm a plant expert; I'm advising Miss Baker on the desert flora." He allows his hand to hang limply from his wrist.

"You're a worthless piece of shit!" Having given his dismissive opinion of Sean, the leader spits on the ground again. "I'm Sheikh Abdul-Muhsi. The rightful Emir of Amahad. You," he waves his rifle at directly at me, "You are now my prisoner." He seems to think for a moment, and this time, the barrel of the gun points at my bodyguard. "We'll take you with us. But we don't need you, Mr Plant Expert, so be very careful. Any heroics and you're dead."

Sean seems to shrink with the threat, but I've seen this behaviour before and understand he's biding his time, lulling the man into a false sense of security. To emphasise the weak front he's portraying he puts trembling hands up into the air. "You'll get no trouble from me," he assures the sheikh, his voice shaking.

Abdul-Muhsi spits again then indicates with his rifle that we should precede him and his men fall in around us. There are too many of them to attempt an escape. We're led across the harem gardens and out through the large hole in the wall made by the explosion. Sean takes my hand to help me across the rubble. Once outside there's a parade of jeeps, their engines idling.

"Wait!" The terse instruction comes out. The sheikh says something in Amahadian, and two of his men approach us, and they roughly grab my hands. Quickly, giving me no time to struggle, my left wrist is cuffed causing a bolt of pain to go through me, and then equally fast I'm chained to Sean's right. Sean's glance of sympathy shows he knows of the weakness in my wrist, and the discomfort the handcuffs cause.

Once secured we're pushed up against the side of the first of the jeeps then one of the men steps forwards while the other trains his gun on us menacingly. Neither of us has a chance to evade the rather too personal body search they subject us too; luckily completely above my clothes, although Sean isn't quite so lucky as his T-shirt's pulled up and his trousers down, as they rummage to find any hidden weapons. Of course, they find his gun and take it away, along with both of our phones. Any optimism I'd retained that we were going to get out of this fades to almost nothing, but I try to stop myself sinking into despair, unwilling, just yet, to give up, hanging onto that one point in my favour. *Ethan hasn't appeared.* Once they search us to their satisfaction, they shove us brutally into the back of the jeep and then with a second pair of cuffs, fasten Sean's left wrist to the door handle on the side. As we're handcuffed together, it's is an efficient way of ensuring neither of us can escape. The man who's been holding his rifle steadily on us throughout the procedure gets in the front and turns to face us, his gun continuing to make the threat clear. The other who'd conducted the search gets into the driver's seat.

"Where are you taking us?" At last, I find my voice though it's hardly recognisable as mine.

The men either ignore my question deliberately, or they can't speak English. The truck pulls away, and I notice the rest of the convoy following. Soon the palace is left behind, and we're heading out to the desert. The jeep bumps across the uneven sand, lurching side to side. I try to hold onto Sean as every time I'm thrown to the side his poor arm is wrenched from being attached to the vehicle.

"I don't generally mind the cuffs, but I can think of many better places to be tied up." Sean's voice is quiet, as he whispers into my ear.

I know he's trying to comfort me. But I can find no consolation in our predicament. "This is nothing to do with Kadar, is it? That man called me a whore, Ethan's behind this. There's no other reason for them to take me."

Despite the jostling of the jeep, Sean stills as though he's reluctant to reply. "Ethan," I breathe the name out, "He's here, isn't he?"

My bodyguard's hand twists and grabs mine. "Zoe, I'm

so sorry, I think he has to be behind this. I can't think of any other explanation. There's no other reason they would take you, no one in Amahad knows that you have any relationship with Kadar except as that of an employee." His fingers squeeze mine, "Kadar will move heaven and earth to get you back. Don't worry."

"I have no relationship with Kadar," I tell him bitterly. "I mean nothing to him." The letter I'd written had been direct and cruel, making it clear I didn't want to see him again under any circumstances. There was nothing in it to make him think kindly of me. I'd had to do it that way. Otherwise, there was a chance neither of us would be able to resist the pull between us. So I killed whatever embryonic feeling there was between us stone, cold dead.

"I don't think you're right." It's clear Sean hadn't read the letter.

"Ethan's going to kill me," I voice my worst fear. But somehow, putting it into words, accepting the inevitability of my predicament calms me, and strengthens my resolve to fight. Oh, I'll fight, I won't go easily. And he won't be expecting that; I've never fought back before.

"He'll have to go through me first." Sean's words sound like a vow to protect me.

"My flower advisor?" For the first time since they'd taken us, I manage a small smile.

"If they knew who I was, they'd have shot me on the spot. I thought it better if I stayed with you." He's quiet for a moment. "It was you who called me a chameleon, Zoe, so just go with the flow if I do anything unexpected."

The sudden jolt throwing me to the side, pulling on my

weak wrist halting our conversation for the moment, but I am so very, very glad I'm not alone.

We're travelling across the sand; I guess we're following a track or primitive road, and we're moving quite slowly which makes me hope that our rescuers will be able to locate us. That's assuming anyone bothers to come. After the way I worded the note to him, Kadar will probably have washed his hands of me. The thought that there's no one else who would care to miss or look for me is upsetting, and a tear escapes down my face. I'm glad for another reason that they brought my bodyguard with me; maybe someone will be concerned enough to come for him. I turn my head so Sean doesn't notice the wetness on my face. I'm trying to stay strong. But with Ethan on my tail, it's a difficult thing to do.

Sand, sand and more sand. The monotonous landscape goes on and on. Suddenly I see something different up ahead. Something is sticking up from the barren landscape. I tap Sean's arm and draw his attention to it. As we draw closer to the object, the shape becomes clearer; it's a helicopter. My heart drops into my stomach. We haven't been driving long across the desert, so we can't have covered that much distance. If rescuers were trying to track us, they might have had a chance to pursue us on the ground or even catch up. A helicopter is something else. Sean's thinking the same thing as I hear him swear under his breath.

I grip his hand again. "Where are they taking us?"

He shrugs his shoulders, "No way of knowing, I haven't heard them say a destination." Moving his head so he can see around the driver and take in the details of the aircraft which we're fast approaching he adds, "It's a Sikorsky, a passenger model, probably the S-76C. If I remember rightly, the range is just under four hundred miles. So taking into account the distance it already travelled to get here, it could take us two hundred miles away."

He's not looking at me and is half talking to himself, "The border with Ezirad is about fifty miles from here, so they could take us a good way into enemy territory if they wanted to."

"But why would Abdul-Muhsi want to take us to Ezirad? It doesn't make sense." I narrow my eyes, trying to think of what I know about the country.

"Who knows how a mad man might act? On the other hand, he could be taking us back to his tribe."

"But you don't think so?"

"That helicopter isn't military; it's civilian. And I can't see that Abdul-Muhsi could have got hold of it without outside help."

"Which brings us back to Ethan," I say, despondently. He'd be able to get his hands on any number of helicopters if that's what he wanted.

The jeep comes to an abrupt halt, throwing me across the seat, again yanking on Sean's hand, but I swallow my gasp of pain. The doors open, the cuff attaching Sean to the jeep is unlocked, and we're pulled out, staggering on the hot sand. Once Sean's got his balance he steadies me, then rolls his shoulders and gives me a rueful look. The rough journey had been tough on us both.

Showing they need no command of English when so

heavily armed, indicating the way with the aid of their guns, our driver and guard wave us towards the helicopter. We're handcuffed together in the middle of nowhere, and there isn't any option other than to obey.

CHAPTER 31
Kadar

We don't meet much opposition as we return from the armoury. It seems the majority of, what we now know are fake palace guards, have fled, or have accomplished a purpose that no longer appears to be waging war on me. The thought leaves me cold, as there could only be one other person that they could have targeted. Telling myself I won't be much help to her if I don't remain composed, I force my head into warrior mode as we move stealthily along the corridors. We only came across one straggler who's shock at seeing us causes him a brief moment of hesitation which Ghalib, showing we can't underestimate him because of his advanced years, takes advantage of, taking him out all by himself; a strong arm round the neck, a quick twist and the man is dead at our feet. Not one of us feels remorse.

Just as we reach our goal, we're joined by Rais and Sofian, and immediately I can see that they bring no good news. Rais quickly fills me in that the attack was direct on the harem itself, and having found no bodies; we can only assume they taken both Zoe and Sean. As the door was locked from inside the palace they couldn't have escaped that way. I push down my desire to rant at their report. It's time for action, not to lament what I cannot change. The only positive is that on their way back they'd investigated a sound and had found, and freed, the bona fide palace staff who the attackers had locked in the ancient dungeon.

Our discussion is interrupted as my phone rings. I answer quickly. As expected, it's Nijad, and he's hopping mad. "Brother. Speak to me."

"Cara's dug into Richard's financials. He received the million pounds for leaking Zoe Baker's whereabouts. But here's the thing, it went into his account the week before we asked him to do so."

"Fuck it!" My companions turn as I slam my fist against the wall. "He was a fucking traitor all along! He sold her out for his own gain."

"Yes, and not only that, a couple of days ago another two hundred and fifty went in—timed to coincide with your plans to go to the Desert City."

One and a quarter million pounds. The cost of betrayal.

Nijad is still talking. "Cara's found his bank account and credit cards were all maxed out. He's been playing a little too hard in our casinos."

Cara is an adept computer hacker; I don't doubt for one minute the accuracy of her findings. "How the fuck didn't we know about this?" I rasp down the phone.

"Because we give our employees privacy."

We do respect the people that we employ but expect loyalty in return. Maybe there are things we'll need to tighten up on, but for now, I've got to deal with the probability that St John-Davies has Zoe in his hands. Unless I find her, she's not going to last long. My gut twists as my mind pulls up different scenarios of what might happen to her. None of them good. With difficulty, I force those thoughts away.

"What else can you tell me?"

"A convoy of trucks left the palace a short while ago. We're tracking them. I've got the drones sent up. They're heading out and getting close to the border. At present, they're a few miles away from it."

"Send me the coordinates and keep me posted. I need a helicopter, Nijad."

"There's one waiting for you. As soon as you can let me know the palace landing pad has been cleared of insurgents, I'll get over it to you."

I end the call and then look at the sheikhs surrounding me. "They're heading for the border. I think they are Muhsi's men, at least one of them was from his tribe."

Jibran's nodding his head, and I again recall the doubts I had about him. It seemed they had some grounding when he speaks his next words, "Abdul-Muhsi dropped some hints about something going down. I ignored him. But it's too much of a coincidence for it to be anything else." That the other sheikhs are shaking their heads in disbelief shows me only Jibran had been party to the traitor's thoughts.

"Who would be with him, Jibran?" I test his loyalty, trying to get more information.

Jibran shrugs and looks unwilling to say. But a growl from the vicious looking Rais makes him change his mind. "I can't say for certain, but probably Fadi and Tamir.

I rub my hand over my face, not knowing how I can cope with all the duplicity around me. I've a feeling I've two battles ahead; one against men wishing to depose me and the other to save Zee. I pray to Allah that I can win both. Or at least prevent harm coming to the woman who's become so important to me, knowing that's more important to me than my position of power. I feel a hand on my arm.

"Tamir and Fadi are easily led, Emir," Rais gives me my title. "But do they, in reality, want Abdul-Muhsi as Ruler? I doubt it. Particularly not Tamir."

There's a murmur of agreement from the others. "Fadi is young and headstrong," Ghalib starts, ignoring the fact that both Rais and Sofian are younger. "Youngsters look for change for change's sake."

I take a deep breath, "They've got outside help."

Rais is nodding as if he expected it all along. "The English woman?"

I appreciate he didn't repeat what he'd heard and thus avoids calling her a whore. "A man called St John-Davies held her against her will; he abused her. Badly. She escaped from him and came to Amahad. I, er, I offered her my protection."

I get five sharp looks directed at me, but Rais is the one to spit on the ground. It's part of what makes Amahad different, women are important to us, and no true Amahadian man would use violence against the fairer sex. If a woman is in an abusive situation, she can divorce, and even remarry. The abuser, however, is forever shunned and would find it hard to find another woman to tempt into his bed. As happened to my brother, Nijad, when his falsely earned reputation for violence had him banished to the desert.

"Who is this, St John-Davies?" Ghalib gets straight to the point.

"One of the richest, most powerful, men in the UK. He's got his fingers in many pies, including communications and the military. And many men at his disposal."

"He will be bringing a private army?"

"We should assume so."

"Your plans, Emir?"

My head's all over the place. I want Zoe back; I want her safe. But I also need to quash any uprising led by Abdul-Muhsi. But until we know where they are heading there's not a lot I can do. A knee jerk reaction to follow the route the trucks had taken driving out of the city might prove to be futile. My phone rings again, giving me a few minutes grace to come up with the plan, and Nijad now provides the information I need to formulate it.

"Brother," I can tell by his hesitation after his greeting that it's not going to be good news. "Speak." I need to hear it, whatever it is.

"The trucks met up with a helicopter; it's in the air now, and appears to be heading into Ezirad." He gives me a moment to digest the information before continuing, "I've notified the army in the desert bases. I'm going to be flying down myself and will be in the command centre. I think, Kadar, we have to assume that this will be an attempted coup."

"And St. John-Davies?"

"I've got Cara trying to track him down. She's working with Grade A Security. Ben Carter is here with me, and he's flying the people he has here team down to you and getting others flown over from England. At the moment, we can't locate St John-Davies, but our gut feel is that he's not arrived in either Amahad or Ezirad yet. His private plane is currently outside a hanger in Dubai. It arrived last night, but he wasn't on it but we assume it's fuelled and ready waiting for him. Cara's keeping a check on all the private and commercial flights heading to the airport."

I thank him for the information and end the call. Calling my fellow sheikhs around me, I quickly update them on the situation. Now is the time to for them all to place their cards on the table. I pull myself to my full height. If I don't have the backing of my comrades, then I'll have difficulty rescuing Zee. At the moment, the thought of losing control of my country is the last thing on my mind. I'd give up my life to keep her safe.

I deepen my voice, "Sheikh Abdul-Muhsi appears to be preparing to attempt a coup. He may well have teamed up with armed forces in Ezirad; whether they are the official military or terrorists jumping on the bandwagon, or a combination of both, we don't know. We can also assume he has the backing of Ethan St John-Davies—St John-Davies wants the woman, and he must have offered something of value to Abdul-Muhsi for him to have carried out this elaborate kidnapping. Something big enough to make him show all his cards. There won't be a place in Amahad for him after this." I hear the growl of agreement around me. "St John-Davies might have provided arms and most probably, men. I would now ask that you give me your support against Abdul-Muhsi. It pains me to admit that trying to use diplomacy to keep him onside has failed. As you will be aware, as a distant cousin to the Kassis family he seems set on making a claim for the throne." I pause and glance around the five faces watching me intently. "Are you with me? Or against me?" I put the question succinctly.

Sheikh Rais moves forwards without a second thought. Falling to his knees, he bows his head to the floor, and then sits back on his heels, his scimitar lying across the palms of his outstretched hands, "My sword is yours, Excellency."

As I nod in grateful acknowledgement Sofian follows suit. After a slightly anxious moment, Jibran and Wahid also pledge me their support.

I cock my eyebrow at Ghalib, a man I have admired all my life. Would he throw in his lot with someone who kidnaps women on demand?

"You are young, Kadar, come to the throne before your time. Have you the wisdom of your father? The sagacity to rule equitably over this country?"

I address his challenge. "We are moving into a modern world, Ghalib. Amahad needs a ruler who can negotiate with foreign governments who would wish to exploit our new found oil fields. A leader who can bring our antiquated laws up to date to attract foreign investment so all our peoples can benefit from education and healthcare. A ruler who not only can consider the needs of the city dwellers but also of the tribes living in the desert. One man can no longer do everything, take all the decisions. Which is precisely why I'm setting up a form of democratic government. A ruler, in today's world, needs to make balanced decisions guided by the wisest of the wise."

He considers my words. "The sheikhs will be part of the new government?"

If it gets his support, I'll agree to that, "I give you my word."

Muttering something about the undesirability of change Ghalib, at last, makes a move to fall to his knees. I put out my hand to stop him. At his age, he need not make the physical show of respect.

With a terse nod to thank me, he just bows his head, "My sword is yours." Although he's come to it last, there's no hesitation or holding back, and I know I'll be able to rely on him. After so much treachery today, I feel some measure of thankfulness and relief.

We hold a brief council of war. The sheikhs already have the men they brought with them and are eager to start gathering other warriors from their tribes. Nijad will soon be here to coordinate the full-time military personnel. As much as I might want to, I can't just race off into the desert after the rebels. We have to wait for more support and more information rather than running blind.

I leave the sheikhs to go back to their temporary camps around the city and start making their preparations, making my way to the helipad. All the insurgents seem to have left the palace now, their objective achieved. The genuine palace employees are walking around looking upset and bewildered, and quickly I locate the Head of Staff and give him the job of placating them. After that, I make my way to the helipad, ready to go to the Command

Centre to wait for my brother.

As I walk, I rub my hand across my eyes and think of Zee, feeling sick at the thought of what she might be going through, and how terrified she will be. The only saving grace is that Sean appears to be with her and hopefully will stay alive to protect her. But my fear is that when they find out he is her bodyguard, how long will he be left alive to watch over her?

CHAPTER 32

Zoe

I t's our second night in this pig sty, a primitive goats' skin tent, God knows where in the middle of the desert. Although we're out of direct sunlight, the inside is stifling during the day, and at night, when the temperatures fall, my thin blouse and light trousers offer insufficient protection from the cold. Sean and I are still together with no option but to stay that way, connected as we are by a chain looped around the central pole; attaching me to one end by my left hand, Sean to the other by his right. We've each got about six feet of free movement, which makes answering the call of nature humiliating and embarrassing, especially since we've not been left with anything to relieve ourselves into.

Even though we've pleaded and begged, resorting to sign language as our guards don't seem to have any command of English and Sean doesn't want to reveal his knowledge of Arabic, they refuse to let us go outside. Instead, we have to use a corner of the wooden hut to relieve ourselves. The only saving grace is that after two days of hardly any food and very little water we don't have to use the corner much. The first time was the most embarrassing; I'd held on as long as I could until I thought my bladder was going to burst. But after that, I felt so weak and dizzy from the heat and lack of food I lost all sense of dignity.

If I had to choose a companion to share this horror with, I could have come up with no better choice than Sean. He tries to keep my spirits up, impressing on me time and time again that Kadar will move mountains to rescue me, but I'm not so confident; my written goodbye to him was too final. And at the end of the day, he's the emir with all the responsibilities that go along with that. I'm only a humble employee. No, all our hopes have to be pinned on Grade A. They won't leave a man of theirs behind.

During the daylight hours, and at night for that matter, there's surprisingly little activity around the camp, the soldiers, tribespeople—warriors? I'm not quite sure what to call them—seem to be waiting for something. Although Sean suggests other alternatives, deep down, I know the truth. *They're waiting for Ethan.*

As darkness falls once more, a sudden change due to our latitude—no lingering sunsets here—I fall into an emotionally exhausted and restless sleep, snuggled up against my bodyguard's side. I start to dream…

Ethan stands in front of me as I'm naked, and stretched across the St Andrews Cross that graces one end of his playroom. My hands and ankles cuffed too tight for comfort. I hear footsteps approaching, and can smell the stale odour of sweat mixed with tobacco so react with no surprise when Hargreaves comes up behind. The grin on Ethan's face looks feverish as though he's overexcited, and I fear this time it's going to be dire.

"The whip, Sir?"

"The eight footer, Hargreaves," Ethan confirms. "You know how much she loves it. It will help settle her. Just like John Tharpe calms his wife, Mia."

Again I hear footsteps as the manservant walks away to the cupboard where Ethan keeps his implements of torture. I lower my chin to my chest, the only movement that's available to me and close my eyes, trying to shut out what I know is to come. Tears start to fall. I'm trapped, there's nothing I can do except try and mentally prepare myself, knowing that there'll be no escape from the wicked tail of the whip slicing through my skin.

"Look at me," Ethan commands, roughly grabbing my hair so I'm forced to face him. There's a manic look in his eyes as he waits for the screams Hargreaves will bring forth, however hard I'll try to suppress them. He loves to watch my body process the pain, and my mind accepting my utter hopelessness. My torture is Ethan's favoured foreplay. He's already turned on, his free hand in his pocket, brisk movements in the material showing he is enthusiastically rubbing his cock. I hope he'll make himself come. Otherwise, he'll use me, whatever state I'm in after my correction.

"How many, Sir?"

"How many, Zo?" He gives an excited laugh, already anticipating my torture and pain, I say nothing. There's no point. So he replies without waiting for me to speak, "Just continue until I tell you to stop."

Will it be this time? Will he forget to tell Hargreaves when he's satisfied? Will tonight be the night he goes too far, and they whip me to death? I tense up, anticipating the blood trickling down my back. It's almost worse now that I know what to expect.

"Very good, Sir. I'll wait for your word."

The next thing I hear is Hargreaves swinging the whip through the air, the loud crack of his practice strike then a deep thud as it hits the stone flooring. Another crack, and then another. I don't know how many times it will be before the lash lands on my back, slicing through my skin. Ethan's manservant might keep this up for a while; they are both aware that the cruelty of the mind fuck can be almost as traumatic as the actual blows themselves. Ridiculously I have to bit my tongue to stop screaming out for him to just get on with it! More tears trickle down my cheeks, and at the sight, Ethan lets out a manic laugh.

"You need a lesson how to treat a submissive." A new voice, but one I recognise. One which manages to be deep and authoritative, but calm and soothing at the same time. Heaven knows how or why, but it's Kadar! How the fuck can he be here? What's he doing in London? I didn't even think Ethan knew him.

"Give me the whip and I'll show you how you should treat a sub!" I flinch, realising this is no rescue, Kadar wants to take part! A long moan of protest comes from my lips as I hear scuffling behind me, it sounds like he's appropriated the single tail from Hargreaves.

Tears fall faster now, my anguish doubled by the presence of the man who'd been so gentle with me. True colours will always out; I should know that by now. Unable to prevent myself from tensing, I wait for the first blow, but there's no crack, no feel of the whip lashing my back, just a gentle kiss placed on my shoulders, then barely-there soft strokes, and caresses of a hand over the whole of my back. A caring hand, arousing me as it circles downwards.

"Relax, habiti, enjoy," Kadar's voice rumbles over me. Ethan and Hargreaves are noticeably silent, as though they're no longer there at all.

His hands reach my backside, starting to rub, then a finger moves lower swiping along my slit. I writhe against my binding, struggling, not so much as to try to escape as somehow to find some much-needed relief. How is it I'm getting turned on with Ethan and Hargreaves in the room? I can't understand it!

As if my squirming is a signal he changes his target area, his talented fingers move up and circle my clit which is very much alive and throbbing, and oh, do I want to come.

He reads me so well; he knows what I need. His fingers are cleverly strumming; Kadar leans over me so I can feel his impressive cock in his robes pressing against my backside. And then, at exactly the right time, the words I need to hear, "Come for me!"

I explode with a scream.

Kadar wipes his hand across my dripping pussy and holds up the wetness for Ethan, who's now moved back in my line of sight, to see. "That's how to treat a sub," he tells him.

Ethan's face morphs into that of a monster. "I'm going to kill you all!" he promises shouting, spit flying out of his mouth.

"Zoe! Zoe!" I can hear Sean's voice and for a second wonder what he, too, is doing at Ethan's mansion. "Zoe, sweetheart, wake up. You've been dreaming."

Sitting up, I rub my eyes, for a moment, disorientated then rapidly remember where I am. Shit! That dream was so real! Oh God, damn! I didn't actually have an orgasm, did I? My body's feeling alive and thrumming. Mortified I turn my head away. What exactly did Sean hear, or worse, see?

"Was it Ethan, again?" His voice is full of sympathy and tinged with suppressed anger that even in my nightmares, Ethan haunts me. I let out a relieved breath I hadn't realised I'd sucked in. As there's no way Sean would equate Ethan with pleasure. I must have woken him up at the very end of my dream.

"Yes." Only able to give a simple answer, as my mind is still trying to process the content of my rapidly fading fantasy. Even now the details fade away, including those I don't want to lose—the fact that Kadar came to save me in my nightmare. I didn't even know my imagination could be that vivid. *I genuinely orgasmed!*

He squeezes my arm and rolls his shoulders trying to get some relief. Being handcuffed with a lack of freedom of movement makes us both stiff and unable to find a comfortable position. "Just keep hanging on in there, sweetheart." Pulling me to him he plants a platonic kiss on the top on my head, "The longer we're here, the more likely it is that someone will come and save us."

He's trying to comfort me, but I'm fast losing hope.

* * * *

Another day passes, then one more. Now we begin to hear sounds of preparation around us as if something is about to happen. But apart from the uncommunicative man bringing us our meagre food and water rations we see no other person. It's a waiting game; I don't know whether I'm anxious for this time to end, or would rather continue as we are, unable to imagine how bad the alternative could be.

We're both weaker now, and our vain attempts to try to fill the time seem too much effort to continue. We've sought to keep our spirits up, sharing stories of our pasts then, when our history was exhausted, Sean started a game of 'I spy'. That didn't work out very well as there's not much to see in the stark tent, but it did help distract me from my dark thoughts. For the first couple of days, we'd made attempts to exercise to keep fit. Attempts that were at times amusing, tied together as we are, but neither of us has the energy for that now. Sean tries to remain positive, but as the days pass I slowly lose hope of any rescue attempt.

Dawn on the fifth day brings a new sound, that of a helicopter flying overhead. As I hear the increase in engine noise when it comes into land, Sean's body goes tense on full alert. *Something's going to happen.* Standing, I know we're both hoping against hope that this might be a rescue. But even I know the lack of fighting outside signifies it's anything but. When the rotors stop turning, an eerie silence follows the fading whine of the blades. Then voices seem to call out in welcome as though sensing no danger or threat. And only minutes later my worst fears come true as the person I dread most enters the tent.

It's been more than three months since I last saw him. In that time, he seems to have changed. His civilised veneer has become tarnished, and the touch of madness I used to discern in his eyes is now far more apparent and accompanied by a twist in his face when he leers at me. Of course, here he isn't trying to act a part, so maybe he's just dropped the façade. I taste bile in my mouth at the sight of him.

For a moment Ethan simply stands and stares, a cruel grin slowly spreading across his face. Quickly stepping forwards Sean puts himself in front of me, but he can do nothing to save me. Surrounded by six fierce looking well-armed men, Sean is outnumbered and would only be committing suicide to try to take on Ethan's bodyguards. But his movements attract attention.

"And who have we here?" Ethan snaps out as he comes further into the tent, but maintaining a safe distance. "Who are you?"

Sean tells him the same as he said last time he somehow had asked him that. Ethan sneers and spits on the ground.

"A pansy gardener! I should just shoot you now."

"No, don't!" I try to push Sean out of the way. "He's nothing to me, nothing to you, Ethan. He was just in the wrong place at the wrong time. Don't hurt him, please!"

For an answer, Ethan raises his gun and points it at Sean's head. As though scared, Sean drops to his knees and lowers his head in defeat.

Ethan laughs, enjoying the show of apparent submission. "I think I'll let you suffer a bit longer, pansy."

Now, his attention turns to me, "And you, my dear little whore. Don't think I don't know what you've been up to. From one rich man to another, eh? Wasn't my wealth enough for you? You wanted to be a rich Arab's plaything instead?"

It takes me a moment to realise he's suggesting I left him for Kadar. When I understand, I have to put him right. "I left you because of how you treated me. You abused me. You beat me, hurt me. You *raped* me!"

I should have known my display of spirit would have enraged him. Motioning to his men he points at Sean, "Watch him!" Six guns come up trained on my bodyguard. Ethan takes another step toward me, his nose wrinkling in disgust, "You stink!"

I hate myself, but instead of pointing out the unsanitary conditions his men had kept me in, instead I do what he's grown to accept, and take responsibility as though I could have done otherwise, "I'm sorry." I'm immediately annoyed at myself and how weak my voice sounds.

"I can't even bring myself to fuck you." He sniffs derisively; then his eyes grow darker, "You shouldn't have left me, Zo. You shouldn't have run. Do you know how fucking long I've been searching for you?" Moving within striking distance his hand comes up and slaps me hard across the face. I feel blood trickling from the side of my mouth. "And that slut friend of yours. Sophie. Where the fuck is she? Would you believe I've been traipsing around America trying to fucking find her?" His voice is getting louder as he starts to lose control, "You wouldn't think it would be hard to find a fucking cripple, would you?" He grabs hold of my hand, yanking it painfully. "Tell me where she is, whore! Tell me where to find her and I might let you live!"

"Why?" I cry out, unable to understand his fixation with Sophie. Hasn't he already caused her enough harm?

"Because I never lose!" He screams out the words, spittle flying from his mouth. He's out of control, and he's terrifying me. This time, it's a punch to the stomach, and I reel from the blow.

"I don't know where she is!" I screech. It's the truth, but I've no hope he'll choose to accept it. Christ, that blow was so hard I have trouble straightening up again. If there were a chance I was carrying Kadar's child, I surely wouldn't be any longer after that.

Our eyes meet for a moment that seems to stretch into hours although it was probably only a couple of minutes. Ethan stares into mine, assessing me. I can't help returning his gaze with defiance, knowing he wants me to break. I'd like to know what was going on in his head even though I'm well aware I wouldn't like it.

With a sudden change of mood, his face suddenly softens, and his hand goes under my chin, caressing me gently, almost an intimate gesture. "I'll find her," he starts in a reasonable-sounding tone, "With, or without your help." I move my head back as his fingers start to push my hair gently away from my forehead. "Where has this defiance come from? Where's my Zoe?" His hand moves down to my cheek again, smoothing it gently, "You used to be such an obedient slave, crawling across the floor on your hands and knees to beg my forgiveness. Taking your punishment so beautifully. My marks will still be on your body, won't they, Zo? Don't they remind me that you are *mine*?"

I try to stop the shudder going through me as he weaves his spell. Part of me wants to blurt out another apology, but I fight it, resisting falling into his trap. The memory of Kadar in my dream, so kind and careful, *loving*. It might only have been my imagination conjuring him up, but the vision of his face makes me feel brave. I'm terrified of what Ethan's going to do to me, but he's not going to make me beg. It might be stupid, but there's nothing I can do which would make things worse. Needing to show him how far I've come since I left him, I blurt out, "Go fuck yourself, Ethan."

He's taken aback; that's clear. But then he laughs, "Common as muck, you filthy, little slut. You whore. I don't know why I bothered with you in the first place."

I hold myself taller. "I'm no whore."

Expecting another blow to come I tense, but instead, his hand grabs my chin, his fingers digging painfully into my skin. "Do you know what they do to adulteresses in Ezirad?" he asks me quietly in a matter of fact voice and then continues without waiting for a reply. His coldness is more disturbing than if he'd lost his temper, "I've been learning all I can about this fascinating country, and some of the practices are, well, they might be thought barbaric in the Western world, but in the circumstances, I believe they're quite fitting. And admirable. Do you know what they do? How they deal with a woman who's left her man for another's bed?" He continues to stroke my face; his touch makes my skin feel worms are crawling over me.

Although my mouth is dry from lack of water, I swallow rapidly. I knew death was inevitable, but am starting to dread the manner in which it might be delivered and what he could be referring to. He's talking about it so indifferently that I grow chilly despite the hot desert air. I have to protest, "I didn't commit adultery. We were never married." I can't stay silent even knowing it's futile to attempt to get him to see reason.

"Here, in Ezirad," he continues as if I hadn't said a word, "Adulteresses are stoned to death. A fitting end for you I think, my love."

"For fuck's sake, man! You have got to be joking!" Sean can't help himself.

Ignoring Sean's outburst, he starts to smile. "You'll be begging to die before long, and it won't be quick. I'll make sure of that. Yes, you'll be screaming and begging and telling me everything I might ever want to know in the hope that I'll be merciful and end it quickly for you. But I'll want to see you suffer. No one gets away from me, Zo. No one leaves me."

"I'm not an adulteress," I tell him again, my head swimming with the brutal sentence he's just pronounced. Is there no limit to Ethan's cruelty?

"As good as! You were, are, and always will be my woman. I own you. Mine, to do with whatever I fucking want. And mine to punish now you've given your body to someone else. No one gets away with that."

I think back to the revelations about his previous girlfriend, Clara, and her very nasty death. I doubt I'll have much chance to escape the gruesome fate he's described, but I make an attempt, denying my night with Kadar, "No, Ethan. You think I'd want another man after what you did to me?"

"Whore!" Spittle flies from his mouth as he shouts the word at me. "Kadar was seen coming out of your bedroom. Don't fucking try to deny it!" Dropping his hand from my face, he turns to call loudly over his shoulder, "Hamid!" A man strides confidently into the tent. I recognise him as one of the servants in the desert palace, the one I had thought particularly surly. Ethan signals him to stop just inside the doorway. "Hamid was a witness to your adultery."

Once! It was once. But it was obviously enough. How Hamid knew what went on between the emir and myself I didn't know, but he'd apparently been spying. And even if he was lying I know that Ethan would take his word against mine.

"Ah, pretty Zo. Shall I tell you what's going to happen to you?"

"Jesus H Christ! Take your hands off of her and leave her alone! Haven't you already done enough to hurt her?" Sean's anger and disgust are palpable.

Without looking his way, Ethan nods towards one of his men at his side and the gun lifts threateningly.

"No!" I shout out, relieved when no shot comes.

Ignoring my outburst, he moves his hand back again, cupping my chin in a parody of a lover's touch. But Ethan long ago lost any resemblance to that description. "First I'll tie your delicate hands behind your back and then I'll blindfold you. You're a woman so we'll bury you in the ground up to your chest. If you can escape I'm afraid I'll have to be merciful, and accept it as Allah's will that you live, but don't get your hopes up of that. It's nigh on impossible. Of course, these brilliant Muslim laws always favour the stronger sex. If you were a man, it would be slightly easier to get away as you would only be buried up to your waist. I've been reading up on it, you see, it is a fascinating practice. But then again, these Arabs know the proper place for women, don't they?" He pauses as if I should congratulate him on his diligent research. "Well, in some countries they do. Amahad is a little different, but Abdul-Muhsi is going to change that. Once Kadar is dead —and yes, my dear Zoe, I'm going to kill him for touching what was mine—once he is gone Abdul-Muhsi will become emir, and he has plans to return Amahad to the dark ages. Frankly, my love, I do not give a fucking damn. You will be dead, and Kadar will be rotting in his grave."

I gaze at him in horror, I should have realised, but hadn't thought that as soon as Hamid had betrayed his ruler, Ethan would want him dead as well. "Please, Kadar has nothing to do with this. With us!" If I can't save my life, maybe I can save his?

Ethan grins cruelly, again ignoring me. "Now where was I? Oh yes, the stoning. Now, Hamid here, as the witness, will throw the first stone. Technically, of course, there should be four witnesses, but Abdul-Muhsi has agreed to act as Judge and has decreed in the circumstances, Hamid will suffice." Ethan's voice is cold as if he's reciting the weather forecast. "Then we'll all join in. I think Hargreaves is particularly looking forward to it. As, I have to admit, am I. The stones can't be too large, or they might help the process along too quickly. And neither can they be too small or they wouldn't be effective. It usually takes up to an hour before your skull is crushed and your brains turned to mush, and all the time you'll be screaming and begging for mercy. To no avail, I assure you. I'll be enjoying every one of your pleas. A fitting punishment for an adulteress, don't you think? You will be dead. And here, in Ezirad, all perfectly legal."

I want to tell him my brains are already mush. How can he stand there and be so cruel? I'm shaking. I feel Sean tense and wonder if he'll try to make a move. I hope he doesn't; I don't want anyone else to die. My death's certain, but if there's a chance he'll survive I want him to take it. I hope he won't try to be heroic.

While the horror of Ethan's plans for me sinks in, a man I know only too well enters the tent. Ethan turns his head. "It's done?"

Hargreaves has a manic smile on his face, his eyes glowing with excitement as he enthusiastically pronounces, "The hole's dug." Of course, he'd have taken responsibility for that.

"Ethan…" I cry out, wanting to plead with him.

"No! Silence, bitch. I've enjoyed our conversation, but it's the last we'll be having. There's no need for further delay." He removes his hand so abruptly I stagger and almost fall. "Bring her! And the pansy can come along as well."

Two of his men cross the tent and taking hold of my arms, undo the cuffs and chain linking us together, ignoring my ineffective struggles. Four days of no nutritious food has made me weak. Behind me, I can hear the other men pulling Sean to his feet. It's the chance he's been waiting for. His legs come out taking down the men trying to restrain him; he's using the same kind of karate kick I've seen him use before. Two men are already down, but that still leaves too many left standing. I hear a gunshot and then another and see the smoke rising from the barrel of the gun Ethan is holding. I daren't look around, fearing Sean is dead.

"Bring him!" Ethan sounds furious. "Drag him. He can witness her death before he dies. Unless he bleeds out first. We can start a book as to who lasts longest."

Amongst the cruel laughter of the men who seem to find Ethan's suggestion entertaining, I hear a muffled groan and heave a relieved sigh. Sean's hurt, but still in the land of the living for the moment at least. Two men pass me dragging Sean along, blood trailing in his wake. They've shot him in both legs and have left him completely helpless, and have again cuffed him with his hands behind his back.

"Now you!" Ethan instructs his men to take me outside.

I kick, bite, scream, but I can't get away from them, suddenly finding energy fuelled by self-preservation but there are too many of them and even on one of my best days, they'd be too strong for me. They laugh at my feeble efforts, discussing what's going to happen as if they're looking forward to the show. Ethan directs Hargreaves to start taking bets on how long I'll survive. And as the men begin calling out anything from a matter of minutes to hours, I heave and retch, but there's nothing in my stomach to bring up.

Once outside I blink rapidly in the stark brightness of the desert sun, my eyes needing time to adjust after living in relative darkness for days. So it's a few moments before I'm able to take in the sight in front of me. When I can, I see men everywhere, a variety of Arab and Caucasian, dressed in tribal clothing or military fatigues. Everyone's rushing to and fro, but even to my untutored eyes, there seems a lack of organisation. In addition to his bodyguards who were in the tent, another group of surround Ethan, apparently the men he brought with him, his personal army. Everyone's brandishing weapons.

Waving on the men who are holding me captive, Ethan watches as I'm hauled over to the other side of the makeshift camp. Not one step do I take willingly; I struggle and fight, using my teeth, getting at least one good bite in that makes one man clasping me swear and drop my arm, but his place is immediately taken by another who holds me slightly further away at arm's length. They're overpowering me, but can't subdue me. This is my life, such as it is, and I'm not going to make it easy for them to take it.

Suddenly a man appears, and I recognise him as the leader of the attack on the harem. Sheikh Abdul-Muhsi's approach causes our small procession to come to a halt. For a second, I hope for a reprieve until he spits in my face. "English whore!"

Ethan laughs, "Your judgement?" He's asking as though to make it official.

"She has committed adultery. The offence is punishable by stoning!"

"I haven't committed adultery!" I scream at him. How could I? I was never Ethan's wife!

"Take her away. And carry out the sentence." He ignores my outburst.

Once more they're dragging me, this time to the middle of the camp where there's a deep hole in the ground. I stand above it, looking down in dread.

"Abdul-Muhsi! Sheikh!" A voice I don't recognise calls out.

"Sheikh Tamir!" Then they lose me as they speak rapidly in Amahadian.

"What's the delay?" There's anger in Ethan's voice. "Let's get on with this."

Abdul-Muhsi addresses him in English, "There's an army coming towards us. Tamir feels we should start preparing and avoid any distractions until we've been victorious against them. Put the woman back in the tent; you can deal with her punishment later."

I hold my breath, hardly daring to hope for a reprieve.

"No, we do this now." I readily recognise the anger in Ethan's voice, his tone showing he will not be moved. "I've financed this operation, Sheikh, so I'm fucking going to do what I want and when I want. Now leave me to do this, or I'll take my money back. Then where would your little coup be?"

Why am I the only one to hear the madness in Ethan's voice? Can't the sheikh see he's a raving lunatic? But the sheikh says nothing; clearly the threat of removing his funds holds sway.

Ethan grabs hold of my arms, pulling them to my back

and tying them together then roughly fastens a blindfold over my eyes. He pushes me over the burning hot ground until my feet falter on the edge of the hole. I struggle, but it's futile. His strong arms surround me, with ease he picks me up, and though I kick out with my legs, Hargreaves grabs them, and they both manoeuvre me and have no problem dropping me into the body shaped pit. Immediately Hargreaves takes a shovel and starts filling in the void around me. I scream for help in absolute terror with no hope that anyone who would or could save me will hear, scrabbling wildly but in vain with hands tied behind and feet unable to gain purchase on the loose sides of the deep hole as the more of Ethan's men come up to shovel sand in around me.

CHAPTER 33
Kadar

It doesn't matter what Zoe wrote in that note to me. On first reading it was hurtful, but I knew she could have worded it no other way, or I would have immediately tried to dissuade her, even while knowing it was the wrong thing to do. And it's obvious whatever her brain told her to say; it wasn't what was in her heart. Although she'd told me in her own sweet way to get lost, there is no fucking way I'd abandon her now. *I love her.* The realisation only hit me when I knew her life was in very real danger. What can happen between us when I save her—and I *have* to save her—I don't know. But she's become my world, my life; she's stolen my heart. How will I go on if I lose her?

When the intelligence comes in that Abdul-Muhsi has pulled together a small army now hiding out in the enemy state of Ezirad, though it goes against the grain, I know it's important to refrain from acting impulsively. As much as I want to have her back safe, as emir I also have a duty to my country, and for everyone's sake, the uprising has to be thwarted quickly and swiftly. And that means waiting for the sheikhs to gather their men so I have a sizeable army behind me.

Over the last two days, my brothers have joined me; Jasim having flown back from England, bring some of the guys from Grade A. Hunter, Ben's explained, is best left to oversee security at the oil field development. My heart warmed when I saw one person in particular who he had brought with him, and I couldn't help stepping forwards and grasping his hand.

"Jon!" I pulled him to me, my arm slapping his back, "I can't tell you how much it means to me that you're here."

He returns my greeting, then steps back, "I couldn't stay away, Kadar, Mia understands. You've got a hostage situation here, so I'm here to give you my help."

With all his years of experience in the elite SAS extracting people held captive all over the world Jon Tharpe's skill set will prove useful to us.

"We'll get the woman out, along with Sean. Grade A don't leave men behind." His confidence that we'll be successful is heartening, and just the encouragement I need at the present moment.

"Our team will focus on the extraction as that's our area of expertise," Jon continues, and I give my response as a nod of agreement.

While it means I won't have an active role in her rescue, I'm comforted knowing if it's possible to bring her out alive, these men—and in particular Jon Tharpe—have the skills and knowledge to do so. Being able to leave such a vital job in their hands enables me to concentrate on putting down the insurgents who threaten my country. With Grade A, my brothers and my loyal countrymen beside me I start to feel more positive.

Hourly we continue to scour maps and aerial surveys. The drones go up time after time, feeding us back valuable information. Between us and Abdul-Muhsi's base, we know there are pockets of the Amahadian rebels hiding out in the primitive villages. We need to proceed with caution, putting down the revolt while not endangering civilian life. I've spoken to Sultan Qudamah of Ezirad and have received his frantic assurance that his army will not be involved in any official invasion of Amahad. In fact, he seemed terrified Abdul-Muhsi might push his country into a full-scale war for which they are unprepared and would surely lose. However, knowing his tentative hold on the stability of his country I wouldn't be surprised if some of his military will be supporting Abdul-Muhsi without his knowledge.

Qudamah seems a frightened man, deeply concerned that the full force of my far stronger country of Amahad might turn on his untrained and much smaller army. The unspoken threat made him eager to agree to talks once the uprising has been put down. And I have no doubt that will be the outcome; the support of the men I have behind me is overwhelming, my army growing in numbers by the hour as more and more tribespeople join us. It seems it's one thing to moan and criticise a leader, but quite another matter to find an acceptable alternative to put in his place.

If I weren't so concerned about Zoe, I would be on a high at this point, my future as emir seems assured, and we may even be able to improve our relationship with Ezirad at the end of all this. But despite the positives, the certainty that I'll lose good men in the battle ahead and the feeling of dread in my gut about the woman I'm so desperately hoping to save, means I'm hard put even to find a smile of encouragement for the troops assembling and being given their orders all around. I've already ruled out the obvious option of aerial strikes on the insurgents' base. I can't put Zoe's life in any more danger than it already is.

At last, the final preparations are completed, and we start making our way across the border. Quickly we become engaged in fierce fighting in the villages closest to that imaginary line in the sand that divides the two countries, but conquer them swiftly and soon we make slow but steady progress to the interior. It's difficult to distinguish friend from foe as Amahadians fight Amahadians while the Eziradians hide in their tents and houses. Hastily laid land mines delay our progress; luckily most so amateurishly deployed they are easy to spot. But Ghalib loses two of his tribesmen in a horrific explosion. It's the first time I've seen him with tears in his eyes, and that, more than anything, brings home to me, that other than dealing with border skirmishes, Amahad hasn't had anything like a war since my great-grandfather's time, the last civil uprising long before that. I harden my resolve to finish this fast.

In one village I'm shocked to find young Caucasian men speaking English, who have no business being here, radicalised youths fighting what they think is a religious war. I couldn't save them; they were determined not to be taken alive.

Saddened by the waste of such young lives we continue. Our progress is slow, but after two days we are nearing the main camp. We split up now, Sheikhs Jibran and Sofian staying back to mop out the pockets of Abdul-Muhsi's men who are still trying to snipe at us, as they continue to fight a war, any sane person must, by now, know they can have no hope of winning. They are unorganised and undisciplined, more of an annoyance to my seasoned troops than any real threat. It will be different when we reach their base, though; I fear that there they will be much better prepared for us.

Fierce fighting men surround me, their sole job to protect their emir. The deserts sheikhs are wary—if I'm taken out of the picture, then it will be a free for all as to who my successor will be—and wish to keep me alive to maintain the Amahadian freedoms and way of life. My blood lust rises each time I'm held back from joining the fray, but I know the sheikhs are right. I'm the figurehead holding it all together.

I'm forced to watch as Nijad proves his worth in hand to hand combat time after time, as Jasim takes a sniper position, picking off our adversaries one by one in the villages we pass through. The Eziradians, on the whole, seem well rid of our opponents, offering them no support or opportunity to hide.

I have to watch my men die, each waste of life fuelling my anger and sorrow. I feel like I've aged half a century in just a few days.

The drones feed back information, and, to our surprise, the terrorist camp seems quiet. It doesn't appear that there's an army coming out to confront us, which strengthens our suspicions of their state of readiness when we eventually reach their base, suspecting their most experienced fighters will be dug in and waiting for us. Our tanks roll and foot soldiers march on, arms at the ready as hour after dreary hour we make our way across the barren desert.

Then the call comes which spurs us all on, St John-Davies, accompanied by around a dozen men, had left England the evening before on a commercial jet headed for Dubai. From there the flight plan lodged for his private plane shows he'll be heading to the airport in Ezirad where one of his company helicopters is already fuelled and waiting for him. Fuck knows how Cara managed to hack into the right systems to find all that out, but thank Allah she did.

Now it is a race against time; a feeling in my gut tells me Zoe will have been kept alive until his arrival as he'll want to deal with her personally, but how quickly he'll then take his revenge is anyone's guess. She'll be lucky to measure her life in hours, let alone days. Or he might whisk her away in his helicopter as soon as it sets down. Unless we get to her before him, I'm likely to lose her forever.

A few hours later unease begins to settle over us as we take stock and consider whether we're running into an ambush. Our intelligence tells us the rebel camp is located just over the next couple of dunes. It's here I'm expecting and dreading rivers of blood to be shed. Instead, it's all too quiet as we approach; our foe seems reluctant to leave their camp. I begin to worry just how they might have fortified it and what traps we could be heading into. And as I glance around me, seeing Jon Tharpe and Ben Carter in discussion with the team from Grade A, and the sheikhs deep in talks with their senior men, I realise I'm not the only one who's worried about what lies ahead.

And then we hear the helicopter approaching, flying low, taking advantage of the sand dunes to hide from our guns. Then the engine noise fades, and in the quiet I realise we've run out of time.

CHAPTER 34
Zoe

I can't move. The dirt filling the hole leaves only my head and neck and tops of my shoulders exposed. Despite my best efforts, I've no chance of any fucking escape! Futilely I try to kick at the impacted sand, but my legs have no room to move. I can't even wiggle my fingers; the dirt is packed down too hard, and almost worse. The only thing I can do is thrash my head, and that at least loosens the blindfold so I can see what's going on, but I don't know if that makes it worse of better.

Ethan has excelled himself this time. The horrors he's inflicted on me in the past don't come close to topping this! I'm beyond scared now, petrified and unable to grasp what's going to happen. There's a pile of stones that have been gathered off to one side, stones which will soon be thrown at my head. Tears flood down my face as I anticipate the terrible pain to come, and I wish fear alone would make me pass out. The size of some of those rocks on their own would crush my skull. And the thought that they'll just keep throwing them, fracturing my head until at last, I'm dead. *Oh my God, surely this can't be happening to me!* It's a worse way to die than any I could have imagined.

Suddenly, an eerie chanting starts to one side of me and out of the corner of my eye I can see a robed figure, his head bowed down as if in prayer. Ethan watches the man almost reverently, listening to his incantation as Hargreaves kneels and whispers in my ear, "He's singing a prayer for your soul, whore. Enjoy the last moments of your miserable fucking life."

Momentarily I'm stunned into silence; then I start screaming and yelling until my voice becomes hoarse. I don't give a damn I'm interrupting a religious ceremony, refusing to go quietly. In between begging and pleading with Ethan to stop this before it goes too far, I'm shouting for help. Ethan roars at me, angry I'm not accepting my fate, but I don't shut up. I make all the noise I can. I hear Hargreaves giggling and laughing, encouraging him on. He's frothing at the mouth and totally mad. Then abruptly the chanting stops. Hamid steps forwards, selects his stone and takes aim…

"*Ma fi asm alllah yajri huna?*" At first, I can't see the man who's bellowing loudly in Arabic in a very voice, or have any idea of what he's saying. But as he moves round into my line of sight he takes the rock from Hamid's hand and throws it away I feel a faint glimmer of hope. "*Rijal Amahad la yumarisun alqanun Shiria . waqf hdha fawraan!*" He roars out, his fury is palpable. I don't understand the words, but it sounds like he's protesting.

Abdul-Muhsi steps up to him. "She is an adulteress. I have passed judgement on her. Sharia law is practised in Ezirad." He indicates Ethan, who is standing behind him and speaks in English, presumably for his benefit.

"I'm not!" I scream, tears running down my face. "I can't be an adulteress!"

The newcomer spares me a quick glance. "Whether the woman is guilty of the crime or not, and wherever we are, Amahadians don't practice Sharia law! We don't kill our women, or our men, in this way."

Abdul-Muhsi switches back to Arabic dialect, and I can't understand a word of what they are saying, but I believe, from his tone, he is furious. The two men get deep into a heated argument. Suddenly I hear a voice translating for me. Sean, who can't even stand, blood running freely down both legs, has somehow managed to crawl on his belly up alongside me, his guards having taken their eyes off of him for the moment. "Sheikh Fadi! Amahad has lost its way. It has become home to the infidels. We must stamp it out. Sharia law must be imposed to restore our country to its Muslim purity." His whispered interpretation at least lets me know what's going on.

"This is madness!" Another man comes up. Sean continues to translate.

"Tamir, I never realised…"

"Sheikhs, you are with me!" Abdul-Muhsi sounds deranged. "You have pledged your support!"

The man named Fadi shakes his head. "Neither I or my tribe can condone this."

Abdul-Muhsi starts screaming. Fadi calls two of his men forwards gesticulating towards me and the discarded shovels, and to my extremely grateful relief, they start digging me out of the hole. Ethan's men try to take their tools away but are in turn surrounded by tribesmen in traditional robes who pull them back. Other men come running from all directions, some group around Abdul-

Muhsi, but there are more surrounding the other two sheikhs. Ethan tries to intervene, but a burly man with a long scimitar holds him back.

Fadi steps forwards. Sean continues to explain what he's saying; I'd have had no idea what's going on had it not been for him. "Amahadians! We are united by our shared blood, although we come from different tribes. We are a powerful and wealthy country. The oil wells will bring great riches to the desert and will enable us to build schools and hospitals accessible to all. Amahad has signed the Universal Declaration of Human Rights, but if we follow the practices of Abdul-Muhsi, we will no longer be able to comply. Is this what you want? Your women subjugated? Flogged for wearing western clothing? Your men beheaded without a fair trial? Western nations will cease their investment in our country. Return to the old ways is not the path to the future!"

A voice calls out. "But Kadar is a weak ruler. He depends too much on the west!"

With a shake of his head, Fadi dismisses what was said, "Kadar is young, but he can grow into his role with our support, and his relations with the West smooth the way for our country. Abdul-Muhsi would return Amahad to the dark ages. Sharia Law is not our way of life."

Abdul-Muhsi swears loudly, and with a battle roar draws his sword and rushes Fadi, who's just as quick, a scimitar appearing in his hand as if by magic. The two men exchange blows, but the fight doesn't last long. The rebel Sheikh is older and carries more weight, from the start he doesn't appear to stand much chance and it's only the strength of his anger spurring him on. It ends quickly, Fadi lunges, and twists his sabre. Abdul-Muhsi hits the ground, his hand covering a wound in his stomach so deep it has to be fatal, red blood pouring out, quickly staining the sand.

Even as the drama's unfolding, some of the men have managed to loosen the sand enough to pull me back out of that ghastly hole and have untied my hands. I stutter over my heartfelt 'thankyous' unable for a moment to believe my life has been saved. Then I turn, transfixed at the scene before me, my eyes held fast by the sight of the man slowly dying as he bleeds out in front of me. I've never seen death close up before. Horrified I watch and I don't notice what's playing out on my other side until a rock hits me on the cheek, splitting it open. I stagger sideways, seeing my attacker out of the corner of my eye. I should have guessed they wouldn't let me escape this easily. It had been Hargreaves who'd thrown the rock.

"Whore!" The shout comes from behind me but I'm too slow to turn and slightly dazed from the first blow I don't think to duck, and the second rock hits me with a crack, hard on the back of my head. I fall forwards onto the hot baked sand and see Ethan walk into my line of vision. "Whore!" He repeats, dropping another stone onto my skull. I'm stunned, immobile.

The fog in my head makes the sound of voices come as though from a distance. There's shouting in Arabic, men barking in English. Struggling to open my eyes, I see the sandals of robed figures getting between myself and my tormentor. Sean crawls closer towards me, trying to protect my body with his but Ethan kicks him away.

I hear gunfire, but the shots sound like they are being fired into the air, no screams mark they've met their targets. Abruptly all sound ceases. The camp is silent. Blackness comes over me.

CHAPTER 35
Kadar

Seeing the helicopter arrive has spurred us on. As it helped them, the sand dunes also serve us well, hiding our approach and enabling us to get closer to the rebel stronghold than we had expected. For some strange reason, the rebels have sited their camp in a bizarrely indefensible position. If he hadn't already reached rock bottom in my estimation, Abdul-Muhsi would by now be dropping down even further. But what's not going to help him will aid us.

We approach with care, our senses alert on the watch for lookouts, expecting them to be posted to warn of our advance. But as we breach the last dune and get our first glimpse through binoculars of Abdul-Muhsi's base, instead of the organised opposition I was expecting, the camp seems to be in chaos. Leaving Sheikh Wahid to form a rear guard, I'm at the forefront of my men, along with Rais and Ghalib. Ben and his team are also in the vanguard ready to face an army. But what we see is a farce. Men are arguing, shouting amongst themselves, and members who, from their dress, I recognise as those from Abdul-Muhsi's tribe are being attacked, ridiculed and beaten by their fellow Amahadians. A man lies unmoving on the ground, and a feeling in my gut tells me he is dead.

Jon Tharpe has directed Seth and Ryan, two members of

the Grade A team and both ex-SAS like most of their colleagues, to come to the front. Dropping to their stomachs they begin to move forward in the military style leopard crawl, keeping low, their desert combat gear camouflaging them well, as they move fast ahead of us to assess the level of threat.

I've got a strange feeling about all this. I know that I have the trained military on my side and apart from, presumably, St. John Davies' men, Abdul-Muhsi is leading mostly unorganised rebels, albeit with a handful of soldiers who deserted from the Amahadian army. But they are heavily armed and must be well prepared to face combat; they would have known I wouldn't surrender without a fight. The desert warrior spirit is in their blood, just as it is in mine. But when Seth and Ryan rise to their feet and beckon us forwards, I start to have a glimmer of hope that there won't be much of or a battle at all. Unless every man in the rebel stronghold is blind, they have to know we're here by now, but they seem more intent fighting amongst themselves rather than making a stand against us. Not what I expected to find at all.

It's with curiosity that I step out and away from my bodyguards, at last leading my men to face our adversaries.

Two men I recognise are coming towards me, Sheikhs Fadi and Tamir. My heart starts sinking at the confirmation that they, too, had risen against me. But before I can speak, they approach and throw themselves to the ground in front of me.

"Rise." My voice is unconsciously imperious.

Sheikh Fadi is the first to speak. "I beg your forgiveness,

Excellency. Abdul-Muhsi was too persuasive. But finding he wanted to take the throne for himself and impose Sharia Law, well, we could not stomach that."

I'm suspicious, "But wasn't that obvious?"

Tamir glances at his companion as if for encouragement, before turning back to me. "He told us your ideas of a democratic government were just a trick. That you were going to sell out the desert to the west and allow westerners to exploit the oil for their own gain."

Rais has come up to my side. He scoffs, "He just wants power for himself."

"Wanted," Fadi admits coldly, "He's dead. I killed him."

Putting his head to one side, Rais asks the question going round my head, "You took long enough to realise. What opened your eyes?"

"What he was allowing to happen to that woman."

"What woman?" I ask, harshly.

"The Englishwoman…"

"Is she harmed?" I can't prevent myself from stepping forwards and grabbing hold of his robe, twisting the material in my hands. If anything has happened to her, I'll kill someone with my bare fists, and he's unlucky enough to be the closest.

As if he realised the danger he's in Fadi explains quickly, waving his hands in denial, "No, no. Well, she's injured, but we stopped it."

"Stopped what?"

He's shaking in the hold of his emir; as ruler I hold his life in my hands. "They were going to stone her."

I throw him away from me and, uncaring about my own

safety, start running towards the camp, my men trying to keep up, Rais and the Grade A team behind them. As I draw closer, I see the rebellious sheikh lying dead on the ground, and two other bodies lying prostrate close by. At first glance, neither is moving. Ben is first to reach me, and steps out in front, but I shove him out of my way, my only thought is to find Zee and see if she's still alive. I tear over fast as I can, without caring I've left the men protecting me behind.

A voice calls out, stopping me in my tracks.

"Kadar! You touched my woman! I can't allow that!"

In slow motion, I see the man I recognise from photos as Ethan St John-Davies come to the front of his team of men. Unlike the rest of the rabble, this group is organised and focused, and I suspect every one of his mercenaries will be highly trained and know precisely what they are doing. Being so desperate to get to Zee, I belatedly notice the gun in St John-Davies' hand is raised, and that it's pointing straight at me. I've exposed myself. Now all I can do try to do is face him and attempt to talk him down.

"You're dead. And the whore's next!"

As he takes the safety off his weapon with an audible click, I know I won't be able to raise my gun faster than his bullet will fly. Time seems to stop, and I even have time to call on Allah's name asking him to protect Zoe. But then, so fast it the very air seems to shimmer, one of the prone figures rises to their feet and launches towards me, the action putting the person I don't immediately recognise deliberately in the path of the bullet heading straight for my heart.

A blaze of returning fire neutralises St. John Davies for good and immediately his team of men drop their arms down by their sides, turn and walk away. Paid mercenaries no longer employed now their paymaster is dead. Moments later a helicopter rises into the air behind the camp.

CHAPTER 36
Zoe

"How are you feeling, pet?"

I bite back a sarcastic comment at the question. Why do people always ask that when you're lying in a hospital bed hooked up to a morphine pump because you're in so much pain? Suffering the indignity of a catheter, because you're unable to make the short distance between bed and bathroom? Visitors, in my opinion, come to be reassured that you can't be feeling as bad as you look, so they can go away satisfied, having put their minds at rest and believing it was worth the visit. I know it's expected of me to refrain from giving the truthful answer, which of course would be 'bloody awful', but to give him what he wants to hear instead. So I lie. "Better, thank you."

Better? Better than what? It's only now that I'm starting to feel I've got my wits about me again, able to take in and understand what has happened to me over the past couple of weeks. Ethan's parting shot with that stone was a doozy, cracking my skull. Luckily they tell me it was only a linear fracture that didn't need surgical intervention, but it was enough to cause a swelling, an epidural hematoma, which meant I spent three days in an induced coma. The bullet lodged in my shoulder had meanwhile caused significant blood loss needing an immediate transfusion as soon as

Kadar's men airlifted both Sean and me to the hospital in Palm[illegible]. Being close to the border and used to dealing with some horrific injuries suffered by the military, the desert city hospital was well equipped and practised in dealing with trauma. Had it not been, I might not be alive.

What I have absolutely no memory of doing, but what's already becoming the making of a legend, is how I apparently managed to raise myself from the grave to save Kadar's life. But the fact remains, had I not acted purely on instinct—ignoring life threatening and what should have been incapacitating injuries, and thrown myself in the path of the bullet—the Emir of Amahad would be dead.

Sean was luckier than me, being up and about a lot quicker than I, disdaining to use a wheelchair and hopping around on crutches despite one leg being in plaster from ankle to thigh as a result of the bullet having made good work of shattering the bone, and the other just having a hefty bandage covering a nasty flesh wound that had required a large number of stitches. Nevertheless, he'll not be completely mobile for quite a while, although the prognosis is good and hopefully he'll be just as competent with his high-kicking routine after a few months' recovery and physiotherapy.

When I first came round, I was just pleased to know we had both survived the ordeal. Fading into and out of consciousness for a few more days, doped up on medication, I wasn't aware of what was going on. But an overheard conversation between Kadar and an unknown man seeped into my awareness, and for the first time in days, I remembered clearly the events leading up to my final abuse at Ethan's hands.

As the overheard words sunk in, it became evident Kadar was being berated for neglecting his duties. Instead of returning to the capital to rule the country, he was choosing to stay if not by my side, at least in [illegible] and visiting the hospital daily. After the note I'd left for him, I couldn't understand why, and selfishly I knew him hanging around was not going to be good for me. So the next time he came to see me, I forced myself to be fully awake, not using my pain medication so I was completely aware and able to talk.

At first, he was pleased to find I was alert and in full command of my senses. But I stopped him before he had a chance to speak. "Ethan's dead." My voice was croaky from disuse, and my throat sore from the ventilator tube which hadn't long been removed. I forced myself to continue through the pain. "I want to go back to England, Kadar."

I watched as he blinked rapidly, my words not being what he'd wanted to hear. "But…"

"No buts, Kadar. We said all there is to say."

"You didn't say anything. You left me a note." His eyebrows arched, puzzled.

If I could have looked away from him I would have, but my weakness had immobilised me, so I was forced to watch the pained expression on his face. "I still meant what I said, Kadar. And I've made a decision, I'm sorry, but I can't finish the harem. I want to return home to England; I want to recuperate there and then rebuild my life." I swallowed, not only to make sure I could get out the next sentence but to hide the lie I needed to tell him, "I want to get out of this country; there's nothing for me in Amahad."

"You saved my life," he says gruffly. "I owe you everything."

Perhaps I would have been more emotionally engaged if I could remember putting myself in front of that bullet, but I couldn't, so it was easy to shrug off the compliment. "Kadar, you're the emir of a country where one of your sheikhs sentenced me to death. Do you think I want to stay here a minute longer than necessary?" I tried to put as much force into my weak voice as I could, willing him to believe me while the truth was all I wanted to do was to stay close to him, and by his side forever. When I left Amahad, I'd be leaving a part of me there, a large part. I'd be leaving my heart. But Kadar's neglect of his duties had already confirmed I'd be making a mess of both our lives if I didn't follow this through. Kadar's future was mapped out for him, and it didn't include me. Far better to leave, and let him get on with his life. In time, I hoped to be able to rebuild mine. It was a mistake to get too close to the emir. Staying nearby would only make it worse.

Whether he believed my reasons or not, or maybe he'd only stayed by my side through guilt, my words had the effect that I desired. Our eyes met in one long glance, and I had to use all the strength I had to force my expression to remain cold and unfeeling. After a few minutes, he gave me a sad nod, looked away and slowly stood, gathering his robes around him and left. He didn't spare one glance back as he went through the door. I've not seen or heard from him since.

He, or one of his employees, arranged a private plane equipped with all the necessary medical paraphernalia, complete with what seemed to be far too many doctors and nurses, and the very next day I was flown back to England with Sean. Once on my home soil, I was taken to, and incarcerated in, a private hospital and given treatment and accommodation that could be described as nothing other than five star. At the time, it didn't occur to me to think of who was covering the expense, but when I recovered the mental capacity to ask that question all I learned was if you saved an emir's life there wasn't much you could want for that you wouldn't receive.

"You pumping your pain meds there, pet?" Sean's amused prompt brings me back to the present showing me I'd spent too long lost in my thoughts.

My head aches something chronic, and my shoulder's throbbing, and while it's tempting, I put off hitting the morphine pump for a little while longer. "Sorry, Sean. I was just thinking about everything that happened. It's good to see you. But how are *you* doing?"

He shrugs, "Fed up with the crutches and the fact Ben's going to confine me to desk work for the next six months. But I'm getting there. Can't wait to get the fucking plaster off, though."

"When's that happening?"

"Another four weeks." He grins ruefully, "Gets me the sympathy vote, I suppose. Hey, I need to have the heroine of the hour's signature on it." Lifting his leg onto the bed, he goes through his pockets to find a pen and hands it to me.

Smiling, I sign my name with a flourish. There's not a

lot of room left to write anything at all, so it's easy to imagine he's been playing on it. "Not sure I've earned the heroine label, Sean. But it's good to see you. You didn't need to come."

"You don't have many visitors," he observes.

This is true. My mother had come over briefly but had had to return to France. She's currently going through a course of marriage counselling with husband number six. I'm hoping for her sake they can reconcile their differences; she's getting too old to start all over again. It was good to catch up with her, but things had been awkward between us. I couldn't explain to her satisfaction how Ethan had got me on his hook in the first place, and being such an independent woman she couldn't understand how it had been so difficult for me to leave, or the lack of contact I'd had with her over the past eighteen months, but she's trying. I'm hopeful we'll get to a better relationship in time.

"So, this is just a social call?" Poor Sean, he's made the effort to come to see me so I ought to give him my full attention.

He lifts his chin, "Ben wanted me to check up on you, and to let you know you've still got protection. We think everything's clear, but just in case one of Ethan's men goes rogue. Hargreaves escaped, as you know. He snuck away in the helicopter with the rest of Ethan's men just after you were shot."

"I still don't think there's any need for that. He was Ethan's employee; he wouldn't have any remaining beef with me, surely?" I frown slightly, not certain how much I should be worried.

Sean doesn't make too much of it, presumably not to worry me, "Well, we're keeping an eye on things for peace of mind. And you've got Grade A on call for as long as you want it." He pauses, "Kadar's still worried about you. He's asked me to let him know how you're doing."

"He gets the doctor's reports." He should; he's paying for my treatment. Though patient confidentiality means he doesn't know everything. I don't like to think of owing him for my treatment; I don't like to think about him at all. It only upsets me. When I close my eyes all I can see is the hurt on his face when I last saw him, but I'd had to make a clean break, if only for my sanity. In a few short weeks, he will be choosing his bride. Better to have ended it when I did. Especially in light of subsequent revelations.

"He wanted an eyewitness report," Sean gives me a gentle smile, "The doctors only report on your physical progress. He wants to know how you're *feeling*."

I go to shake my head and immediately regret it. "You didn't have to drag yourself down here." To be honest, I want to forget about everything. If I could turn the clock back two years, I would. Ethan destroyed my body, but Kadar? Well, Kadar has caused an awful lot of damage to my heart that will take a very long time, if ever, to heal.

Sean looks at me strangely, almost accusingly, "You can't distance yourself from Kadar, however much you want. Not now, can you? Don't you have something you need to tell him?"

My eyes open wide, my heart beating faster. *What does Sean know?*

As my silence indicates my refusal, his face goes dark,

disapproving, "I think Kadar has a right to know."

"To know what?" I try to get away by appearing ignorant. He can't know. No one knows except the medical staff here, and they'd be breaking their Hippocratic oaths and risk being struck off if they let anything slip without my express permission. I didn't have a clue until the doctor told me, after having been starved, beaten and severely injured, it never occurred to me it was possible. It seemed a miracle.

But his next words reveal my secret's out, "That you're pregnant."

"How the bloody hell do you know that?" Forgetting my aching head, I sit up, managing only to get as far as propping myself on my elbows. My eyes are blazing, only to see him shrugging, and not particularly apologetic.

"I read your notes. It's written there." He waves at the foot of my bed. At my look of complete horror, he continues, "Habit, I'm afraid. Part of the job to be curious."

"Fuck, Sean!" Hopefully, I'll have no other nosy visitors. It's lucky it was too early for it to be detected by the doctors in Amahad, and I'd only found out myself forty-eight hours ago. "It's very early days." I'm only just pregnant, and when they told me my only thought was how right I'd been to leave. "I'm not telling him, Sean. I can't do that to him." It was a mistake I'd made, not Kadar, and the ramifications would be enormous.

"He carries so much guilt, Zoe; he blames himself for everything you went through. For trusting Richard, for getting there too late…and now he's the father of your child."

Shaking my head, I refute any responsibility lies on Kadar, "It wasn't too late; I'm alive. And how could he know his assistant was going to betray him? He has nothing to reproach himself for. It's down to me, all of it, for allowing Ethan an opportunity to stir up trouble in Amahad. Ethan was always going to try to kill me when he caught up with me. I'm just sorry for bringing trouble to his door."

"Do you love him?" Sean's direct question shocks me. When I don't answer he continues, "That night, well, it seemed, well, pretty intense. And you risked your life to save him."

Having a conversation with Sean about my love life seems strange. He doesn't appear right for the role of a relationship counsellor, and the thought brings a small smile to my face, but then I grow serious again, "Sean, you know you're killing me here? You want the truth, Sean? I feel such a strong attraction to Kadar that I don't think I'd ever feel anything like it with anyone else. Yes, I think it's love. But you know what his future holds, Sean, just as well as I do. And his future doesn't, and can't, include me." Despite trying to forget it, Sean's reference to it forces me to remember that time when Kadar let me take control. It was then I fell hard for him, and the reason I had to put him out of my life. He is destined for another, and I would only have done more damage to my heart if I stayed with him longer. "There would be a lot of hurt all around if this comes out. I can't go back to Amahad. Have you any idea what kind of mess we'd all be in if Kadar found out about the baby?" I know the implications of carrying the emir's child; if he knew about my pregnancy he might force me to return. I've thought about nothing else is the last couple of days since the doctor had told me I was pregnant.

"It's a fucking mess." Now Sean sounds angry on my behalf. "You'll keep the child?"

My free hand which is not constricted by a sling goes protectively to my stomach, "I will not abort my baby." I leave no room for argument. My first concern had been for the safety of my baby and all the drugs they'd had to give me, but I'd been assured, especially as I was only in my first trimester, that morphine wouldn't harm the foetus. The moment I knew about it I became fiercely protective. There was no doubt in my mind I wanted this baby. The baby that had survived against all odds.

"So Kadar must know." He's equally adamant.

"No." I try to rise above the pain, to get him to understand. "Kadar will be meeting his potential brides, when is it now? In a two or three weeks?" I've lost the sense of the passing days, so I wait for him to nod in confirmation. "He will need to marry someone who'll help him unite the country. One of the tribal leaders' daughters I expect. After being caught up in the insurgency, I've seen the problem with my own eyes. He's got so much to do to make things right in Amahad. An illegitimate heir from an English mistress is not going to help his cause. He never needs to know, Sean."

"Don't you think any man has the right to know he's going to be a father?"

I try to get my thoughts straight; I need him to understand. "Any man, yes. But Kadar's not just any man is he? It would cause too many complications, not just for him, but for Amahad. And that country's fragile enough at the moment. If I'm carrying a boy, well, it would be the heir. And where would that leave his new wife?" My voice falters as I say those offensive words, the thought of Kadar marrying and coming to love another woman makes me want to curl up and die. But somehow I have to find the strength to carry on. "I can't do that to him, Sean. He doesn't need to know."

"But it's his child!"

"He doesn't need to know," I repeat, softly, but emphatically. I fast run out of energy, and lie back against the pillows once more, closing my eyes but remaining conscious of the man sitting next to me in silence, contemplating, as if he's trying to find an answer to my unanswerable situation. Yes, I agree any man has a right to know that he has fathered a child, but in these circumstances, what Kadar doesn't know, and must never find out, is the best path to making sure the knowledge cannot hurt him. And I'll love this child, as much as I'll always love its father.

After a while, the sound of the door opening and closing reaches me, and I know Sean's left me alone. Very alone.

CHAPTER 37
Kadar

Having to visit the hospital today reminds me of the last time I saw Zoe. Well, what doesn't remind me of her? Everywhere I turn, everything my eyes fall on brings back memories of the woman I've lost. Seeing Cara hold her newborn daughter in her arms made me freeze inside as it puts a vision in my head of Zee holding our baby. An impossible dream. I'd gone through the motions, admiring the child who I knew didn't look anything like as pretty as Zee's would have, slapping my brother's back and congratulating him while ribbing him that a daughter was going to keep him on his toes.

They've named her Zorah, meaning Dawn, hoping her birth signifies new beginnings. What began with my father's death has hopefully ended with the opening of a new chapter for Amahad and our family; a chance to start over. My countrymen lacked faith in my rule, but if I'm honest, I'd lacked belief in myself as ruler, thrust into the role far too early. Now I've finally thrown off the shackles of my father's regime, earning my own brand of respect from my citizens.

Taking my leave of my brother and his family, I still can't shake the memory of Zee looking so small and vulnerable in her hospital bed when I last saw her all those weeks ago. When I think what that bastard put her through I want to kill him all over again, but this time it wouldn't be a quick death by bullet. I'd seen the hole, seen the pile of stones waiting, seen the injuries inflicted by St John-Davies and his evil sidekick and the terror of what she must have gone through makes me go cold. Hargreaves escaped, of course, slipping away after his employer's death, flying away in the helicopter along with the mercenaries. Grade A is trying to track him down, and when they eventually find him, he'll be subjected to my mercy, but he can be assured I'll have none.

Zoe doesn't know it, but I remained by her side constantly for the first day she'd stayed in the hospital, even when medical intervention guaranteed there was no chance of her waking. I just needed to see her chest rise and fall as she breathed, to feel her warm hand in mine to convince myself she was still alive. But the aftermath of that fucked up situation in Ezirad got to the point where I could no longer afford myself the luxury of staying by her side. But I allowed myself those first twenty-four hours before picking up the business of state once again. And even then I stayed close by in [illegible]alm[illegible], conducting my business from the desert city, refusing to return to the capital.

When she awoke, I had to go and see her, to watch as she drifted in and out of consciousness, feeling helpless when I saw the pain she was in. And then there was the dreadful day she spoke to me, the final goodbye. When I stormed from her room at first, I ranted and raged, but as I calmed down, I realised that she had every reason to want to leave and that I had to let her go for her sake, even if that was the very last thing I personally wanted to do.

But I would never forget the woman who I'd wanted to make mine, and had done, be it was only for that one glorious night, and the memory will need to last me a lifetime. The bittersweet night that ended up causing her such pain. Fuck! If it hadn't been for my indiscretion and Abdul-Muhsi's man seeing me enter and leave her suite, St John-Davies might never have accused her of adultery, might never have put her in the horrific position she had been—something that will probably give her nightmares for the rest of her life. Though I have no doubt, he'd probably have done something equally terrible. Not that that thought gives me any better comfort.

I should have known something was wrong, should have picked up that Nijad's staff were behaving differently and realised they'd been replaced with Abdul-Muhsi's people, should have read all signs that were there for me to see had I not been so eager to get into her pants. Had I not had a one-track mind I wouldn't have missed all those fucking warnings that under different circumstances would have screamed out at me. No, Zee has too much to forgive me for; I'm not surprised she's no good memories of Amahad or myself and just wants to forget.

As I'd arranged for the medical transport to take her home to England and away out of my life, I realised she was taking a part of my heart with me, and I'm not sure that wound will ever heal. She's there in my head. Every. Fucking. Day!

I shouldn't even have time to think about her; the revolt

headed by Abdul-Muhsi has hit the leaders throughout the country hard. While a challenge to my leadership could seem fair game, the manner in the errant Sheikh had gone about it had shocked everyone to the core. If Abdul-Muhsi hadn't seized his chance when St. John-Davies had requested his assistance in kidnapping Zoe, if he'd had longer to pull together a properly disciplined armed force who knows what the outcome might have been? It could have been a blood bath.

But it was the treatment given to Zoe that had been like a bucket of cold water over everyone's heads. Uniting behind Abdul-Muhsi would have brought Sharia Law to Amahad, along with its derogation of women, disregard for human rights, and an unfair legal system where a man's word was worth fifty percent more than a woman's; a witness statement by a non-Muslim worth near nothing at all. Although the desert tribes are Muslim, the very graphic example of what could happen quite legitimately to innocent women under such an authoritarian religious regime was a stark reminder of what they were supposedly supporting. It wasn't just the mercenaries who had put aside their weapons and quietly slipped away, the tribesmen supporting the insurgency had thrown down their arms without a further fight.

Sheikhs Fadi and Tamir had quickly left, after again pledging me their support, their mood and that of their men subdued and thoughtful. Those from Abdul-Muhsi's tribe were rounded up, and escorted back to the military base in the southern desert, there to stay under guard until a new sheikh had been appointed to decide what to do with them. Surprisingly the tribe took little time making their choice, settling on a young man, one who had been educated in the West. It seemed they had learned their lesson.

Elections would go ahead in three months' time in the cities of the north to elect representatives for the new government. As agreed, the desert sheikhs, already with the authority to represent their tribes, would naturally assume their positions as members. In the meantime, I had appointed an emergency cabinet and Nijad had taken responsibility for tightening up the border controls, it being even more imperative now to keep the jihadists out. Having seen at first hand the level of indoctrination that made young men give up their lives with only the promise of reward in the afterlife to come, my fellow sheikhs and I were even more determined to keep this kind of fanaticism from invading our borders. Amahad was, and is to remain, religion tolerant and multi-cultural. I had gained agreement on that, and my changes to the judicial system had been accepted. And on top of everything else, talks were progressing well with the Sultan of Ezirad, the way smoothed by the offer of a joint exploration of the oil field running beneath our countries. In all my political life was running more smoothly I could have hoped just a month ago.

A knock on my door pulls me out of my reverie. With my permission my new assistant enters—a member of Ghalib's tribe—an intelligent young man who seems to have a promising future. But a man who will have to earn my trust as now I have very good reason to be wary.

We're still trying to trace his predecessor. Richard had fled the country after making that fateful call to remove the palace guard. Cara had worked her magic using her impressive hacking skills to remove his ill-gotten gains from his bank account, but she hadn't yet been able to help us locate him. But find him we will. I need to deal with the traitor, and my retribution will be harsh.

I nod at Ma'mun and indicate he should take a seat. I smiled when Ghalib introduced me, knowing his name meant 'trustworthy' having to wonder whether it had influenced the older sheikh's choice. I hope that he will live up to his name.

"Your Excellency, the final list of attendees."

He's here to discuss that fucking ball where suitable candidates to warm my bed will be paraded in front of me. It doesn't matter that the only woman I want is three thousand miles away; in two weeks' time, I will need to make my choice of another. As he hands me the printout, I glance down the names. Almost all are daughters of the desert sheikhs or close relations; women brought up in the Amahadian ways. Three are suggestions from neighbouring countries, a wedding to consolidate relationships with our allies. I could tell him there is one name missing, but I keep silent, however much I believe Zee is the one perfect woman for me, her heritage bars her from being part of the selection. Apart from Aazeen, daughter of the King of Alair, I don't recall meeting any of them before. And Aazeen is younger than my baby sister. Whatever alliances we need to groom, cradle snatching is something I will not consider.

I hand the list back to him; I can't summon up any excitement at the prospect of meeting my potential bride. "Send out the invitations, Ma'mun. Thank you."

"Do you want to look over the arrangements?"

I suppose I have to. "Talk me through them, though I'm confident that you have everything under control. I'm very pleased with your contribution so far."

As he puffs up his chest in importance, I recall how delighted Ma'mun was when he was told of the opportunity to work in the Palace of Amahad, and so closely with his emir. His obvious pride in his role, and the intensive search into his background that I've had Grade A conduct gives me at least some feeling of confidence that he would be unlikely to betray me.

"The ballroom and state dining room are have been opened up and aired, and cleaners will start next week. The palace chef has some suggested menus for the state dinner…?" He's trying to involve me in too much detail.

I shake my head, "I'll leave the menu to you."

He smiles. "I won't let you down. Now, music. Have you any particular preference?"

I listen, answering his questions with various polite versions of 'you deal with it', and eventually, I'm left alone. I've no interest in this ball, or the proposed outcome, at all. I've given my promise that I'll take a wife for political expediency, now that should be the end of it. Involving me in the detail is a bit like asking a condemned man to tie his own rope.

Rising to my feet I begin to pace the room, wondering for the umpteenth time if there could be any way out of this dreaded union. But again the truth is staring in my eyes, to back out now would be reneging on a promise I'd made my country. The only light on the horizon are the democratic changes I'm putting in place, so an heir of mine will not be subjected to the same debacle.

But Rome wasn't made in a day, and putting in place an elected government will happen far too slowly for it to change my situation. To keep trust in the meantime I can't be seen to abdicate any of my responsibilities, and that includes taking a stranger to my matrimonial bed.

CHAPTER 38

Zoe

Discharged from the hospital I go to the only place I can think of. To Ludlow, to Ida's. This time, the journey is different. I no longer have to hide my face at train stations or buy numerous tickets to conceal my route. The bruises on my face have faded to almost nothing, and even the nasty cut to my forehead has healed to a barely-there scar, so I attract no particular notice during my travels. A nagging, lingering headache is my only companion, but the doctors assure me even that will go in time.

I have no idea where my life will go from here. But I've one less worry at least. I've got money in my bank account now; not only my earnings from my work in Amahad but I'd received an email from Cara telling me the blood money she'd removed from Richard's bank account, the sum Ethan had paid him for betraying me, had mysteriously found its way into mine. Finding I was one and a quarter million pounds richer, I didn't feel at all guilty accepting it, logic saying I was more entitled to it than that traitor ever was. And I certainly didn't want the emir's former assistant to benefit from his ill-gotten gains. He must have known what he did could have cost me my life. It almost seems poetic justice that it's now him on the run, without the funds to ease his way.

Ida offers me a home, my old room, and a job to keep me busy once I've recovered enough to work. It's obvious, though, that my body will heal far faster than the damage done to my heart. Try as hard as I can; I just can't seem to get Kadar out of my mind. As the day draws closer for that bloody ball where he'll choose his wife, I think about him more and more, remembering the night we had, the things we did constantly playing around my head.

In a moment of weakness I googled the Emir of Amahad, and immediately wish I hadn't. The first page showed pictures of the likely contenders to be his wife, and I tortured myself by studying the bevy of beauties from which he'll make his choice, running my hand over my growing breasts and ample hips, knowing I'd never have been able to compete. An interesting aside in one of the articles informed that the sixteen-year-old daughter of the King of Alair was not going to be in the running, after agreement by both the King Asad and Kadar. That she'd ever been considered was shocking in my opinion. But whoever he ends up with, the very idea of him touching any woman the way he touched my body haunts me.

But I'm carrying his baby. The fact I have something of him with me to keep and cherish helps me to stay grounded. This baby is going to be loved and treasured more than any other ever born. It's part of him that I won't ever allow to be taken from me.

I potter around the nursery, doing light jobs where I can, trying to manage without my sling. *Oh shit! Fucking wrist!* I curse, as again the old injury causes my wrist to fail me and yet another plant pot bites the dust, smashing into smithereens on the concrete path. Hating being so useless, I bend down to pick it up, trying to scoop the soil back in. It's a permanent reminder of Ethan's cruelty. But I've decided I no longer have to live with it as I've got the money now and can look into getting it fixed. I can go private, and won't have to rely on the National Health. Although I'd prefer to avoid an operation, I don't want to risk dropping a baby. The thought makes me smile, thinking that's one good reason why I've got to look after myself now, as well as giving me the strength to get up and cope with each day. A miracle baby surviving my ill-treatment at Ethan's hands.

As I kneel, scooping the compost back into the pot, my mind planning my future, a pair of expensive looking shiny shoes come into my line of sight. I stare at them, for a second panicking before I remember Ethan is dead and buried three thousand miles away in the desert, no one having volunteered to bring the body home. I raise my eyes and follow the line of trousers up, see the tailored jacket covering a large body, and then focus on the face. *What. The. Fuck?*

Sheikh Rais had visited me in the Desert City hospital, his mission to thank me for saving the emir. Which would have been all well and good had I the slightest recollection of doing so! Coming round from the coma the last person I'd expected was to see this wild looking man of the desert looming over me, but his comforting manner, so at odds with the roughness of his voice, had quickly put me at ease. And now he was the very last man I ever expected to see on English soil.

It took me a few seconds to place him, so far out of his environment and his traditional clothes. His hair is neatly groomed and tied back in a bun, his beard trimmed and he's dressed in what looks like an Armani suit. He looks almost civilised.

He leans down, offering me his hand. I take it, using the brief time as he helps me to my feet to try to fathom out why on earth he's come to visit me.

"Sheikh Rais," he introduces himself, apparently having noticed my confusion.

I nod and smile, "It took me a moment to recognise you." Once on my feet, I acknowledge him and quickly brush the worst of the dirt off my knees. "I'm surprised to see you. What on earth are you doing here? How did you find me?"

He stares intently, taking in my appearance. Embarrassed, I'm only too aware of my well-worn jeans and a baggy top, hardly the height of fashion. I'm also muddy; carrying plant pots around will do that to you. But then I wasn't expecting a visit from a desert sheikh today. Suddenly his face breaks into a broad grin, an expression which transforms his rugged features. "You're looking good, Zoe Baker. Are you well?"

Apart from suffering morning sickness at any time of the day—a fact I'm clearly not going to share with him—I'm feeling much better now. My shoulder and wrist ache when I overdo it, but I'm mostly mended, so I answer him honestly. "All healed up. I still get the odd headache which the doctors tell me is only to be expected, but I'm getting there."

"Good," he nods again.

"Sheikh Rais, I don't know why you're here?" I'm mystified why he's turned up, "Surely it's not just to check up on my health?"

He looks around the greenhouse and apparently noticing there's an office area he waves towards it, "Can we talk in there?"

Not sure what I have to discuss with a formidable sheikh so far away from his home country, I nod and lead the way. Once we're inside, I point him to a seat and decide I should be sociable. He's made a very long journey to come to see me. I just can't imagine why. "Can I offer you a drink? Tea, coffee?"

He declines but sits down. I'm relieved when he's no longer towering over me. I'm having difficulty trying not to stare at the way he's attired. He looks entirely different, yet somehow not completely out of place in his western suit. Again he regards me with intense scrutiny, and then, as though I've passed some test, he nods slowly. I feel uneasy as I take a seat on the other side of the desk, and try to curb my impatience as I await the explanation for his visit.

"You and the emir were close. Very close."

I lift my chin; there's no point denying it. And it wasn't a question, so I don't offer any answer.

"There is a ball, next weekend. Prospective brides are going to be presented to Emir Kadar."

I stand abruptly. What does he think of me? "I'm well aware of that!" I snap at him, unable to help myself. From his previous words he must know I have feelings for Kadar, so why torture me like this? Why does he bring up the one thing that's never far enough away from my mind? I just wish the bloody thing was over so perhaps I could forget it and move on with my life. "Is that why you're here? To warn me off? Do you think I'm going to make trouble for Kadar?"

"No, no," he reassures me, his hands fluttering up as if to emphasise his denial. "I don't believe you'd ever want anything but what's best for our emir. But don't you wish something could have come of your relationship with him?"

Although it would be rude, I feel like walking out, leaving him and going back to my work. Why is he here to torment me? Why is he asking questions about the impossible? I have to force myself to be polite and be calm, though I'm close to losing my temper, "Sheikh, the emir was upfront and honest with me. There was never going to be a future for us."

"But nevertheless, Kadar started a relationship with you."

One night, we had just one night. Without thinking my hand goes to my stomach as I remember the result of our coupling. I take my hand away quickly as Rais narrows his eyes.

"You're in England for business?" I attempt to change the subject.

"You could say that," he leans forwards, "Paramount state business." He chuckles quietly and leans back again. "You see, one of the prospective brides for the emir happens to live in England. I'm here to take her back to Amahad."

I close my eyes as my head starts to throb. *Why does he keep reminding me? Why is he torturing me?* It makes sense now, of course, he's stopped off to make sure I won't cause any problems for Kadar; Rais is obviously deeply involved in the arrangements.

"Kadar has decided on a short engagement," his tone is conversational, and I don't know why he thinks I would be interested, "He seems confident that he'll settle on a bride on the night, so preparations are already underway for a state marriage."

"Won't his fiancée want something to say about that?"

"Kadar's not expecting a love match. It will be an arranged marriage for political reasons only. His bride will be expected to go along with his plans."

Another thought hits me. *Is he going to suggest I could be the woman on the side?* Someone to comfort the emir in his loveless marriage? My anger rises, and I'm not going to suppress it. I'd never put myself in that position.

As I open my mouth to blast him with my rage, Rais continues, giving me no time to vent, "Kadar needs a wife to support him, a wife who's prepared to put her life on the line for the country and the emir. A wife who'll give him the family he needs, not only to provide an heir but to also make him a better man. The woman who marries the emir will need to be an extraordinary person."

For fuck's sake! I'm going to explode if he says one more word. Doesn't he think I know that? Isn't that why I left? To clear the way for Kadar so he can find the type of marriage he needs for himself and his beloved country?

I risk a glance at him; Rais looks both grave and

oblivious to my distress. In a deeply serious tone he carries on, "There are ten desert sheikhs, Zoe. Nine of us have led our tribes for many years now; one is new to the position. But each and every one of us is unanimous in our preference of bride for the emir. Instead of each presenting our favoured women as would normally be our custom, we will present just the one we have chosen to represent us all. With such a wealth of support behind her, we expect Kadar will have no option but to agree our choice. Peace within Amahad will depend on it."

CHAPTER 39
Kadar

Why I needed new robes for tonight I've no fucking idea. It is going to be a cattle market, and it's the women who should be preening themselves, trying to make the most of their assets to attract *me*. I'm the emir of a developing country, with a personal fortune making me one of the most eligible bachelors in the world. But my advisors seem to think I, too, need to polish up and present an image to entice them—as if my money and prestige weren't enough on their own. I'm not a vain man, but I know I'm not uneasy on the eyes, so why go to this extra trouble for this fucking debacle?

When the issue of my marriage was first raised, I wasn't particularly concerned about it. In the beginning, I'd no real qualms about who would warm my bed; I could never have imagined anyone would capture my heart. But at that point a particular woman hadn't yet entered my life or taught me how to feel like a man.

And there I go again; she's all I seem to think about. It almost seems like another lifetime, so long since I last saw Zee. If I catch the scent of roses it reminds me of her, and it's as if it all happened just yesterday. *Shit! No more!* I have to put her out of my fucking head!

Looking down at myself I see my cock lying limply,

dressed to the left as normal in my new trousers. It would be laughable if the emir couldn't provide an heir because he couldn't get it up for his new wife. Perhaps that should be the test? Whichever of the women causes my fucking dick to twitch should be my selection. The trouble is, the way I feel at the moment I have doubts any of them will have much chance of success. The only time my cock rises to the occasion is when I allow myself to think of Zee, and of our one night together. Perhaps the only way I'll be able to procreate is to imagine it's her lying beneath me instead of my actual bride. And what a fucked up travesty of a marriage that would be.

Oh for fuck's sake, I need to get on and get this started. I take my freshly ironed gutra and put it over my head, checking in the mirror to make sure the crease is dead centre. I pick up my golden agal, looking at it for a moment in reflection. Then I put it over the gutra. Tonight I'm told I need to look my best, so double check that it's properly in place, my thumbs smoothing out the material around my face. Finally, I throw the sides back, one over the other, so the material falls down my back. My reflection stares back at me, freshly shaven, except for the small beard I've allowed to grow on my chin, trimmed professionally for tonight of course. I give a mirthless chuckle then enjoy my final moments of solitude. I'm ready like a lamb for the slaughter.

As I leave the royal suite of the Palace of Amahad, the personal guard waiting outside dips his head, and then falls in behind me. Feeling more like he's escorting me to my execution rather than to a banquet given in my honour, I walk unhurriedly down to the anteroom to the state banqueting suite, where guests are already assembled and waiting for me. I enter, and the crowd greets me with the proper protocol for my station.

As the assembled men and women bow low, I acknowledge their obeisance with a dip of my head. Pasting a false welcoming smile on my face, I move forwards. *Let the farce begin.*

Nijad comes to my side, Cara with him, looking weary which I put down to caring for a new-born. He throws me a sympathetic smile. My sister-in-law tosses me a look of disgust, to which I shrug ruefully, hoping nobody else in the room has caught sight of my action. Despite the fact that their successful relationship was a result of an arranged marriage, it doesn't encourage me, and I know I haven't managed to hide my misgivings from Cara in particular. She has strong suspicions about the depth of my feelings for a certain Englishwoman who's conspicuous by her absence tonight. Cara's unspoken reminder causes me to rub my temples. The evening hasn't even begun, yet a pain has started throbbing in my head.

"Jasim?" I force myself to speak.

"He's not coming." It doesn't surprise me. Jasim doesn't agree with the outmoded traditions we continue to follow in Amahad, and I understand the statement he's making with his absence. Nevertheless, however much sympathy I have for his views, it doesn't ward off my responsibility to do my duty. To fulfil what was possibly a rash promise to the sheikhs on the day of my father's funeral.

Drawing a deep breath and nodding to my youngest

brother, I take another step into the room knowing this is it. The commitment I'm making tonight will last a lifetime. I have to make an effort, wear a mask that looks like I'm enjoying myself, and to show I'm taking the situation seriously. To do any less would be a mockery for both myself and my future life partner.

With that in mind and once again blocking thoughts of Zee from my mind, I start making my way around, getting my first glimpse of the hopefuls all done up to the nines. The main meet and greet has been arranged to take place with a formal receiving line after we consume what I expect will be, a tedious dinner, so, for now, I just acknowledge those who come up to me, knowing there's no expectation for me stop and make lengthy conversation.

I have timed my entrance well, hardly having had a chance to speak to anyone before the gong sounds, and we make our way into the enormous dining room. The table set for fifty guests. Everyone stands behind their chairs, waiting for me to seat myself first. I do so quickly, not wanting the formality to hold anyone up. As the wait-staff commence setting out the first course, I take the opportunity to glance around the room. The desert sheikhs are all in attendance with, what I take to be their hopeful candidates, sitting by their sides as well as diplomats from other countries with various women sitting next to them. Names on paper now come to life but I don't even feel the slightest glimmer of interest now I see the contenders in the flesh.

Ghalib seeks my attention, his age and rank mean he's seated to my left. He engages me in the business of the proposed new government, and I welcome the diversion, which serves, for a short while, to take my mind off the purpose of tonight's gathering. As the starters are eaten and plates removed my mind comes back to the reason we're here, and my eyes flit around the table, noticing women in ball gowns in western fashion, and women in traditional robes, and one, seated far down the table with a full veil over her face.

As the servants place the main course in front of us, I find my eyes being drawn time and time again by the one woman who isn't flaunting her assets. I wonder who she is, and why she keeps her features hidden from my sight. The simple answer is probably due to her upbringing and religion, but that's strange as veils are rarely worn in Amahad, or at least, not in Al Qar'ah. There's something about her that keeps capturing my attention. Maybe it's because she's the only one who hides from me? Of course, I couldn't take such a shy, devout woman for my wife; she'd be unlikely to be able to cope with the difficult life as the wife of an emir, conducted very much in public view. But she intrigues me. She's sitting next to Rais, and I notice when her plate is taken away, she's hardly touched her food.

The meal lasts a wearisome two hours; my chef has outdone himself judging by the comments from around the room. I couldn't tell; everything I've eaten tastes like cardboard. Waiting until the last spoon is laid down on the plate, and the final coffee cup placed on its saucer, I heave a silent sigh of relief then give the signal the meal is at an end, and I rise, leading the way to the ballroom. It's time to make my choice.

Music is already playing as we enter. The principle guests along with their suggested offerings for my consideration have eaten with us, another couple of hundred guests—foreign dignitaries, my advisors and senior staff, so called friends and officials from other countries far and wide—have been invited to join us for what is being described as a celebration tonight. For myself, it's anything but.

The room is noisy as I take my place up on the dais, ready to be introduced to the women vying to become my wife. What kind of woman would give herself to a man she didn't even know, except by reputation? One attracted only by the thought of wealth and power I would expect. *Okay, you can do this, Kadar. You can do your fucking duty.*

As the first is brought in front of me, I give myself a silent lecture and try to plaster something resembling a smile on my face. I'm the emir, and this is my pre-ordained life. I give my attention to the bubbly pretty enough thing who simpers and blushes when I take her hand. There's no spark; my cock doesn't even twitch. Schooling my features, carefully hiding my thoughts as the woman moves on, I glance up ready to greet the next.

Looking down the line, it's shorter than I expected. Perhaps I won't have as much choice as I hoped. Strangely I notice some of the women who'd accompanied the desert sheikhs aren't lining up. Don't they know what to do? I'll need to ask Ma'mun, who's bound to be hovering close by, to remind them to take their places when I see him.

I open my mouth and say something polite to the second girl who's looking at me with a hopeful expression on her face. I'm civil, as I was to the first. I get into a routine, and the line passes along. My prick lies nestled in the V of my pubic bones devoid of all life. I'm hoping against hope that someone will wake him up.

The last girl is greeted and moves on. I'm full of dread. If this is the only selection, there's been no spark, nothing at all. People watch, and I can see the surprise in their eyes. I haven't even found one woman I've even wanted to talk for more than a few seconds let alone take to my bed, so the line has moved fast, the evening's entertainment completed within only a few minutes. I start to panic. This isn't right; this isn't the way it should have gone. I notice Cara, the look on her face now one of sympathy as though she understands my plight.

Suddenly there's noise to one side of me, a congregation of men. My head turns sharply, the memory of the uprising still fresh in my mind and I'm not comforted when I see that all ten of the desert sheikhs are moving towards me; an impressive and intimidating group of warriors each in the ceremonial robes of their tribes. Automatically my hand goes to the scimitar in my belt, tonight it's for decoration, but despite the rubies and diamonds which decorate it, the blade is sharp and could separate a man's head from his body just as well as any not so extravagantly adorned.

The sheikhs form a line in front of me. With the attempted coup so recent I feel a flicker of uncertainty looking at their grave faces. But then I notice Sheikh Rais following slightly behind, his hand gently resting on the back of the strangely veiled woman who'd captured my attention back in the dining room. Her head bowed so low I can't even see her eyes.

And it's Rais who steps up to address me. "Your Excellency, the most exalted Kadar, Emir of Amahad and Ruler of the Southern Desert." My head goes back in confusion as he greets me with the outmoded title, the one that was used in times past to recognise the ancient division between desert and city. But before I can pull him up on it, he continues, "It is the tradition for each of the desert sheikhs to present the woman whom they would wish to be the one to be chosen as the emir's wife. The woman to be by the side of the emir, supporting him in his role, caring for him and his country, giving her life for her ruler, her husband, and the lands over which he presides. Tonight," he pauses his solemn speech, to indicate his compatriots behind him, "Tonight we stand united."

Have they decided not to take part in the proceedings? Is this an indication that the southern desert tribes wish to split off from the cities of northern Amahad? Is this night going to end with the threat of civil war?

"We stand united," Rais continues, a twinkle comes into his eye which I'm not totally sure puts me at ease, "United in the choice of the woman we propose to become your bride. We present not ten choices to you, Your Excellency, but just one." He puts his arm around the woman, pulling her forwards. I notice she moves stiffly as if reluctant, unsure of her place here. I'd dismissed her as being an unlikely bride for the emir, but should I take her unseen just to keep the peace? If I reject their united choice there could be a rift in our country. What is it about this woman who has caused the sheikhs to band together for once? These fierce men who usually guard their independence so vigorously? Suddenly I'm curious to see what's so special about this woman to have made her the desert sheikhs' choice. Who is she, and what has she got that's led to them singling her out as the favourite of them all?

She stands before me, her head still bowed. My hand reaches out, and I place my fingers under her chin, gently raising her face until I'm looking into steely blue eyes, eyes so deep I could easily drown in them. *Eyes that I remember.* My hand drops away to brush over my face. I'm hallucinating, I must be. I think I know those eyes, know who they belong to, but they can't, can they?

Shaking, I replace my now not too steady hand, resting my palm against the side of her face, feeling reciprocal trembling as I touch her skin. With mixed feelings of dread, the expectation that I'm going to be disappointed, a sense of intense joy and with the desperate hope my eyes are not deceiving me, I start to take hold of the veil. She makes no protest as I unclip one side, and then the other. Then I brush back her hijad, setting her sleek blond hair free.

I'm speechless. Blood rushes through my body, the sound almost deafening in my ears, heading south so fast it makes me feel faint and dizzy. My cock jumps to attention, throbbing hard in the confines of my clothes.

She stares at me, the joy in her eyes fading as I can't seem to regain my ability to speak. I realise she doesn't know what I'm thinking, doesn't understand she's the most precious thing in the world to me, doesn't know that she's my life. *And she's going to be my wife.* My future. There'll be no more running from me now. *She's mine!* Together we'll heal each other. We'll take this second chance together. As I see her fear of rejection increase, worry lines deepening on her forehead, I can wait no longer. My arms go out to her, pulling her to me, holding her tight, so fast to me, I must be crushing her. She doesn't flinch, doesn't try to move away and I don't give a fuck that her tears are causing her makeup to run, quite possibly ruining my new robes.

"We need to talk." I hope she heard my words, my voice now found still isn't working too well, and I refuse to lift my head from its resting place on top of her head. But I raise my eyes, my gaze taking in the boyish grins on the ten faces in front of me. I shake my head in disbelief. A united front from the southern desert? It bodes well for the country. And my choice of bride is theirs? They are accepting an English woman to take her place by my side? Words are inadequate, so rather than struggling to find the right ones, I clear my throat and gasp out a simple, "*Shukraan.*" It seems insufficient when really I'm thanking them all from the bottom of my heart.

But they obviously understand. With nods and smiles, and a couple of rather crude suggestions that I'm glad were spoken in Amahadian rather than English for Zee's sake, the sheikhs move back, giving us space.

"Come, Zee. I need to be alone with you." Glancing round I see Nijad and Ma'mun already have my back and are clearing the way for our exit. Ma'mun's indicating a curtained doorway, his wide grin showing he had a hand to play in tonight's affairs. I should bawl him out for his deception, but instead, I'll give him a pay rise. Without wasting one second more, I pull Zee with me, behind the curtain, and through the doorway. We end up in a small room, obviously one used by the staff, but now empty except for us. A small table, cushions, a bottle of champagne and two glasses have been set out.

Suddenly as my earlier tension of the evening evaporates I start to laugh, "What if I'd preferred someone else?" I'm joking, of course, there could never be anyone else.

She's giggling, "That would have been awkward!" Her mirth fades, "Actually, Rais wanted me to be presented to you first, but I asked to go last. Just in case another caught your fancy…"

"Habiti! Stop right there. There could never be anyone else for me!" I cup both my hands around her beautiful face. "Every day apart has been torture. I've wanted you more, loved you more, every fucking day. You've never been out of my mind."

"You love me?"

How can she doubt it? I stroke her cheeks, running my fingers over her lips. "I fucking love you. And now I'll be able to show you how much until the end of my days."

She covers my hands with her own, leaning into my touch. "I love you too, Kadar." Then she looks down and away as if there's something on her mind. But whatever it is can wait.

I start to reach for the bottle. "If there was ever a time for a toast then this is it!"

Her hand touches my arm; she stops me. I'm so attuned to this woman I feel the change in the atmosphere immediately. There's a grave expression on her face, so solemn it worries me. I can't think why. If she didn't want me, she wouldn't have taken part in the charade.

"No champagne."

"No worries, habiti. If you don't want to drink, I'm sure we'll find some other way to celebrate." I waggle my eyebrows suggestively, wanting to make her giggle again. It was such a lovely sound, and well appreciated by my dick.

A tremulous smile comes and goes in recognition at my comment. She's starting to worry me now. She licks her lips and swallows as if trying to summon the courage to speak. Whatever the fuck it is she wants to tell me I'm not going to let it ruin the best day of my entire fucking life! I still can't believe she is really going to be *mine!* I give her time to gather her thoughts, to say what she needs to say. We've got time. We've got the whole of our fucking lives now. *I can't believe it!* Once she's said her piece and I've accepted her apology for a transgression she certainly hasn't committed or anything else that might be on her mind, I'll scoop her up, and we can get on with the evening's celebrations. Our own personal way.

"Kadar, I…I don't know how to say this any other way than how it is."

"Just say it, Zee." Nothing she can say can faze me at this moment.

"You have to tell me now, Kadar." She speaks with determination. "I need to know now what you feel for me. Do you really want to marry me? This, this is what this evening's been about, but am I just the best of a bad lot? Would you have chosen me, if you had the choice? I know how pressured you must feel to accept the choice of the sheikhs."

How could she doubt it for one fucking minute? Closing my eyes for a second, I realise what I need to do to convince her. Sinking to my knees I take her hand. "Zee, the moment you came into my life I was attracted to you. I fought my feelings all the way until I no longer had any fight in me. I don't know when I fell in love with you, only that I did so somewhere along the way. When I thought I'd lost you, I thought I would die along with you. When you left me I thought I could live without you, but every day was a struggle, and I was doing nothing but just existing. You took my heart with you when you went. Now you're back, finally I feel whole again. Our marriage was meant to be. It's our destiny; we cannot fight it. Zee, Zoe, habiti. Will you do me the immense honour of agreeing to be my wife?"

For a second she says nothing then slowly she folds herself down and kneels in front of me, enclosing my large hands with her small ones. It should be the other way round, but at this moment, she holds all the control as tightly as her physical grip. I find it hard to breathe, waiting for her to speak. *She's going to say yes, isn't she?*

"Kadar, oh my love, Kadar. I want to marry you more than anything I ever wanted in my life. I want to be by your side, helping and supporting you." Then she looks at me with a glint in her eyes. "Just don't make me take too many bullets for you."

I groan at the memory of her suffering for me, and the

fact if it hadn't been for her I might not be here at this moment.

"Kadar, I have something to tell you."

I nod my encouragement for her to continue. Whatever it is can't be that bad.

She's looking down, caressing the backs of my hands with her fingers. "That night in the desert palace, you told me I took a piece of your heart with me. Well, I took something else as well." She swallows, and looks up, just as I start to wonder whether she's admitting she's stolen something from me, and then I realise my stupidity as it's written all over her face. She's not admitting to taking one of my possessions, or nothing that is yet in existence. It hits me like a physical blow, the reason why she refused the champagne and I reel.

"You lied to me. You weren't protected." The look on her face tells me I'm right.

"I didn't want to worry you, Kadar. I knew then the issues it could have caused."

I rise to my feet, pulling her with me then release her so she's standing in front of me. She's looking down like a naughty child. "You're pregnant!" I straighten to my full height, my arms folding across my chest, my feet apart. "You're fucking pregnant, and you didn't think to tell me?" She looks worried; then it suddenly hits me. An explanation for what's happened this evening. "Rais knows, doesn't he? That's why the sheikhs…" Fuck what a mess, she isn't their choice, they were forced to accept her as she carries my heir. What's this going to mean for the country? None of us had a choice.

I'm confused when she sadly shakes her head, "No. Rais nor anyone else in Amahad knows. No one at all, except for Sean and Ida."

My relief is immense as I hear I'm not the only one in the dark, and that if the sheikhs didn't know, she really *was* the one they wanted for their future emira. But was she still mine? I'm trying hard to fucking understand this, and bite down the urge to rant in fury. "When did you find out? Did you know before you left Amahad?"

It's hard to make out her answer, her tears making her voice husky, "No, it wasn't until afterwards, when I was in the hospital in England."

"But you told me you were protected…"

"I didn't know," she wails, "My periods had been so irregular I didn't know if it was a safe time or not. Then, even if I had been, Ethan had hit me so hard… with everything else that happened, I thought it wouldn't have been possible; a baby couldn't possibly have survived. It was a shock to me, Kadar."

Devastating thoughts hammer into me, the idea that bastard Ethan could have caused her to lose my baby before anyone even knew of its existence. But why hadn't she told me, all those weeks ago when she first knew? "Were you going to keep the child? Were you thinking of an abortion?"

"Never!" The vehemence of her response convinces me, and I don't need her further explanation, but she continues anyway. "Kadar, that last time Ethan raped me, he didn't use a condom. I wasn't on the pill, I've never been able to take it, it makes me ill. The very first thing I did the next day after the rape was to make sure I wasn't going to get pregnant." She pauses to wipe tears from her eyes, "It was the complete opposite with you. I would never have planned it, never wanted to bring a child into the world without a partner by my side, but I knew if that were to be the outcome, I wouldn't, *couldn't*, do anything to prevent it. I was so sure it was impossible; it seemed a miracle when they told me. I never thought for one minute of having a termination. As soon as I knew, I started to love the baby, and I knew I was going to keep it. To keep part of *you*. And if that makes me selfish, I'm sorry."

As I stand there trying to understand why she's kept this from me, and why I wasn't the first person to know, it's at that point the most chilling thought hits me. "Were you ever going to tell me?" I growl, "If Rais and the sheikhs hadn't have chosen you for my wife. Would you ever have admitted you were carrying my child?"

Sinking to her knees once again, she sobs into her hands. "Noooo." Her admission comes out as a wail.

Fuck! Fuck! Fuck! *FUCK!*

CHAPTER 40
Kadar

No. That one word echoes around my head as I turn away, walking to the far wall and thrusting my fist into it, hard. The ancient brick doesn't give at all, but the pain in my hand helps me focus. I stand, my head bowed, my hands steepled below my chin. I'm unable to even look at her. The woman who would have hidden something so precious to me. The woman who lied to me and who would have kept that crucial secret from me for the rest of my life. If it hadn't been for Rais bringing her back, I'd never known I had a child, possibly a son, *my heir*, living and breathing in another country. A royal child, one who should have been brought up on Amahadian soil. Could a greater act of treason ever be committed? And if she'd told me, I could have dispensed with that mockery of a cattle parade; I could have just married her instead without tonight's circus. Could have been saved the heartache of the last few weeks and just had the woman I loved as my wife. *Couldn't I?*

As she stays weeping noisily on the floor, I'm unable to turn and go to her or offer her any comfort. My knuckles throb having come off worse than the wall, and idly I smooth my other hand over them, hoping to ease the physical pain which is so much easier to alleviate than the damage done to my heart. *I trusted her.* Out of everyone I knew I thought she was someone I could rely on. How could I forgive such a betrayal? Her admission she was going to keep something of such great consequence from me?

Thoughts and memories rush round my head, tumbling through my brain. Tonight has made me feel too many emotions, far too many for a man who doesn't do emotion at all, who was taught from the moment of my birth to think and not to feel. From my depression when I accepted tonight's inevitable outcome, my elation when I found Zee was chosen for me, the choice I would have made myself. The euphoria that swept through me when I made my impassioned proposal, the joy at her acceptance then, the horrifying realisation of the implications of her devastating revelation. An intolerable number of emotions for a man not accustomed to dealing with sentiment at all.

And haven't I always known that's what causes problems? A leader of a country should never be swayed by his heart. Now is not the time to be bound or driven by passion. Now is the time for logic instead. Emotion must be pushed aside.

Ignoring the sobs of the woman kneeling on the floor, I force myself to do what I do best, to think, to analyse, to consider problems and options from all angles. To bring into play the traits of an emir as I'd been taught. Not to rush headlong into a knee-jerk action without digging beneath the surface, as to react without looking at issues from all sides is the way to start wars.

Bringing my hands down by my side, I uncurl them,

willing myself to relax, and roll my head on my shoulders. *I should never have put her in that position in the first place,* I reflect, as I remember the night I forgot to use a condom. And why was that? It had never happened before. I'd always abided by my teaching that the royal seed was precious and must not be wasted. Sure, she'd been in charge that night, but it was still down to me to be responsible. But something about her had made me lose my mind. Fate? Or instinct? Had I, even then, subconsciously wanted her to be mine, and deep down had hoped that by impregnating her with my heir I'd be able to keep her by my side? When she lied to me, told me she was protected, hadn't that been a kernel of disappointment that I'd felt?

Why had she lied to me? Why had she hidden her pregnancy from me? Now I risk a glance towards her, still sobbing as though her heart's been broken. Fuck knows what she's expecting me to do now; I don't rightly know myself.

As I stare at the woman I love, the woman just moments ago I was so elated to know would be my wife, the ideal woman to support the emir. The woman who risked everything to save me. She shielded me then, didn't she? Even when I failed to keep danger away from her.

And then it hits me like a sledgehammer. She was protecting me. That night, she lied to save me worry. And then she'd continued to safeguard both me and Amahad, by concealing her pregnancy, leaving me free so I could follow the path that had been laid out for me. And there could only be one reason why she'd done that. She did it out of love. She hadn't aborted my child but was prepared to raise it alone, unsupported, taking on all the problems that went along with that, for just one reason. Because she loved me.

Because what would have been the alternative had she told me? All hell would have broken loose, the ramifications would have been so great, would have caused such complications I'm not sure I'd have been able to keep my throne and the country could well have fallen into civil war. She lied and kept a secret. But out of love. And here am I, a fucking bastard making her cry.

As I realise the enormity of the decision she made and the reasons why she had done so, I can hold back no longer. With a roar I spin around, go to her and pull her to her feet and into my arms in one swift move. "Zee, I'm not worthy of you!" I tell her, fervently, taking her lips against mine, moving my mouth over hers, using little nips with my teeth to make her open for me. Taking advantage of her surprised gasp, I thrust my tongue inside, pushing into her mouth in the way my steel hard cock wants inside her tonight. When we're both out of breath, I pull away. "You are mine, Zee. Mine. And there is nothing, *fucking nothing* that will ever keep us apart again."

Breathing hard, she looks into my face and straight into my eyes. Her brow furrows as though she can't quite comprehend what I'm saying, and it's confirmed as she says quietly, "I thought you'd hate me; I didn't believe that you would be able to forgive me."

I throw my head back, my eyes automatically closing as I draw in a deep breath and let it out with a sigh. Looking back down at her I tell her, "I was angry, Zee. At first, I could see nothing through my rage. But what had you to gain by keeping the baby secret from me? Then I understood. You thought by telling me I would lose everything. You amaze me that you could be so strong, so determined and have my best interests at heart and those of my country." Smoothing my hand over her beautiful face, I continue, "I understand loyalty, Zee. But I might need a little help dealing with how much I fucking love you. I'm out of my depth here. With all of my fucking undeserving heart, I fucking love you."

The minx considers me for a moment, and then gives a self-conscious smile and in a whisper dares to say, "I think I like the sound of the fucking part."

I snort in surprise. "Zee, I'll be as gentle as I can…"

She puts her hand to my lips, "Kadar, I've had a long time, too long, to think about this. That night, when you gave me control, it was what I needed then, but I didn't know what to do, how to please you, how to take my own pleasure. It's not how I've been thinking of you in my fantasies, and I want you now to bring those to life. I want you to take control; I want you to be my Dominant. You'll never hurt me; I want to try *everything* with you. Just like you said, 'all the things you want to do to me'."

I'm taken aback by her frankness and honesty. "Are you sure?"

A slow, but deliberate nod, "When Ethan died, it unlocked something inside me. A realisation that I had to start afresh, that men like him are very few in the world, and you, Kadar, definitely don't number among them. I love you, and I trust you. Now, will you take me to bed?"

Her eyes sparkle, and like her, I want to stop the talking and to get to the action part, but first, there's something I need to do. "Don't doubt it, we'll be getting to that soon, but now we have to re-join the party. I need to claim you officially as my future bride."

The smile fades. "You are certain you want to marry me?"

"No backing out now. You said yes."

After a quick scrutiny as though she's assuring herself of my sincerity, she straightens her clothes and tries to clean up her face with a tissue. I take it from her, dampen it with my saliva and gently wipe away the dried tracks of her tears, and the blackness where her mascara has run. Her makeup might not be as perfect as it had been, but the woman herself is perfection to me. I take her hand and lead her back into the ball. With a simple hand signal, I gesture for the music to stop. The sudden silence has everyone looking towards the small stage. I pull her up beside me.

"Ladies, Gentleman, Sheikhs, Sheikhas. May I present to you my chosen bride, Zoe Baker."

Our prior exchange with the desert sheikhs had not been seen by the majority of those present so a surprised buzz of conversation started around the room. Rais steps up to my side, "Take your fiancée and finish what you started, Kadar." He gives a pointed look to Zee's clearly ravished lips, "My brother sheikhs and I will make sure everyone comprehends the wisdom of your choice."

As grateful as I am, I have to frown at him and elicit a

promise, "No bloodshed, Rais."

"You spoil all my fun!" he retorts with a snort.

At his feigned look of disappointment, I pull him into me with one arm, my free hand slapping his back. No further words are necessary to show how profoundly thankful I am to him, knowing he had to have been behind getting all the other sheikhs on side. Then I waste no time taking him up on his suggestion. Zee and I have a lot of catching up to do and damn it if my woman wants a good fucking that is what she is going to get.

As quickly as we can make it through the vast palace, we hurry together until at last we arrive at the royal suite. I can't quite believe it; she's here in my fucking rooms. In my fucking bedroom. Protocol be damned, she's staying her until the wedding and forever after, never leaving my side again. I can't let her go.

I turn her to face me. "Zee, I don't know how gentle I can be tonight," I warn her again as I place her hand on my cock, hard and throbbing with the urgency to get inside her. "I don't want to frighten you."

Her beautiful face turns up to me. "I trust you, Kadar."

"Do you? Do you trust me to know what you need? Do you trust me as your Dominant? Because that's what I'm going to be for you."

There's only a slight flicker of concern in her eyes, and then it's replaced by conviction, "You will never hurt me, Kadar. I know that. You would never take advantage of me."

"I need control." She has to understand what I'm asking.

"You've got it." Her soft words, spoken with confidence, nearly undo me. She's giving me herself, completely.

Pulling her close to me I take her mouth in a punishing kiss, so much emotion flowing through me, words are insufficient to express the depth of my feeling for her. When I release her, I touch my finger to her chin and turn her face up. "As you're pregnant…" I stutter as the implication of what I've just said hits me with a force that almost brings me to my knees. "Fuck, Zee. You're carrying my child inside you." I can feel my eyes glistening with tears.

She gives me a wicked grin, and her head moves sideways left to right, then back again slowly. "It's perfectly safe for the baby, Kadar. You're not getting out of it that way!"

She thinks I'm backing out? Nothing will stop me being inside of her tonight, even if the desert sheikhs wage full-scale war with the cities. "There's no escape now, Zee. But I will have to hold back on some things." I decide to push her, "No spanking, whips, canes or flogging." I wait for the signs of panic remembering what she'd been put through in her past, but instead I see a flash of disappointment. Deciding to lay down some ground rules I tell her, "Whatever we do will be consensual, Zee. You know that, don't you? We'll talk about your limits, things you want to try, and things you absolutely don't want to do. We may be restricted for the next few months, but I warn you, habiti, once the baby is born the gloves come off." Her eyes flash with excitement. "I want you to have a safeword—when you say it, I'll stop."

"Ethan."

"What the fuck?" I bark a laugh of disbelief and my eyebrows lift as she says the name I thought she'd never want to voice again. I wouldn't like it if she ever said that, my cock would deflate in seconds as she'd be comparing me to that monster. I can understand why she suggested it, but I'm not having it.

She sees I not enamoured by the idea. "I'll never have to use it."

"Why don't you just say 'red'?"

A little nod, her precious smile, and she agrees.

I look around the room, my mind racing as I consider the possibilities while knowing I have to take things slow. A chuckle escapes as I plan the scene in my head, causing her to regard me suspiciously. "I'd like to tie you up." I raise my eyebrows quizzically, wondering if it's too early to ask her for this.

After a moment processing my request, she gives her agreement by dipping her head. I continue looking at her, and she remembers I need to hear the words. "Yes. I think I'd be okay with that."

Putting my forefinger to my chin, I study her. Yes, she's ready.

"Undress for me, Zee."

As I wait for her to comply, the way her mouth turns up at the corners I know she remembers the time when she asked me to strip for her. I wait for the flicker of concern as she remembers how St. John Davies had used her nakedness as a form of humiliation, but that flash of memory doesn't come. Instead, the shudder she gives and the flush that covers her body shows me how aroused she is already. But I want to check. "Are you wet for me, Zee?"

Her cheeks grow even redder, and she answers with a nod.

"I need words, habiti. You need to speak to me so I know what you're feeling."

"Yes, I'm wet. For you, Kadar. Only ever for you. All the time I was away from you, I thought only of you. I want you so much, Kadar."

Fuck, how she unmans me. My cock feels ready to burst, my balls already drawing up in anticipation. It takes every amount of discipline I possess to will that over-eager part of me to be patient. Seeing her standing naked in front of me when I never expected even to see her again, causes my breath to catch in my throat. She's so beautiful. And she's *mine.*

"Lie on the bed. On your back." My voice is deep and low.

She follows my command with only a second's hesitation, but without argument or discussion. It will take time to train her in the ways I like to see submission, but fuck, we've got a whole lifetime to explore. Once more I'm overwhelmed by the notion. As she turns away from me, the just healed scar on her shoulder where she took a bullet for me comes into sight, and it hits me all over again. She would have sacrificed her life for mine. There could never be anything more humbling. Then I see those silver scars where she'd been whipped so cruelly. They make me even more determined she'll only know pleasure for the rest of her life.

I go to my wardrobe and take out two scarves. Moving across to the bed, I take one leg and tie a scarf around one ankle. I tie the second scarf to the other. She holds her legs closed, hiding from me, but I grin, thinking she'll be unable to conceal anything in a moment. Gently I bend her left leg at the knee until the sole of her foot is flat on the bed. Taking her hand, I encircle her damaged left wrist with my fingers; it reminds me she needs to have this fixed. "Does it hurt?" I want to make sure I'm not going to cause her pain.

"Not much. Not anymore."

Gently stroking it, I tell her. "We'll get it sorted, Zee. Erase every trace of your pain and memories." Then I continue, tying her wrist to the other end of the scarf so it's almost touching her ankle. I take a moment to read the expression on her face, knowing this is all new to her. I see a little anxiety, so I lean over and kiss her. When I feel her relax, I do the same to the right side, checking to make sure the bindings aren't too tight. She's now completely open to me. For a moment I just stare at her beautiful face. Then I check in. "Are you doing okay?"

"Yes."

"Are you at green or yellow? Do you need me to slow down or talk about what we're doing?"

"Green! Frigging green!" Her husky voice with a touch of laughter in it gives me the answer I want to hear, and the flash in her eyes looks suspiciously like a sign of impatience.

I grin. Lowering my eyes and focusing in on that part of her I've wanted to see for so long. Her pubic hair is neat and trimmed, but I'd like to see it bare, maybe one day I'll shave it myself but not tonight. There's no hurry. Her clit is still hiding beneath its protective hood, but I know it will soon be coming out to play. Her labia are a beautiful pink colour, framing her opening like the petals of a flower. As I continue to stare I see her wriggle, either in discomfort or embarrassment. Deciding it is more likely the latter, I proceed to take her mind off the vulnerable position I've placed her in.

Unable to resist any longer I put my mouth to her clit and suck lightly, then I move back and blow a warm breath over the top. She twists and comes up off of the bed. *Yes, that's it.* Anticipation has increased her excitement. I lick from clit to slit, delving my tongue into her tight pussy, like a cat lapping up cream. Her salty, musky taste taunts my tongue and sends a wave of desire right down to my balls. As I work her with my mouth, my fingers caress her clit. And there it is, coming out of its hood, glistening with her moisture. She moans, and twists again, thrusting her hips up trying to encourage me to apply more pressure, but she's going to have to wait. This is my show. I place my free hand on her stomach and hold her in place.

"Kadar, please," her breathless voice begs me.

"Don't come until I tell you to," I tell her sternly and then go back to working my tongue into her slit, lapping as more and more moisture comes from her. My fingers work her clit, and I feel her tense, her muscles growing taut, and then I pull away. She's panting, her head moving side to side, and I feel her stomach muscles clenching beneath my hand.

"Kadar…" She begs me again, but I'm ruthless. The longer she holds off, the better it will be for her.

I massage some of her wetness down to that forbidden place; gently I rim her arsehole with it. I feel her tense.

"Has anyone ever taken you here?"

"No!" I hear the mortification in her voice.

I chuckle, "Not yet, but soon. This will be mine. All of you will be mine." She squirms, as I continue to rub gently around her puckered hole, pushing my finger gently inside. But she's not trying to get away. *Fuck me; she's pushing back into my hand!* "I think you're going to like that, habiti. But not tonight." Though her body's reaction sparks an idea.

I switch my attention back to her pussy, curling up my fingers inside her, trying to find that special bunch of nerves. As I locate the right spot, her body goes rigid, so I press down on her clit. "Come for me."

As if she was only waiting for my authoritative command she explodes with a loud scream, her pussy clenching around my fingers. "I've got you," I tell her, as her muscles contract and release time and time again. "Let it go; I'm with you." I keep a light pressure on her clit, bringing her back down. Just before she relaxes I press firmly again, my fingers on the inside, my thumb just on that right spot outside. Another strong orgasm hits her and again continues for some time.

"Kadar!" She screams as if she can take no more.

This time, I have mercy on her, and let her come down completely, and move up her body, taking her mouth with mine, letting her taste herself on me. Momentarily she seems surprised at the saltiness on my lips, but with a groan, she toys her tongue against mine as though the taste of her essence is turning her on all over again.

"My turn," I tell her. I stand up and remove my clothes, her hungry eyes watching my every move. Seeing her staring greedily at my cock I slowly rub myself from root to head a couple of times. She seems to enjoy watching me pleasure myself. Grinning at her, I climb onto the bed, placing my knees either side of her face and moving the head of my cock over her lips. Her tongue comes out, licking the drop of pre-cum off my slit. Now it's me unable to suppress a groan. Again my balls tighten, and I'm not sure how long I'll be able to hold off my release. I decide to tease her. "Never say I don't take care of the needs of my pregnant woman."

Her eyes open, her pupils are dilated with the pleasure she's received, but her expression is puzzled. "What?"

"Extra protein." I laugh. As she opens with an O of surprise, I take advantage and push in through her lips.

Her mouth is everything I remembered, the thoughts which necessitated me pleasuring myself in many long, lonely showers. But tonight it is the real thing! Taking a light grasp of her hair, I tilt her head back so I can get further inside. She stills as if I'm forcing her, and I wonder if it's too much, but then her tongue slides around my cock, and she sucks me in. I pull out, wanting to make sure, but the smile on her lips shows me that she's doing fine. Gently I start to thrust in and out, fucking her face. She responds enthusiastically and before very long I feel the blood flooding into my prick making it expand and the tell-tale tingling running down my spine. She moans around me, and for a second I'm undecided whether I should pull out, but she's working me hard, not struggling to get away.

"I'm going to come," I warn her, but for an answer she swallows, her throat muscles massaging my cock. I can't hold back; my balls contract and my cum rises so fast pulling out is no longer an option. With a roar, I explode deep in her throat, and she drinks me down, every drop, and then continues to lick my deflating cock clean. I lift myself up. She's grinning.

"Not too much?" I know I got carried away and need to make sure she's alright.

Her grin widens, "Well, there was a lot to swallow…"

"Fuck, woman! I was asking you if I pushed you too far." I'm laughing too. Her cheeky expression makes me start to harden again. I want to get inside her before her arms and legs get too sore from being bound.

Her earlier reaction has given me an idea. "Wait here."

"Well, I'm not exactly able to go anywhere."

"Respect, woman!" I growl in my deepest Dom voice. Sex has always been serious before, but I like the fun she brings into it. I take a moment to drink in her beautiful features, to remind myself again that this woman is mine. And I'm hers. I could never want another woman after her.

Remembering my objective, I leave the bed and return to my wardrobe, this time opening a drawer at the bottom which contains a bag I've not used for a very long time. I fumble through the toys, all new in sealed packs and eventually find what I'm looking for. Grabbing a tube of lube, I hide both items in my hand and return to the bed.

"Ready to feel me inside you?"

Looking at her I can see her getting wetter at my words, her pussy glistening in the light. Seeing the plainly visible evidence, for once I let her get away with a nod.

I apply a line of lube down her crack. She tenses. "Relax."

"I don't…"

"Remember your safeword."

As I remind her, she has an out some of the tension eases out of her muscles. I massage the lube into her hole, pushing it inside with my fingers, making sure it's properly coated. I then remove the item I'd selected from its protective wrapping. It's small and slim, and shouldn't cause her uninitiated arse any problem. After applying more lube, I gently push it in. Her muscles tighten against me.

"Push back."

"What is it?"

"Just relax. And do what I say."

I continue pushing, watching her carefully as she scrunches up her face I know she's feeling the slight burn, but it is very slim. But effective. Once it's firmly seated, she breathes out a deep breath. I'm so proud I've been able to push her this far; so proud of my woman.

My cock's recovered now, and then some. It's pulsating with almost painful need to be inside her. My patience is running out. I press the button on the remote.

"Oh!"

She exclaims loudly at the vibrations inside her arse, her

face reddening, her mouth opening as she starts to process the alien sensations. Giving her no time to adjust I thrust the head of my prick into her wet and ready pussy. Her muscles start to suck me in. I can feel the vibrations coming from her rear channel and even though I've already had one release I know I won't be able to last long. She's tight as fuck, but I push gently, gaining a little ground each time I thrust until I'm all the way in.

"Fuck me, Kadar!"

I'm not going to reproach her for telling me what to do; she'll learn the discipline I expect in time. But tonight her needs match mine, and there is nothing I want to do more. I thrust harder and harder, then start hammering inside her. She starts moaning as her orgasm begins. I'm so close that when her muscles spasm she takes me over, my shout combining with her screams of ecstasy, my cock emptying my all inside her, wave after fucking wave of sheer delirious pleasure.

Somehow I remember to switch off the remote control, and then take a moment to come back down to earth. I don't think I've ever come so hard in my life. Pulling out of her I'm delighted to see her laying back looking so satiated, and more than that, at peace. I look to her comfort, removing the bullet from her arse and quickly untying her, rubbing her arms and legs to prevent any cramping. She slumps back exhausted on the pillows, a small smile on her face showing her contentment. My love, my future wife, the mother of my child. I feel a warm glow inside of me, and allow myself a moment to drink in the glorious sight. Can there be a luckier man in all the fucking world? At last, I remember I need to see to the rest of her needs. Going to the bathroom, I get a washcloth and return, cleaning her up. When she seems oblivious to my actions, I realise that I've put her into subspace. The Dom in me beams with pride.

Disposing of the cloth, I scoot up the bed and take her in my arms, just so very grateful for everything that's brought her back to me. The death of that monster has freed her, has given her the potential to blossom again, and I'm determined she'll do so in my arms. I vow here and now nothing will ever hurt her again.

She's fast asleep now, my arms tighten around her, holding her so close, knowing there's nothing that could make me let her go. Zee is the perfect woman for me. Her responses tonight overwhelmed me and open up infinite possibilities for things for us to explore. There's a new spark within her that wasn't there before, and I will do everything I can to nurture it and see it grow into a fire. No one will ever again get close enough to douse that flame.

CHAPTER 41
Zoe

Sometime later I wake to find I'm half lying across Kadar and half against the beautifully embroidered cushions at the head of the bed. We're both still naked, but I feel no embarrassment at all. The chill of the air conditioning disturbed my rest, so I inch closer to my man to share the warmth of his body. *My man.* I'm so happy I'm sure I must be dreaming, unable to believe this is really happening to me. *I'm going to be Kadar's wife.* The sheer utter glee of the realisation makes it impossible for me to be still. I wriggle, and my slight movement disturbs him. "Sorry."

"Why?"

"I woke you."

He kisses my head. "No, habiti. I wasn't asleep. I was thinking."

"What about?"

"Us, my family. *My* family." His hand strokes my still flat belly. His obvious delight about my pregnancy gives me a warm feeling inside.

"What about your family?"

He's quiet for a moment. "About my father. And his wrath if he had known I was going to marry an Englishwoman, particularly one without blue blood running through her veins."

"I…"

"Shush." His fingers cover my mouth. "I'm not my father. And I'm not going to live his life or even try to. I've been too set on following the path he set out for me, tearing myself up when I couldn't do the things he did. I've got to make my own way. And do things as I wish to. Not as he would have done. You, and Rais, and the rest of the desert sheikhs have shown me that. If they can move forwards, there's hope for us all."

"Deep thoughts," I smile.

"Very," he laughs, "And I was also thinking it's about time Jasim surrendered and joined his brothers in marital bliss."

"We're not married yet!"

"We soon will be."

He hugs me then lets me go. Then after getting out of bed, he comes around to my side of the bed and lifts me in his strong arms. After he sets me on my feet, he turns down the covers on the bed, revealing the silk sheets underneath. "Get in; it's been a long day."

I do as he says, and he places the covers over me before going to his side and sliding in. As he does so, I can't help but think how my life has changed. I wish to God I'd never met Ethan, but meeting him led me here. I wouldn't want to go through all the pain and fear again, but eventually, it was worth it, my reward is this fantastic man.

Then I frown, as niggling doubts hit me, "Kadar, I want to finish the harem."

"Hmm?" he sounds like he's dozing off, "No worries."

He doesn't mind me working. Good.

"And I want to wear what I want when I want. I want to have friends, and, I'd like my mother to visit."

"Of course!" he sounds bemused that I'd even ask.

"Just wanted to make sure," I snuggle into his side. Ethan and Kadar. They couldn't be more different; I can't understand how I ever could have thought they were similar. There's no comparison.

As his body relaxes and he starts to drift off, a thought hits me. "Cara, Cara will be my sister-in-law!" I say with delight.

"Allah help us! Yes, she will. Ni and I will have no chance once you two get together." His voice is sleepy, but I hear the smile in it, "And you'll have another, my young sister, Aiza if she can pull herself away from Switzerland. And two brothers-in-law. You didn't meet Jasim when he was here, did you? You've got that debatable pleasure to come."

I giggle, for all that he said, I can tell he loves all his family dearly. And now, by some miracle of fate, that includes me.

"Welcome to the Kassis family, Emira Zoe." Leaning over, he kisses me. "Now go to sleep, habiti."

Emira? It hadn't dawned on me I'd have a title. Me, of such insignificant birth. It takes a moment for it to sink in.

After the exhausting day, my eyes feel heavy, but before I let them close, I've one last question for my future husband, "Kadar, what does habiti mean?" I've often wondered.

Sighing, he sits up and gazes down at me, his hand reverently caressing my face. "It means 'my love', Zee. You are my love, my only love." His fingers still and his dark eyes start to glisten as he tells me, in a deep voice almost as though he's making a vow, *"Sawf 'ahabbuk hatta alnnujum tasqut mmin alssama' w tasjud lak hatta nihayat alkawn."* Then he offers the translation, "I will love you until the stars fall from the skies and worship you until the universe ends." Another kiss, then just before I succumb to sleep he tells me as if I needed further assurance, "I'll love you forever."

THE BLOOD BROTHERS SERIES

Each book in the series can be read as a complete standalone, but characters from one book may well appear in another, and you may enjoy reading the whole series to get a better understanding into their backgrounds.

- *Stolen Lives* (Blood Brothers #1)

- *Close Protection* (Blood Brothers #2)

- *Second Chances* (Blood Brothers #3)

- *Turning Wheels* (Blood Brothers #3.5 / Satan's Devils MC) – coming soon

- *Identity Crisis* (Blood Brothers # 4) – coming soon

Sign up for my newsletter to hear about new releases in the series: http://eepurl.com/b1PXO5

TURNING WHEELS

Sophie

All I did was try to help my best friend Zoe escape from Ethan St John-Davies, her abusive boyfriend, but neither of us realised the power he has until a hit and run accident punishes me for the aid I'd given her, leaving me in a wheelchair. I don't want to live anymore, what's the point? I can't do the things I used to, and no man will want me now.

Then, almost at my lowest point of despair, I find my nightmare is only beginning when Zoe escapes again. Now Ethan wants me as leverage to get her back.

But even as she ran, Zoe made arrangements to help me, and that's how I end up under the protection of the Satan's

Devils, an outlaw motorcycle club in Arizona. The woman I was would have been in her element among a group of handsome, rugged bikers; the disabled woman I am now feels scared and vulnerable, and soon I find this isn't the safest place to hide.

But there's a contract out on me, and useless as I am, there's nowhere else for me to go.

But there's one reason for me to stay, the VP of the Satan's Devils who teaches me to feel like a whole woman again.

Wraith

She doesn't fit into our world. Fuck, even if she wasn't in that damn wheelchair she'd be out of her element. Our American ways are foreign to her, let alone those of bikers. But as soon as I saw her something attracted me to her, even though our Prez made it clear we were protecting her, and she wasn't fresh meat for the boys.

I knew from the start I wanted her, but also that I would have to be patient. She thinks she's undesirable, is scared of taking a man to her bed as though her disability defines who she is. I'm going to need to teach her she's wrong.

Sophie is broken in more ways than one, but as she regains her independence, gradually the woman she was starts to emerge and it's then I take my chance.

But that's the point when it all goes to shit. She's under our protection, but we fail to protect her from one of our own. And when a contract to abduct her is taken on by a rival biker club and one of our prospects is killed, it becomes more than just about her, we have to protect our club.

Blood Brothers #3.5: Turning Wheels

Brothers protecting their own

IDENTITY CRISIS

Sean

When a 'package' is left for me at Grade A's reception, I hardly expect it to be a baby, nor to discover after DNA testing that she is mine. Fuck, me with a daughter? And I've no idea who the mother is – I've always been so careful! But the wording of the note left with the baby suggests whoever she is she's in trouble, so now I've got to discover her identity and then find and help her. All I know is that I was working in Amahad when the baby must have been conceived, so I return to that Arab country to call on the help of my old friends, members of the Kassis royal family.

Ben teams me up with Vanessa – I've no idea why. She hates me. It will be her first time investigating in the field and I know she isn't prepared to be thrown into something like this. Together we start our search not realising it will end up with lives at stake, including our own.

I've always fancied Sean, well, who wouldn't? But when I discover he's fathered a child and has no idea who the mother is it brings home to me his manwhoring ways. He's never going to change, is he?

And then there's the baby. It's not that I have an aversion to children, but any young child reminds me of a past I'm ashamed off and brings back many painful memories I'd much rather forget.

So when Ben offers me my first job out of the office, I protest going anywhere with Sean, but my boss is insistent. Then in Amahad I grow to see the man underneath the shallow exterior and it gets harder to resist my attraction to him. Gradually he learns my darkest secrets and the key to my heart.

But our search for Mollie's missing mother leads us into danger. Will we be able to stay alive long enough to explore what could be between us?

Blood Brothers #4: Identity Crisis

ACKNOWLEDGEMENTS

Again thanks must go to my beta readers, Kirsten, and Christy who helped me get the plot in shape and gave me the encouragement to continue, and once again I'm extremely grateful for the help and support from Kate Marope of The Ribbon Marker Editorial Services.

Cover design and formatting by Freeyourwords. Lia, once again it was great working with you!

I'm grateful for all readers who have read the previous two books in the series and have given me such lovely feedback and encouragement to continue writing. Knowing you are enjoying Blood Brothers spurs me on to write more. If you have enjoyed this book, please take a moment to leave a review. Writing is a lonely life, and I can't express enough how much I appreciate all feedback I receive.

Finally thanks to my husband who takes the time to read my books and along with his encouragement and support, helps pick up on some of the inconsistencies which I've missed. Any left in there are completely down to me, and not to him!

And, as always, thanks to my wonderful son – it's nice to know that he's proud of his mum.

ABOUT THE AUTHOR

After commuting for too many years to London working in various senior management roles, Manda Mellett left the rat race and now fulfils her dream and writes full time. She draws on her background in psychology, the experience of working in different disciplines and personal life experiences in her books.

Manda lives in the beautiful countryside of North Essex with her husband and two slightly nutty Irish Setters. Walking her dogs gives her the thinking time to come up with plots for her novels, and she often dictates ideas onto her phone on the move, while looking over her shoulder hoping no one is around to listen to her. Manda's other main hobby is reading, and she devours as many books as she can.

Her biggest fan is her gay son (every mother should have one!). Her favourite pastime when he is home is the late night chatting sessions they enjoy, where no topic is taboo, and usually accompanied by a bottle of wine or two.

Email: manda@mandamellett.com

Website: www.mandamellett.com

Connect with me on Facebook:

https://www.facebook.com/mandamellett

Photo by Carmel Jane Photography